A TRILLION DOLLAR MAN

MAN

By
Angus Kennedy

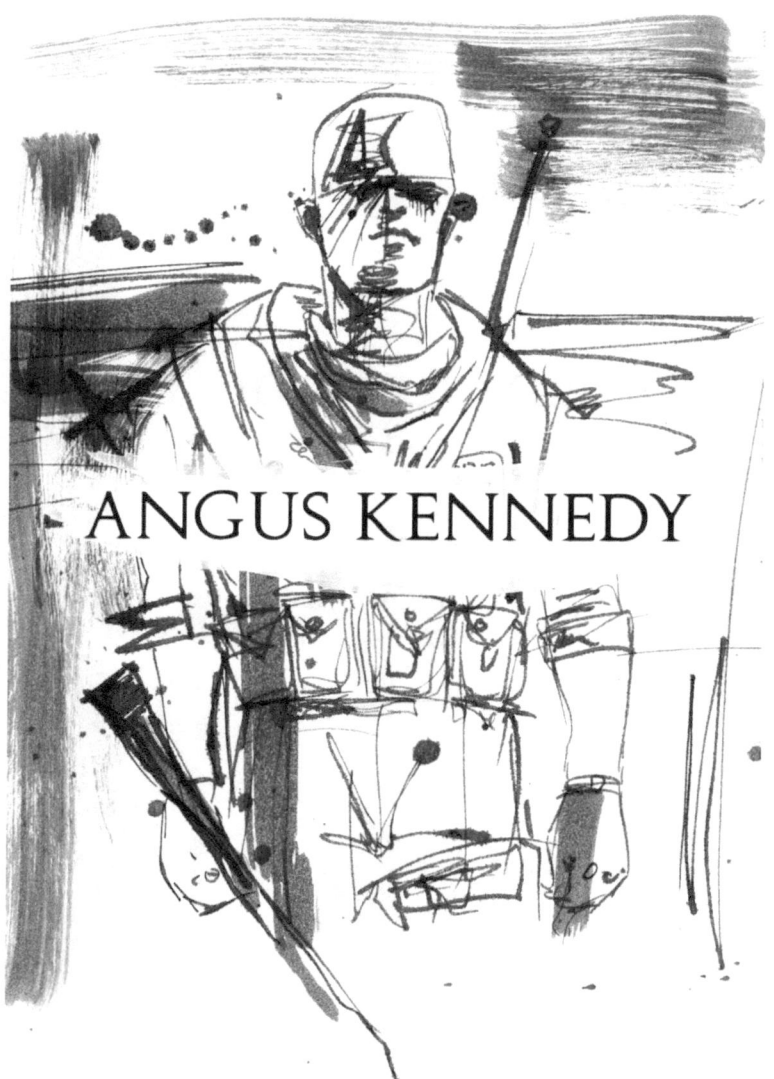

ANGUS KENNEDY

A
TRILLON
DOLLAR
MAN

A TRILLION DOLLAR MAN LAUNCHES A NEW TYPE OF HERO

THE FIRST TRILLIONAIRE GOES OUT IN THE WORLD, AND LIKE BILL GATES FIGURED OUT, HE LEARNS TO MAKE A BONA FIDE DIFFERENCE

1000 BILLION DOLLARS EQUALS A TRILLION

A SERIES OF DYNAMIC BOOKS

The Trillion Dollar Man books are a series. He is retired Marine Force Recon & joins forces with the black sheep of a wealthy blue blood family, a Shaolin Priestess. This supercharged team change things fast. They take down the bad guys who are in charge—not the little guys underneath—and become true 21st Century Heroes.

SPIN SCARES POLITICIANS

The Butchers File, a thick, in-depth report mandated by the Senate is being hurriedly wrapped up in San Francisco at a globally esteemed research center.

THE GOVERNMENT HAS KEPT THE MATERIAL BEING RESEARCHED UNDER THE TABLE

- The gang on the hill has kept the politically dangerous information under the radar. But the facts are nasty, and not just in foreign lands.
- The true grit is happening at home, right there in the United States of America on the Pacific Rim.
- How long can they keep it hushed?

THINGS ARE ABOUT TO GET WICKED

- The true grit is taking place at home, right there on shore in the United States of America, on the Pacific Rim and all across the country.
- How long can it be covered up?

Classified top secret because of the shadow of hacking and commercial espionage with China, US marshals will pick up the file and ferry it to the capital.

CATASTROPHE SETS IN

As the hour for the Federal Marshals to ferry The Butchers File from San Francisco the senator draws near, full out catastrophe strikes.

The Chief of the Think Tank is discovered on his living room floor overlooking San Francisco Bay, murdered with an exotic, military, .12 gauge shotgun.

His home looks like a war zone, and the story explodes as the Trillion Dollar Man hunts down the perp.

FORCE RECON

WHAT IF
- You were trained as a special op by Force Recon?
- You retired from the Marine Corps, from Force Recon?
- You re-directed all that can-do from the Corps.
- You put it into the money markets.

DOES BEING THE RICHEST MAN ON EARTH CHANGE THINGS
- Yes, but once a Marine, always a Marine.
- You're bored like crazy.
- The lives of the rich and famous seem empty and pointless.
- You stick to your ranch in Texas, raising quarter horses with an old Comanche named Four Fingers.

LIFE AMONG THE WEALTHY IS BORING BUT

WHAT IF
- Your best friend is head of the think tank doing the Butchers File for the senate?
- He is dead on his living room floor.
- Some weird military weapon has destroyed his home.
- His personal assistant is a 10th degree Shaolin Priestess.
- The two of you burn into hot pursuit of the perp.

A Trillion Dollar Man
Angels Gate

Solid Footing Press
5451 East 2nd Street, Suite 1
Long Beach CA 90803
angusk@outlook.com

Ordering Information:
Quantity sales. Special discounts are available on quantity purchases by The Department of the Interior; any Environmental Group, globally; all groups working for the welfare of animals and nature; The Marine Corps, corporations, associations, and others. For details, contact the publisher at the address above.

Orders by U.S. trade bookstores and wholesalers. Please contact Angus Kennedy above.

Printed in the United States of America

Publisher's Cataloging-in-Publication data
Kennedy, Angus

1) A title of a book: *A Trillion Dollar Man* by Angus Kennedy
ISBN 978-0-9903071-0-5

2) A title of a book: *Angels Gate* by Angus Kennedy – first two chapters as release example for next novel in The Trillion Dollar Man Series
ISBN 978-0-9903071-2-9

The main category of the books — Fiction – Novels

Cover Art
Chase Wood is an illustrator born in Hollister and finds residence in Southern California. In his work, he channels his skills and particular attention to detail into his communicative imagery. The idea of trying to evoke a clear message in his work is what attracted him to the illustrative side of art. He mostly enjoys taking one small bit of subject matter and letting his pen do the rest, getting lost in detail.

Fonts by Luke Davies
The Davies brothers grew up with an American mother and an Australian father in Melbourne Australia. Though they are ten years apart in age, they have always been best friends. This connection was never more apparent than when the two played guitar together throughout their teenage years. After a year at Berklee College of Music in Boston. Luke decided to take a summer off and come visit his brother Jake in Long Beach California.

Countless late night booze fueled jam sessions ensued. Each day the Davies brothers would wake up hung over and play back all the riffs they had forgotten they wrote the night before. The music was pouring out of them faster than they could record it, each new riff trumping the last. It became abundantly clear to the brothers that this sound they had found together was important. Not just to them, but to music. This blend of hard rock with a punch of catchy pop melodies was something they hadn't heard before. It sounded like Alice in chains fucked Michael Jackson. It was raw, it was fun, and it had the kind of balls that seem to have been castrated from all rock music of the past 15 years. There was no turning away from this. Not now. Not ever.

CreateSpace formatting and ebook conversion by Niall Gray
Niall is a music, literature and art lover. He is currently interested in all things publishing-related, and has honed his skills in ebook conversions and print layouts over the past eighteen months. If interested in a conversion quote, please feel free to contact Niall at niallpatrickgray@hotmail.co.uk

FOR PHILLIP JOHN KENNEDY,
A BONA FIDE TRILLION DOLLAR MAN

CONTENTS

There is always the howl of the wild creature we actually are, and there are always a million petite bourgeoisie commandments that, de rigueur, require the slaughter of that free range savage within. Always—and without doubt —the cardinal law for a human being is to learn to continually sort enough data to keep that wild critter well-oiled so it can spring forth and rip the hide off the ghastly ego of the petite bourgeoisie's commandments without being killed or caught, while—during every heartbeat keeping the soft thing inside fat and sassy.

Lucky Esposito
Notes from the Cathedral

ONE

Billy Clayton stood riveted to a 30-inch computer screen displaying an undercover documentary of two men wearing camouflage uniforms. The men dug the gall bladder out of a black bear then hacked off its body parts with chainsaws. The corpse lay on the ground and they moved fast, tossing the contraband into the bed of their pickup parked next to an entry sign for Shenandoah National Park, not a hundred miles from the Oval Office.

Jenny Warren walked out of the computer room and down the hall. Grabbing a set of field glasses off the coat rack, she stepped through the door and crossed the accounting office in three smooth strides. She eased up a single slat in the blinds with an index finger and peered down across Grant Avenue where a new pair of men sat watching.

"Come in here, Billy," she said in a hushed voice.

As he entered, the streetlight's glow highlighted the thick scar snaking down from his hairline, dropping across his nose to his cheek. She signaled him to the window, and at six foot four, he stood three and a half inches taller than Jenny. He leaned in to see what concerned her, and as she handed him the binoculars, he recognized the scent of a fine French lavender shampoo, like his grandmother's, from her hair.

The fading afternoon bore down with the bone-numbing cold of May fog beginning to roll in off the bay. Thin traffic eased along with caution as North Beach rested before the nightlife revved up.

The men outside sat calm in a plain rental car, wearing off-the-rack suits, cheap white shirts, dull ties, and short, military-style haircuts. From time to time, one or the other glanced up and scanned the windows.

Sam, Billy's huge black lab, skittered in from the hallway and went straight to Jenny. Billy examined the men's faces: mouths cast in dour expressions; doughy, fast-food skin color; phlegmy, dull gray eyes, all resting on necks thick as stumps. Jenny scratched Sam behind the ears, and the stout dog wiggled as Billy shook his muzzle while they walked out of accounting and back down the hall.

Early that morning, before Billy had volunteered to help, Jenny reviewed her checklist for tying up Animalfund's massive senatorial report, Operation Butchers Data. The study was for Senator Marlin Hicks, a man seriously concerned about corporate slackers trying to sneak around limitations related to sustainable business practices.

Senator Hicks had made it through three assassination attempts—the Secret Service took each perp down on the scene. They had all been labeled terrorists and the National Security Agency black holed all information.

Jess Hayes, CEO of Animalfund, had been Billy's best friend for many years, and they had both been close to the senator and his wife. Jess had been in Washington for a week, ferrying the first half of the report with him under the protection of federal marshals.

Saturday afternoon, and there was still a lot to do. Jenny, in her meticulous style—the demeanor that had whisked her through Cambridge University twenty years earlier—had used her skill to insure the report's accuracy, but she had begun to wonder how they would ever finish on schedule, considering the tasks that remained to be done.

The report boiled down an in-depth investigation of poaching, smuggling, marketing and uses of parts butchered off of large, wild mammals around the world, with emphasis on how the United States fit in the chain of supply and demand. Working through weekends, Jenny had spent over a year spearheading the extinction study for Senator Hicks' Committee on the Environment. As the last few weeks crept in, deep exhaustion had dulled her, and the frequent return of the doughy men kept her edgy. But as she began to near the end, she felt a fresh boost of energy. The study's schedule

4

required US Marshals to courier five hard copies with accompanying flash drives of the entire report to the capital at 10:00am, Monday morning.

The staff was so bone-weary they had begun to make time-consuming mistakes, and Jenny sent them home at noon on Saturday. Within 42 hours, she planned to tie up the remaining graphic inserts, pass out under a throw on the lush corduroy couch in reception, and once refreshed, edit the index, burn the flash drives and print the copies in time for the marshals.

A passionate global sailor, Billy had been gearing up his 30-meter yacht, *dead latitudes*. He kept permanent anchor in Sausalito—an excellent shelter from storms and just a hop across the bay from San Francisco, his favorite city on earth.

He had flown in from Austin, Texas and was prepping at his mooring, readying with his ship's captain. They would take Animalfund's staff on a trans-Pacific sailing expedition to celebrate the report's completion—and the Senate, at long last, paying attention to the end of big mammals. They planned to escape to the wild forestland on Russia's Pacific coast for a survey of the handful of existent free-range tigers north of Vladivostok.

All dedicated naturalists, the Animalfund team trained a skeleton crew to keep things running and arranged for a year of basking in some of the Earth's remaining, authentic wilderness while doing their research. The plan included producing articles and video for the Smithsonian and *National Geographic*, as well as compiling data on the Siberian tigers for an appendix to Operation Butchers Data. They intended to set sail Tuesday morning at daybreak— around 6:30am—just twenty hours after the marshals marched in for the pick up.

Not long after Jenny sent the staff home, Billy rang to get a final count on how many people planned to go to sea. She gave him the total, and told him about her time crunch for wrapping the report on time. To her amazement, he drove straight over from Marin County and rolled up his sleeves the minute he walked in the door. Together, they pulled the thick document right back on schedule. Billy didn't complain at all. She had been astonished; the richest man in the world, the first trillionaire, and he behaved with a smooth and impeccable demeanor, not even a little bit peevish about grunt work.

Jess—Billy's longtime friend and CEO of Animal-fund—had been gone all week. An emergency call from the Hill, direct from Senator Hicks and his wife Claire, had pulled him out of his torturous schedule without fore-warning. He had red-eyed to Washington and been there for a week. When Claire Hicks pumped Jess about the most pressing danger zones in the huge report, she insisted that he come aboard and help them raise money to stop the animals being murdered.

Jess stayed on to help Claire and the senator outline a new, nationwide campaign to save the American black bear from long-term extinction. He had planned to return to Animalfund by Saturday afternoon, early, and help wrap things up with the senator's report.

"Has Jess called?" asked Jenny.

"No, I had Nuke sail on over to the yacht club so we can launch right from the party at Jess' house."

"Nuke?"

"He's the new captain of *dead latitudes*."

"So Nuke can go up and check on Jess," said Jenny.

"Yeah, for sure. He'll be over there waiting so we can load everyone's gear on board straight from their rides then walk up to Jess' house for the party's going on."

"That's weird; it's not like him," she said.

"No. It *is* weird; but it's DC and politics as usual."

Back in the graphics room, Billy and Jenny glanced at one another in silence. He punched more images up on a screen. Though a calm man by nature, Billy had to strain to keep from gazing at her. She dressed smartly but comfortably, wearing jeans with a French-T and flip-flops. She wore a trace of makeup, and had pulled her thick, chestnut hair back in a wide, sterling silver and turquoise clasp. One eye shone hazel and one a brilliant light blue. The contrast amplified her natural beauty and made her face hypnotic.

"The first time I noticed the men waiting outside was on a Sunday. It was raining. They checked me out as I walked up Grant to work, and sat still. They came back for a month or so, just looking up with those dead eyes. Then they disappeared for a while, the rain stopped, and they never showed all summer."

"What did you do?"

"I told Jess, and he teased that I was getting paranoid from city life."

"But why would anyone stake a wildlife think tank? You're not enviro-cowboys like Animal Liberation Front or even Greenpeace; the fibbies wouldn't be after you," said Billy, remembering the fresh scent of her hair, the shiver he'd felt when he got so close to her.

"You're way out of touch, Billy. The planet is owned by corporations who use their puppet politicians to brand the environmental movement as terrorists. With a covert iron fist, they chip away legislated protection of natural resources so the corpo-types can loot public land. They've sicked the fibbies, and more nasty hyenas like the NSA, on all tree huggers."

"That's why Jess Hayes and Jenny Warren are being called *The Bourne Identity* gone green?"

"You got it. But, it's kinda dumb because Jess kicks butt with lawyers rather than fancy martial arts moves."

"Conspiracy Theory, right?"

"Mr. Clayton, that was a complete non sequitur and you appear to be a decent guy, but your understanding of the global situation is a bubble off plumb. Jess says you are now the richest person on earth, with no chance of anyone catching up for a real long time? The first real-world trillionaire?"

Billy grinned again. "I've earned a couple bucks."

"Don't run the dumb Texan routine on me! I had to listen to Dubya play lame long enough to make me puke."

"Lord, Ms. Warren, are you a bit paranoid from these two thugs watching you? Like Jess would say, they're just some fed snoops making sure Senator Hicks' report is safe."

"Our research shows serious greens being slapped with the handy terror label to legally hamstring all efforts toward demanding corpo-sustainability."

"But Obama's a bleeding heart; it's not like the Dubya days."

"Come on Billy, don't dumb down on me. You've snatched a trillion dollars and built cash stashes in dark places all around the planet, maybe on Mars too—there's no way you could have missed the fact that all politicians are owned by the uber-rich." She moved closer to the computer screen.

"Those two down in the car aren't like these video creeps." He pointed at the faces of the men on the screen. "Look at how these cedar choppers are all bunched up with hurt feelings, anger and that red glow of their skin from hangovers. They're pouty little boys. But the boys down in the car are not in pain, they simply don't have souls. They're not alive at all. They're fed zombies."

She looked at the screen closely. "Yeah, they don't look like they're feeling well."

"They are voids of humanness due to booze and controlled substances?" he said.

The both laughed.

"Quite observant, my dear Watson," said Jenny.

"They don't organize anything past the night's methamphetamine, Holmes," said Billy with a rather impressive British accent.

She continued laughing. "I don't feature them pulling a complex operation together."

"Thank you, Holmes. Your two tormentors down there are obviously on a different team than the bear whackers in the vids."

"Yes, quite so, Watson."

"Why in the hell didn't you call in the senator?" Billy asked. "Marlin and Claire Hicks are among the few honorable people in Washington. I imagine either one of them could fetch the Secret Service on those two, on anyone who threatened you in any way."

"My dad was old-line Connecticut Yankee and taught me to buck up, keep a stiff upper lip and all that hog wash." She looked at him closely as she continued. "They are dogged. They've even caught up after I ducked through lobbies and lost them for a while. My address is in their database for sure. You can bet they know where Jess lives, where we all live," she said.

Billy stopped to scrutinize her as she spoke and then turned to another display. The huge, flat monitor streamed a video of a group parting out a black bear. One man cut off the paws with a chainsaw and tossed them up into the bed, still dripping blood. This truck also sat next to a Shenandoah sign.

"You know how Jess reacts," she said. "Never was a born-again. He's an honest-to-god, old-line, walk-the-talk Christian. You know he doesn't care what anybody thinks about him."

Billy's eyes lit up as he thought of his good friend. He could hear Jess's voice and mimicked it aloud: "Follow the golden rule. Do unto others. Practice kindness. That's all you need."

"You've got him down exactly," she said. "We've always been so busy we'd forget about Dumb and Dumber, but before long, they'd show up out of nowhere."

Billy stood transfixed again, grimacing at the men mutilating bears.

Jenny continued, "Jess called a couple San Francisco cops, old friends of his family. They staked out the stakeout. But every lead about the watchers melted into a labyrinth of cyber information, the police said they were dealing with some kind of black op. Old-line San Franciscans are protective. I guess several squad cars trapped the pair and beat the hell out of them. Then, all of a sudden, the cops clammed up and Jess heard that the mayor had come on strong, demanded that Jess' cop buddies close down the whole mess."

Their eyes met as Billy said, "So, what did Jess say?"

"He always made some glib comment and changed the subject."

"He suffers from FDD," said Billy.

"FDD? Is that some sort of a Texas homeboy acronym?"

"No way, Jenny, it's from the Mayo Clinic, Fear Deficit Disorder, FDD," he said, grinning.

She slugged him on the arm and laughed as she agreed. "FDD. He definitely suffers from that." Then she imitated Jess with impressive accuracy. "'Supposed to be a free country, Jenny.' He'd shrug, raising his eyebrows. 'Let 'em snoop. Who cares who they are? Some bureaucrat half-wits like fibbies or maybe NSA stealing code off the hard drives because they're too lame to write it themselves.'"

"Are the bear gall bladders hard to sell?"

"Lord, no. Wild parts are an instant sale."

"Wild parts?"

"As opposed to captive. Even the bile from the milking farms sells like crazy."

"Milking farms?" asked Billy, tightening his face.

"Yeah, they cage 'em and stick tubes right into the bladder."

"Good god!"

"You don't even want to hear," Jenny said.

"So we're talking whopping cash?"

10

"Next biggest illegal market to sex slaves. Drugs are third. Media figures say nine billion, but Jess thinks that's Rupert Murdoch's math—that global parts sales are really at around a hundred. The only problem for the big pushers is they don't have a central database of their supply train."

"Just-in-time inventory?"

"Correct," said Jenny.

Billy walked over to a different workstation and touched the keyboard. A fresh image stream—another group of cammy-types next to a Yosemite sign—flooded the screen. They acted with calm, as unruffled as people congregating after church. Devoid of emotion, they carved the jaw out of a black bear with a chainsaw. Just as another man pulled the huge rack of teeth loose, a dim rattling arose through the speakers. The sound grew in intensity and took over the room.

"What's this?"

"Part of the report your friend Luther Four Fingers inserted."

"You know Luther?" Billy asked, surprised. He had known Luther for many years.

"Are you kidding? He helps the whole staff, especially with computers. Jess says he's one of the ten best supercomputer programmers on earth."

"What, you mean Jess and Luther are buddies? I didn't know he had time to be in with y'all. He raises world-renowned quarter horses on my father's ranch."

"He told me," said Jenny. "He loves animals and never charges us a dime. He hammers out code when I'm swamped. Last month he wrote a sorting patch for the database so we can grab frames from videos, do captions, and insert them as photos at light speed."

Coiling up from the shot of the man holding the jaw, a thick, dark timber rattler filled the screen. The tail shook as it crawled toward them. It coiled, struck, and then disappeared.

11

"Jeez, that's Luther for sure," said Billy laughing.

"I know. I don't think we should keep it on the flash drive for the report, but Luther wants to rattle the politicians' cages, to scare them, to make them fight with the fat men that own them. He always says, 'Save the planet is bullshit; the Earth doesn't give a hoot about Homo sapiens. She'll belch us right off like the dinosaurs. Save the humans is more accurate. Don't mess with Mother Nature.'"

A new screen opened up after the rattler. Another pair of men cut into a black bear's abdomen with special ops combat knives.

"Those two in the car aren't like these guys at all," he said.

"Look closer," said Jenny, joining him. "Imagine this pair cleaned up. Limit the whiskies to one per evening. Cut out the methamphetamine. Take the pained, raw edge off. Now check the zombie glaze. Play like they've dropped the cammies and gone to a discount suit place. Put some fat on them."

Billy laughed, "That's right. When you focalize on the eyes, it's obvious that they've all got the same chipped gear." He turned his head and gazed out the windows. "Wait here, I'll be right back. Sam, you stay."

Jenny followed him into the hall. "Billy. What are you doing? We've got to get this report off; we all want you to take us sailing." Sam whined as Billy strode under the exit sign and on down the stairs.

Billy shot through the passage between the Animalfund building and the structure next door. Jenny moved back to accounting and raised a slat. Billy walked along far side of the street. He approached the rear of the vehicle, moving swiftly.

He dodged between two automobiles parked several spaces behind the men. Jenny gasped at his boldness. From Jess' conversations she knew that stereotyping Texans as heartless swine that only cared about profits didn't apply to Billy. She grabbed one of the fund's cameras off a hook, spread the blinds and began to film.

She knew Billy had established an irrevocable trust of 100 billion dollars for Animalfund. Coupled with the substantial endowments from Jess' family, Animalfund had become weighty nonprofit. Billy and Jess both came from a long line of deep assets; they had met at one of Jess' grandmother's events on Knob Hill.

What fascinated Jenny, being a trust fund brat herself, was that Billy pitched in, not grousing at all. It was simple for a zillionaire to write a check, but Billy dove into chores without flinching.

Jenny didn't really know anything about Billy except that he popped into the city on a private jet to visit Jess. She knew that Jess admired Billy greatly, but they always took off to some dangerous place for sailing or windsurfing. Jess spoke of Billy from time to time, saying that he was one of the few people he trusted. When the two showed up together, their closeness stood out with a glow.

She watched Billy as he walked straight up to the car door and rapped on the window. Dumb and Dumber both jerked their heads toward the noise. The one on the passenger side whipped an automatic with a sound suppressor out from under his jacket.

Jenny quickly dropped and grabbed her canvas boat bag. Sam, sensing her urgency, took the lead down the rear stairs. As she stepped into the alley, her stomach sunk at the gaseous *whompfff* of the gun. There was the sound of metal hitting metal that made her cringe. She ran faster, until she caught sight of the car and the two men inside.

The driver collected himself, and pulling his eyes off the hole his partner had blown through the windshield, shoved the door open with a lunge, knocking Billy away from them. The man popped the car into motion as he tried to slam the door shut again. But Billy sprang hard and grabbed the driver's jacket at the shoulder so he couldn't close the door.

Instead, he gassed it in reverse. Billy hooked an elbow around the guy's neck. The vehicle crashed into the bumper behind. The lurching yanked Billy sideways, but he tightened

13

his grip by grabbing his own wrist, and managing to keep on his feet.

As the car bounced, the man tugged the wheel left. Trapped under Billy's weight, he humped the gas and bolted out of the parking space. Billy was dragged along the street. The driver struggled to break Billy's hold around his thick neck. He jerked and huffed, choking all the time, barely maintaining his seat. Billy dug his hand under the man's collar. The thug on the passenger's side tried to steady the pistol for a clear shot.

Suddenly, Sam jumped and grabbed the driver's left forearm. The man roared with pain. Sam's weight forced him to lose the wheel, but he steadied the vehicle with his right hand. Billy saw Sam dangling, his body scraping along the pavement.

"Sam, let go," he yelled, dropping his grip on the man's collar and taking hold of his dog. He released the driver's neck and pulled Sam in close. They tumbled onto the asphalt. Both of them rolled over and scrambled to stand up. Billy didn't even glance back at the car as it barreled along Grant Avenue. He ran hard in the opposite direction.

His Dodge Ram sat in the yellow zone in front of the Animalfund building. He beeped the locks before he got to the gunmetal gray pickup and didn't bother with his seatbelt. Jenny hopped into the passenger's side. She put her arm around Sam who sat between them with his tongue hanging out. She pulled his body close for warmth and to protect him. Billy yanked the gear stick. He checked Jenny's door lock, and his eyes paused on her for a brief second. He glanced at Sam, dug down on the pedal, and the Dodge burned out on Grant Avenue spinning into a sizzling U-turn.

"What the hell are you doing? We can't follow those creeps. They've got guns." She dug in her coat and flipped her cell open. "I'll call the cops and we can stay back and guide—"

Billy snatched the phone from her and slipped it into his pocket.

TWO

Billy and Jenny burned through San Francisco and tore across the Golden Gate after the pair who had been watching her. The thick-necked watchdog's car went 90 miles an hour on the bridge, barely missing the rear bumpers of vehicles as they passed, but Billy pushed after them doggedly, fishtailing through traffic.

On the other side, the watchdogs dropped off Highway 101, down the hill past Fort Baker into Sausalito and roared along Bridgeway Boulevard. They kept giving Billy the slip, pushing forward into the fog, but he caught them every time.

Finally, in the middle of town, the men shot past a red light, and Billy had to slow for cars coming through the green onto Bridgeway. He eased into traffic, and drivers pounded their horns. By the time he broke lose, the pair had moved out of sight. He floored it. Jenny slipped her window down and filled her lungs with the cool sea air in quick tiger breaths—a mind-stilling practice she had learned, and needed to use, many times during her Shaolin training.

Billy's personal duffel—packed specifically for their Pacific crossing—sat on the floor beside Jenny's leg. As they tore along Bridgeway, he leaned over and shuffled with the zipper, digging out a huge handgun: a .50 caliber Israeli arms Desert Eagle, and a slim box of surgical gloves.

He stuffed the Eagle in his jeans and mounted a pair of gloves. She cocked her head to the side, staring in disbelief. He returned the box and pulled out a liter of Negrita rum. He wolfed down a big gulp, glanced over at her and paused for an instant. Her eyes locked on his like a bird of prey.

"What in the name of heaven do you think you are doing?"

15

"I am in extreme pursuit of what appear to be jack-booted thugs from the government of the United States of America. If so, they are merciless stalkers and ruthless murderers with extensive training. I intend to perform a citizen's arrest and leave them completely exposed to media coverage. They have been endangering you and my best friend in the world, all the staff at one of his trusts, the most effective platform for elephants, rhinos, tigers . . . well you know all of that—and have now attempted to murder you, myself and my fine dog."

Jenny looked out at Bridgeway then back at his face. She broke into a slight smile and shifted her eyes back to look out the windshield.

"Will you please pay attention to the road?" she said. "You can't drink and drive."

He chugged again and handed her the bottle. She took a long pull off the dark liquid and returned it.

"You look like an Australian shepherd," he said.

"Come on, Billy."

"Right! I guess they all have to say something dumb."

"Be real with me. Why did you put that massive artillery piece in your pants, and what's with continuing to chase these guys? I told you to call the cops."

"I just explained it. Is there something in your ears? Nobody's supposed to stalk you or shoot at us."

"Oh, okay! We are set. Not a thing to worry about, right? Gee, let me get a handle on everything. This is a film script, right, and you have everything all under control? Alrighty then, thank you, Mr. Transporter."

"Whoa, wait a minute, not Mr. Transporter. You have to say, *the* Transporter."

"Oh, well Lord Almighty, thank you so much for your mastery of the details of the history of cinema—that irons everything out, right?"

"Jess already tried the cops."

"So what's the big macho plan? Catch 'em? Run 'em off the road? Jerk 'em out of the car? Call in your favorite French police officer like Transporter? I mean, come on! What do——?"

"Relax, Jenny," he interrupted. "You are in danger and policemen are not dependable for serious matters. I won't let these men follow you—not you, not Jess, not anyone. And you don't say Transporter. It's *the* Transporter."

"Relax? Oh, well sure, I'll just break into song. He wants me to relax. Right. That's right. I'll lean back and take things in stride while these weirdoes that you have now pissed off royally stop and murder us."

Billy drove the inside lane next to the curb. He moved as fast as he could, but the fog sat thicker than in San Francisco and obscured his view. He took another pull off the rum and handed it back to Jenny. Just as she grabbed the bottle, the glass exploded in all directions. She held the jagged neck in midair; none of the bottom remained. Bullet holes embellished both the windshield and the rear window.

"Where are they?" asked Jenny, sounding amazingly calm.

Billy didn't have time to answer. The sound of rounds thudding into the body of the pickup came again, and in the hint of light from the holes, he noticed the deep, red spot of color on Sam's shoulder.

"Are you okay?"

"I think it's just nicks on me and Sam both," she said.

A Humvee glided out of the fog like a phantom. The serious-looking black vehicle eased toward them on the wrong side of the center median, rolling along in the slow lane to the right of the truck. Billy tromped the gas to get around, but the Humvee swerved and braked, coming to a halt at an angle across both northbound lanes.

With precision, Billy jerked the wheel left so his pickup bounced over the median, cutting past the front of the Humvee. His tires dug through the grass, fishtailing in the damp topsoil. Billy thought he would lose control for sure, but he stayed with the motion, and they flew off the curb, facing southerly traffic.

The Humvee driver speed shifted the rugged military vehicle, whipped a screeching right and hurtled over the island. He crunched into the southbound fast lane, ending up behind Billy, and plowed into pursuit.

Out of the fog, a GL-Class Mercedes was approaching head on toward Billy and Jenny. Billy hit the brakes hard and the Mercedes swung into the slow lane, its horn blasting. The Humvee slid to a stop behind Billy, pulling up at an angle to avoid his rear end.

A woman switched on the cabin lights in the Mercedes and turned, reaching behind her. Billy knew that the Humvee occupants had noted everything from within the dark vehicle. The couple in the Mercedes appeared to be in their 50s. The man sported a chopped, waxed, trendy haircut and wire rimmed glasses—a serious business type: wiry, fit and demanding.

His wife's hair framed her features in a short, high-fashion razored style. She came off as a more strident, female version of the man. He still wore his tux from an evening on the town, but had pulled the tie off. He pushed and let up on the GL's obnoxious horn in a pounding, discordant series of blasts. The veins stood out on his neck.

"Jesus H. Christ," said Billy, "these boomers are frickin' clueless." He threw the door open and Jenny grabbed his arm.

"Billy, come on, don't do this." She tugged hard. He stepped into the night.

The woman managed to yank a gym bag out of the back and into her lap. She hugged it up tight, and the man attempted to snatch it from her with one hand, while shaking a fist at the Humvee and moving his mouth fast. The wife started shouting too. Then she turned sideways to yell at her man. He grabbed the bag, struggled with her and the zipper and pulled out a black Glock automatic. Screaming, the woman tried to take the pistol away from him.

The veins on the man's neck made him look as if he would detonate. The woman's fury contorted her face wickedly. From her expression, Billy discerned that she was not mad at the Humvee occupants, but thought that her husband was behaving like a perfect ass. She did not want to stop and mix with the troublemakers driving in the wrong lane.

The passenger's window slid open on the Humvee, and an arm extended into the night, calm and steady. A hand sheathed in a surgeon's glove held an STI Grandmaster with a long, engineered, lethal-looking sound suppressor snugged up on the barrel. He waited as the man's unruffled fist drew a bead with the handgun. The driver's side headlight on the Mercedes exploded. The arm moved slowly, steadily as the man shot the other headlight.

The first gunshot ripped through the quiet, and Billy looked on in disbelief as the wife pulled a matching Glock out of the bag. Holding the pistol, she dug in her purse and retrieved a cellphone. She punched three keys while sliding into the driver's seat. Billy knew that the 911 call would get the law to this wealthy neighborhood pronto. Her husband stood beside his car, gun hand down to his side, frozen.

Terror overwhelmed the woman's face. At the sound of gunfire, the man turned abruptly and ran away from the Mercedes. He dropped to the island, flat on his stomach. He crawled around in a circle and assumed a prone shooter's position. He zeroed in on the arm coming out of the Humvee. He let go of a round and it missed the vehicle entirely. The pistol in the passenger window of the Humvee pivoted toward him. When the laser from the gun spotted on his forehead, he screamed.

The Mercedes engine fired up and it burned away from the ruckus using its reverse lights, and Billy's enormous handgun shattered the deadness of the fog. The now empty STI was jerked back into the dark cab of the Humvee.

Billy lurched through the Humvee's passenger window, grabbed the driver by the larynx and punched the side of his temple three times, splitting the white latex glove on his hand. He took the other man by the hair, pulled his torso over his friend, pounded his head against the door panel twice and slugged him so hard he passed out.

On his feet again, the Mercedes driver stood paralyzed on the island, watching his GL's backup lights turn to a distant glow in the fog. Billy sprinted to the passenger side of his truck. Jenny flipped the lock, and he yanked the handle.

"Billy. Billy, listen. You've got to get a grip on yourself."

He dug into the sailing kit, grabbed two of the fifteen bicycle chains and padlocks packed for sailing and ran before Jenny could finish. He yanked the car door open. The passenger started coming to, but Billy popped him again and jerked a chain around his neck loose enough to keep the man alive, but tight enough make him gasp for air. He repeated the action with the other man. Moving fast, he wove the links in and out of the steering wheel and the steering column a few times. He forced the men down tight against the padded surface and locked the chains.

"Boys, you've gotta behave and stay here for the press," he said. He grabbed a loose cell off the seat, searched for the *San Francisco Chronicle*. "You've got to get someone out on Bridgeway in Sausalito fast while the cops are here. It's a big story. There has been an altercation between citizens and some weird government spooks. Right, they are there waiting for you, tell your reporter to shake a leg."

While patting them down for another cell, for more evidence, Billy said, "Wow guys, I hear the reporters coming already. I'll be back when they have you in a cell. My lawyer will be itchin' to know you. You'll like him. He's a swell guy."

Billy searched the car. He flipped open the glove box, but there was nothing but a cheap, metal flashlight. He searched the floor and under the seats. Nothing.

"Oh Jesus, dude you stink," said Billy, taking the gun away from him with no resistance and stuffed it in his waistband. "You need to go home with your wife. I don't know where she went, but you need to bathe. Forget the Vin Diesel routine—it's definitely not you." Billy pointed across Bridgeway, away from the ruckus.

Billy pointed to the roadside, "I want you to go over and hide in the bushes on the shoulder where nobody can see you. Stay put till the cops are swarming, and you are sure that they are in control." He turned the zombied man around and pushed him. A car almost hit him as he traipsed across the asphalt.

Muffled by the moisture in the air, the wail of sirens arose in the distance. Billy hopped into the truck. "Fish a plastic bag out and put these inside," he said, handing her the flashlight and the cell he found in the Humvee.

"I wrote the plates down on this napkin out of your glove box. I'm putting it in with the flashlight."

Jenny looked out at the night as the engine jumped to and purred.

"What are you doing, Billy?"

"I'm driving to Jess'."

"No, you have to tell the police what happened."

"No can do."

"What?"

"They'll take us in."

"And?"

"And, they're dumb and politically driven, and all of you are in big danger."

"The cops take care of the danger. That's how it works."

"They may be the danger, too."

He gunned the pickup north, toward Jess' house.

THREE

Sam ran ahead and broke into a pained moan as Billy and Jenny walked up to the front door Jess' stately home in Tiburon. Hearing them, Nuke, the captain of Billy's sailboat, swung the great, oak door open. Without stopping, he strode back through the foyer in three steps, bellowing, "Shut it fast," over his shoulder.

On the living room floor, in front of the sweeping view of San Francisco, rested Jess's still body, a fresh nasty wound in the center of his chest.

Already knowing the outcome, but unable to stop himself, Billy knelt to try for a pulse. At the same time, Jenny, trying her best to avoid the blood and not disturb the crime scene, stooped and put her hand on his forehead.

"Oh, Jessie. Oh no," she sighed deeply. "No. No. No." She collapsed on her knees, lifted his head into her lap and stroked his brow. "Oh no. No, no, no," she moaned, slumping over him. She stared into the big man's eyes, placed her fingers on the lids, slid them closed, and broke into tears.

"I berthed down at the Peninsula. The whole place was quiet, empty as yacht clubs ever get, and you and Jess didn't show," said Nuke, watching Jenny.

"So I walked on up figuring you might be here. I knocked and nobody came, but the door was open. I shouted out his name, 'Jess? Jess Hayes! Billy! Hello!' Standin' on the porch like fuckin' Goofy, yelling out. Not a good scene. Me, a big old, scarred-up dude of African heritage with a record, right here in the middle of all these white-boy mansions. What are the cops gonna say? Hey boy, you Django, with a D," said Nuke, shaking his head.

Billy's whole body had gone numb. He thought he should comfort Jenny, but he couldn't. Overwhelmed with the scene, everything about him had short-circuited. Not only had Jess been shot, someone had cut off one of his hands and the remains appeared to be missing.

Billy toured the room looking at everything closely, then slumped against the fireplace. He scanned the damage to the house. Shotgun blasts had destroyed big sections of the plastered walls and knocked out the picture windows overlooking San Francisco Bay.

"Check out how the wall mess is more scattered than Jess' wound," said Billy.

"Something's weird," said Nuke. "The wound's from a .12 gauge slug."

"No," said Billy, "it's from a FRAG-12. They're warheads, little rockets with fins for Special Forces. Hit the market in 2004 or so and changed combat forever. A guy on foot can take out armored vehicles without bringing in air support and drawing attention."

"So you're saying this is military?" said Nuke.

"I don't know, but they used two different FRAG-12 loads, so they are heavy hitters." Billy pointed at the walls and windows. "It's so messed up because they used a fragmentation load that's designed to shoot through a window on an armored vehicle and wipe out everybody inside out with an explosion of ball bearings."

"Fock," said Nuke, "if ground soldiers could stop armored vehicles the whole battle would change."

"Exactly. This is heavy shit."

"Come on, Billy, you're telling me Special Ops came after Jess because he saved bears?"

"Right. Nothing adds up. The hole in Jess is from the load for piercing light armor and that can take the driver out in vehicles built with steel as thick as half an inch. The shell delivers a compact hole, and the projectiles that pommeled the wall would have blown his body to smithereens. Look how the plaster debris is all over the room. It's not the result of a concentrated spread like buckshot," said Billy.

23

He turned back to Jenny as Nuke disappeared into the kitchen. Jenny still held Jess' head in her lap. Her crying brought on tears of his own, and the anger came out with them. Of all the people on the planet, why single out such an extraordinary person? A truly kind man; a real gentleman who took care of so many humans and creatures; a passionate citizen who funded trusts caring for large numbers of each new generation of the elderly in perpetuity; a philanthropist who had rolled up his sleeves long before Bill Gates and Warren Buffett turned from acquisitions to charity, and had made sure the cash supported the boys and girls or went straight to the aged and not to bureaucrats.

"No shells, so they picked them up," said Nuke. He returned from the kitchen with three tumblers, a bottle of vintage calvados, a box of latex gloves, a roll of paper towels, and window cleaner. Already wearing gloves, he joined Billy at the fireplace, placed the supplies on the mantle, and poured the old apple brandy. "This'll keep us out of shell shock."

He handed out gloves, towels, and glasses of calvados. "I used to steal boxes of these damn things from the doctor's office because they were hard to find. Now anybody can be a perp—they've got 'em at frickin' home warehouses." Nuke pulled on a pair of gloves and pushed the latex in the valleys between his fingers as he spoke.

"Let's do this. Start with wiping everything you touched. Prints are body oil, so the window cleaner takes them right off. But be careful. Don't mess up anything for the crime scene gang."

Nuke stopped still and examined Jenny who was still on the floor. "You going to be alright? We've got to get out of here fast." He pulled her up.

"Let's check the whole house," said Billy. "There's no sign of the little propeller slugs, so they must have picked them up too." His voice rang out, but in his head, everything sounded distant. He forced his eyes to start surveying the scene again.

The gruesome mutilation of someone so close to him was surreal. Sam whined and licked at the blood pooled next to the wound from Jess' severed hand. Jenny stood, looking at the body. Sam moved next to her and whimpered more. A long, reciprocating saw sat on the floor next to Jess' shoulder.

Billy tried to work through the obvious. The perp used a shotgun, no question, and Billy understood patterns well enough to know the wound resulted from something other than typical double-ought buckshot or a slug. Even fired up close, the shot would spread, and this hole was smooth and compact. But what about the walls and the window area? The heavy destruction was weird like the aftermath of focalized explosions, not buckshot penetration. It had to be a FRAG-12. Whatever took place, a lot of rounds were spent, and each made a thunderous noise.

After blowing Jess away, why would anyone want to stand and empty a .12 gauge? Slide and fire...slide and fire. Billy had emptied many a round in the Marine Corps. No way the shooter would want to empty the gun. The urge to run before the cops showed would have been tugging at him. The damage had to be a symbol of power. The shooter reloaded the magazine with loose shells, probably in a jacket pocket, or, maybe it was an automatic like he'd tested that had been specially loaded.

Did he, or she, fire one round, start dismembering Jess, and then stop to blow the wall out? No. He would have done Jess and blasted the wall as a token of his power. Next he'd have started cutting up the body to demonstrate his ruthlessness, but he had must have been interrupted by Nuke and left the saw behind to escape. Or maybe he remained hidden in another part of the house until they left, or perhaps he stood waiting for just the right moment to get the jump on them. Billy couldn't stay with his thoughts. The pain over Jess was so overwhelming that fear couldn't even jumpstart his survival instinct.

He gulped straight from the bottle, the burn of the old aged apple brandy causing him to snap to, but he couldn't even sense the effects of the booze after the first burn, except that the hit of calvados made his thinking clearer.

He straightened up off the hearth. Transfixed, Jenny stood over Jess. Billy started to pace. He glanced out at the city. The winds off the Pacific had thinned the fog, lifting the bank so the gray whisked along right at the skyline. San Francisco: pristine, celestial, sparkling, as if she floated on the water, deceptive in all her beauty. Many dark tales squirmed just below the surface of the City by the Bay.

Billy gazed across the water at the Embarcadero, at Coit Tower, at the whole skyline thrusting eerily into the night. He felt as if he could reach out and touch the famed landmarks. A premonition similar to when the Humvee first rolled out of the fog flooded him again, a bizarre but profound intuitive sense of enormous forces at play in the background, a reading coming from so deep in his fiber. He shivered. He understood that he must fight these forces alone.

Yes, he had good friends and a lot of help awaited his call. Nuke would automatically take control of any *de rigueur* revenge all by himself. But Billy understood his position as the thrusting force that would bring the connected, cash-laden people who lurked behind the scenes to task.

He would have to jumpstart the jurisprudence machine and continue to hammer on the players himself if he wanted the perpetrators to be taken down forever. And he grasped fully the importance of many critical moves taking place very quickly, because the trail leading to the real killer would be brushed clean quickly.

"We've gotta figure out what we're gonna do and get out of here." Nuke's voice boomed like the shockwave. Everyone slipped back into the moment.

"I'll call 911," Jenny said.

Nuke's broad, black brow tightened into a deep wrinkle—a rare event for the captain.

"No can do, Jenny! Billy will tell you the story," said Nuke.

"What are you talking about?" she asked.

Nuke took Jenny's arms with his broad hands and looked right in her eyes, "Last year in Malibu a sneaky little bitch, Nora, shot his woman, Melissa. The DA tried to drown Billy with the murder rap. I already knew not to bring the law in on anything, but he didn't have any street smarts. He's just a dumbass, cowboy jarhead. None of the cops or the DA's office guessed who they were messing with: a trillionaire? Billy shot in under the radar because he doesn't like very many rich people and never mixed in the social circles. The media didn't know about him because he wasn't like Trump and Gates and all the cutesy boys. He likes his privacy like me." Nuke laughed. "He was a shadow for the investigators, but without Harlan, Billy would be up at Pelican."

"Harlan?" asked Jenny.

Nuke took off for Jess' study towing Jenny, and Billy followed.

"Yeah, Harlan Jenks." Nuke looked at Billy, and they both grinned.

"Okay," said Jenny. "What's the joke?"

"Harlan's serious, baby, you'll meet him. You've never met anybody like him," said Nuke. "He's the best trial lawyer in the world."

"Hey, guys, get a grip. This is—"

Nuke pulled her over to the window before she could wrap up her thought. He eased a drape back. "Check out that Humvee."

"Humvee?" asked Jenny.

"Hummers are the civilian car for wannabe tough guys. You are looking at a military vehicle," said Nuke.

"Oh my god, it's what tried to kill us."

"Another Humvee?" asked Nuke.

27

"Down on Bridgeway in Sausalito," said Billy. "We chased a pair of guys from Animalfund. They had staked the building for months. We lost their car in the fog but another Humvee came out straight at us. They moved like droids, like NSA, like CIA thugs.

"Look at my truck," Billy said to Nuke.

Nuke looked at Billy's bullet-riddled truck in the driveway

"Holy shit. They dumped a lot of rounds. Assault rifles?" asked Nuke, stepping back from the window, moving to the hallway and signaling for them to follow. "Come on, get away from the window. Don't take any chances with them seeing you."

"Naw, he had an STI Grandmaster with lavender grips," said Billy. "Good piece with the eighteen-round clips, but the purple handle? That's for girls."

"Don't be a punk, Nuke," said Jenny. "The correct term is *women*, not girls. *And*, plenty of women can outshoot the vast majority of men. Pathetic statements are for wimps, not you. Besides, lavender is a smashing color."

Nuke smiled, "Hey, no contest, your honor."

Jenny winked at him. Nuke laughed and then asked Billy, "So, what happened?"

"We left the guys tied up in their truck. The law was blowing in fast, but Jenny got the plates." Billy pulled the piece of paper out of his pocket. "8V13657 and 8V13658."

"I wonder how many the state made in the series," Nuke mused.

"Good question. Harlan might find something there. The plates on the car with the two characters from Animalfund are," he read from another note. "5PDD559. They've been watching Jenny, Jess, the whole staff. The Humvee had to be in contact with the pair we chased. They looked like government. Maybe NSA but not clean-cut preppy types."

"We've got to search this place and jam," said Nuke.

"You take *dead latitudes* to Wilmington. I'll drop Jenny in the city, get rid of the truck, and cash out a car. I'm going to find these people."

"Time to go. That one across the street sees your shot up pickup and watched you enter. If he starts shooting, the neighbors will call the cops. They may have already because of the noise."

"Let's look around for a minute," said Billy.

He had hired Nuke as captain of his sailboat the year before. Nuke grew up on the streets of South Central Los Angeles. Mother and fatherless, he stayed with a hard-drinking aunt. Like many young entrepreneurs without anyone, he ran with the gangs.

As he aged into his 30s, the drive-by death of his baby daughter caused Nuke so much grief that he hunted down the young men who shot her. The bereft father tracked each of the killers to their homes, walked right through the front doors, and strangled all four with his bare hands. That same evening he left Los Angeles, completely devoid of interest in the life he had been living. The deep, throbbing knowledge that his own activity triggered the murder of that baby girl—cut short of the years with those special father-daughter things like eating ice cream cones— left a knot of pain in him.

Nuke drove 1,700 miles straight through to live with his grandmother on her farm near Buda, Texas. She had named her grandson. She told Nuke's mother that it would be Martin Evers Moss, a combination of Dr. King's first name and the stately Medgar Evers' last. Since the 1960s, she had invested money from growing organic herbs and ended up very comfortable.

During the stay, Grandma Moss guided Nuke toward his inner strength. She taught him to read quickly and with ease, made him practice piano, gave him English lessons, put ten dollars in a mutual fund for every day that he could go without using any *ghetto-babble,* her term for thoughtless languaging.

"You drop that trash and become a man," she told Nuke. "Then, after you break the habit, you can learn to use hoodie language and the powerful knowledge of street smarts as an advantage. Never try to be one of those old stiff ass white men—but you must never allow them to smash you because of what rolls off your tongue. Always got to stake out old Whitey; no matter the bullshit he spews out like poison, he's a ruthless son of a bitch."

With the blessings of the fine, old, high-toned Texas woman, Nuke returned to LA and etched out a new life. He loved the ocean and sailboats, and instinct told him that he had to remain removed from the earlier patterns in South Central. He decided to make a living brokering yachts and moved to San Pedro. Every street-smart kid is an astute businessman. Finding product and clientele were already familiar activities; the only difference was that now he pushed legal merchandise.

After Billy retired his global takeover business—the wealthiest man in the world and completely unknown and carefully cloaked from the pop-tabloid, business gossip like *Forbes*—his father died, and he made a vow to his mother, another high-toned, old Texas woman. They sat on the kitchen floor after the wake, and laughed and cried, and talked more intimately than ever. They drank ancient Armagnac straight over from Gascony out of French jelly jars.

A sizeable trust would be launched that would teach hungry youngsters how to make a living at something they really had passion for, to figure out what the word "fun" means, and to keep their sense of wonder alive.

That same spring marked the beginning of Nuke's new career. The two met in Wilmington where Billy had heard a Norwegian, catch-rigged yawl from the early twentieth century was docked. He ran into Nuke on board and they couldn't stop talking.

Billy wanted him to spend time with his mother, and Nuke took Billy to get close to Grandma Moss. Austin and Buda sat very close, and Billy knew his mother would be blown away by Nuke, would set him down and make him explain how he managed to find the will to persevere in such an amazing career change.

Billy could hear the questions. She had spent time immersed in the efforts of one of Freud's most profound protégés, Roberto Assagioli, whose work related to using willpower. Billy's mother always wanted to learn more about people who had developed the ability to use the willpower in ways that transcended the typical, clichéd, how-I-made a million drivel.

Billy had to go to Hong Kong on business, so Nuke wrapped the deal, buying *dead latitudes* for Billy. They rendezvoused at Nuke's grandmother's home in Buda, Texas. They grew even closer, sailed together, and Billy offered him the position of captain, with a hefty salary he used to jump-start himself as a yacht broker.

With his natural savvy, Nuke concentrated on selling to black professionals, athletes, musicians, and celebrities and they proved to be a solid market. At the same time, Billy couldn't have found a more methodical guardian for his yacht.

After they waded through Melissa's murder, Billy offered him a perpetual salary better than any yacht broker could hope to earn, and all the cash he'd ever need to take care of his grandmother. With the ad guys under wraps, the two men talked a lot. They enjoyed the sleuthing and the chase. Got their rocks off big time as Robin Hoods. Nuke loved the Easy Rawlins novels: his cool, his style, and his helping people, going past his own little sad story, short-circuiting the cops, and finding the real lowlifes. As younger men, they had both greatly enjoyed the Travis McGee novels by John D. MacDonald and one night—moored in Wilmington, California, laughing over a couple bottles of Coppola claret—decided to honor Trav McGee by becoming salvage.

As Nuke stood in Jess' study with Billy and this completely class-act, knock-down sexy woman, he wished they could just get away on the big sailboat. Wished they could go to the Caribbean, pick him up a beauty for himself, and island hop.

31

"What the hell are we going to do for Jess?" Jenny asked. "We have to call the cops; he can't just lay here and rot," she said, looking at the corpse and breaking into tears again.

Billy started pacing again like Jess would have done. Jess' vibes swarmed all around, and the great man's spirit filled the entire room as it prepared to move on to the other side, to push on through the gates of Bardo, starting the parting phases in *The Tibetan Book of the Dead*. Jess' spirit prowled like a great circling mist in the room—a sworl of pure energy.

By instinct, Billy wanted to be as close to Jess as possible for these few moments. He saw that this was the only ceremony they would be able to attend. An impulse flashed through him, as if Jess were right there.

He moved over to the Bang & Olufsen sound system. A vinyl 33 rpm of John Coltrane's *My Favorite Things* rested on the turntable atop the CD player. Billy fiddled with the controls, bringing the music up. The oozing little soprano sax took off and he started crying. He could hear Jess speaking: "Coltrane can bring you home, Billy. Tuck you right in out of the cold." Trane squeezing out the title track, the completely grounding flight of *My Favorite Things* made it as if Trane and Jess both stood before him. The emotions swarmed like mad.

Jess' voice kept coming back. "Whether we can remember or not, we live in the moment, Billy; you should sense that by now."

"We have got to go," Nuke said. "The law's on the way. I smell 'em. The rich watch their stuff close 'cause it's all they got. A wannabe cop's probably called in already."

"We *have* to call 911 and tell the truth," Jenny insisted

"No way we're gonna do that," said Nuke. "The neighbors own the DA and the judge. He'll want to wrap it up real tight, real fast, and they've got a retired gangster at the scene."

"We'll leave the saw," said Billy.

"Right," said Nuke, picking the long instrument up with his gloved hand and touching the trigger. "Man, oh man, that is some nasty shit. Harlan can get everything from CSI. We're going to hammer this dude."

Jenny started for Jess' office and Sam followed her. Billy roamed through the rest of the house with Nuke. It was immaculate, which meant Jess hadn't been home for a while. There were no piles of books or clothes anywhere

His housekeeper must have cleaned recently. All the shelves and tables were free of dust.

Jess usually loved being at home. He enjoyed having friends visit for days on end. Billy had never seen the house as tidy as this. Why had Jess been away so much?

Jenny called out, and Billy followed her voice into Jess' office.

Sam had led Jenny to Jess' little pocket date book under the couch.

"Sam went right to it, right here, just under this skirting. He must have dropped it when he heard the intruder coming," she said.

"He could have kicked it on purpose so they wouldn't find it," said Billy.

It looked as if Jess had been in a big hurry, opened it, and scrawled fast. Billy read the day's entry aloud, "Neeley at Tosca at midnight." He wasn't sure what it meant, but he slipped the little book in his pocket and looked around the study.

Jess had installed a lot of computer equipment since Billy's last visit. A massive, corporate-type laser printer, several CPUs, frame grabbing and scanning gear, video editing tools, and gear for mass producing internet files, CDs and loading flash drives.

Jess came from old San Francisco stock. His grandmother gave him his first name. At his birth, the spirited, Knob Hill dowager predicted that he'd be the proverbial wild child with a heart of gold like Jesse James.

As the years ticked by, every word from the woman proved true. Jess survived his teens in the '80s—an extremely torrid time in a sizzling city. Always industrious, he dealt marijuana to the newly burgeoned computer industry, working with old friends and hippy growers in Northern California. He barely slipped past numerous encounters with the police.

He put together a fortune on top of his inheritance. Kilo-by-kilo he built his trade with ordinary people, alongside the Silicon Valley types, the executives who used the pot to come down off cocaine and the hundreds of born-agains and good-old-boy types, the working-class Christians who liked to smoke a joint, watch the game with a six-pack. The dogs and burgers always tasted fantastic after a doobie.

But Jess lost interest when the fun, innocent pot smoking wore thin; business people dove into cocaine with a vengeance and turned into yuppies. The meth labs, crack heads, and speed freaks flooded the Bay Area from the East Coast. The cops and courts turned drug misdemeanors—as harmless as public drunkenness—into felonies and Jess dropped drugs completely.

Being a California native, naturally frugal and conservative, Jess put aside large sums of capital and with real estate passed on by relatives, and ended up a wealthy man. By the time Billy knew him, he had tied all the realty up in trusts, frozen forever as open space or affordable housing; rentals that paid the taxes and covered management but never to be used for profit. He set up bond funds to live off of and invested a vast fortune churned from pot money into trusts for children's sanctuaries, offering full support for those facing duress.

At times, Jess Hayes tried everyone's patience. He never couched the truth, which proved overwhelming at times. Ordinary, working people simply thought him eccentric and let go of their pretenses in his presence. But officials, socialites, newspeople, bureaucrats, politicians, and anyone hung up in their personal rhetoric were threatened by Jess' straightforward nature. Though indifferent to social mores, he had performed more acts of kindness than any one person Billy had ever known. He actually put his life, not just his funds, right into the projects.

Among the items Billy had never spotted before were piles of CDs and external hard drives on the two worktables. Jenny stood beside him, looking at a small shelf above the workspace lined with the spines of numerous CDs. Each carried a stick-on label lettered in Jess' hand: rhinos, African and Indian elephants, Siberian tigers.

Both Jenny and Billy examined the titles closely of the disks standing in a slot by the equipment on the table: 2025 - The End of Wild Bears - Kodiak, Grizzly, Black, and Brown; 2025 - The End of Tigers; 2015 - The Extinction of Pachyderms and Black Panthers. All three had notes written on the printed labels with a fountain pen. Jess always carried a thick, black Mont Blanc.

Billy pulled the pachyderm disk off the shelf. In a corner of the label the word "Neeley" was scrawled in small print, as if an afterthought. He squeezed it and the others into his vest pockets along with the notebook.

Billy sat at the keyboard and flipped on the computer, the rubber gloves making it difficult for him to move his hands. He inserted the external drives and scrolled through the directories. There were files, but they were not labeled with types of animals. They were labeled with names.

Jess had stored the files on the main drive and removable hard disk. A light blinked on the laser printer, and Jenny pushed a button to empty the buffer. The device began to purr and click, gears turned, and a piece of paper came out.

Jenny read aloud: "Slade is poking around, doing something weird—something big is going down. He is not a happy boy. Why is he mixing with Neeley? Why is Neeley pissed? If I can't make it, Billy and Nuke could...too much dangerous shit. I have to do it. He will be at a table in the back of Tosca at midnight. We have to stop them."

As she read, Billy heard Jess' voice, saw him pacing the room like some free-range creature stuck in the throes of modern life.

Jenny furrowed her smooth brow. "Who is Neeley?" she asked.

Billy shrugged. He tried to reason through why Jess would have bothered to type this out, to send the thing to the printer. Was he in trouble already? Was some obscure meaning hidden beneath the text, something he assumed Billy would understand?

The music swept through the house. Jess' presence swarmed with it. If he had been in his study working, he would probably have been listening to John Coltrane. Billy ached all over.

He willed himself to control his feelings as they rolled through in waves. He had to get a grip on what to do so he turned the computer off and slipped out the removable hard drive.

He peered out the window at the Humvee hunkered out there, dark and still. He noticed the lights that glowed from the house across the street.

Nuke's voice resounded in a muffled growl from the basement. "Billy, Jenny, come here."

Sam took the lead down the stairs. Billy cringed when he got to the bottom.

A cardboard box full of bear paws ripped off at the wrist—ruggedly scarred as if amputated with a chainsaw—rested on a bear's hide. Sam began to whine. Strings of big teeth and heaps of gall bladders mingled with the revolting pile of remains.

"Good lord," said Jenny. "This stuff's all from the trade. What the hell is it doing in Jess' house? He'd have brought this to the office. Someone is setting him up."

Nuke held up a shotgun shell. "This was right outside." He pointed to the basement door and said, "The dude who picked them up left through this door."

Nuke held the shell casing and a small, stainless steel object in his latex gloved palm. Fins were mounted on the back and three O-ring-like gaskets circled the front.

"FRAG-12s are made by a Brit company and are going to change combat forever. That's heavy ordinance for a hit man. Gotta be some deep strings attached."

"FRAG-12s?" Nuke looked closer at the shell. "So all the military, spooks, the Hill, the whole gang is anteed up for this," said Nuke.

"We're talking a river of cash," said Billy. "After I was inactive, I was called up as a non-person consultant, and sent on a black op in Afghanistan to test the AA-12 using all three loads, and I can tell you, they blow your mind."

"What's an AA-12?" asked Nuke.

"An automatic, twenty round, .12 gauge."

"Fock, man, they wouldn't even need the Air Force or artillery for backup."

"Exactly," said Billy. "A foot soldier becomes his own military force."

"So what's it got to do with Jess?" asked Jenny.

"We've gotta go," Nuke insisted.

"We've got a hell of a lot of questions," said Billy.

"The guy up in the Humvee might have a pocket full of these things," said Nuke.

"What are these?" asked Billy, pointing at the gruesome artifacts.

"Dried bear gallbladders," said Jenny.

"Damn, man, these guys are some nasty dudes."

"They are as ruthless as people get," Jenny agreed.

"Jenny's right," Nuke said. "They wanted to ruin Jess in every way. This is a frame up to destroy Jess' good name."

"No question. Jess' new foundation, Free Range, makes Greenpeace like Bambi. They have won hundreds of lawsuits, making an unbelievable mess for sleazy corporate types," Jenny explained.

Nuke scooped up a necklace of what appeared to be vertebrae spread across a pile of dried bladders. "What's this, Jenny?"

"A rattlesnake spine."

"It's a sacred Comanche talisman," said Billy. "Jess killed the rattlesnake barehanded with Luther to learn the sacred practice. It took days for him to find and catch the right one. He had to eat its flesh to become one with the snake. No store weapons allowed, so he used a sharp bois d'arc stick to clean it."

"These rituals were okay when there were a couple billion people, but now it's an industry," said Jenny.

"I like old Luther, but the son of a bitch is kind of off the deep end," said Nuke.

"Who's not off the deep end, Nuke?" Billy asked.

"Aw, come on, Billy. I'm messin' around."

"Luther made Jess apologize to the rattler for having to take its life, jerk and eat the flesh, thank the big diamond back for the sustenance, boil the spine and dry it, " said Billy

"Old Four Fingers blows your mind completely."

"Four Fingers?" asked Jenny.

"Luther Four Fingers," said Nuke.

"He makes you do all this to learn to stop holding onto the petty little trips we cling to. We go around trying to defend crappy stuff to prove we're okay. It's sort of like Force Recon training using psychotropics so the mind is opened up and purged. The ceremony is so intense you have to give up on being cute, stop acting out habits, drop everything, and get into present tense with your speech and your feelings. Afterwards, Luther gave Jess some jade beads."

"This is our Luther, right?" asked Jenny in disbelief.

38

"Luther Four Fingers is Comanche—the People. His family has managed the remuda on my father's ranch, Moon Willow, for over a hundred years. Luther has an old buddy named Milarepa Da Mo over in Chinatown who gave him the beads. They're 500 years old."

Jenny shook her head. "Doesn't make sense."

"What?" asked Nuke.

"Milarepa is a Buddhist Saint from the sixth century. He killed a couple dozen people before he became ordained. Da Mo is Bodhi Dharma, the guy who brought Buddhism to Japan. The real-world founder of Zen and the Shaolin postures."

"Yeah. Mo's dad honored both saints with his son's name. Nobody you ever met is anything like Da Mo. . .well, except Luther. Da Mo even stops Harlan dead in his tracks. Doesn't have to say anything. Nobody slows Harlan," said Nuke.

"He's an authentic, all Chi—mighty scarce in this day and age," said Billy.

"How come you know so much about all this Chinese stuff, Jenny?"

"I'm just lucky."

"Lucky?" Nuke smiled warmly. "You're somethin' else, girl." His big, dangerous face and kind eyes shone in the dim light.

"You remind me of Dr. King," she said.

"Damn, I believe that's the nicest thing anybody's ever said to me. But I'm no preacher."

"He's not as handsome as Dr. King," said Billy.

"Were you with Luther and Jess?" asked Nuke.

"I was."

"Do you have a rattlesnake necklace?"

"I do."

Nuke laughed. "We're gonna be continuing this conversation in jail if we don't get out of here soon."

"Some Chinese think jade brings good luck. Luther put the beads on the necklace for that purpose. The rattlesnake spine brings power. So we've got Luther who is a descendent of Quanah Parker and—"

"Who's Quanah Parker?"

"An amazing Comanche prophet," Billy explained.

"So these people trade in animal parts, too?"

"No. They would only kill the snake, eat the meat, and do everything by themselves."

"Billy, the Earth's population will be twelve billion 2035," Jenny said. "300 years ago a person collecting something like this for his own use wouldn't cause tremendous damage, though it still would have been murdering a fine creature for some lame superstition. But today's not 300 years ago. With Homo sapiens being such serious breeders and so vicious, slaughtering these animals will lead to their extinction."

"Rattlesnake. The whole backbone just like the Predator. Damn, Luther and old Da Mo are some real spooks. They've got to be up to something. They know who killed Jess. I can feel it. This spine makes my hand hot when I squeeze it," said Nuke. "We've gotta get all these leads down in a computer. List everything in a time table with notes and right away."

"Why would such an intimate possession of Jess' be down here with this . . . this, uhm . . . this horror?" Jenny asked, feeling ill. "His things had to be planted because Jess started Free Range. I mean, wouldn't the bear parts come from some other location? And, wouldn't one of Jess' very special personal possessions be stored right here in his home?"

"Maybe one of the perps found it in a closet, tried to steal it, but it gave him the creeps. Or maybe his boss slapped his hands." Nuke tossed it back on the pile.

Billy slipped one of the dried bladders and the shell casing into his pocket beside Jess's date book. A great, carefully concealed, dark cloud had crossed over Jess permanently, and all of their lives would be changed forever.

FOUR

Across the cold, swift water of San Francisco Bay, slightly farther north than Jess' house in Tiburon, two US Fish and Wildlife undercover agents crouched over the beam of a black, metal flashlight as they paged through a folder. They waited, tucked up in a thicket of live oaks. Wind hissed past the doors of the old pickup. The blacktop road they watched wound about the rugged costal woodlands, only a short distance from the Animalfund office in North Beach.

US Marshals had ferried their copies of this preliminary file straight from the Hill and barely caught the agents as they locked their field office door. From time to time, they glanced up at the turnoff from the blacktop to the dirt, but then continued to study the high priority op that had brought them to Marin County.

Operation Butchers Data...it was a gruesome case, but Clarence Henshaw and Desi Sandoval dealt with sickening situations regularly. Ghastly discoveries had become normal. Illegally sold tiger penises, rhino horns, bear bladders, deer fetuses, leopard paws: they had seen it all. There were mountains of completely disgusting contraband under everyone's noses. Within three months they had found two-dozen dead bears, some of them only cubs. The carnage took place for just a plastic bag full of gall bladders; the harvesting had grown worse every week since the recession began. Cedar choppers did the dirty work, performing their task for some stranger somewhere in a distant, expensive home, who took doses of the bile and for nothing but a high. The gallbladders worked better than Viagra for men. The sellers were no longer confined to strangers in Asia, bound by old traditions, so now the buyer might be a corporate wimp in America starved for a boner. Clarence and Des both knew that if the guy stood with

41

integrity and kindness like a real man, the hard-on would always be in place when required.

As the courts let the perps off, and years slipped by, their faith in human beings had oozed away. Nothing stood sacred within the US any longer. Wild, natural liver bile from the American black bear flowed straight out of the once-venerated national parks.

Clarence raised his eyes to check the road again. His massive body looked like he should be outdoors, not cramped by a truck's cab.

The thoughts of all the carnage pained him. The job with Fish and Wildlife and his family were his whole life, the only one he'd ever known. He felt his hands were tied as lobbyists controlled politicians and convinced them to turn away from the issue. Presidents, senators, congressmen: they were all dupes for the money. Their thirst for office made many of them spineless shadow puppets lost in an endless thread of broken promises and disgusting poli-babble.

Clarence always stood strong even though the atrocities piled up in his head until it throbbed. The new op focalized on the rapid decline of the American black bear population. The slaughter of the grizzlies still received some scattered media attention, but after the black bears started to come back during the late 20th century, all went quiet about them.

Clarence felt trapped working for the government; he couldn't do anything but watch. The mega-corporations controlled anything a worthy secretary of the interior might want to accomplish, so the rape of the wild had been continually hushed. Nobody would broadcast a canned hunt on TV, a slaughter with US senators and their corporate donors using illegal, automatic assault weapons out of a chopper to blast a magnificent grizzly with her cubs loping behind. With the recession, population growth, and real estate developers, timber groups, and mining interests lobbying, the Fish and Wildlife budgets were on the endangered list. Clarence knew from experience how extinction creeps in, and now even the national parks mascot was front and center on extinction row.

Clarence glanced at Des, who had only been with the Department of the Interior for five years. Young and strikingly handsome, Des turned many girls to mush as they tuned into his big, brown, lounge-lizard eyes, his thick black, wavy hair, and glowing teeth. When around the ladies, he swaggered with confidence.

As he continued to thumb through the paper, Des pulled the collar of his jean jacket up to shield the cold. Clarence checked the roadway.

"So, what's it say?"

"The usual crap, but they're paying a little attention to how big it is, saying parts trade is at six billion a year."

"Try 200 billion," said Clarence. "There are six billion trades just in the US."

"Even the left wing politicians want low numbers. If the end of Smokey gets out to their fellow Americans, they're dead meat. Six billion's just the petty cash that parts traders spend in bars and whorehouses."

"Yep, you're catchin' on, but why Operation Butchers Data? Does that mean there's a guy named the Butcher and this op's his story, solo, or do they have records NSA grabbed from the Butcher, or that some spooks have a new load of data about all the butchers?" said Clarence.

"Must be all the butchers."

"Parts or live animals?" asked Clarence.

"This isn't the whole thing," said Des. "The rest'll be sent out this week with some marshals."

"Must be parts, nobody knows about the live ones, all that stuff like the bile farms."

"Can't tell—must be parts—butchers cut up dead animals, so we're talking the stuff they get when they dig out organs and whack the saleable inventory off the carcass, not live trade," said Des, continuing to read. "It says the market's global and you and I are heading up this whole op."

"Black bear parts only?" asked Clarence.

"That's it. Says that this bunch knows what a strong cash cow black bears are, not enough grizzlies around, I guess."

"So it's business as usual? We start here and build a case with no funds."

"No. That's weird too," said Des. "The funds are open ended at this time."

"Say what? We're not even going to have to pay for tires with our own plastic?"

Des laughed, "Strange, right? With some money, we'll be able to find them fast."

"Right. Bust the big guy; he'll buy a high-priced mouthpiece and fix a judge. Next, the jurisprudence system pats his butt and turns him back out on the bears," said Clarence, looking impatient as he peered out into the night.

Des shook his head. "I'll read the whole report when it gets here." His hair glistened in the slight glow from the light. His keen eyes reflected shrewdness. "What do we do this shit for, Clarence?"

"We're dumb-fuck, tree huggers. Ask any corporate wuss and he'll tell you how lame we are, how we're screwin' up business, destroying jobs."

"You reckon?"

"What I don't get is why a Cubano stud like you isn't out in a band shakin' your booty. Oh man, all those hot hips and swaying chichis."

"I'm old."

"Spare me. Mick Jagger's still on stage or something. He's a band guy."

"Come on, let's get outta this truck," said Des.

Clarence pushed the door open with a huge, weathered hand and his ruddy face came to life as he

44

stepped into the ocean air. He slipped on his brown denim jacket and pulled up the corduroy collar.

"The Butchers File...why no apostrophe?" he wondered, gathering up the sound dish and recorder. "Must be all the major dealers, not one big, bad wolf named the Butcher."

"Guess so." Des checked his Beretta's action. "Talks about Animalfund sending a global report on traffic to the Hill this week."

"Animalfund. That's Jess Hayes."

"Right," said Des, "Good people. And man, I've never seen so many dolls in one place. These aren't the Betty-bubble-brain, Hugh-Hefner chicks or the bimbo or Pepperdine, business-speak bozos. These are the class-act, UC Santa Cruz and Sorbonne grads, not the in-your-face with the boobs types."

"What the hell is wrong with Hef's girls, Mr. Big Shot?"

"Come on Clarence. Don't mess with me. Poozle's never real good 'til you're with high-IQ chicks."

"The only animals you ever think about are two legged. You always want everything partner: 200 IQ and three-inch spiked heels." Clarence cracked up, pulling a .50 caliber Desert Eagle out of his belt and checking the action.

"Man, that's no lie. Can you imagine? Living in Tiburon—isn't that the richest place in California? Kills me. Jess does his tree-hugger shit like us, only he's up in his mansion."

Clarence grinned, "If he's as dumb as we are how come he's got so much cash?"

Des looked at the time on his cell. "They ought to be here pretty quick."

A dirt road broke from the main asphalt highway and wound into the woods. The men followed a trail that ran parallel, hidden from view by live oaks and scrub brush.

"So what do you think?" asked Des.

Clarence considered the folder they had left behind in the truck. "Same old shit. Government as usual."

"But they *are* throwing money at us."

"Come on, Desi, votes rule. Animalfund or Wildwatch, some enviro-trust's getting ready to blow the whistle on how fast we're losing bears. This president would get his *huevos* chopped off by his beloved public for letting parts traders in Asia murder Smokey."

"You are way jaded, Clarence."

"Won't be any big mammals in the wild by 2050. Don't play dumb with me, Des."

"All you ever think about is how fucked everything is, big guy."

"No, partner, I've been grubbin' around out here so long I can *feel* all the bullshit."

Cloaked by the tree line, carrying their surveillance electronics, they eased along the footpath, away from the thicket where the pickup sat concealed. They waited until three black Humvees pulled off the Marshall-Petaluma blacktop onto the unpaved surface. The vehicles traveled in tight formation, barely slowing for their turn. They swept off the asphalt and plowed the dusty roadbed.

Clarence and Des followed the trucks, but had trouble keeping them in sight because the scrub was thick. The craggy, windswept coastal hills of Marin County provided excellent cover.

The officers knew the area so well that they didn't run to catch up. They always started stakeouts early and scouted the environs closely. A dead end lay just ahead.

. . . .

The Humvees filed along swiftly in the fog. They rolled into a big clearing and raced around the live oaks that lined its perimeter. They circled like frontier people ringing up wagons for the evening.

46

A husky man with a full beard and weathered cheeks briskly stepped out of the second Humvee. He wore jeans, work boots, and a green and black plaid wool jacket. Urgency propelled him, but he did not rush. He moved to the back smoothly and mechanically.

Both of the rear vehicles hauled heavy steel cages in their beds and additional men climbed out. One carried a Mossberg, slide action, riot gun. The man next to him held an HK MP5 assault weapon. Two more sentry types slid out of the last Humvee. All four slung their weapons over their backs to help the husky man unload equipment.

He threw an industrial extension cord over his shoulder and jacked it into an electric outlet on the Humvee's front bumper. In the circle he unwound the coiled cord onto the grass. One of the other men brought him another loop and he spread it on the ground. In the center, he placed the remainder down in a neat pile.

The bearded man returned to the vehicle and checked the gearshift and the parking brake methodically. He flipped the ignition and the engine idled smoothly. He circled around to the back of the Humvee, remaining intent on the work at hand. His face never changed expressions.

The others finished unloading rolls of plastic sheeting, ice chests, boxes of latex gloves, and more equipment. All of them dressed the same: work boots, jeans and jackets. The only variation was the color of the plaid. The husky man leaned into the back of his vehicle again and pulled out a long, D-handled, reciprocating saw with a twelve-inch, fine-toothed blade already attached. One of his associates grabbed an industrial searchlight in each hand and accompanied him out to the center of the circle.

They got juice from the cords, and the halogen lamps flooded the clearing. The man plugged in the saw. He held the long, heavy tool up in front of him as if saluting an unseen sky god and squeezed the trigger. The thin, fast-cutting blade sped in and out of its housing.

As the men finished working with the equipment, they moved to one of the vehicles and hefted a large, thick, steel plate to the ground. Another man pulled one of the other Humvees out of formation and backed it up to the sheet of trench covering. A small crane slid out, and the man lowered the hook at the end of the crane's cable. Another slipped it through a hole in the steel. He backed across the clearing to an oak, stopped, and the machine leaned the formidable rectangle against the trunk of the tree.

A pair of men dressed in black SWAT gear had remained seated behind the smoky glass in the lead Humvee. They stepped out at the same time, paused, slipped their caps on and adjusted them. One, thin and wiry. The other, trim but powerfully built, was six foot five and glanced down at his companion. They both had long black hair that was gelled straight back over their heads. The patches on their ball caps and vests read ANVIL.

While the husky man and his crew continued their field review, the men in black scouted the entire area. Quick and sinewy, they moved like a pair of weasels, turning their heads about rapidly, surveying everything closely. After touring the outskirts of the clearing twice, they took off their hats, crawled back into their vehicle, and sat talking on cellphones. They wrapped up their conversations and scrutinized the crew. Their faces shone gaunt and pale with serious expressions in the glow from the ten million candle lamps.

With sudden urgency, they stepped down out of the trucks again. They snapped their caps back in place. Both stood erect, with their hands down at their sides, radiating an attitude of grim authority. They studied the clearing carefully. With quick and penetrating eyes, they surveyed everything, every inch of the hideaway. The crew seemed entranced by the movement of the saw and paid little attention to the two men.

With a southern drawl, the tall one in black spoke to the bearded man, "You all set, Cosmo?"

"Yes, Brother Maxwell," the husky man replied.

The others exchanged nervous glances.

"When did you bring him in, Cosmo?" asked a tall, clean-shaven man.

"Brought him in yesterday, only it's not a him; she's a sow."

"A sow?"

"Yep. Couldn't find a male."

"She got cubs?"

"That is affirmative. She has two," said Brother Kramer.

"Oh lord. Well...I guess we've got to carry through. Brother Slade wants these bozos trained pronto," said the clean-shaven man, reaching deeper into his pockets and kicking at the reciprocal saw. The rest of the men fidgeted.

The pale, serious pair circled the field again, talking on their phones.

"No, the Italians are late. Yes, an hour. They have a lot of attitude, too," said Brother Maxwell to the phone. "Why are we calling these people Italians if the boss is named Neeley? From England? So they're mixed? Germans? Colombians? Sicilians, too? I thought all those types hated each other." Brother Maxwell dropped a beat, thinking. "Well, Brits are sometimes super smart and really nasty, but why would an Italian work for one? He what? With tree pruners? That's disgusting, explains why he's boss. Right, okay and the best at distribution. Yes, you're right Brother Slade."

Brother Maxwell stared off toward the horizon, thinking. "Yes, of course I'm on a safe phone, Brother Slade," he said, tensing his jaw and pausing.

"No. You've got to be kidding. No, of course you wouldn't kid about anything so serious." His face contorted as he continued. "Where did he come from? You what? ANVIL investigations can't find anything? That's hard to believe."

Brother Maxwell watched the men in the field intently as he continued. "The truck's registered to a Gold Coast corporation that owns six tankers under and Indian flag?

What's that? Is the guy a Muslim? Who the hell is he? Damn. He went right over and beat the hell out of two ANVIL ops. I can't believe that."

Brother Maxwell walked toward the others. His southern drawl grew thicker.

The shorter man, Brother Noah Army, followed. He also held a cellphone to his ear. Brother Maxwell's black hair shined so thick with gel that nothing, not the night, not hiking around the site, no activity could have moved even a strand out of place.

"Is he from India or something? He's white? The woman was in the truck too? Damn, who is this guy? The cops have our ops? So the judge will soon get a call from the Hill, from the Senate."

His face strained as he tried to think through the twist in plans. "So, our only worry is the Animalfund woman taking this invisible shipping-tycoon-gone-postal up to Hayes' house."

Brother Maxwell inspected the men in the circle as he neared them again. "Yes, of course, Brother Slade, but that's covered, because Zeke is out front and he's getting ready to go in the house to check on the NSA exterminator, make sure the tree hugger is cut up and hauled off."

Brother Maxwell examined every person.

"Right, Brother Ezekiel Army. He would call the second he saw anything weird. So the shipping tycoon must be eliminated with the girl. No, of course not, the NSA can't have any exposure at all. Yes, I understand. Right, I'm going down to the house myself. Yes, Brother Slade. Yes, of course." The man shielded his voice with his hand. "Yes, I'm leaving now."

He stopped short of the men. The shorter man paused well behind him, and Brother Maxwell turned around and walked back to him.

Maxwell said into the phone, "Yes, Noah is talking with Ezekiel. Yeah, okay, I'll tell him right now."

50

Maxwell looked at Brother Noah and shouted, "Tell Zeke to go on in the house."

Seeing that Brother Noah understood him, Maxwell wheeled around to survey the field preparation and see if he could leave. "Right, Brother Ezekiel. That's right. He's on his way in to check on the NSA op."

Maxwell slipped the phone in his pocket and stepped on into the group. The men in plaid still stood transfixed, quietly staring at the saw, hands in pockets.

"I hate to take out a sow with pups," said a square-faced man. "I guess we have to get used to production, but..."

Maxwell overheard the comment as he moved in among the men, surveying the equipment.

"Gentlemen, we are chosen to train these new recruits. This is not about personal decisions. We are working with much bigger matters. This is how you set yourself free with your maker. The Book of Revelations is upon us. You have been given an opportunity from God's hand. This is ANVIL: The American National Vigilance and Investigation League. We are here to make the Earth whole again. We are administering God's science, gentlemen. You know that, Brother Kirby," said Maxwell to the square-faced man.

All of the men in plaid pulled their hands out of their pockets and straightened their posture as Maxwell continued. "You are chosen. You are now a part of a greater whole. Brother Slade has a system, God's word, the Science of Man. The world has been out of balance for several millennia, and Brother Slade has been chosen to execute the true meaning of Christianity with science through God's word. Human behavior is being changed forever. We will have true systems, the command for the new millennium. Nine-eleven brought us the new order. Christianity has risen again. The false religions will be disposed of by God's command. We are his servants. We are ANVIL. September eleventh, 2001 was a great date, gentlemen. Its pain launched the return of the United States of America."

Unable to move, mouths ajar, the men stood transfixed by Maxwell's charismatic baritone.

"Let none of us use disparaging language. Remember Brother Slade's words, in the name of true Christianity, by the science from God which is the new scripture, The Science of Man. Dwell not on negatives, for they are from the workshop of the devil."

The circle of men looked down at the tools in an effort to avoid Maxwell's eyes.

"Glitches are always a part of any system, gentlemen. Though created by the Almighty, we remain men. Our mission includes immediate alternative action," said Maxwell, looking at each of them. "Are we all prepared for this event, my brethren?"

"Ah, Brother Maxwell, have you decided what to do with the cubs?" asked the square-faced man, his brow furrowed with concern.

"They are part of the inventory of man, Brother Kirby. True science is performed by the modeling of data in robust corporate style for the resurrection of Christianity. All of you are supposed to be skilled with procedure by now. Why do we have the cages with us?"

Maxwell did not threaten Kirby. He spoke clearly, without any blaming overtones. He smiled warmly when testing the man on product handling protocol.

"The youngsters become inventory and you will take them back to the Washington State Command Center, to Fort Rainy. While young they will be raised safely at one of the command centers. Then, they will be released back, east of Lake Ross as stock," Brother Maxwell grinned and raised his brow. "Can't let 'em out so little. Something'll eat 'em without their mom, and we've gotta protect our inventory."

The group laughed nervously, and as the men in plaid struggled for their senses of humor, two black Chrysler 300s with smoked windows pulled off the dirt road and eased into the clearing. Without hesitation, Brother Maxwell turned and walked toward them. Brother Noah strode to move up alongside him.

Like phantoms, the cars moved into the circle. The passengers could not be seen, but when the trucks stopped, four men in cashmere overcoats stepped out, one out of each car, with slide action shotguns.

FIVE

The huge house sat among a group of multimillion-dollar estates perched over the Pacific Ocean a few miles south of Laguna Beach. Nothing in the environment hinted at the home's proximity to the grating hustle of Los Angeles an hour and a half north.

The entire south coast shimmered in full autumn glory. The sun, the moon, the water, the bright blue days, the gossamer evenings, the tourists returning to the heartland: fall ushered in the part of the year when the coast belonged to the locals. Time seemed to stand still.

Mattie Slade felt close to God as she swept her eyes over the lights dotting the coast above Mussel Cove. The miracle of His presence swept through the thin blonde woman. On the northwest horizon—big, thick, and dark with water—a few cumulus clouds stood out with rings of moonlight around their edges. They moved through the heavens lazily, hopefully foreshadowing the coming of the winter rains.

Mattie wondered why the storms were late. Would they come at all? Were the Revelations unfolding? The weather seemed so strange. The sun shone so hot each winter. Would the southland run out of water? Men did such horrible things to the Earth—were the drought, the heat, and the hurricanes all signs of the coming retribution. She thought her mother's old songs: "God gave Noah the rainbow sign. No more water but fire next time . . ." The planet had begun to burn with global warming. Was it true? Were they watching the Apocalypse move closer every day? Were the horsemen galloping home? Were Americans causing the fire by being so lost in greed?

Mattie walked along the deck diffidently, and then stopped because the grandness completely overwhelmed her. Tears came to her eyes. As she witnessed the sweeping beauty of His vastness, she understood God with every fiber of her being.

Small and lean, but invincible of spirit, Mattie always persevered. Her rough, strong hands bore calluses and remained ruddy from harsh cleaning chemicals. She refused to allow anyone to clean her home even though her husband now knew tremendous financial achievement.

The lockup of others in servitude, indenturing them to perform one's personal chores did not fit Jesus' plan. Trained to bear witness from birth, Mattie never allowed herself to be a slacker. She practiced what she preached. The miracle of God's creations possessed her so overwhelmingly she clinched her fists at her sides and shivered with vibrations. Then she tucked her hands under her biceps and hugged herself.

But even in this moment of inspiration, a cast of blankness clouded Mattie's face. Not a vague emptiness, but a frantic edge running in slow motion—a countenance unique to people who spend many years ingesting mind-altering, prescription drugs doled out freely by their doctors.

She recognized her overindulgence in thoughts, scooped her dust rag and bottle of lemon oil off the rail and padded gently upward on the risers of the outdoor stairs that ran from deck to deck, heading up from the lower parts of her home to the main floor.

In the living room, she eased toward the dozens of yards of wooden bookcases, all solid cherry, surrounding the eight-foot wide, stone fireplace. She passed her husband, Jet Slade, who sat at his computer. Slade studied what was on the screen.

The on-screen image laid out the entire planet with exhaustive precision. Proficient, centered and tireless, Buster Bush—global director of IT for ANVIL—applied Richard Buckminster Fuller's Dyaxiom Map Projection of Earth for the design. Buster was a fan of Mr. Fuller and knew that he would have been as appalled by this application just as Dr. Einstein had been appalled by the United States' creation of the bomb.

Buster was proud of himself for being brilliant enough to comprehend Mr. Fuller. He had started with the Earth as a sphere in order to capture a model of the surface. He then laid it out on an icosahedron. Next, using the twenty triangular planes of the image folded out flat, he produced a single visual of the blue planet's land mass—a simple, fully-realized, world map.

A classic example of Buster's brainpower was that he knew Mr. Fuller's searing genius was manifest in the fact that the chart was a cinch to use because one experienced only the slightest distortion of the existent continents. As Slade commanded, ANVIL thrived and provided accuracy via a healthy mix of God and science.

Slade grinned broadly, looking at the screen. He punched his mouse and icons of tigers, bears, elephants—all the creatures of the wilds—popped up on the continents they inhabited. Then, with another quick flick, the images of the animals turned into spreadsheets, into inventory counts of the species in each area. He peered at Buster through the equipment racks between them.

"This separates the men from the toddlers. Just-in-time distribution makes wild animals a better racket than the God business; I don't even have to preach or talk to the customers at all. JIT inventory gives us a perfect global supply chain, and, we have free product.

"The nations pay for our manufacturing and warehousing. The harvest of product is performed by idiots and costs nothing. Damn, Buster, we are good. I went into God as a business because the end user is addicted—but it's better than beer or drugs because the product is almost free. The horrible part is that I have to babysit all of the congregation."

"So what about the gun, boss?"

"Now Buster, you know what the Lord said about impatience."

"No, I don't, boss. Besides, what the Lord said was in the pre-computer age."

"Well, now we have the ministry and this wonderful, global inventory out in the woods. They are cash cows for the support of growth. After our presentation at the ranch, the wonderful world of weapons opens to us. Not only do we lock in a third revenue stream but our potential for vigilance will be augmented exponentially."

Slade punched his mouse fast and the screen refreshed instantly, truncating down from the overview to the local habitat: the Americas, North America, the United States, Virginia, black bears. Glancing at a screen, he could spot the habitat of each species of animal that would become part of ANVIL's product line.

He clicked again and the US map popped back up. On-screen, the cursor eased up to Alaska. He double clicked, and rack upon rack of computer hardware whirred and came to life flashing, downloading and uploading through the ANVIL systems. Lights blinked, motors whirred, and hard drives strained as the trunk line blew data through the internet, scoured local area networks, searched mountains of information, and loaded graphics files. Slade's face pinched up at the brow in a knot of wrinkles as he watched the screen.

Mattie surveyed Slade's workstation nervously and looked briefly at her wiry spouse and his companion. Buster sat at an identical computer rig. The workstations stood back to back. Slade slicked his crow-black hair straight back over his head with a comb. His vintage, Ray-Ban Aviator sunglasses spread a yellow tint over his eyes. His father gave him those shades and they were the one possession he treasured. He wore a black silk shirt, black jeans, and black cowboy boots.

Buster slouched in a swivel chair. He hammered strokes on a cordless keyboard resting on his lap. His black boots sat on the floor. His stocking feet rested on a shelving rack. He also sported black jeans, but wore a fluorescent, lemon yellow T-shirt. The silk screening on the back read:

NO FEAR IS BULLSHIT

IT'S ALWAYS THERE - RIDE IT & DON'T PLAY COOL

The silkscreen above the aphorism highlighted a lone surfer on the face of a humongous wave.

Muffled microphones projected from the racks, making the workstations look like a disc jockey's studio. Audible input from other ANVIL centers as well as men's voices filled the room through studio speakers. It overwhelmed everything.

Mattie's body jerked ever so slightly each time a new sound flooded the room. She saw her husband connect to the phone lines through his headset and frown. She hunched her shoulders up, pulled her elbows toward her body, shivering at the sounds of the digital equipment and the sounds barking through the speakers.

Slade dialed Brother Ezekiel Army. Deep in thought, he held his sunglasses up and pinched the bridge of his nose. "I never want to have to tell you this again, Brother Ezekiel—we do not make mistakes at the American National Vigilance and Intelligence League. How long have you been trained as an ANVIL professional?"

He leaned back and rubbed his small round belly with pride. The years of being scrawny—especially as a boy—had etched some deep scars into his psyche. All his old wounds remained raw sometimes. Dull, but hurting around the taut edges of the mental damage, the areas where he had been forced to place the sutures in his thinking to keep his mind from bursting.

Slade watched various animal screens as he spoke to the microphone. He touched the controls and Brother Ezekiel Army's voice flooded the speakers, booming in from the Humvee where it sat in front of Jess Hayes' home.

"But Brother Slade, the gangbanger type came right in out of the fog."

"Had you locked the door behind you, Brother Army?"

"No, I hadn't locked the door. I went to make sure everything was okay with the NSA op; in and out was the plan. I left the door ajar just a bit for speed."

"Brother Ezekiel, I am very concerned."

"Brother Slade, it was a heavy oak door and I left it open in case I needed to exit fast."

"So you left yourself vulnerable to whomever decided to walk in off the streets and interrupt your mission?"

"Right. This big, deep, black-guy type of voice started yelling out for someone named Jess and another name too. Billy, I think. So I ran."

"Alright, that means this intruder knew the tree hugger, that's Hayes. So Billy's gotta be the pickup truck character that is so aggressive. How soon did this Billy guy drive up?"

"I don't know. When I got back to the truck, a pickup was already in the driveway."

"Was Hayes dead?"

"Yes, but only one hand was cut off, and the NSA guy was headed out the back."

"For god's sake, the body was supposed to be parted."

"Just the hand. But the NSA perp blew the shit out of the houses."

"Did you get the plates off that truck?"

"No, I ah, I was watching the house really close after I got back up here. And then they were gone."

"Lord, Zeke. What the fuck's going on?"

"I'm just watching to see if they leave."

"So you followed the NSA op down through the back."

"Right."

"Where was he parked?"

"Don't have a clue. The guy was a phantom, really fast."

Slade's voice deepened into a basso profundo. "So your effort at being expeditious was interrupted by an intruder." The sound system delivered so well that Slade sounded as if he spoke from the throne of the Almighty.

Mattie shivered and applied lemon oil to the library cases, bringing up the warm, hand-rubbed finish of the cherry shelving. She moved frantically, never looking up.

"Yes, Brother Slade, now I am watching to see where the black guy goes."

"Okay, Zeke, I mean Brother Ezekiel. Brother Noah and Brother Maxwell are on the way. The minute they get . . ." The phone thudded as if dropped. Ezekiel's voice grew distant and ragged, and there was another voice in the Humvee—a deep, unfamiliar voice.

Slade got up and started to pace as he listened to the beating and yelled into the microphone, the situation was chaotic enough to get anyone's attention.

"I've got to go up there; it's all gone to shit."

"Somebody's beating the shit out of Zeke, probably that deep-voiced guy that walked in on him and the NSA fuckup."

"Run a voice trace. Find out who this guy is."

"It's already started."

The sounds of the struggle only continued for a few seconds longer before a deep voice said, "You motherfuckers better run, because you are under surveillance, and you'll soon be mine." Then the phone went dead.

"Did you get a run on that voice yet?"

"My people aren't finding a thing."

Slade dialed Maxwell but didn't get an answer. "This whole thing has a really bad smell to it. Maxwell's not picking up, and we have two lose cannons."

"Three with the tree hugger girl," said Buster.

"Two of our brethren are wrapped up with the law in Marin County. Those are ANVIL ops, retired SEALs, the best. And they're also really fucking expensive," Slade exclaimed, losing his temper.

Slade's voice caused Mattie to tremble.

"They cost an unbelievable amount of money, and now they must be eliminated."

"Can you trace the black Afro guy?"

"He is a black hole, probably erased himself from the radar for past crimes on purpose," said Buster.

"Who is in the pickup?"

"Gotta be the Free Range bunch again. Fucking Hayes," said Buster.

"Your Thursday meeting in Long Beach is set for 10:00am at Christy's with the Fish and Wildlife guy. What's his name? The Cuban one. With Hayes gone, we'll get rid of Free Range. They bounce their tactical plans into web chats, all kinds of blogs, information sites, spread it out all over, so they're rough to get a handle on, but all those portals leave holes in the setup, and my NSA hirelings send the stuff right to me every time."

"How can they be so smart? In those pictures they look like some biker gang, not tree huggers," said Slade.

"Yeah, and they're rough too. Even Neeley said they fight like barracudas."

"You sure about the Fish and Wildlife meeting?"

"Thursday at 10. Christy's. Long Beach. Apparently the place belongs to Sonny Bono's kid."

"Godamnit! What's next? Stinkin', nosey, power-tripper cops have an ANVIL Special Ops team; some gang banger interrupted the NSA exterminators before they cut Hayes up into parts; SWAT teams falling apart, gangbangers, bikers, tree huggers, too many loose ends."

"No, boss, they call themselves oxygen protectors or some such crap, now."

"Right, and now I'm dealing with these nincom-fucking-poop oxygen assholes all the time. What the fuck is next, Buster?"

Slade loved the sound of his deep, resonant, pulpit voice. He hated snafus by underlings interrupting the trance created by his magnificent words, hiccups that forced him to think. He looked at his display and jabbed the mouse again. The Dyaxiom Map refreshed without interruption and continued to fill the screen until he double clicked on a tiger in a national park in India.

"Buster, the data's not popping up when I hit tigers in India."

"The linkage is tight boss, but the Indians are dragging their feet. Not getting me the data. And their accuracy sucks," said Buster, pulling a cigarette out of a pack of unfiltered Camels.

"When are you going to stop smoking those damn things?" asked Slade, getting up. He walked over toward the windows to the wet bar. He popped the cork on a bottle of scotch and poured off a couple fingers.

He turned and walked back to Buster. "Give me one."

The programmer looked at him, surprised. "I thought you quit, boss."

"I've told you a million times not to call me boss. I am your fellow citizen, your ANVIL brother, and your spiritual advisor."

"Okay . . . boss . . . ah, Brother Slade."

Buster plugged away at his keyboard, wrapped up in the screen again. The entire country of India jumped out of the Dyaxiom Map. Icons of various animals dotted the whole country. Buster hit a few keystrokes and computer code flooded a pop-up box on his screen.

"Got the downlink from the satellite, but I still get bugs in the links from data to graphics. This only happens part of the time. Shiva Digital is pretty good, but I think that the boys and girls at Bollywood Data are smoking hash or something."

"So?" said Slade, sipping some whiskey.

"Lined up Karma Data Corporation. Heard good stuff from the IT boys at a couple major internet providers. Lester over at Globelink says they're smooth."

"Sounds like a bunch of fucking hackers," said Slade.

They are not concerned about people, but about pumping the animal parts cash flow into arms trade. I've gotta go down to the ranch with you, too. The Cray isn't conversant with the Marseilles facility. Keeps dropping the link."

"Fly over and get those Indian hippies herded up. Steal their hash and sell it in DC. Those neocons gobble the stuff up like junkyard dogs."

"Yeah, I'll turn the operation around. That new EU-TWIX database in Belgium is gonna make us a fortune."

"I can't keep up with all those letters, the ah, what'd'ya call it—CITES and all that?"

"I know, too damn many acronyms now; drives everybody bat shit."

"So tell me again."

"Big database. All twenty-five European Union states. Center is Brussels. Right by our office. The BFP, Belgian Federal Police, lists all the crooks in the animal trade. We grab names right off the thing and cut deals so they go right out and get parts for us. I gotta couple Rumanian hackers on it. Money from heaven, boss. I've already moled through."

"Damn you're good."

"I know, and that's not half of it; we'll use the same lame-os to connect with arms dealers. We'll buy and sell ordinance all over Europe. I'll go next week. Bayonne needs some link work, so I'll hop right on over from New Jersey. Hong Kong and Singapore are just fine, but something's wrong in Seoul and Shanghai. And, I have to bounce around India again."

Mattie started to cough from the cigarette fumes. She looked as if she might faint.

"Darlin', did you go get your 'script filled?" asked Slade.

She reached into the pocket of her apron, held up a medicine vial for him to see and then padded out of the room silently.

Slade went back to his workstation. He brought up a working model that showed all of their computer stations on a traditional, rotating globe. The network of ANVIL centers covered the earth. Slade amazed himself. All this in a few, short years. He had dropped offices and would add more, but the network stood solid.

He loved his own idea of using mob types like Neeley for handling the distribution of the products—again, pure genius on Slade's part. They had always performed as serious businessmen and the powers-that-be would watch thugs, not ANVIL. American National Vigilance and Intelligence League—the ring of truth for everyone.

More Slade genius. The perfect acronym. The powers-that-be couldn't argue with hammering out the truth on steel. And the big bonus—Homeland Security needed all the help they could get.

A flow line the color of blood moved through each ANVIL work station on a Dyaxiom Map and up and down from the satellite. The line broke and blinked at all areas with system problems. Slade took a deep drag off the unfiltered cigarette, a pull off the scotch and walked over to Buster who shook a couple more cigarettes out of the pack. Then Slade walked out toward the deck.

He edged up to the rail and lit another smoke off the one he held between his fingers. His eyes looked like two onyx circles, steady and hard as he gazed out over the dark Pacific. Slade's mind slipped back to Texas, to the fields and streams he knew as a boy. To a simpler time, hunting, fishing, lazing in the sun. He felt a longing for a life that allowed him to relax, that provided a less demanding environment. As a boy, he charmed every adult—such a bright-eyed, helpful child, so sweet, so kind.

He took another swill of the amber liquid and walked over to the oval-topped dove cages. They hung from the roof beams over the deck. He looked at their soft bodies, at their piercing eyes and the melody came to him as always. The words from the old song poured through his mind: "On the wings of a snow white dove, he sends you his pure, sweet love. Oh, he sends you his love, on the wings of a dove."

Sweeping thorough his every fiber, the deep-throated cooing made his skin crawl. He couldn't even see that young boy, that sweet-faced thing he had been, any longer. The images slid down into the chasm and the sound of the doves crying overwhelmed him. He remembered Mattie as a girl. He remembered their baby dying. His mind could never stay with that thought. He remembered his mother, his father, Mattie's mother, her father—them leading the two children out to the barn after church. In front of them stood the Maxwell's, his best friend's, parents. Lucien, three years older, oh so much stronger, standing in front of him, between his own mother and father, Deacon Maxwell and wife, all born-agains. Lucien stared right at Mattie, then helped his parents. Slade's parent's hit him, his little baby boy skin. They were church people, the so-called adults. Each time it happened Slade's fire for revenge grew deeper. And poor, helpless Mattie: they would take her little church dress up from the knees. Each time he vowed to make Lucien Maxwell his servant. Lucien talked tough, but Slade could always hypnotize him with words, with his voice.

Then the throaty cry of the doves came over him so intensely that he threw the glass and the cigarette. Put his hands over his ears. The cooing grew louder and louder and louder, swarming all over Slade with the information that already jammed his head so tight his body throbbed all over.

In an instant, he felt so horny that he tightened his thighs to put pressure on his genitals. All arose in him quickly, wrenching at him like mad, a horrible, throbbing desire. He felt as if he would explode with the dove sound—that the thoughts would obliterate him just like erasing a file on the computer.

Slade walked back into the house fast to get away from the doves. He grabbed the bottle and poured more of the blend. He marched over to Buster with his hand out and didn't say a word. Buster gave him the whole pack.

Slade went straight to the kitchen where Mattie sat on the stool, looking through the massive windows, out over the ocean. Slade took her by the hand and the sound of the doves disappeared. He led her down to the master bedroom, to the special corner over by the French doors. A sturdy tabletop upholstered with fine silk damask. Slade placed the cigarette in a candy dish on one nightstand, next to a box of latex surgeon's gloves, and he placed the whiskey on the other wooden surface immediately adjacent to a slab of sweet butter.

Mattie bent over the cushioned surface at the waist. Slade slipped on a pair of gloves, eased up the back of her skirt and slid her cotton briefs down. He grabbed the white mounds of her hips and nudged up against them. He took a hit of whiskey and a big draw off his smoke.

Slade slid his zipper down and dug through his white briefs. He lubricated with the unsalted butter, then took hold of Mattie's hips and moved into the rhythm. The procedure took but a scant moment. Mattie supported herself with her arms without any reaction to the invasion— she stared at the Berber carpet.

Slade pushed the lid up on a pack of baby wipes, lifted several out delicately and cleaned himself. He shivered as the cool cloth removed the liquids. He peeled off the gloves, slid Mattie's cotton underwear back up over her hips, slipped her frock back into place, and then patted her backside primly. She arose silently and walked away, toward the bathroom while thinking about the kitchen, about a deep cleaning of the stove.

SIX

The four men in cashmere topcoats held their .12 gauge, Mossberg, Marinecote riot guns at the ready position—fingers on the triggers. Four more men with identical weapons—also wearing elegant coats—stepped out from the cover of the other car's smoked glass. They walked over to the two men dressed in black SWAT gear, bearing their arms down at their sides as casually as a businessman totes an umbrella.

The foursome with the slide actions on the ready flanked the others in a guardian formation. They all proceeded to examine the surroundings. They wore fine, wing-tipped shoes and gabardine trousers. After a first scan of the situation, they nudged one another and laughed.

"A fuckin' bear hunt . . . a, ah . . . what does he say?" asked the sole blond man.

"I dunno, Heiny, but we can't stay too long. We gotta get over to Tosca for the meeting," said the biggest of the men.

"Hey Leonard, fuck you and all the meetings you rode in on. You're gettin' awful pushy," said the blond man.

Leonard moved in close on Heiny.

"So who the fuck are you, Heiny? Turnin' Nazi, some SS-type thing—Heiny the Stormtrooper? Checking out who's naughty and nice?"

All the men laughed and Heiny pushed Leonard away.

The tall man in SWAT garb, Brother Lucien Maxwell, scrutinized them with a mindset of rancor. *How can any species be as stupid as Homo sapiens?* he thought, but he kept a straight face. "Gentlemen, you're late," he announced.

The men in topcoats all eyeballed him, taken aback for a moment by his commanding presence, then snickered.

"Yeah, well, you know. Shit happens," said Leonard, straightening up to his full height. Sizing Brother Maxwell up, barely moving his ruthless, pallid face. The men with shotguns raised them, slid the actions, chambered shells, and they all shuffled and sniggered.

"You the big cheese around here?" asked Leonardo.

"I am in charge of the operation," said Brother Maxwell.

"You oughtta know better than talking on a cell. They leak like sieves—hell, you could crush garlic through 'em," said Leonard. He grinned at the other overcoats who laughed, and turned back toward Brother Maxwell. The shorter man, Brother Noah Army, stood right up beside him.

Brother Maxwell kept his deadpan expression even though the men were like a group of insecure high school boys trapped in the paunchy bodies of grown men. "Shit doesn't happen in our work. Anyone who understands technology at all knows how and when to use cellphones, and would immediately recognize an apparatus of this size as a unit that is most probably protected. All of our security is state of the art. Any phone we use is risk free. Mr. Slade doesn't believe in excuses. Also, punctuality is very important, gentlemen, and I expect you to remember that in the future."

The toughs all looked at him with smirks on their faces. They laughed and elbowed one another.

"All right gentlemen, you've come here because Mr. Slade is a thorough man. He understands your potential in distribution, and he wants you to understand the parts business very well. The parts business is now one of the top revenue providers of the so-called 'illicit' enterprises—right up there with weapons, child labor, indentured servitude, smuggling people, humans for prostitution and the narcotics trade. It is a global industry with steady growth each year. Since you are now going to become such an important part of our work, you need to have a thorough understanding of production," said Brother Maxwell, wishing that he could get in one of the hoods' cars and leave these imbeciles, leave all of it behind.

68

Leonard's nostrils flared and his lips twisted with anger, but he managed to transform the energy into oratory. "The news estimates animal parts bring in six to eight billion a year, but he says the actual global cash flow is at least 200 billion. He figures the US all by itself is at about 40 billion 'cause we're global. The beauty is that Americans see enviro-types as bad guys, as tree huggers. Fish and Wildlife are the only watchdogs and they don't have enough funds to buy truck tires. Not enough Smokeys out there. The courts just slap your hands. The judges kiss ass to the politicians who all suck up to the lobbyists. It's perfect—nowadays, every last stiff in government, right up to the president, is a crooked, back-stabbin' chickenshit—we go about our business, and they play kissy face with the rich and each other. The real beauty of the whole setup is that the dumb-fuck, workin' stiff, my fella Americans, pay for the whole party."

Ready to barf at this swine's coarseness, Brother Maxwell kept quiet for the entire discourse. "That is all true. It is refreshing to talk with someone who is well informed," said Brother Maxwell. "I'm sorry, but we didn't introduce ourselves. I am Brother Lucien Maxwell, and this is Brother Noah Army."

The men in overcoats all shook hands with the brothers and introduced themselves, looking one another up and down. Then they reformed into a circle, cleared their throats and shuffled on their feet.

"We will make California the center of all product control. And pick up several billion in harvest right out of the national parks, off hunting ranches and out of the ports. We'll use snitches to spy on Fish and Wildlife, put a couple Smokeys on payroll and pick up all the product they leave behind because they don't have enough staff to handle inventory from busts. No matter what happens, they can't do anything but slap hands. It's fucking heaven." Heiny lifted his head and looked at the thugs, striking a baronial pose.

"Your knowledge of product disbursal is unparalleled, gentlemen. We have researched your capabilities in depth. Now, let's take a close look at how our inventory will eventually be handled in the field. Naturally, we have a lot to learn and technique will change on the various continents and with the different types of merchandise and field reps."

Brother Maxwell walked toward the lights. His voice had started sounding distant, muffled, as if he was in a padded chamber. His longing to get in one of the Chryslers and leave had grown stronger and stronger for months on end. When he got over to the gathering of men in plaid jackets, he paused. "Technical Command Leader, Brother Cosmo Sinclair is going to demonstrate how it's done," he said, pointing to the bearded man who had unloaded the equipment.

"Alright gentlemen, we will now move out in pursuit of three items to secure as inventory. First we have to flush them out," said Brother Sinclair.

Leonardo's men laughed nervously.

"Hey, we can move fast as frickin' Boy Scouts. We've done stuff in the woods that would scare you choirboys to death. Ain't that right Heiny? Heck, Heiny here's your original scouty-two-shoes type thing . . . know what I mean, Cosmo?" said one of the men with shotguns.

"There will be time for levity after we are finished, gentlemen," said Brother Sinclair to the men. "We are going to drive her back into the clearing and Brother Randy Gates, there—who is an expert marksman—will terminate her to be parted out."

Brother Gates walked toward the light briskly carrying an aluminum case. The man behind him carried a pneumatic sedative rifle. Brother Gates laid the case on the grass near the reciprocating saw. He flipped the latches, and a Stoner rifle, an automatic SR25, was snugged into the foam.

The gaunt, silent, careful man pulled the butt piece out, attached the upper and lower receiver, and the long sound suppressor with amazing speed. He sighted in on an oak branch, just visible, far across the clearing, fired off a round, and the branch fell from the tree with a distant thud. Immediately, he jammed another round in the rifle and blew a six-inch limb off the oak against which they had leaned the plate of steel.

"Fock man, did you see that thing?" asked Heiny, his mouth hanging open. "It's frickin' Deadeye Dick." All of the men in overcoats turned their heads in unison to stare at Gates. He stood, self-assured but reserved.

"Hey, Randy boy, we got a job for you. And we got better bennies than the fuckin' Boy Scouts, here. We got girls and candy for the nose. You can wear real clothes. You don't have to be out here crawling around with the friggin' spiders and fag-boys and stuff. How about it? How much is the den mother payin' you?"

Guffawing, the overcoats danced around nervously. Randy did not respond. He walked over to cover at the edge of the clearing and hunkered into the bushes with the rifle and sedative gun.

Brother Sinclair spoke in a commandeering voice. "Your cavalier attitude is not appropriate here, gentlemen. Do not get in the way. Put your weapons back in your cars. No one other than Brother Gates will be shooting."

The overcoats looked around at one another for a signal to destroy this new authority.

"As we return from the bush, the sedative gun and the sniper's rifle will both be discharged skillfully. However, the direction of fire will not be known to you. Do not re-enter the clearing until the product is down. At that time all firing will have ceased. You will be safe to join us for the parting."

Reluctantly, the men with shotguns put them back in their vehicles. But just as the final sentry leaned to place his in the car, Leonardo grabbed it swung the barrel up, over Brother Gates' head. With a thundering sound, he blew a branch off a tree. As the limb fell near the man, Leonardo slid another load into the chamber and the empty casing fell at his feet.

"Hey, see that shit. Don't go Adolf on us with your cute little woodchuck beard. We don't need no fuckin' dictator," said Heiny. "We put the riot guns away but we're gonna keep our heat. Hell, maybe we can catch some DEA geeks down there in the woods. Part out a couple feds." The men laughed as he slid a thick, black, SIG Sauer—an automatic pistol with a sound suppressor—out of his shoulder harness. He pointed it at the tree off of which Brother Randy Gates dispatched the limb. Heiny eased the trigger toward himself and the limb next to the stub from the one Brother Gates hit dropped to the ground.

One of the men pulled his hand out of his overcoat and he still had his riot gun. He chambered a shell, raised the gun and shot a limb of a nearby oak. One of the men wearing a plaid jacket already had his shotgun in the air. He blew a limb out right next to the first one. Both men chambered again.

The attention of every man moved back and forth from the pistol in Heiny's hand to Brother Sinclair and Brother Maxwell. The only sound came from the idling Humvee. Eyes wide, all of the ANVIL team had slipped into a hypnotic state.

Leonard watched his men and the ANVIL crew closely. Suddenly, he broke into a wide, mocking grin. "Hey, fellas, fellas, don't get your little scout-o-rama panties all bunched up on us just 'cause Heiny can shoot better than your marksman. We just wanna have some fun, you know. Make some money. Know what I mean? Why should ol' Brother Randy get all the kicks? Why should we start right off takin' orders from some cedar chopper fucks?"

Brother Maxwell looked at the ground, then up at the sky. He struggled to keep his expression deadpan. He longed to feel the wind blowing on his face as he drove to nowhere in particular, inhaling the freedom of not dealing with human beings. He looked straight in Leonard's eyes.

"Absolutely negative on that subject, gentlemen. There will be no indiscriminate use of firearms. This event will, under no circumstances, turn into a wanton display of violence. This is business and it is to be treated as such. Brother Gates is retired US Infantry. He is a highly-skilled

72

marksman. Random shooting damages the product. Makes it defective for the market place. Your weapons will be confiscated if there is a threat to product."

"Damn boys. You hear that. We got a boatload of Adolfs gonna take our cannons. Listen to me, all you woodchuck fucks need to drop a chill pill. Take some Valium. I got some right here. A lot of people have wanted to seize our hardware: judges, cops, bad guys—you name it—and you can guess where they are now."

The toughs all laughed. Brother Maxwell looked straight through Leonard as if he were product. His face was so pale it seemed to glow in the darkness. His dead expression made everyone nervous. He was almost 60 years old and there was not a wrinkle etched into his face. He never blinked and he never flinched away from Leonard.

The man with the tracking device looked up suddenly and said, "Okay, I've got her. Turn the Humvee off. She's down in the bottoms, in the creek bed. Let's go."

The men in plaid put their weapons away and took off at an unfaltering pace, leaving the thugs behind, moving down through the oaks and brush. They traveled through the thickets fast, into the darkness, toward the bottom of a valley created by the course of a streambed.

Brother Maxwell hung back, watching. He flipped his cell open and talked as he walked toward the trees. He watched a man in an overcoat bend and pick up his spent shell. They all put their weapons in the cars and moved out toward the others.

"They are here. Yes. They act like they're sixteen. Yes, I understand that they are effective. Okay. Right. Jesus. You're kidding. Somebody interrupted the NSA guy. Okay. I'll get Brother Army. Yes, pursuing the product. It's okay, I'll phone him," said Brother Maxwell. He stopped moving toward the woods, hung up and dialed another number.

As the coastal forest closed around them, the terrain became rough with rocks, fallen limbs and brush, and made every step tricky. The city dwellers in their expensive, calfskin shoes began to slip and fall. They breathed heavily, trying to keep up with the woodsmen.

"Goddamn," said one of them as he stumbled on a large rock, and hit the ground hard with his knee. "I'm not a fuckin' woodchuck. I don't need this shit."

As the gang caught up, the men in plaid all heard their clumsy movements and smiled as they neared, disgusted with the event.

"What the fuck are we out here for? Let's go back," said Heiny as he skidded down into the stream bottom, ripping his 1,200-dollar trousers.

From nowhere, Brother Army appeared in the streambed and surveyed the overcoats who were gathering themselves from the decent into the bottoms.

"Gentlemen, let's get some composure here. You need to maintain silence or you will disturb the product and we will not be able to run her in for parting. Please try to get a grip on your emotions."

"Hey, another frickin' bossy boy. You guys pop up just like fungi. This ain't no emotion shit. This is a goddamn place for a warthog, not for people."

"Gentlemen, shut the fuck up and try to maintain our pace," said Brother Noah Army and he took off running.

. . . .

The creek bed flowed downward toward a convergence with another watercourse. The men in plaid split up and covered ground quickly and quietly. The thugs moved along, trying to maintain the pace. They were quiet now, except for their breathing and the occasional scuffing of their shoes on sticks and stones.

In the distance, the two watercourses converged, forming a wide gulch. And there, scraping in the roots for grubs and rodents, the bear prowled. Alarmed by their noise,

74

she stood right up on her hindquarters. A large, native, American black bear, she weighed in at about 250 pounds.

She stretched her thick barrel of a nose out on the foggy air and adjusted her ears, listening to the wind. Her two cubs played at grubbing, stopping here and there to listen like their mother. They batted at one another and scuffled. It took only a moment for the cubs to pick up the concern of their mother. The mother sensed deeply, down in the recesses of survival instincts that had been passed to her from all of her ancestors—from all the black bear mothers that had padded along the Pacific coast for thousands of generations—that something odious, some threat to her cubs closed in toward them.

Her entire body shuddered as she lurched her forelegs back toward the earth, swatting at her children to come to attention and flee with her. The cubs grunted at the pain from their mother's swats but ran downward into the lower part of the basin.

Two of the men in plaid looked out from their cover, into the clearing created by the convergence. They had the bears flanked. The mother turned abruptly and bolted up a steep bank, out of the bottomland, up, up, upward through the scrub brush. The cubs whimpered at the strain of following their mother as she bolted through the dense growth.

The cubs ran through an eddy of air that carried the human scent. Their alarm took them over. Up the bank, fast, skittering on moving rocks, pushing hard, straining with all the might in their small bodies, they chased their mother toward the bench of earth that sat above the steep bank that carried them out of the creek bottom.

When the mother reached the flat area above the grade, she pushed up with her hindquarters again and put all of her senses to work on the darkness, on the air, through the wispy fog. The cubs reached the top and joined their mother on the wooded knoll above the men.

The cubs whined from the exhausting climb. Their mother craned her neck, listening, straining for the scent on the air. Her great chest rumbled with an uncontrollable growl. She batted her children again, wheeled around, lowered her forelegs, and loped up the ridge above the creek bottom.

She backtracked automatically. Her unparalleled, natural sense of topography sent her upstream. She ran above the men, flanking them, backtracking in a paced climb. Up, up, up. Upstream, back toward the source of the streambed, toward the clearing where Brother Gates waited with the light off, the Humvee off, and the Stoner rifle in hand.

The men began the rugged ascent of the steep bank, up the route by which the bears had fled. They moved quickly, in silence. Leonardo's men, unable to talk due to the grueling upward path, moved quietly.

The three bears galloped along the top of the streambed easily, backtracking toward the clearing. With supreme effort the men rose from the creek bottom. The city men hurt badly. Their fingers and toes ached with the cold. Their bodies overheated from the climb, they gasped for air. Halfway up the slope, they could hear the other men scoot over the top of the ridgeline.

The mother stopped a couple of times and rose to survey the position of her pursuers. She took off toward the upper reaches of the streambed.

The men in plaid jackets moved along the edge of the ridge, directly above the descent into the creek bottom as fast as they could dodge through the oak forest.

Leonardo's men grew so winded and distressed by the steep climb out of the creek bottom, that—for the first time in his life—Heiny could not find any words. Completely exhausted, he was overwhelmed by the bone-cold chill of the fog. The cold had moved into his feet, his ears, his fingers. He listened to the men above. His trousers were snagged and ripped on jagged limb of a fallen oak as he stepped over it. He just grunted and moved on, upstream, in the direction the bears had gone.

The rest of the crew stumbled along through the woods, doggedly, following the sound of Leonard breaking a trail through the soft, coastal woodland. The other group, well ahead of them, forced the mother and her children to flee. The bear padded nimbly, onward, upward with her babies.

She ran on and soon she came to the break in the timber. She looked back to see that her cubs were clear of the wooded area, then continued into the center of the clearing. As she moved into the open area, she sensed danger again and rose on her hind legs. Just as she picked up the scent, the sniper rifle kicked and the gases propelled the projectile with just a trace of sound.

The bullet slid through the fog, flattening a bit as it contacted the mother's skull. Her children heard her great body thud to the earth. They whined as the smell of blood contacted their nostrils. They stopped for a moment and loped on, whimpering. They traveled as fast as their small paws could move over the grassy clearing. Then they picked up the strange odor. They froze in fear of the dreadful predator, but were overwhelmed by the familiar smells of their mother. They looked at their mother's form lying heaped on the ground, motionless. They ran for her, whimpering. They sniffed the blood, and started to whine and yelp.

And then they flinched at a strange stinging bite into each of their small necks. They growled and barked and snarled and strained to get to their mother. And then all went dark.

. . . .

Brother Gates kept the sow in the night scope in case she was still alive and ready for a fight. He approached her with caution. The cubs lay still and sedated. As he drew near, the mother did not move. She had become a part of the inventory of products to be moved in the global marketplace. Her big fur coat over a heap of bones and organs would be sold.

She could now be parted.

Seeing that the bear was indeed dead, Brother Gates put away the sniper rifle in its aluminum case. The engine of the

77

one Humvee that was being used as a generator popped to life. The pistons purred and the big light switched on as the men in overcoats moved out of the woods and into the clearing.

The men in plaid had already started to work. One pulled a Colt Serengeti Skinner out of the scabbard on his belt. He rolled up his shirtsleeves at the cuff, above his long surgical gloves. Then he slid the knife's blade along his forearm, shaving off hair in order to make certain that the blade remained razor sharp. The men all gathered around the downed mother bear as he plunged the knife into her and ripped open her belly. He reached inside her and started cutting out organs. Another man stood by with a plastic bag. He labeled and collected the bear parts. Another entered the listing of parts into a satellite-linked, palmtop computer.

Leonard and his men huffed up to the center of the circle, panting hard. They stared at the skinning, their clothes filthy and ripped, and every part of them exhausted. They stood for a moment, mouths open, as another man in plaid picked up the reciprocating saw and pulled the trigger to make certain that it was working. The saw lurched and purred, the blade thrusting in and out fast. The man with the saw grabbed one of the bear's paws and pushed the blade down through the wrist, taking it off quickly.

"Oh, god I love that smell." The man with the saw looked up at the hoods, grinning an insidious grin.

"There's nothing like the smell of that coil spinning and mixing with the smell of fresh blood on a dark, foggy night," he continued.

Leonardo's men looked at each other, grimacing.

"Hey, dumb fuck," said Heiny, "that's the war movie, by the guy that made *The Godfather*, the guy that was consigliere, only he was a marine or something."

"Duval—you fucking guys are sick like that weird guy Brando played," said Leonard. "The one up in their in the jungle. Hearst or something. But it's Duval that says it. What's it . . . what's he say . . . 'Man I love the smell of napalm in the morning.'"

78

"Right," said Heiny. "See, you fucks are sick like those weirdoes at the end of the movie. Man, cuttin' up bears . . . fuck. . . ."

"You're right Heiny," said Leonard, "What the fuck are we doing with sickoids?"

"How come you don't use a chainsaw?" asked Heiny.

"I hate chainsaws, they make too much noise, they damage the inventory and I can't stand all that splatter all over me. Too messy, noisy, smelly, and you'd need to carry gasoline. It's not a professional method," said the man with the reciprocating saw.

"So what do you do with the hide? I'd like a big bear skin rug to do the wild thing on," said Heiny. They all laughed.

"The local scavengers and insects take care of parts like the pelt. They go back into the ecosystem. With shipping and possible spoilage, at this time skins are too cost intensive for effective profit. However, we don't approve of waste and are doing a low-level study of ways to cycle them into production," said one of the men in plaid. "But only the furs from exotic species: big cats, lynx, ermine, currently have a worthwhile margin."

"Jesus H. Christ. You fucking geeks are disgusting. Too weird for me. Digging around in guts. Fuckin' up Smokey the goddamn bear. Now what are you going to do with the saw?"

"Stand back tubby, it's—"

Leonard grabbed the man with the saw by the back of his jacket collar and popped him in the mouth, hard. He threw him on the ground and started kicking him in the face and ribs. The sawyer swung at Leonard's leg as it continued to kick and Leonard's cuff got caught up between the blade and the guide-foot of the reciprocating saw. Leonard hopped back, the bottom of his trousers frayed.

The man with the saw went after him, ready to bury it in Leonard's stomach. Brother Kirby, the clean-shaven, square-faced man in plaid who had doubts about killing the sow grabbed the man with the saw.

"Gentlemen, that is enough, we do not let our petty differences interrupt God's work," said Brother Kirby.

Leonard pulled his automatic out of his holster, feinted toward Brother Kirby, but grabbed the sawyer's collar, pulled him close and, stuck the automatic in his eye. Everything but the Humvee idling in the distance grew silent. The men loading the cubs in the trailers locked the gates and turned to watch.

"Where the fuck are those weasels, Adolf and Adolf junior?" asked Leonard.

"Brothers Army and Maxwell have to tend to a very important matter," said one of the men in plaid.

"Brothers Army and Maxwell. Brothers fuckin' Army and . . . man, will you cut all this crap . . . you weirdo . . . geek, motherfuckers!" yelled Leo. "Don't ever call these goddamn Boy Scout faggots, *Brother* around me. And don't say you work for God. That is frickin' blasphemy. Don't say it. Don't be a bunch of fuckin' loony bin, cammy, Aryan, terrorist, motherfuckers with me. Never, never, never say that Brother shit or mention the Lord in vain again."

Spittle flew from Leonard's lips as he spoke. His face puffed out swollen and red. He looked around for Brother Maxwell and Brother Army while covering both of the rest of the men with his pistol.

"Listen you fuckin' woodchuck, you tell that big weasel, that Dr. Mengele or Hitler, or whatever the fuck he is, that he is not the boss. I am my own boss and I only take orders from God. That is the end of that. This ain't nothing about brothers. This is a bunch of fuckin' robot droids. You tell your boss beaver that I will personally part out the next one of you that starts calling people little chummy, chummy names . . . but before I do the woodchuck, I'm gonna start with little Hitler, capiche?"

80

As Leonard turned, before he could holster the pistol, the sawyer sprung to his feet and started to amputate another paw. Leonard brushed himself off and looked at his watch.

"Hey boys, we've got a meeting in the city. We don't need to watch these pervs anymore."

Brother Gates walked back from the Humvees, toward the area where he'd placed his the aluminum case for his sniper rifle. He carried another case and lifted a thick, modern-looking weapon out of its container. The overcoats had never seen anything like it. It looked much like a US Armed Services, typical combat weapon, the AR-15, but thicker, bulkier. He jammed a large rectangular magazine into the bottom of the gun and opened up on an oak tree. The automatic fired fifteen thunderous shots and the tree fell over. The gaunt man immediately jammed another magazine in the weapon and fired at the thick sheet of steel. It blew a sulfurous smoke, burning holes right through.

Leonard looked at him. "Hey, thanks. Wow. What a guy. Chief Little Big Deal." He turned without saying another word and walked off toward the Humvee. He walked quickly and jumped into the beast. The rest of his men followed without looking back. The 425 horsepower engine jumped and they pulled out fast.

SEVEN

Nuke, Jenny and Billy stood in the basement of Jess' house over the pile of bear parts in silence. Billy and Jenny slid off their latex gloves and stuffed them in their pockets. Billy pulled his dog's head up to his knee and scratched his crown.

"Stay here with Nuke, Sam. Keep him in line." Billy winked at the sturdy man as he pulled the thick Lab up.

Jenny and Billy hugged Nuke.

"Call me as quick as you get out from meeting with this Neeley guy," Nuke told them.

"For sure," said Billy. "We've got two quiet phones in the truck."

Nuke crouched and put an arm around Sam as Billy and Jenny headed through the basement door.

Billy lead Jenny around the house and up toward the driveway.

Nuke already stood in the study, watching the Humvee for any sign of movement. His two friends inched toward the truck. Billy grabbed the Desert Eagle out of his waistband. He ran from the cover of the house to the passenger door, opened it, and walked around the vehicle in an effort to draw fire. He hurried back to where Jenny stood in the shadow of the house, grabbed her torso, hefted her up over his shoulder and tossed her in the passenger side.

He backed out of the drive, and as they reached the road, Jenny pulled a labeling pen out of her pocket and jotted the Humvee's plate number on her wrist. Billy drove slowly out of the wealth-laden Tiburon Peninsula. By now, government thugs were gathering to swarm past the mansions to Jess' house. Jenny kept turning to watch for cops and Humvees.

"Quit looking around," he said.

"What are we going to do if the cops cruise by?"

"Keep your eyes straight ahead and act dumb."

"Now there is a foolproof plan. Do you say that to all the girls?"

In the dim glow of the lights on Paradise Drive, Jenny smelled the rum, surveyed her clothing, glanced at Billy's condition, gazed at the bullet holes, and then stared straight ahead.

She wore a black nylon, equestrian vest, old Wranglers and an ancient pair of rawhide, Leddy cowgirl boots. Billy wore a gray nylon, riding vest ready for a run through the cleaners. Like Jenny, he wore Wranglers and beat up Leddys. His face bore a day and a half's stubble. Their nerves had spun on past fully ragged to the calm truly powerful people experience after battle engages fully. Billy reached into the duffel and heaved out a fresh bottle of Negrita. He took a long pull off the dark liquid and Jenny followed.

"Quit worrying, Jenny. People in San Francisco tend to be dignified enough to leave another person to their own devices. They won't notice us," said Billy.

"Oh for god's sake, Billy, look at us. Did you look at this truck?"

"That's right, it's a damn good color."

"Well thank you Professor Einstein. What are you going to do, put a sign on the roof that says 'This is a brand new truck, good people on board' so the choppers will catch on? We're going to Union Square, to the Saint Francis. One of America's Grand Dame hotels, not the buckaroo lodge in Dodge City. I think they are going to notice the bullet holes," she argued.

"I already miss Sam," Billy said, shaking his head.

"Are you listening to me? He's much safer with Nuke. What are you going to do with this truck? Driving it into the ocean is an excellent idea," she said.

"We don't have time to steal a new ride," Billy insisted.

"Tomorrow. Tonight the beast hides in the garage and we take a taxi," she said, fishing her cellphone and a credit card out of her vest.

"Wait. Cellphones leak like strainers; you can use them for your tagliatelle." He pointed to the sailing gear in the back seat. "Get the black zip case out of my bag. Only use the safe phone. Also, dig out a card. They're all from my own banks in Oceania—impossible to trace."

"Your own banks? The things all have different names on them," Jenny said as she flipped through a stack of credit cards.

"A business requirement when working in the Far East."

"Are you the Bourne Identity or something?"

"Naw, I'm an ordinary working stiff. More of an anal retentive Boy Scout than the Bourne Identity."

"Jeez, I hardly drink at all and I can't even feel this rum," she said.

"Adrenalin produces sober drunks, the reason cops and special ops, those action dude lushes, enjoy so much job satisfaction." They both let go with a deep, over-the-edge cackle.

"Why are we laughing?" she asked.

Billy turned to her and grinned. "We better put the Negrita away; driving with an open container is against the law."

They both broke into the hyena laughter extremely sturdy people can pull out of their medicine kits when they face radically dire straits. A much needed relief valve. Jenny barely got the words out. "Right, right, we sure wouldn't want a cop to bust us for DUI on such a calm and lovely—"

She couldn't finish. They roared until their jaws ached, and without warning, Jenny burst into tears.

"You okay?" Billy asked.

She was silent for a moment.

"I can't believe they cut Jess' hand off," she said softly.

84

Billy just shook his head. It was something he couldn't bear to think about right now. Not when he had a mission.

She picked up a credit card and the cellphone. She began to dial.

"I need the number of the Saint Francis Hotel. Yes, dial me through. Hello, may I book a pair of adjoining suites. Right, up high, overlooking the bay? Yes, in about 45 minutes. Henry. Patrick Henry. No, of course not, he's my husband." Jenny read the number of the credit card and finished the reservation.

"Why are we getting rooms?" he asked.

"I told you. We will be about an hour and a half early. What are we going to do? Panhandle? Sit in Tosca all exposed and get drunk?"

"Sounds right."

"Don't be a jerk."

"Jesus, we don't know squat about what these guys are doing, who followed us, who's watching us, what they'll do if they trap us in a hotel room, or—"

"Lighten up, Billy. We are at the Saint Francis. It's not the most high-end place in town, but we'll be safe. Unless they followed us, they'll be clueless about our location. We require bathing and rest in order to remain effective after this meeting. And, no way am I going to hang around in this damn truck. This brute will be in the garage and we will take a cab to Tosca."

"Jess and I used to sit at the bar for a nightcap," said Billy.

Jenny started crying. She tried to choke back the emotions, and the tears came out harder. She hunched over, leaning on her knees.

"Jess is dead, Billy. They desecrated his body. Who are these people? What did we stumble into? I can't—" Her tears came in waves.

"Seems like the whole world is screwed up. Everything is about grabbing, grasping for more possessions

85

with no concern for others," Billy said, and he put his hand on her neck and massaged the taught muscles.

"Oh lordy, thank you. I'm so uptight." She sat up straight and inhaled slowly, drawing the air clear down to her pelvis. Then she exhaled, emptying her lungs. She repeated the exercise ten times and continued with deep, level breathing.

"Where did you learn to breathe?"

"From a teacher."

"What kind of a teacher?"

"A Tantra teacher."

"As in sex?"

"As in Vajrayana Buddhism."

"Tibetans?" he asked.

"Yes, the Tibetans." She didn't pause before she changed the subject. "We're assuming Neeley, and anyone with him, none of them, know Jess' face, and this is their first meeting, right?"

"Right, so chances are they won't recognize how he dresses or anything except, maybe, a phone voice," said Billy.

"So it's a long shot. Is Neeley the big boss? Did he order Jess' death? Who were those Hummer dudes in Sausalito?"

"Those are Humvees: the bare-bones Hummers the armed forces use," said Billy.

"Nuke said those two are NSA. Those two staked at Animalfund had to be, too. Our office phones are, like you say, colanders. There's a first-rate Gene Hackman and Will Smith movie, *Enemy of the State*. It shows how disgusting the NSA is for Americans."

"I bet the end made you happy all over."

"It's so kick-butt when the mob turns the table," Jenny said, smiling.

"Its hella' good," said Billy.

"Those thick-necks are NSA."

"A bunch of pencil-dicks slinking around, perving on citizens of the United States—none of them have the balls to stand up and face things like a man. The Bill of Rights is now meaningless."

"Yeah. You could be labeled a terrorist for listening to jazz musicians like Gil Scott Heron. Maybe Animalfund is on the terrorist list. Those two in the Humvee had to be NSA Special Ops," said Jenny.

"Free Range brought them around. The whole group is bound to be labeled as terrorist. Some corporation wants the money from the parts business, so they've fetched Homeland Security on the dealers. Some corporate type wants to be dealing in hacked-up animals big time."

"So who are we actually meeting at Tosca? What if there are photos of Jess? Or someone saw him in *The Chronicle*? Or in *The New York Times*?" she asked.

"No time to think it all through. First thought, right thought."

"That's a Tibetan notion too," said Jenny.

"How do you know all this Eastern stuff?" Billy asked.

"I'm not your average bimbo."

Billy laughed and changed the subject. "We've got to stay on the trail. We can't let up for a minute. Dust blows over homicide trails real fast."

"Billy, take a chill pill. I am not suggesting we go to the Caribbean for the winter. But think: would Jess go to a meeting in a vest with bloodstains and jeans all mussed up and torn from gun battles in the streets? And this fucking truck is out of here. We will go to the guest shop at the Saint Francis and buy some tourist clothes or something and take a cab to Tosca. I've still got blood on me from pulling Sam's head into my lap."

"Yeah, okay. We can shower and get ourselves a bit more put together," he said.

"What if the guy in the Hummer—"

"Humvee. The combat vehicle."

"Billy, cut the crap and listen to me. Rest assured, the guy out in Marin called headquarters and reported our upset of his plans."

"Let's hope it's a different guy, and he didn't talk to Neeley," said Billy.

"We'll be in way too much danger. It'll be nothing but a trap if they know Jess at all."

"Jenny, calm down. I'm going, no choice. You can't let a big lead pass. Stay in the cab," he said.

"Don't be ridiculous."

Billy didn't like the idea of Jenny going into Tosca with him but didn't say anything. His mind shot back to Jess. He would call and say "Meet me at the clock"; the phrase people all around the world had used since the rebuilding of the Saint Francis Hotel after an earthquake.

The clock had been installed in the lobby, and locals and friends all knew what the expression meant. Billy and Jess spent a lot of time at the Saint Francis. They'd sip a cocktail at the clock, grab a taxi over to Tadich Grill for dinner, and take another cab down to Tosca, where they would stay until last call. His friends flew in from all over the world. They would take two or three suites overlooking the bay. A think-tank of people in from everywhere: Paris, Buenos Aires, London, Manhattan, Milano, Beijing, Prague, all over, would gather. They would spend a couple of weeks discussing world issues, partying and going out on the town.

They also enjoyed many quiet times when they walked and talked, exploring San Francisco. Jess sounded like a history book when he spoke. His great-grandmother lived at the stately "old girl" as his family designated the Saint Francis. Jess beamed when he told San Francisco stories: "When the Crockers opened up in '04, my family moved in to several suites and shuttled from their houses up on Knob Hill. They called San Francisco 'The Paris of the West.'" Jess loved the legend of his great aunt, Nevella Hodge. She had been shaken awake by the quake and gone down to find Enrico Caruso—in a post-performance state—staggering in from some other hotel with a group of the Metropolitan Opera. The world-renowned Chef Hirtzler, served them in the morning and John Barrymore came in for breakfast, but had enjoyed such a rugged night of partying that he retired to his suites until the fire alarms began.

When they arrived at the hotel, Jenny gave him the key cards and Billy headed straight up to the room. She went to the lobby to shop for clothes. Billy tried to get his mind off Jess with a shower. He wrapped up in a towel and tried to spot clean the rip-stop nylon vest with a washcloth. But the blood had set, making the project hopeless.

Wrapped in his towel, Billy sat down at the desk with every clue they had gathered. He had just pulled a pad and pen out of the drawer when Jenny knocked at the front door. She rushed in with a bundle of clothing. Radiant with laughter, she spread out the items out on a bed: puce-colored, plaid trousers and a blue jacket for herself, and a lime green sport coat with a pair of yellow slacks for Billy.

"Do you actually expect me to wear this?" Billy asked.

"No choice, Mr. Clayton. The place is a poodah pants store," said Jenny as she took in the expression on his face. She cracked up so hard tears came to her eyes.

"A *what?*"

"A pooh—" Jenny doubled over with laughter.

He stood, picked up the slacks and held them up to his waist. Jenny noticed all the ragged, nasty scars on Billy's shoulders and abdomen.

"Jeez. Are those bullet wounds?" she asked, before she could stop herself.

"Yes, and other things."

"Are you some kind of CIA or something?"

"I'm an ordinary working guy," he said, paying attention to the pants.

"How did you make a living while you studied martial arts?"

"I was doing takeovers with some front money from my dad. How about you?"

"I have a PhD in computer science from Cambridge University."

"Lordy, a digi-geek."

"Yes, I write in assembly language. I compiled software written in C. They called me Data Girl."

Billy doubled over with laughter. He roared and could barely get through to the words. "Did you study fashion at geek school, or—"

"That will be enough from you, Mr. Clayton."

"What is this style called? Golf Geek Chic? Maui Lounge-lizard, Moderne? Torrid Fairway Casual?"

Jenny laughed aloud. "Don't be obtuse. I had to beg. Got the woman to open the bloody door, didn't I? She interrupted her inventory. It's one of those cubbyholes for the hair-piece set. My grandfather, a Maine fisherman, called country club attire the 'poodah pants' style. I'm sure the expression is quite obscene, but he never explained," she said.

With a resonant belly laugh, Billy examined her. "I think that I would have liked your grandfather, and I've got to cut you some slack. You're trying to keep Neeley from freaking out. Fair enough. But wouldn't he expect Patagonia or maybe Sears moderne on Jess? Wouldn't messy Wranglers and boots be closer to what tree huggers wear?"

"Like you said, we can't possibly think everything through right now. We're in the heart of the city and we will tidy up a bit," said Jenny.

She went in to shower. Billy sat back down at the desk. He took in the panorama from the big windows, out over the fog-muted lights of San Francisco. He couldn't get a grip on the motives. Being pissed at Jess Hayes made perfect sense, but offing him didn't compute. The clincher had to be enviro stuff.

It had to be Free Range pounding major corporate shareholders with massive litigations from huge funds.

Granted, flamboyance went with Jess' nature, at times he talked too much; he could be obnoxious, and he always remained deeply involved in the indigenous sorcery of the Americas, with heavy American Indian practices like the peyote rituals.

He never turned violent, he never offended people, but he openly disagreed with the ideas they held. His eccentricities were not reasons for murder. Free Range issued the death warrant for sure. Jess had taken jillions in lawsuits from them and angered even more big-money thugs by using the Free Range nonprofit to scoop up huge parcels of wilderness, then giving wild animals free range and paying a slew of high-priced lawyers to smash anyone that endangered the security of the reservations. Filing massive actions against wilderness rapists was definitely something he would do.

Jenny returned from bathing, long boned, calm, with color back in her cheeks from the shower. She put on the clothes she had purchased from downstairs. Even in hokey golf clothes, she remained an extremely attractive woman.

"You look very well refreshed, Ms. Poodah Pants," said Billy.

She giggled. "Yeah, I feel a lot better, but I've got to eat."

"We'll get something at Tosca."

Jenny snapped up the phone in the black case and dialed Grace Jones, copyeditor for the report. Animalfund's project still had to be completed for the marshals that would deliver it to Senator Hicks.

"Hi Grace, it's Jenny. Hope you are getting your bearings a bit. Listen, I'm in a pinch and I'm in bad need of some help. Yeah, a tough emergency. I need you to take some friends, at least three to the office and get the rest of the report off to the federal marshals. Just trust me, Grace. I know, but take friends. Yes, I named it *The End of the Black*

91

Bear in the Americas. Really. You really do like it? Sounds kind of dowdy to me. Okay. I'll take your word that it's hot. Yes, I'll explain all this as soon as I see you. Yes, they'll be in at ten on Tuesday. Thanks, sweetie, I'll see you real soon."

Jenny hung up the phone and brushed her hair. Billy flipped on the lamp at the desk, fished out the rubber gloves and thumbed through Jess' belongings. Jenny walked over and stood next to him.

"We've got to go through all of this stuff carefully," she said.

"For sure," said Billy. "My computers are on *dead latitudes,* but I'll buy us laptops."

He punched in numbers on the safe phone.

"Estelle, hi. Yeah, good to hear you, too. Will you please tell Harlan he needs to get ready to come out? Yeah, head up an investigation and build a case for some underfunded, politically-frightened prosecutors. Murder in the first. Yeah, I'll call back real soon. I'm going to be hard to find for a bit. For sure. That's right. I am incorrigible, Estelle, and I don't foresee change coming any time soon. Tell the old fart that, like the Predator, 'I'll be back.' Oh, you're right, aren't you? The Terminator. Okay. Love you, Estelle. Yeah, Mom's in Italy. I'll definitely tell her to call you."

He hung up and punched more numbers. No one picked up the phone on *dead latitudes.* Then, he tried his close friend Angel Orozco, but had to leave a message with the Los Angeles County Sheriff's Department. Finally, he called Luther Four Fingers, the manager at Moon Willow, his deceased father's quarter horse ranch near Austin. Luther picked up.

"Yeah, she's still in Rapallo. I think she's going to the Caribbean for the winter. Yeah. Of course. We all do. I mean, I miss Dad something awful. Yeah, I know you do. No kidding? Yeah, you're flying on a horse in my dreams. I had a timber rattler coil on me, too. Much thicker than a diamond back. Right. Thicker, darker and real serious. You're kidding me. You already know about Jess? You already feel the bad guy? Okay, I will be out ASAP. I'm tailing some crud balls right now, but I'll be there soon. I'm going to fax you a note that was in Jess' LaserJet. Yeah, Harlan's flying out to set up the case."

Billy hung up, leaned back and watched Jenny. He liked her a lot. She stood close to him as she went through Jess' things. He turned to watch as she moved back to the mirror and started brushing her hair again. Though torn by Jess' murder, something about Jenny made him feel very much alive again.

"The bear claws are a plant for sure," said Jenny, looking in the mirror. "Time to get dressed."

"Yeah, right, but why are you so sure all the sudden?" Billy stood and examined the goofy pants.

"It all has something to do with hunting down people who are involved in the Free Range Foundation. A lot of very powerful people really hate the foundation. The litigation has been hugely successful and many square miles of land are now held in seamless, irrevocable trusts. The defendants are out many millions in legal fees. The trust's assets are at least 50 billion, and I guess some of that came from you. The lawyers file hundreds of environmental lawsuits against corporations every year, which really pisses the shareholders off royally."

"You could buy a hell of a lot of open land every year, just off the interest," said Billy.

"Precisely. And, fund very sharp lobbyists, not just lame car-sales types or off-the-deep-end liberals or neocons. The capital finances a pack of very intelligent, dogged lawyers and pays for the activities of a lot of angry environmentalists.

"The major power freaks have never seen anything so uppity. All the litigation and the locked up land along with Jess being articulate and speaking his mind at all times is some wicked hoodoo. I've seen Senators turn away from him to save face because they were too slow witted to keep up."

"There's motive, even if it's a bunch of conspiracy theories," said Billy, walking out of the bathroom in his new poodah pants.

"No clue what the cops know."

"Just left a message for a friend who helped me last year—Angel Orozco. He was an LA County Sheriff then, but he moved up to San Francisco. Must be a homicide detective in San Francisco now. Harlan will also be able to dig deep and fast."

She examined his outfit closely and laughed. "God, you are one dashing fella."

"Why, thank you, Miss Jenny, but keep your hands to yourself."

"Yes, hatred due to deep cash flow has got to be the motive," said Jenny. "Power freak, money grubbers running Free Range participants down like rabid dogs, backed by Washington. Doesn't matter whether it's murder or through the courts. They are rich vigilantes."

Billy put his possessions, his old vest and wranglers, in a laundry bag and slid his attaché case in with it.

"You better stash your belongings in here. We'll put them in the truck, behind the seat."

"The duffle's out there already, all sotted with rum and full of weapons," she said.

"It's not *full* of them!"

"Come on, don't be obtuse, William Clayton. That bag is an immediate lockup in Guantanamo. And why are we putting these things behind the seat? The bag won't fit," Jenny responded.

"Put your vest and jeans in. We have to wear our boots with these delightful outfits. I'm putting all these clues in, too. We can't leave anything here. What if we don't come back for some reason? "

"That is a very morbid thought, Mr. Clayton."

"Just realistic. Harlan will find my truck with Angel, and they'll do it real fast."

She pulled the brush through her hair again, and then looked at Billy.

"The perp planted the bear paws and all to make Jess look like a sickozoid, tree-hugging creep who had turned to cash flow from his professed love of animals?" she said.

"You got it. To frame him as a liberal who turned to crime."

"But it won't work. We'll get to the editors at *the Times*, *the Post*, and the *Christian Science Monitor*, all of them. There are some benefits to being a rich girl. Did you know about Jess' work with children?" she asked.

"I was one of his first contributors; my mother and I both kept up with his work through the years. My father died last year and my mother transferred a hefty chunk of his estate into a trust for Jess' work with kids," said Billy.

"He was an ace at setting up nonprofits, and unparalleled at keeping them well funded and running smoothly. His outrage about the trade in dead animals ate at him constantly just like the horrors of mistreated children."

Jenny looked round from the mirror and locked her eyes on Billy. Then she continued.

"'A child dies for unnatural reasons every three minutes, Jenny, and we don't care at all.' Jess stopped and said that ten times a day, no matter where we were. A lot of power and money grabbers avoided him at functions because he would say it right in the middle of dinner or a conversation."

"Did you work on Free Range yourself?" asked Billy.

"No. Come on. We've got to get going."

As they stepped into the hall and headed for the elevator, Jenny said, "What do we do while we wait?"

"Like everyone else, we talk. Loosen up. Slide with everything and fake it. We play like we were dispatched as emissaries from Saint Francis of Assisi. He was the saint for the animals and the environment. It's perfect, and we'll do whatever it takes."

"Oh, well thank you, sir. Stalking. Murder. Mayhem. 'Just loosen up,' he says. Get back to the roots, right. Down to the bone. Texas on down. That's how Armadillo people do it, right? You just talk, right? Talk your way through everything, like the politicians."

"Texas on down—where did you hear that locution?" asked Billy.

"It was one of Jess' favorite expressions."

"I'm from Austin."

"I know. Jess loved it down there. He loved the music and the Texas women."

The elevator came and they continued as the doors whooshed shut.

"My people go back a lot of generations in Texas. Nuke's family does too, indirectly. He was raised in Watts, but his mom was raised by his Grandmother Moss, who lives in Buda."

"Buda. No shit. There is actually a Buddha, Texas? What an oxymoron. Texas is a weird place. When did you come out here?"

"Last year. It's not Buddha, like Siddhartha. It's B-U-D-A. My mother would like to think it's named after the Buddha himself. She's into in all that Taoism and Buddhist stuff. And the American Indians, the indigenous peoples' shaman stuff, Toltecs, the same things Jess was into. They turned me onto all of it."

"No kidding. My parents were wrapped up in it, too."

"That's where you learned about Tantra?" Billy asked.

"Let's say my parents sparked the interest. But I spent a lot of time at Cambridge enchanted with math, and then in corporate trying to learn how to remanufacture a wild thing like myself, transmute me into a 'good girl.' It took quite a while to ignite their spark, to come to my senses."

96

"No kidding. I did the same thing. Corporate is a real thorough waste of time. All you do is pile up a little bit of cash. You never have an actual, visceral life. Just a bunch of computer screens and pathogenic, lying cowards completely lost in stroking one another's egos. You might buy a Shelby Cobra, but you never blow it out across the desert with a fast woman. You just dream of doing something real. And you can't make real money."

She looked around at him and grinned as they drove. "Jeez, Mr. Clayton, are you always so temperamentally disinclined to fully express your opinions with precision?"

He looked at her, raising his eyebrows. "What are—?"

She grinned, slugged his arm. "Hey, don't go all serious on me. One does not often run into people that have the intestinal fortitude, or know themselves well enough to express their actual thoughts. It's quite refreshing."

"It was my DI," Billy explained.

"Your DI?"

"My drill instructor. He enlightened me. I dropped out of corporate and joined the Corps because everything else seemed lame. So, you've worked with a teacher? That's where you learned to breathe? Vajrayana Buddhism?"

"Yes, and Shaolin."

"That's why you're branded with the tiger and the dragon."

"Correct."

"Lordy, an extremely high Buddhist?"

"A Human Being," said Jenny, laughing, looking in his eyes and smiling warmly.

"Yes. Human Being training."

"I like the way jazz people phrase it: '. . . a seeker of wisdom and truth.' But truth is having a hard time now. Where did you step onto the Path?"

"Force Recon."

"What's that?"

"Marines, Force Reconnaissance."

"How could soldiers be on a spiritual path?"

"Dropping ego. Doesn't matter if it's Shaolin, Taoism or what."

"But you were in the Marine Corps. Is that where your scar came from?"

"Operation Desert Storm—the first invasion of Iraq."

"So what does that have to do with spiritual studies?"

"I was behind enemy lines for a long time."

"Okay?"

"My mother. She heard Alan Watts in Paris in her twenties. She didn't really want to be the wife of an oil baron, but she never had the guts to take off on the Way while Dad was alive. I learned about Buddhists and Krishnamurti and all of those types of things from Mama. But my first major Satori happened behind the Iraqi front."

"What about the next one?"

"I had gone to Singapore to grill my chief accountant. He showed me my net worth had exceeded one trillion dollars."

"Makes you well over ten times the wealthiest man on earth; the people on the Forbes list are wannabes. But we're talking little boy games—what does cash flow have to be with being on the Path?"

"Exactly. What did my life have to do with the Way? I was asking that when I joined the Corps and when I started getting closer and closer to a trillion."

"Okay. So your mother really put you on the Way?"

"Right, and you are the first American I've ever met who was raised in the middle of true spiritual thinking. Mama is a real Texas kook, a free thinker. There are more of them in the Lone Star State than you'd ever dream if you listen to politicians."

"Well, I thought my folks were kooks when I was a kid. Then I fell into the hype of the business droid: the Wall Street Journal shuck-and-jive two-step. The business types think they do something, but in reality, they just push widgets around in carts and rip off the middle class. So I did put on a suit and do some corporate—but I ripped off my pantyhose next to the 405 freeway when I stalled in the morning traffic. I marched up on the hillside, sat down in the ivy, put a rock down them and hurled those pantyhose as far as I could. A CHP jerk gave me his personal pickup card and tried to put the make on me.

"I went to the Third Street Promenade, got drunk with a girlfriend, called work, told them to take the job and shove it, and never put pantyhose back on.

"So now, here we are. I've been on the Path, the Way, for a long time. Funny how many of Mom and Dad's ideas proved true with the passing of time," said Jenny, smiling fully for the first time that night.

They parked the truck and grabbed a cab.

"Will you please take us down to Tosca?" Billy asked the cabbie.

"Best bar in town," said the driver, moving out.

"Best bar in the world," said Billy.

"You got me there, pal. I just know this city. If you live in paradise why go hunting around for something better? It's an old Bob Dylan song: 'when you see your neighbor carryin' somethin', help him with his load, and don't go mistaking paradise for that home across the road.'"

"Great song. Great album. John Wesley Harding. 'The Ballad of Frankie Lee and Judas Priest'. Can you wait for us right out front at Tosca?" Billy dug an enormous roll of hundred dollar bills out of his pocket, slid off five, placed two in the man's hand. "If I don't return with her, the lady must be driven back to the Saint Francis no matter what you see happen. When you deposit her safely, with or without me, follow her instructions to the letter, she will give you the other three prints of Mr. Franklin."

"No problem at all, my friend. I'll be right out front, even if we have another big one, an eight-point-zero. Your lady will be escorted back to the Clock," said the cabbie.

"Alright, thank you," said Billy.

"No problem. In my opinion, she's the finest hotel in town. Your boomer types might think they're hipper at the little cracker box places but there's nothing like these old girls for class."

They took a place at the bar just as a couple walked away.

"You should have stayed out there with the driver."

"Billy, the cab is waiting. I love it that you are a true gentleman, but have faith, I can get back to my driver if something—"

"Alright, I will trust you. You were going to tell me if you worked on Free Range."

Jenny looked around the interior of the venerable establishment. "No. We've been on the report for months. Jess kept it to himself, but I don't think that the Hicks report is what launched this. Free Range is at the root of everything. I can feel it. I know that there is a massive array of information related to it. He compiled every database we found into one. He worked with the Belgian Federal Police on their new Trade in Wildlife Information Exchange—EU-TWIX. It is a real model for protecting indigenous creatures."

"There were a lot more CDs in his office."

"I know, but I think those three were down in his work area for a reason."

"Jess' has to be the biggest animal database in the world. He merged all the public ones from the whole planet."

"But what's the bottom line?" asked Billy.

"I don't know. My guess is that it's the biggest database about wild animals and trafficking in the world, and that in all that data he had discovered something malignant. And that he jumped into the mess and went after the beast. He had hired detectives and some black op investigators. He also worked close with some guys from Upwind, a splinter group from Green Peace. They're all ex-marines like you, and they are sick of the uber-rich owning everyone."

"There are no ex-marines, only members of the Corps who are not on active duty."

"Okay, that's right."

"These were very heavy dudes. Very rugged. They come to town on big dirt bikes. I think that Upwind wanted Jess to distance himself from them—he could do so much with straight people because he could pick up so much cash."

"The rugged enviro-types just wanted to kick butt, so they would endanger funding for groups like Animalfund and were so savvy that they knew to keep distance, to protect the groups that tried to open the eyes of the middle class. They knew that with all the antiterrorism propaganda being used to keep the neocons in office, the Patriot Act, Homeland Security and the NSA would be used to keep Jess' organizations under tough scrutiny."

"Jesus, you need to tell me everything, maybe the big power grabbers are already using the Patriot Act to detain enviro-types. Maybe those guys that are after us are all Special Ops. Maybe Neeley works for NSA or DEA or some fed bunch," said Billy.

"I'll tell you everything as we go along. Where is Neeley?" she asked, looking around.

"Jess told me that he had something important that he wanted to talk about during the trip to Vladivostok. Must have been the Free Range Foundation," said Billy.

"What does Neeley look like? Do you know?" The worry wrinkles opened up and Jenny's brow shone fair and smooth in the light, as if it had been chipped from marble by a renaissance sculptor. She left her thick hair down for the evening and it swished each time her head moved. They both paused and scanned the crowd.

101

Then, as if he had been telegraphed by Jess, or been swished into some form of voodoo understanding, Billy felt pulled. He got up, and on the way over to the jukebox, he honed directly in on Neeley.

Neeley saw Billy in the same instant, and by impulse of knee-jerk habit, flexed a bicep, showing his strength for the entire room. He sat with several big men. He leaned over to the closest and pointed at Billy while speaking into a big man's ear.

Leonard crossed the room fast and walked close behind Billy all the way to Neeley's table. Leonard stood there, off center. His expensive gabardine trousers were a mess: dirty, ripped and stained. Dirt ringed the cuffs. He looked as if he had been in a scuffle, as if he lived in a scuffle, as if his entire psyche equaled a continual scuffle.

The man didn't have a clue what to say, so he launched his habitual paranoia and elbowed Billy in the ribs.

"This is Mr. Neeley," said Leonard, sweeping a hand toward the boss awkwardly.

Billy stood steady. He knew that every offense presents its own, specific Achilles tendons, and that they are present long before they are seen—always, in every moment of the person's life, no matter how tough the person may seem.

"Mr. Neeley, where the fuck have you been? It's been way too long. I just wanted to make the . . ." Billy didn't finish the sentence. His shoulder shot out a howl of pain as a very strong man snatched it behind his back in a hammerlock and wrenched upward hard.

"That's it Heiny. Keep this criminal detained. A citizen's arrest," said Neeley with a strong British accent.

Leonard now stood in front of Billy and winked at his accomplice. "Listen, Jesse boy, you need to watch your tongue. Being polite is a very good habit. You know what I mean?" He opened his topcoat and put his hand on his pistol.

Neeley's vicious, pasty face stood out from everything in the old bar. His small onyx eyes looked through Billy like some type of laser surgery unit. Billy swept the area to observe his odds. Leonardo had hold of him. Heiny had a grip on his pistol. Neeley's seven men lurked in various places throughout the room.

Indignant over Jess' death, Billy felt anger rear up like the hood of a cobra. But anger is simply an ego trip, never allowed by a true warrior. Billy inhaled unnoticeably, unwaveringly, clear down to the floor of his pelvis and let the air out again, slowly. He touched into the anger, and it dissolved.

He required information from these men and had to stay in character. All leads required that he move forward for swift engagement. His psyche clicked into the brain nodes that weld intent into a circuit. He would find Jess' killers and whoever threatened Jenny. No matter what it cost, how long it took, who had to go down. No question about it.

EIGHT

Nuke listened to Billy and Jenny's feet on the concrete stairs as they went up to the yard from the basement. Sam moaned for Billy as Nuke coaxed him up into the house.

In the study, Nuke eased the drapes apart with his finger and watched Billy and Jenny slip into the truck and leave.

He watched the streets for a while, looking to see if a tail would come out of hiding and jump them or try to trail the truck. He knew that anyone shadowing them would have had to roll out fast because soon Jenny and Billy would disappear down the winding streets.

When no one followed them, Nuke let out a sigh of relief, even though he knew that the character in the Humvee had seen Billy and Jenny, and probably already divulged the truck's license plate number over a cellphone.

Nuke watched the black Humvee. It, and whoever was inside, had been there when he first toured the house after discovering Jess. And now, as Nuke remained alone with a decent white guy dead on the floor, the menace remained perched in the glow from the streetlight. The big, ugly vehicle waited to confront Nuke. He knew that he should get down to the yacht club and power *dead latitudes* out through the Golden Gate before choppers swarmed overhead.

But adrenalin was pumping in his body, and he felt like he was about to go nuclear. He shot back down the stairs, through the basement, and approached the bear paws. He stopped and grabbed the rattler necklace off the pile. He watched Sam for a moment, then cringed as he focused on the box. He stared off across the room. He held a vertebrae and one of the old jade beads between his thumb and forefinger, then squeezed the whole totem in the palm of his thick hand. His entire body heated up. Nuke slid the necklace into his pocket.

"Sam, you've got to stay here. I'll be right back."

The Lab watched closely as Nuke bolted through the door, but he didn't move.

Outside, Nuke paused beneath the deck. He fished out Jess' rattlesnake vertebrae and held the string up to the light from the basement window. The ancient jade was lustrous, and had a certain aura that shone in the orange light. He still wore the rubber gloves, so working the clasp was awkward. As he put the necklace on and the vertebrae spurs dug into his neck, everything seemed to change. The entire evening felt airy and light, as if some gas had been released or some force had taken over. With newfound determination, Nuke shot out from under the planking.

As a boy, he had spent a lot of time skulking through neighborhoods. Cutting through rich peoples' yards was simple compared to the small, crowded lawns of his home. At home, the thin walls throbbed with the sounds of people. But in the neighborhoods of the rich with the big houses, the huge lots, the trees, the space and quiet, getting around was easy.

This neighborhood was similar to the ones he used to prowl. He felt confident. He moved over Jess' wall, trying to judge where to cut through to get to the Humvee out on Bellevue Avenue.

He cleared the second wall, and a dog galloped out of the dark in a full-out charge. The big dog's breath pounded like a machine. A deep rumble of a snarl came from its throat. Without even looking around, Nuke could tell it was either a Bull Mastiff or a Rotty because of the depth of the growl.

It blew him away how his instincts came back instantly. He turned on the big mutt and as he'd suspected, the clueless owners kept a collar on it. He grabbed the wide leather band like a handle and picked the stocky creature up. The Rottweiler twisted, snarled, and snapped, trying to grab human flesh with its teeth.

105

With Nuke holding it up by the collar, the dog choked and slowed down, gagging. Nuke loved dogs, though he hated what the owners did to them.

Still dragging the dog, Nuke approached the basement door of the house, turned the passage handle so he wouldn't damage it, and then pushed through the lock with his hip. He tossed the dog back into the depths of the basement, wishing he could take it out for a run behind a good horse.

But he never got bogged down in sentiment when he went nuclear. He ran and cleared the second wall, expecting another dog. Nothing. He ran hard, diagonally across the yard toward the street. He cleared the front wall on the other side of the mansion and ran for Bellevue.

Brother Ezekiel Army sat in the driver's side and continued to talk with Slade: his cellphone in his right hand and his pistol in the left. A glow from the streetlights provided some vision through the sparse fog.

Nuke moved fast, feinting, watching his course, sprinting like a linebacker. The Humvee emerged from the fog. He hoped the driver was a typical, dumb, white guy on a macho trip and that had gotten out to walk the street, but hadn't bothered to lock his door.

He moved straight and fast. He grabbed the handle. Jerked the door open. And Brother Ezekiel dropped the cellphone on the passenger seat gripping his weapon with both hands.

Nuke looked into the small, dark hole and recognized exactly what he faced: a cop's weapon. Nuke could do a field breakdown on it with his eyes shut. It was a Smitty. Smith & Wesson made rugged pistols. But a .40 caliber. Not Nuke's tool. Not enough stop. Nuke liked a handful: A piece that put the kibosh on whatever it hit immediately. A big old .50, a magnum. A Desert Eagle like Billy packed for the trip to Russia.

The young men in South Central hung the name Nuke on him because he exploded massively. Fights never took place with Nuke involved; everything simply blew apart at the seams. His cohorts didn't romanticize. They called things as they went down. He was a thermonuclear reaction, primed and ready blow.

Slade's voice cackled through the cell, but no one heard it.

Nuke did not hesitate. He grabbed the weasel-looking man's pistol, pulling his forearm into the frame and slammed the door on his wrist so hard Brother Ezekiel Army soiled his trousers, and his finger squeezed off a round involuntarily. Nuke heard the slug break a window in the mansion behind him. The Smitty bounced in the gutter. An alarm resounded from the home.

"Aw, man, that's disgusting. You stink," said Nuke.

The stench flooded the car. Nuke bunched his nose as he grabbed the man's hair and bounced his head on the steering wheel. He pounded it four more times, rapidly. Still using his hair, Nuke yanked him out of the car and threw him on the ground. He put his foot on Brother Ezekiel's throat.

"Where's your boss?" he demanded.

Suddenly, sirens blew in toward them fast. A lot of sirens. Lights came on all over the neighborhood. The little man spat at Nuke.

"Who's your boss?" asked Nuke, grinding on Brother Ezekiel's neck, but the man simply spat again.

Nuke stooped, took hold of him by the ankle, and hoisted the man up, bouncing his head on the curb and throwing him back in the Humvee like a rag doll. The sirens drew closer by the minute. Nuke pulled the man's handcuffs and his black combat knife off his belt. He raised Ezekiel's left ankle over his head and cuffed him through the steering wheel to his right wrist. He gripped the man's ear and ripped the serrated area of the dark knife's blade along the backside of it in a semi-circle. Ezekiel screamed.

"You did something real bad. You killed one of the few decent human beings left on this little planet. I thought I had myself out of all this shit. I started reading and studying and going somewhere. But you pulled me back into the suck. I'm gonna have to work on you so you don't practice your evil on others. Not ever again, man. And besides, I know you saw my best friend's truck."

Nuke sawed on the ear cartilage. "Talk to me. Who is the big man? Did you call in the plates on the truck?"

Ezekiel spat again.

"Alright tough guy. Your boss is responsible for some wimp taking Jess' hand and I was gonna take both of his just like the good book says: two fuckin' hands for one of a righteous dude's. But since you are going to run all this loyal-to-your-boss shit on me, I'm going to take yours."

Nuke started sawing. Ezekiel could smell his own blood and spat once more.

"ANVIL will take you out, nigger," he muttered.

"Aw, man. What's with you Klan-type pussy-boys? How come you're so dumb? Here I am with your life in my hands and you use the nasty old word on me. People of African lineage do not go around calling your kind ugly, maggot-colored, pencil dicks.

"You just feel inferior deep inside 'cause you're not good at lovin' your women, and that makes so you hate a sensual black man so damn much you got no control. My grandmother told me about all that psychology shit. She said to watch gimpy whites like you real close. Not have a knee-jerk reaction. But I want to kill your sorry ass. I'm not sweet like my grandma." Nuke loosened the ear more. "What's ANVIL? Who killed Jess?"

"Come on, man—don't take my ear. ANVIL's a Christian brotherhood."

"A bunch of Nazi gimps, right? Where are they located?"

Nuke ripped at the guy's ear with his hand.

The man screamed. "Nooooooh! Anaheim. Temecula. All over."

"What's 'all over' mean?"

"Look online. Out by Pechenga in the wine country. Don't cut it off—I'll look like a freak show."

"You're already a freak show."

The sound of sirens blew up at the end of the Tiburon peninsula. Nuke sliced off the rest of the ear, and Brother Ezekiel started to sob.

"Here you go muthafucka," he said as he tucked the ear in the man's shirt pocket. "You can thank my grandma for your life. I'm trying to follow her as my guru." Nuke put his face right down in Ezekiel's. "I'm gonna make it worse than being dead and leave you here to talk to the law. After they're done, you get to talk to your boss."

"Come on, let me loose at least. A government spook did the deed . . . I mean . . . I don't have a clue who the guy is. We're nothing but surveillance. Everybody wanted the tree hugger dead."

"Alright. That's all the time I've got now. I'm not gonna kill you, but remember, if anything happens to the people in that truck, you better commit hari-kari because I will find you and I will harvest everything so you move around on nubs with your dick sewed up to hang out your mouth. Have a nice fucking evening."

Nuke slammed the butt of the knife down on Ezekiel's trachea and the man passed out. He took Ezekiel's flashlight, used the tips of his thumb and forefinger to put the Smith & Wesson in his pocket, and searched the floor. He found a ballpoint pen on the mat near the edge of the seat.

Barely any blank space showed on the barrel of the pen because of all the words printed on it. Nuke held the light on it and read it, and couldn't understand at all why a murderer would have himself incriminated by a pen. Who could he be advertising to? More dumb, white-bread trash? These hate-filled Klan-boys just did not compute for Nuke. Nobody carries a pen with their fucking name on it to the site of a first degree.

The writing on the pen read:

ANVIL - THE AMERICAN NATIONAL VIGILANCE AND INTELLIGENCE LEAGUE - ANVIL SPECIAL FORCES - BROTHER EZEKIEL ARMY - PO Box 14251 – TEMECULA - 5220 Seventh Street – 714-621-2631 - Costa Mesa CA 92130 - vigilance@anvil.com

Special forces? What kind of sick, Aryan nutcases did this shit? The Klan resurrected? Nothing else in the Humvee offered any information about the man or the vehicle. He stuffed the ballpoint in his pocket.

. . . .

Nuke disappeared into the yards of the estates just as the lead Humvee from the bear parting in Marin cruised up and stopped beside Brother Ezekiel's Humvee.

Brother Noah Army and Brother Maxwell, wearing surgical gloves, slid SIG Sauer automatics with sound suppressors into their belts. The untraceable pistols came off the streets of Houston.

They opened the door on the other vehicle quickly.

"Good god," said Brother Maxwell. "Who did this? Get him loosened up. They're ANVIL cuffs. Get the master key. Get a couple sniffers outta the first aid kit, too."

"Brother Maxwell," said Ezekiel with relief in his voice as he began to wake up.

"We've gotta get out of here real fast," said Brother Maxwell as Brother Noah Army loosened the man's wrists. "We're just going down to the yacht club. To that same sailboat Hayes went to when he got home."

"That same nigger who walked in on the NSA guy, the one off that boat. He's the one who jumped me. Oh, god," he said, reaching into his pocket and pulling out his ear. "We've gotta go to a surgery unit."

"We can't," said Brother Maxwell. "There are too many cops after us. We'll use our medical kit to clean it up, get rid of bacteria, then I'll sew it on after we board the boat."

110

"Jesus, Maxwell. You don't even know if it'll stay in place. What holds a fucking ear?"

"It'll be okay. We can't stop now. We'll have to go south. Get out of the bay area."

. . . .

Nuke could usually empty his mind when he needed to focus, but so much had taken place so fast that his head was spinning. Who are these people? Oh, man, Jess. Jess Hayes. Helped more little black kids make it in jazz and dance and art than I ever saw. You get one white man in a thousand who isn't all fucked up and supports Afro-American shit, and they have to off him. Black, White, Mexicans, Asians, and Indians, like Grandma says: "All our row boats are in this shit up to our elbows and it's so thick we can't find the little tweaky motors."

He leaned back against the wall of the house. Brought his pulse back down. He wondered why the big dog didn't come after him again. He loved animals and hoped he hadn't killed it. He could smell serious white racists, feel every tick of their beings. They got all spastic with hate. No matter how hard they tried, American honkeys just weren't good at hiding their shit. They never had been forced to.

Jess Hayes never had a trace of any kind of racism in him. Nuke would have picked up the scent. He could see the big, kind white man laughing: "Hell Nuke, everybody's a racist of some kind. You know, like Sly Stone says, 'There is a yellow one that won't accept the black one that won't accept the red one that won't accept the white one and different strokes for different folks . . . I am no better and neither are you . . . we are the same whatever we do . . . you love me, you hate me, you know me and then, you can't figure out the bag I'm in . . . 'cause I am everyday people.'" Jess had been a friend, a real friend. He was so far beyond all the petty-ass bullshit that most people are bogged down in. He was just like Nuke's grandma.

Tears welled up. He hadn't known how to release tears since he was a little bitty, baby boy. Not until he picked up his dead daughter in his arms. Grandma Moss had talked him through gallons of tears about lots of things. She took

111

him back through his life like a shrink, and guided him through the stuck places. He could see her so clearly: her beautiful long, cocoa fingers; her eyes as big, warm, and soft and pure as the shiny shell of a chestnut; her thick lips moving as she talked to him; her fine eyes looking at him.

He ran through his options. The fastest way back to LA would be an all night drive. He could steal a car and cruise off the Tiburon Peninsula, out toward Highway 101, being careful to stay at the speed limit, but not too slow, either. He didn't want to be noticed by any cops.

Nuke once got a ticket for fucking impeding the flow of traffic. He was only sixteen. The whole scene remained fresh in his mind. LAPD. Their eyes dead from hate. The same species of thugs as the killers on the street, the only difference being that the badges made them legal. Two black and two whites. Four sets of nasty, void eyes. One cop said, "Out nigger. On the asphalt motherfucker. Spread 'em."

Nigger, Nigger, Nigger. Nuke rolled his shoulders, pivoted his head on his thick neck, trying to ease some tension. He stretched out and tried to slow his pulse down further. He had to be calm. Anger could not be present when a person had to fight to survive. Anger always amounted to self-indulgence. It was a waste of time.

But his mind burned with anger. Aw man, Jess Hayes. One healthy white man out of a thousand and they gotta . . . What the fuck. Man, oh man, oh man. Nuke stared at the big stucco fence across from him.

"Thinking, thinking, thinking," he said to himself. He had to empty his mind.

But he had run out of time. Two squad cars burnt the road up, screaming toward the Humvee. They would find the weasel for sure but did they know to go to Jess'? Maybe he should jack a car and go straight back to Grandma Moss.

No. He had made a vow to be a PI with Billy. Alright. That's it. He would be the best damn PI ever. Salvage consultants. Nuke laughed. Fucking Easy Rawlins gone nuclear. He and Billy would find these scums. The law wouldn't do anything. There was too much politics. But they could take them, and Harlan would make the judge roll over like a pup.

Nuke wanted to be at sea. He would go straight for *dead latitudes*. Out at sea everything felt so real, so calm, so powerful, so far away from human bullshit. Then, he could get his head around it all. The decision made him calm. Lights flicked on in the mansions all around. The sound of hefty, high-strung dogs flooded the night as they loped out of the big houses. Nuke vaulted the fence into Jess' yard.

NINE

Sam exploded from Jess' basement. He whirled and twirled, and thumped everything in his path with his tail.

Nuke grabbed him and hugged him up close, rubbing him hard. He understood the big Lab. After all, he knew all about the feeling of being set free. They ran all the way to the Peninsula Yacht Club together. At the eight-foot stucco walls, Nuke scooped Sam's butt up with his hands and heaved him over.

Behind the club's walls, feeling protected from anyone watching, Nuke stopped to get his bearings. He wondered what had happened in the street up by Jess' house. The Humvee still bothered him. The little, white-assed, weasel wore black SWAT gear. The man fought real hard—stood strong and tough for his size. ANVIL Special Forces? Did they operate an ongoing training camp out by the casino? Must be thousands of these fuckers. Did they come from all over the country? American National Vigilance and Intelligence League? Fucking Django with a D?

It had to be one of those Aryan things with the nasty acronyms. Gonna hammer you into shape if you don't do it their way, if your skin ain't white. Better write it down in case he lost the pen. No, no need. He'd never forget a bunch of vigilantes. Or was it some government thing? The NSA watching Free Range? Billy said that a Humvee caused all the damage to the truck with a Grandmaster. The ear guy had a Smitty. Did they buy their own? What were they assigned? Billy also said that they were seriously aggressive and didn't care if civilians ended up in the mix. Billy did not exaggerate. If he called them badass, they had to have Special Op training.

But why Humvees? Why not plain old Hummers like Arnold? Why look like the Army is loose on city streets? Does the law stop you for being in a Humvee? Why not a plain rental? They had to have a lot of cash to buy the things.

Could anybody off the street buy a military vehicle? Drugs were the only place that much money came from. The animal stuff had to be a front to throw the fibbies and the DEA off. Or maybe they were DEA, or part of it. Or in *league* with them—VIGILANCE AND INTELLIGENCE LEAGUE. Vigilantes.

He felt the pen in his pocket. Really creepy shit. There could be a whole hell of a lot of them. The thought that they might already be following Billy and Jenny made him feel like puking.

He led Sam back up out of the yards toward the street, weaving through the outbuildings, and on down to the front of the yacht club grounds. When he got to the top corner, he pulled himself up on the perimeter wall to see if they had been followed.

He could see light and commotion from a couple of cop cars that lit up the neighborhood. The beams of their searchlights and flashlights drifted about, sorting through dark places. He heard more sirens screaming in the distance headed toward them. The 911 call had to have come from some really rich dudes, judges or politicians or something, to have sirens wailing so fast. Someone must have heard the .12 gauge that dropped Jess. But where was the shotgun? There had to have been another vehicle. Was it up on the street when he went into the house?

Nuke had been near so many shootouts that he understood the way cops worked. He knew that the second wave of sirens would be an army and they would lock down the whole place. The sweep of the neighborhood would include choppers.

He knew that the big sailboat needed to be out in the bay before they would think of it as an escape vehicle. *dead latitudes* moved very slowly and it had to be out in the open ocean, under the Golden Gate, far enough away that it would not be associated with the murders in any way.

He pushed off in the dinghy and rowed fast toward *dead latitudes*. Sam hopped toward the bow and curled up on

115

a tarp piled in the bottom of the little boat. He nestled in and watched Nuke as they slid through the water. Once they reached the sailboat, Nuke tied the dinghy off to the stern and helped Sam over the rail. He could secure the little boat as they plowed toward the Golden Gate.

On board, he began to check everything on the sailboat. The old diesel engine jumped immediately and began to idle with a gentle, purring rhythm. Nuke demanded perfection from everyone that touched the old girl. He owed his life to being a very thorough man. He was a man with a remarkable ability to pay attention to details. Immense patience went hand-in-glove with his scrutiny of each small part of the whole. He only went nuclear when the situation demanded an immense force be applied with all possible haste.

. . . .

Back out at the entrance of Peninsula Yacht Club, Brother Noah Army opened the gate. Brother Lucien Maxwell and Brother Ezekiel Army eased the Humvees down the drive, and hid them behind a storage building under a big awning designed for trailers with small boats. Brother Maxwell dug into an electrician's nylon tool bag and pulled out a street pistol: a .40 caliber Smith & Wesson to replace the one Nuke had taken from Ezekiel. The other two men followed as he cut a Boston Whaler loose and they headed toward *dead latitudes*. As they neared the old yawl, he killed the motor.

. . . .

Nuke moved through the pilot's area inspecting everything quickly: navigation, communications, all systems, and then he headed down into the cabin. He checked the galley briefly, even examining the burners on the stove. Nothing looked awry. Sam followed him all the way to the fo'c's'le. In the forecastle, he rummaged through supplies and rigging to make certain that the ANVIL people had not been there to wreak havoc with anything. He checked his extra equipment for going out on the Pacific. He and Billy had been through it all several times, readying for the trip to Russia. Everything sat just as it should.

As Nuke straightened up to go above and raise the anchor, a deep rumble rose from Sam's chest, and the hair on the back of his neck stood up. Nuke didn't know what had Sam's attention. With the noises from the bay and the diesel engine, he couldn't pinpoint any sounds. Nuke pulled a door open on one of the cabinets and grabbed a Desert Eagle. He turned and jacked a cartridge into the chamber as he headed for the galley. Sam skipped ahead of him, growling louder.

"Sam, stay. Stay here, Sam," hissed Nuke.

But no command dampened Sam's protective nature. Nothing other than a demand from Billy could have held him back. He sprung through the galley and up toward the cockpit. At the top of the stairs, he turned sideways as if he had someone trapped. Nuke slowed and eased toward the opening.

Sam lunged around the doorway and the sound of a scuffle and a loud whimper set Nuke off. He made it up the stairs in two strides and turned in the direction of Sam's whine. The big dog lay still on the deck, and a man rose, removing a rag from Sam's nose, with a bottle in his other hand.

"Don't think about anything," said Nuke to himself, leveling the pistol. He blinked his eyes and shook his head. The little rodent of a man he had manacled to the steering wheel stood before him, only his ear was now in place

"What the fuck? I just tied your sorry ass down for the cops."

"You cut my brother's ear off, nigger. What a mistake. You breached an ANVIL operation at the tree hugger's house, and you and all your friends are personally going to suffer for a long time," said Noah Army.

Nuke slapped him across the jaw with the pistol so hard that teeth flew out of his mouth. The man yelped with pain. Nuke grabbed his hair and stuffed the barrel in his mouth.

117

"You don't call anybody nigger, maggot-boy. Never. Not ever. You're gonna—"

Nuke was interrupted by the other man, who rapped Nuke hard on the head from behind with a lead-cored sap. Nuke fell. The intruders had waited on either side of the door, using Sam as bait.

Ezekiel stepped around, next to Brother Maxwell. Noah crawled about on the teak, searching the planks closely. "My fucking teeth," he said.

"Brother, you must watch your language," said Ezekiel Army. "Just look at my ear."

"Fuck both of you whining simps," said Maxwell. "Fuck Slade and this whole pathetic ANVIL scam. Jesus was about love, not rules. Selling citizens a pseudo-Christian wrap that the preacher doesn't even believe, and cutting up freakin' Smokey, and selling weapons, and . . . "

"Brother Maxwell, you have to get a grip on yourself."

"Shut the fuck up, you little pussies. Get up off the floor, Noah, and lace him with chloroform. Besides, what are you gonna do with your teeth, put 'em under your pillow for the tooth fairy? We've got important shit on our hands. We must find who owns this boat. Is the titleholder the same guy who owns the pickup? Where is this tub registered?"

"It's my fucking teeth, Lucien. He knocked them out."

"Get up! Gas this asshole. Your teeth suck anyway; they're butt ugly. The dentist will screw in some shiny plastic things on a couple pins. And for now, the look will go great with Zeke's ear."

Maxwell laughed deep and harsh. Noah jumped up, grabbed his shirt and pulled his fist back for a swing, but Brother Maxwell kicked him in the groin and he bent over holding himself, groaning.

"We've got much more important shit here than teeth. We got to get this damn boat out to sea and ditch the Humvees," said Maxwell.

118

"I gotta get my ear back on."

"Let's just throw the dog and this big, ugly thing over. The bay's full of leopard sharks. After they perform their vital recycling task for the ecological balance, we can put the sharks in inventory. The jaws and fins are a quick sale. Heck, their livers or some of their guts must be worth something, too. Those Asians probably make a hard-on drug with them. You know, we'll up the cash flow."

As always, Brother Maxwell stood erect, his hands straight down at his sides. He radiated authority. He studied Nuke's body carefully, with the same intensity he applied at the bear parting. He surveyed every square inch of the situation. Then, again, his concentration returned to Nuke's body. He pulled out his comb and slicked his hair back into place perfectly.

"Come on, we'll heave them off the back," said Brother Maxwell.

"You know that we can't do that," said Noah. "We must always call Brother Slade."

"Jesus, Noah. You don't even talk like a man anymore," said Maxwell.

"I've known you for a long time, Lucien, and I see Brother Slade changing too. I know what you're saying, but you know why we're doing this."

"No, Noah. Sometimes I have real strong doubts about just what we *are* doing. Things aren't like they were back in the day. Jet has changed. It used to be a brotherhood, but now he's more interested in dealing those fucking shotgun shells. Cash flow has taken him over. Working with Homeland Security and real citizens has lost the front seat. Cleaning up America is no longer important. He's getting bigger and more powerful, and he likes it. He really likes running with these freakazoid, NSA fucks."

Noah looked down at Nuke. The gas had knocked the man out.

"We need to get these two down below," Noah concluded.

"What for?" asked Maxwell.

"Because we can't have bodies topside when choppers come by, and we have to call Brother Slade and tell him that all is secure."

"Yeah, we'll call Slade. That's right. Call old Jet right up but we don't need this thing," said Maxwell. "Why should we get a hernia hauling a rhinoceros downstairs?"

"Protocol would be to secure him down there where he is not visible, and the dog with him, so we can investigate the scene as professionals," said Noah Army.

"Oh fuck that. We'll just push him over and the sharks will fatten up, or he'll be a floater. The cops will think there was trouble in the hood. It doesn't make any difference. We'll leave this big, slow tub of a boat here with all the other rich fuck's toys. Nobody will think twice."

"No. We have to secure him and call Brother Slade for instructions," said Noah. "The helicopters will be here any minute. We can't have a floater. Besides, we have to question him and find the guy with the girl."

Maxwell sat down on a rail. He reached in his pocket and pulled out a long, mother of pearl cigarette holder. He fished a pack of unfiltered Camel cigarettes out of his pocket. He flipped out a cigarette, put the pack away and proceeded to tap the unlit smoke on *dead latitudes'* mahogany railing. He stared out at the night. He inserted the Camel in the holder and pulled out a death's head Zippo. A skull sculpted in platinum with ruby eyes, was branded onto the lighter. The 22-karat gold lettering above the skull read "101st Airborne." Below the skull was the words "Manifest Destiny." Maxwell flicked the lid open, then lit the cigarette and took a slow, deep draw.

"How long have I known you, Noah? And don't fucking call me Brother Maxwell."

"Jesus, Lucien, come on. This is no time to—"

"It is always time to think through what you're doing, Noah. In fact, it's high fuckin' time we did. Haven't you ever heard the saying, 'the ends do not justify the means'?" asked Maxwell, after a slow pull on the cigarette.

"For god's sake, Lucien, what are you talking about? That's the kind of crap liberals say. I think Bill Clinton made that up after he got the blow job."

"Aren't there policemen all over there?"

"There are, and the helicopters will be here any minute."

"Noah!" shouted Maxwell.

"Lucien, what the hell is coming over you? You've got to get a grip. We came out here to board this boat and find clues about the guy and the woman in the pickup."

"I am getting a grip. It's time we all got a grip. Slade told us to come out here, but what's the point? We're letting the pickup get away," said Maxwell.

"The pickup is under surveillance, Brother Maxwell. We are onboard to find information about the driver and passenger. You're losing it. We have to sail this boat out of here in case we need to use it to find out who those two that got away are. We need to work on this big one and make him talk. I don't know what we do with the dog, but they'll have spotlights shining down here any minute now, and we've got to get rid of those Humvees."

"Whoa Noah. Whoa, whoa. Slow down, son. This is when people really fuck things up."

"Slow down? The Humvees are sitting up there and they're registered to us personally. ANVIL won't get in trouble. We will."

"Noah, Noah, Noah. That's just what I'm saying. Now slow down. You're working too hard. This ain't Watts. Those rich people don't want choppers intruding on their private property. That's a ritzy yacht club," said Maxwell.

"We have to get out there under the Golden Gate so the cops don't associate this boat with that house," said Noah.

"What for? The cops come aboard, which they won't, it's some rich guy's yacht. And it's not connected to Hayes' house at all."

"But the cops just picked up the ANVIL Humvee in Sausalito—not Brother Slade's NSA people—and they will see ours and put two and two together," said Noah.

"They are safely tucked away," said Maxwell, taking another hit off the cigarette.

Noah grabbed Nuke's wrist and heaved. He could barely budge the solid body with all his might. He dropped the arm and tried a leg.

"Where the hell do you think you're going? The three of us can push the nigra over the stern, there. Then we'll flop the dog over, and we'll take off in the Humvees," said Maxwell.

"But they saw the vehicle in Sausalito."

"Not these cops that are up here."

"Forget about it. I'll tell you what would be real dumb is if we got busted for trying to sell animal parts. We take in plenty of cash from our fellowship—the tithing is abundant and it's fine for our mission. Brother Slade has fallen in love with wealth itself," said Maxwell.

"Well . . . "

"Yeah—you say *well*, Noah, but *duh* is more like it," said Maxwell.

Noah stood there staring at Nuke, then up at Maxwell, then back at Nuke. Ezekiel looked as if he'd checked off the planet as he reached up and felt for his wound.

"We have to tend to my ear or I've got to get to a hospital."

Maxwell pulled out another cigarette. He threw the spent one into the water and started the smoking ritual all over again. Ezekiel pointed at his ear.

"What the hell are you doing? Are you just going to sit there and smoke?" Ezekiel asked.

"I am going to sit here and think through what to do, and then I am going to act on the intelligent conclusions resultant of my ability to reason," said Maxwell, flicking his Zippo shut.

Noah Army stuffed Nuke's ankle under his own bicep, locked his arm against his ribs and tried using the strength of his legs to pull the body. Nuke heaved a few inches, but Maxwell grabbed Noah and pulled him up close.

"Sit your scrawny little ass down here and try some reasoning yourself," he demanded.

Noah Army jerked loose from Maxwell's grip and adjusted himself. Maxwell took a long, deep draw, cocked his head and examined Nuke.

"Get your gun out, Noah."

Noah whipped the pistol out of its shoulder holster, grabbed the tailpiece and locked a round into the chamber.

"Did he move?"

"Nah, I slapped the hell out of him," said Brother Maxwell. "He's got the skull of a rhino, but the persuader slowed him down. It's that spring steel shank. Then you hit him with the chloroform so we've got a long time. If he comes to, knee-cap him on both sides."

"Jesus. What are we gonna do?" asked Ezekiel Army. "We've gotta call Slade, ah, Brother Slade."

"Slade. That's right. Say it like it is. Jet Slade. Now, what is he?"

"He is a Christian."

"Come on, Noah. Christians bugger choirboys, so it don't mean you're good if you call yourself one. And, he is not the fuckin' Lord God Almighty. He's an ex-trailer-trash, spam sandwich from frickin' Alabama: a down-at-the-heels, country preacher who's slunk into some money and fallen for the power that comes with it. Cash don't make you anything—you're still just another turd in the punchbowl. That's it, my man: do you catch on, Zeke? For Christ's sake, look at you. You look like a freakin' geek out of a sideshow without the ear. We've gotta sew it back on," said Maxwell.

"We have to call him," said Noah.

"Alright. I'm sick of this. You two are lost. We're gonna call him. First haul this thing down below with the dog. It will be easy to get the truth out of this big one with him out on the open ocean. Ezekiel will use the drug and get the truth fast," said Maxwell.

"Okay. Okay. Okay. I'm going to look for a first aid kit after he's secure," said Noah Army.

Brother Maxwell flipped his butt over the rail and lit another smoke. He raised his head upward toward the night sky and pursed his lips around the long cigarette holder. He held it up, with his elbow in the air and his head cocked to the side. He lifted his chin and watched the stream of smoke suck up into the breeze off San Francisco Bay.

"We are going to sew up your ear." He looked up at the man as he spoke. "After we fix your ear, you two are going to motor on out under the bridge by yourselves with the prisoner. You can throw the dog over when you are out to sea so the sharks tidy up for us. We don't want anything behind us here in the bay. No cops are going to bother you. You are going to cuff the negro really well and then you are going to get the information from him. We will join you in Santa Cruz, or farther south if need be."

"But what about my ear, Lucien? We really need to go to a hospital; I can't go around—"

"You know I was a Special Ops medic in Desert Storm. They transferred me after I beat up a colonel. The fuck was all embarrassed that a medic whipped the hell out of him. I didn't get trained all the way, but hell, there are no moving parts with an ear. I'm gonna make you look better than Brad Pitt. Now haul these bodies down and get the medical tools."

"You shouldn't curse, Lucien."

"Let me settle with the Lord in my own way, Zeke."

Maxwell pulled some plastic, flex cuffs out of his vest. "Put more of these on the dog too. Do them both real tight. I don't want him to take you again." He kicked Nuke. "You are going to knee-cap this rhino on one side to make it start talking. Then you are going to question it. After you find out why it was at the tree hugger's house, why it came out to this boat and who the dude with the chick in the truck is, you are going to push it over the side. We can't part it out and sell it, so we'll feed the shark inventory. After you get out to sea and finish your questions, you're gonna throw the pup over with it."

Noah came back up with a professional triage medical unit.

"Look here, Zeke, I found it for you. This is one hell of a seafaring medic's kit. You *are* in luck. It's even got all the sewing stuff."

"I'm going up to secure the vehicles myself after we get that ear hitched up. Come on, sit down Zeke. You are going to sail this boat out the Golden Gate, find all the paper on board, let his highness, Mr. Jet Slade, decide what he wants to do with it," said Maxwell.

"We can't make all these other decisions without Brother Slade."

"Sure we can, Noah. Just you relax. They are already made and you can blame it all on me."

TEN

Not fifteen miles from Pechanga, from the Indian reservation and the throb of the casinos, rested the small valley hidden out of the view from most travelers who drove through on the country roads aching to lose their money.

The driver had to pull up into a pass and then head down sharply through a series of tight switchbacks. In the daytime, the gentle hills of Northern San Diego County rolled off before the travelers' eyes in an unexpected view of some of the most beautiful country in Southern California.

From a crow's eye, the sprawl of the rapidly growing community of Temecula, California and the vineyard gold all around the expanding city would have been visible. But night covered everything and his plane sat at the ranch. He rode in a caravan of three Cadillac SUVs. They rolled down the winding road smoothly and quickly. They wound through the chaparral and dropped onto the valley floor where ANVIL's main camp, White Dove Ranch, sat.

The American National Vigilance and Investigation League held rallies on the grounds. Sometimes 10,000 people swarmed in around the basin to hear Slade's sermons. Vigilant investigation of all things kept the members safe from Armageddon. The Four Horsemen rode their trusty steeds fast and headed straight for anyone not prepared. All the major magazines, newspapers, television and radios covered ANVIL and its rapidly expanding membership.

As Jet Slade's entourage moved into the valley, the halcyon countryside sat quiet. The squat, wood-frame, camp-like buildings seemed to glow in the night from the lights of the ranch. They each had a coating of thick, white, semi-gloss paint.

On a sunny day, the vast expanse of lawn looked out of place among the indigenous species of vegetation. The grass covered fifteen acres and the tending of the vast lawns and golf course relied heavily on an aquifer beneath the ranch.

Slade missed the excitement of the revivals with thousands of members on board. His caravan shot past the lawns off of the perfectly maintained asphalt roadway, straight up toward an immense four-story gothic house which was painted the same bright satin white as all of the outbuildings in the encampment. The structure loomed above everything.

The Caddies headed through the lights toward the circular drive, which provided automobiles entry to the structure. A southern gothic porch extended twenty feet out, beyond the front of the building. Covered with tongue and groove lumber, the gray enamel floor of the porch glowed.

Six-foot swings hung from chains attached to the porch ceiling on either side of the front door. A woman with a fair complexion, black hair and pale blue eyes perched on one of the swings. She pushed off the gray floorboards with one bare foot and swung gently. She wore a thin, white, cotton frock with a loose bodice snugged up around her ample bosom. Her skirt lifted in the breeze as she swung. She arched her long creamy neck and turned her head when she noticed the approaching SUVs. Immediately, she got up and walked into the white house.

The caravan swept around the drive and came to a quick stop. Jet Slade stepped right out of the second vehicle with his cellphone to his ear. Buster Bush slid out the opposite door brusquely and popped his phone into his hip pocket.

"I'm going down to the Crays," he said.

"Yeah, I'll come down after I get finished upstairs. I've gotta figure out what the fuck is going on at the tree hugger's house."

"Is Zeke's phone still on?"

"Brother Ezekiel! And yes, but the voices are muffled. Something's really weird. Maxwell's not calling me. The whole operation has gone to shit."

"Okay, boss," said Buster, and he took off toward the out buildings.

Slade walked directly up the steps and into the house. Inside, the mansion was Spartan and clean, with hardwood floors and oriental rugs. The structure screamed with silence. To the right at the entry, a cavernous parlor spread out offering straight-backed furnishings to guests.

He headed up the circular staircase and through a door on the second floor. The office he entered sported white paint like everything else. A gray plastic work table took up much of the room. The table was attached to the wall like a kitchen counter without any cabinets. Computer equipment, including scanners, printers, and laptops covered the surface. On the walls, wire-shelving racks supported masses of digital hardware with blinking lights.

He sat down at a keyboard in front of an enormous monitor. He smoothed his greased hair with his hands, and then he rapped on the keyboard. His face pinched up severely. He adjusted his Ray Ban Aviators, pushing the sunglasses up on his nose. He undid the neck button on his black silk shirt, squirmed in his gabardine trousers and kicked off his tasseled Italian loafers.

Buster came right up on the screen. He sat erect on an egg-shaped chair with an ergonomic keyboard in his lap. He wore a day-glow lime-colored t-shirt with the words "The Cyber the Infinite" silk-screened on the front in white. An image of a cowboy on a roan stallion with a keyboard in the horse's side scabbard instead of a rifle was printed above the words.

Like in Slade's home office, studio microphones hung from the racks, making it like a disc-jockey's workspace.

Buster's voice flooded the room through studio monitors.

"How many people are you going to have at the hunt in Texas?" he asked.

"Very few. We'll keep it low key. I want to get down to serious business with the arms men and the senators."

"How about Virginia and Bayonne?"

"A lot. Probably a big crowd down from the Hill for the Virginia hunt. A bunch of kiss-ass politicians. Bayonne's the biggest. New Jersey's perfect for both New York and

Connecticut. We'll have the big money boys that own the politicians. We're gonna blow their minds with the Steeler and the Buster."

"Damn, boss. I'm gonna be known all over the world just like Superman, able to cut through steel with a shotgun and able to rip armor plate with one shot. Every chick in every bar where the weapons groupies hang out will want a piece of my action."

"Mr. Bush, I want to tell you that we are never gonna have to think about money again. The war boys are gonna quake, Buster. Quake, man, quake I tell you. They are gonna drop to their knees, bowing down for the guy who's already got the plants in Asia. And, funny thing: the Koreans are big shotgun nuts. I've got the same guys that distribute my bear bladders doing it with shotgun artillery. Hell, North Korea's a great market.

"And these Brit wise guys, this Neeley, can sell to the Mideast and China. Can you imagine? China. The US is already tied up, but fuck 'em. We are not just talking an ordinary dumb product that costs us an arm and a leg for marketing."

"Jeez, boss, you're preachin' to the choir. Are you kiddin' me? A lightning-fast, debugged, camel-rugged, recoilless, armor-piercing, automatic shotgun that uses fifteen-round clips or neoprene belts with endless loads? Boss, you are a fuckin' genius just like me."

"I am a genius, Buster, and finally, in this lifetime, these dumb big shots can see. Preaching is a loser's job. Look at what it got the Lord himself. All those goddamn losers nailed him on some boards in the hot sun."

"Thankless is the word, boss."

"Buster, quit calling me boss—the Big Boy is boss. I'm just a humble servant. Think about it—North Korea is just across the border from our manufacturing: Russia, Saudi Arabia, China, and Africa. Damn, we're gonna give Bill Gates a run for top dog in the billionaire's club.

"Right after we train Neeley in the parts business, we'll let him handle this weapon here in the US. May take a while to get in with the military, but every redneck, gangbanger, wannabe mobster, robber, cop and his pooch will want one."

"Seventy-five max, in Austin with the help and all?" asked Buster.

"Yeah, it's a good number that I can schmooze real smooth and easy. I'll get finished up here and I'll be on down."

The rattling started softly. Slade grabbed the sides of his keyboard. He squeezed until his knuckles turned white, holding as if it would steady him from a great imminent calamity.

He looked at the monitor in terror as the sound amplified. The rattling became more ferocious. Even a person who had been face to face with the noise would know that searing danger arose. Slade pounded his keyboard, but it had already frozen.

He grabbed the cellphone and punched the speed dial to ring Buster.

"It's here goddamnit! The fucking thing is going to pop up any minute now. You've got to get rid of this sound. Of the whole fucking thing," said Slade into the phone.

"Okay. Right. The network is tight. It's just some popup thing. Came right in off the trunk but. . . ."

The rattle began to overwhelm the room.

"Don't tell me about this hacker shit. Just get this thing away from me," screamed Slade.

"Okay, boss. I just—"

"And goddamnit, don't call me boss."

Slade threw the phone across the room. A huge, frighteningly realistic, computer-animated, timber rattler appeared on his screen. The creature slithered toward him. Its rattle stood in the air. It stopped and looked directly in Slade's eyes. Slade wanted desperately to run from the room, but he couldn't move. He trembled and broke into a sweat. Slowly, the snake coiled, raised itself, and everything but the rattle stood breathlessly still. Within Slade, an eternity passed. He couldn't move any particle of his being. And then, like a bolt of static electricity between huge clouds, the demon's jaw opened wide for the strike. Pulling its head back, it vanished.

Slade stood, and as he walked toward the door, whipped his white monogrammed hanky out and wiped the sweat from his brow.

"Lucinda," he shouted.

Immediately, without making a sound, the woman from the porch swing appeared on the stairwell.

"Yes, Jet," she said softly.

"Will you bring me a bourbon and branch, darlin'?"

"Sure Jet. Is everything alright?"

"Yeah, ah, yes darlin'. Everything's fine. Just been a long day."

"Okay. I'll be right back up." She spoke with a rich southern drawl.

With extreme effort, Slade made himself turn around to face the terror on the computer screen. He massaged his furrowed brow. Then, he returned and sat at his workstation. He hesitated but forced himself to grab the keyboard. He logged into his email from the ANVIL facility in Bayonne, New Jersey. Everything worked perfectly. He checked on the Manhattan and the Austin facilities and the connections zipped right through.

From Austin, the ANVIL team confirmed that the contractor had pulled through. In preparation for the first hunt, he surrounded the new acreage up in the Hill Country, Paradise Ranch, with a 25-foot stainless steel fence. Topped with razor wire, the fencing buzzed with a 40,000-volt charge at all times. Low amps prevented injury, and steered Slade and Anvil clear of legal hassles.

The inventory for Paradise flowed in from zoos all around the globe, especially the US, where the zoo breeders pumped out stock for inventory every month and always had throwaway animals.

The Germans said they looked forward to the hunt and to seeing the facility. In fact Wolfgang Vorn, who would be the first to buy shotguns, cracked up—he had already cleaned his .460 Weatherby Magnums for the event. Vorn explained further, saying he had never shot a tiger and the cash sat in aluminum cases, bundled neatly for the dead tiger transaction. "I vont to have zee entire penis dried just for me. For von hundred fifty thousand Euros, I should get a fucking couch made from the hide." The fat man laughed hardily and hung up.

Slade couldn't pay attention. No possible way Jet Slade would allow a dumb cartoon like that snake on his screen slow him down. Some joker in the ANVIL crew smoking too much grass. Maybe some kids using their mommy's credit card to torment businesses.

Buster would find the tormentor with some of his hacker crap. Whoever thought the joke was so clever had an eighteen-foot sieve-fenced pit waiting for him at Paradise. The floor of the pit provided a haven for dozens of diamondbacks and the hackers would be forced to join the snakes. Ah, such poetic justice, thought Slade. Whoever thought the graphic was funny could discuss it with members of ANVIL's poisonous reptile inventory.

Slade had decided to place a hundred toxic reptile pits all over the property. He had already experimented with rattlesnake expositions, which provided excellent cash flow. The patrons had a real hard-on for eating the flesh and letting the blood of any rattler. He advertised in churches and the revenue stream proved a healthy cash cow. The demand for viper venom rose monthly and some patrons wanted poison snakes for pets. Jet Slade always marveled at what a dumb fuck a human being could be.

The stumbling block had been hunting the snakes down. It was too damned labor intensive. There were too many drunk hunters and shit-faced cowboy types. No way to count on them. But now the snakes could be inventoried for on-demand fulfillment. And the true glory was that vipers already existed globally, the manufacturing and warehousing only required compact spaces, and the reptiles could be placed way out in the boondocks. A pit full of vipers would serve as the best execution chamber ever designed. "Oops. The poor bastard must have slipped."

Lucinda whisked into the room with no noise but the sound of her skirt. She handed him the drink and his eyes fixed on her full bodice.

"Thanks, sweetheart. Is everything alright for you?" asked Slade.

"Oh yes, Jet. My first batch of hydroponic tomatoes are coming in from the hothouse," she said.

"Lord, darlin', you are such a wonderful creature. So darn organic. A real, lovin' Christian girl. I don't know how you do it. So wholesome and fascinated with such wonderful things. Lord Almighty, everyone should be as healthy and radiant as you are."

"Why Jet Slade, I do believe that you are the most charming man I have ever met," she said.

"I'm just after your juicy tomatoes, darlin'."

"Why you naughty boy! I must serve some up before you leave," she responded.

"I'm afraid that I can't do it this time. We've got to leave in a couple hours."

"But I can help you and Buster both. At the same time. You both love that and you definitely need to ease some tension."

"We'll sleep on the plane."

"Well alright, but you better get back here real soon."

"We will. Thanks darlin'." Slade turned to the keyboard and Lucinda padded back out the door.

He grabbed the cell phone off the floor. He dialed and put it on speaker before he laid it on the desk.

"Did you find the thing? What? What the hell is going on? No! Don't go off with the trapdoors and randomness, none of that crap. Find this son of a bitch. I have a gift waiting for him on the ranch."

"It's probably teen hackers."

"Good. They'll enjoy the gift even more than some old geez."

Slade hung up and dialed another number.

"Where are you?"

On the other end of the line, one of the NSA surveillance team's men, one of the pair with the non-descript serious faces who watched Jenny in the Animalfund office, spoke with a slow gruff voice.

"Tiburon," the man said.

"Tiburon, are you insane? The whole peninsula has to be swarming with cops. Did you get the two in the truck?"

Slade wolfed the bourbon down. He placed the glass on the gray work surface and rubbed his small round belly. Things had never gone off course with ANVIL. Mixing with the feds was a mistake. They were all fuck ups. He told himself that problems always accompanied growth. He would learn to expand and to whip any problem.

"Naw, we were looking into something. A big sailboat down at the yacht club took off about the same time the cops started to roll out on the peninsula."

"I am telling you what to watch. You are NSA which means that you are too stupid to make decisions on your own."

There was a long deep silence on the other end of the line.

"So, you're tellin' me that after the cops took Fermin and Miller down there in Sausalito, you went up to Hayes' house and lost those two again?" the voice asked.

Slade took a drink off his bourbon.

"You call them Brother Fermin and Brother Miller, do you understand? I don't care if you guys are feds and the best Special Op spies in the universe; you have to get with the fucking program. These men are brethren in a fraternity ordained by God. At this time, you are servants, too."

"Right, boss."

"And don't call me boss. The Lord is boss."

"Right, Brother Slade, we talked it over with Maxwell—ah, Brother Maxwell. He told us where Hayes—ah, Brother Hayes—"

"No! Not Brother Hayes. No brother there! Hayes was a fucking infidel. You said that you are both Christian. Now let's snap to."

"Right, Brother Slade. Brother Maxwell guided us from Sausalito. But he went down and when we got back to the house, our guys were gone. The chick and the pickup dude were gone, and some gangbanger had showed. Our guys didn't even finish the deed," said the man.

"Your chief told me that NSA is the one group that doesn't mess up. But obviously, you are just as stupid as any other so-called Intelligence. Maybe as dumb as the FBI. How could you possibly miss one guy in a pickup?"

"Brother Slade, we have to stay transparent."

"Jesus H. Christ. That man interrupted a very important antiterrorist action," Slade yelled into the microphone and his voice boomed through the whole building.

"What about the gangbanger?"

"I told you to eliminate him."

"You told your men to do him."

Slade rolled his eyes as he listened.

"Yes, I told you both because you're all fuck ups. Maybe one of you can perform.

"So where is Maxwell, gentlemen? I haven't heard from him." Slade calmed his voice and it dropped into the rich basso profundo of a sacred eulogy.

"We lost the pickup down by the Embarcadero after they left the Hayes house. We followed them back across the Golden Gate. It looked like they were headed into the middle of the city, right downtown, not back to North Beach. Could have even been Union Square. We went back to the Animalfund office but there was nothing."

"Gentlemen, you are serving as part of an ANVIL surveillance team. You were highly trained by the United States Government and then the Russians and the Jews. Are you losing it completely? This is not a tea party for federal bureaucrats. It's what we do out here in the real world," said Slade and again, his voice shook the building.

"No sir, we, ah . . . it's just that too much stuff piled up at once . . . there were too many unexpected—"

"No. That is pur-dee bullshit. This guy in the pickup is better than you are," said Slade, sucking on the whiskey. "I want to know who trained him. This is the first time that ANVIL has faced an error, the first series of snafus in God's plan for the ANVIL system. I am reaching out for His hand. I will ask Him for the great power of forgiveness."

"Jeez. Thanks Brother Slade. We'll grab them right away and we'll bring them in to you, sir," said the man.

"Who has the new weapon? Did they cops find any of them in Sausalito?"

"It doesn't sound like it. We have audio teams listening to everything."

"Does Maxwell have his shells accounted for?"

"We assume that he does."

"Assume?"

"He's your field boss, so we're taking for granted that—"

"What about your Kane guy who went in?"

"He's missing the one full round he had left."

136

"He fired four, right?" asked Slade.

"That is correct."

"Tell him to call me. No, tell him to call your boss. I'll call him, too. This Kane guy should be offed. He's a serious fugitive now for a very conspicuous murder."

"We will do it immediately upon hearing from him, Brother Slade."

"Alright gentlemen, but remember the ANVIL motto: Precision Creates Perfection. Pay attention to what you are doing. And just think about where the hell two disposable humans like you are going to earn a million dollars a year. Not from the feds." He spoke deeply. Slade felt as if he were in the pulpit.

"Yes, Brother Slade, to the mission at hand," said the man.

"Our mission is the Great Revival of the United States and now it is soiled. You may consider yourselves above the law, but you are Americans and you have lost two brethren to the law. It is time to put an end to mistakes."

"Yes, Brother Slade."

"Alright gentlemen. I will be in Texas for our first domestic tiger hunt. Keep me posted. I expect these three people to be apprehended and flown out to me. I also expect all of our brethren to be free by the time I call. You must work closely with Brother Maxwell before he comes out."

"Yes, Brother Slade."

"Find Maxwell, ah Brother Maxwell, before you do anything else and tell him to call me immediately."

"We will."

Slade threw the cellphone right through the window, shattering the pane. He finished his whiskey and began to type furiously at the keyboard.

"Buster, bring me some cigarettes," he barked into the microphone, not worried about snoops.

Lucinda came running into the room, her face flushed and the top two buttons of her summer dress undone.

"What happened, Jet? Are you alright?" she asked.

Slade's eyes snagged on the top of her breasts that were bulging out of her bodice.

"Yeah darlin'. I hope I didn't frighten you. I just lost my temper due to some business problems," said Slade, his voice steady. "I will go into the chapel and pray before leaving for Texas."

"Anyone might lose their temper if they worked as much as you do," said Lucinda. She walked over and started massaging his shoulders. He relaxed and let out a deep sigh as her body slid up against him.

"There, now. Atta boy. You just take a deep breath and relax," she said.

He sighed again, deeply, and let his head fall back onto her breasts.

"Now, there's my boy," she said, digging into his shoulders. "You just get rid of some of that nasty ol' tension."

Slade's entire body slumped into relaxation. He moved turned his head, settling it into the cushion of her chest. He reached back and took hold of her thighs. Lucinda wrapped her arms around his shoulders, engulfing him, and massaged his pecs.

Buster walked in and she straightened up and patted Slade's arms.

"There you go, hun. You need to rest," she said.

Buster moved on into the room with the Pall Malls outstretched in his hand.

"The Lord is my rest, Lucinda," he said.

"You are such a good man, Jet Slade. The boys will fix the window tomorrow. Can I get you anything?"

"Another bourbon, darlin'. One for the road. I'm gonna take off right away. Some things have changed, so I need to get right on out to Texas and make sure that all will work out right for the business meeting."

Lucinda left the room and Slade took a cigarette.

"Got the bot diggin' deeper," said Buster.

"You are a smart guy. Will you please explain to me why people make it so difficult for a guy who is just trying to make the world a better place? The ANVIL Ministry: a little recreation for the burdened businessmen and the hardworking politicians, a piece of military ordinance that puts battle in the hands of the ordinary foot soldier. These are the things I am linking together. Now I am taking on an animal husbandry industry, just like dairy, like hog ranching, like poultry—"

"Whoa, Boss, I'm your computer guy, so I've got to keep it straight. You're talking about animal husbandry, but you're dealing with wild animals, not domestic."

"Nonsense, you just stick to programming. There's no such thing as a wild world now, that's all romantic thinking about the past. It's all domestic now. Humans won the war with the wilderness; it's all ours now. I am spreading just-in-time inventory—the tool all corporations use—to an industry that is a hundred years behind. Bears are a domestic harvest nowadays."

"Hey, whatever, man. It's your thing."

"I'm getting out of here right now," said Slade.

"Aren't you gonna come down to the computer room?"

"No. Things are messy up there in Tiburon. I'm going on to Texas. I've gotta get things tied up out there, then get back to meet Neeley on Thursday. Then I've got to go to the *Queen Mary* to make sure everything's set for the Smokey the Bear crap with Hicks and the Senate stooges. I've got to go to Virginia real soon, too. We've got to rev up the logistics for the East Coast hunts. In order for us to stay on our timeline, the deals with the buyers in Austin have to be locked in globally before the event at the *Queen Mary*. But I've got a feeling that I am going to have to find this fuck in the pickup myself."

"Okay. I've got a lot to do. The bot first, and then the uplinks still keep falling apart. I'll have this Cray talking to all the stations right away and without the frickin' cartoon. I'll do Austin, Bayonne and Manhattan before you get to the ranch," said Buster.

"Oh, I'm meeting this guy from Fish and Wildlife on Thursday at ten in the morning. It's in Long Beach at Christy's. The guy Neeley met in Vegas. Some Cuban."

"Cuban?"

"Yeah, Desi Sandoval, just like the old Lucy show on TV. A Smokey on the inside is just what we need. Dig into records and find out about him."

Lucinda brought the cocktail in, fanning the cigarette smoke out of her face. She had also poured both Slade and Buster coffee. She handed them the beverages and padded right back out of the room.

"Damn, darlin', you are such a thoughtful person. How do you do it?" asked Slade.

"Yeah, thanks Lucy," said Buster.

Slade fired up another cigarette, took a deep drag, a hit of the drink, and chased them both down with coffee. He could hear Mattie's doves out on the veranda, calling on the soft evening breeze. They sounded as if they were singing some hideous curse. His head screamed with data overload. His horns needed filing again. He tightened his groin thinking about Lucinda. He had to get on the Gulfstream, had to allow the smooth corporate jet to sweep him away from all of it.

ELEVEN

Right in front of Tosca on Columbus Avenue—one of San Francisco's true landmarks—the ominous black Chrysler 300C idled. The darkened windows sat dead and menacing like Neeley's eyes. Two gunmen from the bear parting took over for Leonardo at the entry doors of the cafe. They shoved Billy into the back next to Heiny. The bulging, square-faced, blond Teuton had come straight in from his field training.

Neeley sat across from Billy. He unbuttoned his gray cashmere topcoat. Leonard slid in beside him, next to the door, and undid his coat just like his boss.

The giant character perched on the seat, broad and still, and spewed swamp breath whenever he opened his mouth. He glanced sidelong at Billy for a long time and finally belched. The rancid odor flooded the car.

"Jesus, Heinrich, try one of these." Neeley's Brit accent rang out rich and strong as he pulled out a tin of breath fresheners.

Leaning forward for the mints, Heinrich belched again. Neeley grabbed a lapel of his cashmere coat and to shield his nose and talked to Billy.

"Please excuse Heiny. These Krauts are loyal, and they are excellent marksmen, but they don't understand class. Not at all. So tell me, how are you, Jess?"

"This is a fucked-up procedure for a business meeting, Mr. Neeley," Billy ad-libbed since he had no clue of what had already taken place between Neeley and Jess.

"You're right, Jess. Heinrich, listen to this guy. We are engaged in a professional get-together not a barnyard brawl."

"You need to make an appointment before you take me off in an automobile. Your assistant did not speak with my office," Billy continued.

"You're talking to Mr. Giacomo Neeley, funny guy. Let's stay on our p's and q's here. Mr. Heinrich Mueller is my name, and I make Mr. Neeley's appointments." He leaned forward, hands spread on his knees.

Billy pulled his head back, concerned about having to take another whiff of the man's breath.

"You're moving out of your league, Jess," said Neeley.

"The league is determined by the skill of the players."

Quick as a cat, Heinrich slapped Billy so hard a thin stream blood spurted from the corner of his mouth and left a delicate spray on Neeley's shirt.

"Heiny," said Neeley, straining to inspect himself, "settle down for god's sake. Check out my fresh laundry job. You spoiled the look."

"Jesus, boss, I'm awful sorry. The guy is a wiseass. I'm helping him not be a punk," said Heiny. "You're fooling around in the majors, asshole, and you're from a sandlot team." Heiny sounded like Arnold Schwarzenegger only he had a deep voice, a basso profundo.

A warm stream of blood trickled down the side of Billy's mouth. He licked the metallic liquid as well as possible. He didn't have a clue where to go with this script. "Fuck you Heiny," he said.

Neeley raised both hands to protect himself as the heavy hand popped Billy's head against the seat again. "Smartass is not the best approach around here. Heinrich is a rather proper type guy even with his lack of culture."

Neeley leaned back and gazed out at the street with his brow tightened. "Hey, Heiny, stop the goddamn slapping. I'm wearing a Wilkes Bashford shirt, and now just look." He pointed at the fabric. "Look closely, Heiny, look at the little spots of blood splatter you've got on the front."

Neeley moved his perilous gaze from Heiny to Billy. "You're betting on what's gonna be a bad roll Jesse. We know you're looking around in Asia for product. But even if you find it you don't have distribution experience, and you don't have a

142

strong organization for stability: you are lost. This is the third time asking you, son. You stall and stall and stall. We've tried to keep this gentlemanly." Neeley's rich, dignified accent made him seem credible and elicited trust. He drew a slow breath, sighed and kept his expressionless eyes on Billy.

"I am now the source. You have to recognize this fact, young man, and you also need some management training. An extremely reliable contact informed me about how you burned your first supplier by going around him for product."

"You go where the supply is strong and the price is competitive," said Billy.

Heiny's hand flew through the arch again. Billy jerked his head away involuntarily, but the broad hunk of beef caught him, and the bleeding increased.

Neeley kept looking at Billy without expression. "The boys from down in Southern California keep me posted, Jess; I always get the skinny on your affairs. Gotta hand it to you, good move setting this up so you smell like part of the environmental movement. Some true flair, you're quite the impressive young man. The setup reminds me of myself as an upstart."

"We're gonna take a ride," said Leonard.

The dark vehicle jumped away from the entrance. As they swept away from the curb, Billy spotted Jenny mixed with the crowds mulling at the door into Tosca. She honed in on Neeley's car for a moment; her eyes attached themselves to the 300C with falcon-like intensity. She had planted herself among the people for cover, observing everything as a high-strung creature on the hunt would do. Her body changed. She moved like a raptor right out of *Jurassic Park*. Her nostrils flared as if she fixed a scent on the vehicle. Her attention was riveted on the Chrysler. Then Jenny melted away and nothing remained except the different colored eyes locked in primal concentration.

Billy wanted to break Leonardo's neck and go to her. But he understood how tough she was and that the

143

discovery of the facts depended on them as a team. He let the thoughts slip out of his mind; he couldn't lock his attention because Neeley might notice. He leaned back and the driver wasted no time.

"Don't fool around with this, Jess. We've studied your history rather carefully, and the fact is you would never have to work for a living at all. We don't catch on. Why mess with scum, try to buy from fools to save pennies when a real supplier is now in place? You don't know anything about these Orientals. Let me tell you, they are ruthless fuckers, and the language is all gobbledygook. I just don't get it; you don't even seem lame. Are you stupid or greedy?" Neeley's face actually showed concern.

"Is this a thing to get your rocks off? A thrill for the rich boy? You can chair a couple healthy causes the way you've been doing and go with our fine service organization? No reason to run with Hong Kong sleaze. You're wasting your own time."

Neely's logic made sense. Not only was the man articulate, but with his rich voice, he sounded like an investment banker.

"Jeez, you got me," Billy admitted.

Neeley nodded to Leonard, and a cudgel of a hand shook Billy's jaw badly and he felt as if something would soon crack. Billy licked at the blood on his lips, trying to slow the flow.

"Heinrich already told you not to get cute," said Leonard.

"Darn, Leonard, must have blown right in one ear and out the other side."

Leonard popped him again, and the gash in his mouth got big and mushy. Leonard appeared to be capable of hitting Billy forever without taxing himself. Billy slurped up more blood.

"Things are going over the edge this time, and you are experiencing a little taste of what can happen during

144

negotiations. Your predecessor seems to have disappeared. He dove overboard into a school of sharks or something. And this fucking Free Range stuff is coming to an end. They are nothing but a pack of adrenalin chasers. You now get to pick up their dirty work because you are part of the supply chain. Do you understand?"

"Not quite."

Neeley stopped Leonard's arm before it collided with Billy's face again.

"What do you mean, 'Not quite'?" asked Neeley.

"I don't have a clue about you. You could be any old geek. I can see you have some hired bullies, but nothing is clear to me yet. You're covering your ass in the market place. And I have to assume you want me to be too scared to let net profit be the guide to business procedure."

Clueless, Billy staggered on through the menacing situation, grasping for words. He was amazed that Neeley didn't push him out the door. He grappled for lead ins so they could start hobnobbing, but nothing synced. He hoped Neeley would grow more animated, and tell him what he dealt in and with, whom and where. Was Jess actually selling drugs? No possible way. Billy sat there on pins and needles with the most looming question—why didn't they know that Jess lay dead on his own living room floor? The car dropped down toward the Embarcadero. Billy turned away from their dead, raw pork chop faces. He considered his odds against all of them at the same time and noted that the only one without a pistol bulge in his coat was Neeley.

He thought of Jenny. He could picture her thick hair and still smell the lavender. What had she done after they pulled away? Her strange brutal countenance, like a hawk readying for a swoop downward to grab a snake out of a field, stayed with him. He knew that she stood in front of Tosca sorting out a plan. Could he keep her from being dragged into something worse than they had already been through?

"Being so global, you've got a healthy clientele established, Mr. Hayes. Your enviro front is a brilliant tool, and as you know, after Mr. Daltry's disappearance, we are open for some help with distribution. And we know you don't want to be stuck with Hong Kong or Seoul for product. Do you think you can trust those people? What if they decide to crap on you?"

Billy wanted to bitch slap this pathetic excuse for a human being really, really badly. He barely restrained himself. He kept looking at the man's trachea, imagining the feeling of crushing it with his left hand. He breathed slowly so that the air pressed to the bottom of his pelvis and calmed him down.

"Either way, you are going to be an example for everyone. On the one hand, if you choose to continue to be an asshole, you will become a demonstration of what happens to a person who is receiving product inappropriately. If this meeting is successful, you're a shining model of how to obtain inventory correctly and establish a strong business."

In the center of Leonard's flat face hung a big triangular bulb for a nose. Two deep wrinkles furrowed his brow, making his eyes severe. He sat still. Out the window, the city flew by as they shot north along the Embarcadero, past the docks and toward Fisherman's Wharf.

"Are you listening to Mr. Neeley, bozo? Like your fruity pals say, 'Do you get it?'" Leonard sat perched on the leather, ready to pounce.

"I do believe I got it, Leonard."

"You are real slow. And remember, I told you to cut the cute guy stuff."

Leonard popped him again. The inside of Billy's mouth felt pulpier each time the hand came around. The bay floated by, the big steel ships inched past like phantoms. His mind started to run with speculation about where they were going.

Neeley crooned out again, calm and collected. The air inside hung thick. Everyone except Neeley exhaled swamp

146

breath, though Leonard's was no competition for that fetid gas that came from the Teuton. Neeley's voice sounded like a low-pitched drone hovering between Billy's ears. One could float off to another plane on it. *Reverence. Belief. Reverend Neeley. Danger.*

"You are a bright young man, Mr. Hayes. Bright young men often find the most trouble in life. Cleverness can be carnivorous. Don't play the fool by pouting and acting out, trying to be the clever rebel. I'm giving you a chance. I don't know why. Maybe it's that you remind me of that rowdy kid I used to be. It is not solid business practice on my part, but you'll have a little breather anyway. I'm being soft because I've learned to indulge when I wish. We won't be on this earth for long, so it is good to treat ourselves to its treasures like cutting people some slack here and there.

"I'll be taking care of a few things, and these gentlemen will provide for you until I return."

Lifting a lapel in each hand, Neeley adjusted his coat.

"I was a bright boy, too," he continued. "The trait evokes empathy in this particular old man, but it won't in all of them, rest assured. I'm making you a good offer because you have talent. Don't let a strong hand float past you, son. They are not dealt that often in life, not as often as young men think."

Neeley checked for lint and crumbs on the front of the wonderful coat. He ran his hand over the fabric. "You can be a success. You are involved in a business with a staggering cash flow and I don't even think that greed is your problem. It looks like we've got—you'll pardon such an ancient cliché—the old 'bigger than our britches' syndrome in the way here."

Neeley gazed toward the streets and back at Billy, leaning his head to the side.

"Take my advice. I like you son. Reach for something your claws will sink into. Joy rides won't carry you too far in life. In the end, they get tiresome. I know. I got into the

147

work for the thrills, just the same as you, but they only have a limited appeal.

"I'm outta here for a meeting, and I hope to sit right down on the banquet beside you and shake hands when I get back."

His black eyes scanned Billy like obsidian radar dishes, but Billy didn't think that Neeley could read him. And he thought that the puzzle irked Neeley. Did Neeley know that the truth was that there was nothing to pick up on? That Billy didn't know anything? That Billy didn't want to do anything but leave?

The looming car flew alongside Fisherman's Wharf, around Fort Mason, past Marina Green, and seemed to be headed onto the 101 headed north, across the bridge and up to Jess' house. But just before the 101 access, it hung a right at Yacht Road and headed toward the Golden Gate Yacht Club. When the car stopped, Neeley gently placed a thick pink hand on Billy's cheek. The hefty Burmese, ruby ring on his hand sparkled in the harbor lights as he touched Billy's flesh, then he took his hand away.

"Don't disappoint old men, son. It's not good karma. My colleagues will be your hosts until we rendezvous later."

After stepping out of the vehicle like a statesman in his great coat, he walked onto the deck of a big old wooden yacht and shook hands with a herd of associates. They disappeared into the cabin of the stately vessel.

"Nothing cute, kid," Leonard ordered. He gave the impression he would enjoy ripping flesh more than pounding it. He moved over to Neeley's seat, across from Heinrich the Teuton and Billy, and the driver eased them into the eerie yellow glow from the streetlights.

They flew back around under the Bay Bridge, clear to the end of the Embarcadero and swung onto Brannan Street. Somewhere near China Basin, they pulled into the drive of an old brick industrial building as big as a city block. A steel truck door clanked up its track automatically, and the car stopped in the center of a warehouse space full of machinery.

Another Teuton, large and silent, wrapped Billy's wrists behind his back with duct tape. Then he strapped Billy's elbow with the tape, which put a severe strain on Billy's arms. The man slammed a couple pieces of tape over Billy's mouth and looped them around his head over his hair. As if Billy were a human barbell, the driver curled his 240-pound body up, setting him on a metal table used as a big punch press.

With precision, the man lifted Billy's trouser legs and bound his knees, then slid his socks down to get the leg hair and secured Billy's ankles. The four men joined another at the plant's squat office structure. They flipped on the lights and moved through the door and Billy started wondering about Jenny again. He breathed ten full tiger breaths and settled on the steel dais.

The inside of Billy's cheek had been ripped deeply by his canines when they had smacked him, and with the tape in place he kept swallowing the warm iron taste of his blood. His ankles hurt. His arms throbbed. And there was no real way to sit in a comfortable position, so he straightened his spine. He couldn't have been there terribly long when he heard an odd sound from somewhere off in the cavernous building. Something dropped from a window in the rear of the immense room and landed on another something with a thud.

The men inside the office did not seem to be affected by the loud noise but the tape giant did come back out after a few minutes to survey the situation. He walked over, stared with the severe eye of a beached tuna, and then rejoined his company.

As the sentry turned, Billy noticed a motion like a colossal, quick, rodent dart past the shadow of a massive metal shaping machine near the area framed off as office space. Then he saw a shadow float up against the offices. In a moment glass exploded with a thunder as huge steel bolts flew through the large factory windows lining the walls of the building. The gang spewed from the office into the warehouse, fanning out. Heinrich and Leonard ran to Billy's throne, and their companion disappeared toward the windows.

"What the fuck's going on, cute boy?"

Leonard couldn't resist giving Billy an upper cut right below the rib cage. Billy could have rolled off the press and become a tight ball on the floor without any trouble. But then it would have been easy for Leonard to kick him. He worked on getting his breath back.

Leonard ducked around the punch press, the Teuton slid into the dark warehouse, and silence moved in with a net of tension. A pigeon cooed somewhere off in the truss system, and a metal door clanged softly in a surge of cold night air. The wind, carrying the foreboding fog, moaned through the cupolas on top of the structure. Somewhere, down toward the far end of the building, past the office partition wall, a dull thud resounded, followed by a gasp and the sound of a body toppling to the floor.

A pistol blasted the stillness, and the projectile ricocheted off thick steel three times.

"Down there, Willis." The Teuton pointed for the driver to join in the chase, and they wheezed into motion. Their heavy feet scudded off somewhere beyond the office area.

"There," Heiny grunted and another pistol report rang out from a big weapon like a .44 magnum. The bullet stopped dead as if it had struck a disintegrating mortar seam between the old brick. Quiet overwhelmed the world again. Billy started a slit in the duct tape on a metal ridge behind him.

"Fan back there." Heiny took command.

Billy had very little leverage with his wrists. He could have ripped the binding with his forearms after he got a cut started in it but his elbows were taped. He struggled with his hands.

"Down at the other end. The fucker's nuts." Heiny's voice was unsteady due to his loss of orientation.

Neeley's men's shoes pounded concrete quickly with slovenly thuds.

A shot tore at the silence again and the slug bounced off the big machine tools like mad. Then there were a number of meaty contacts followed by the tumble of bodies. And the silence returned heavier than ever. Billy struggled with his wrists.

"Quick," said Jenny.

Billy's wrists came loose.

Jenny slit the elbow, knee and ankle binds with a packing knife. Just as she finished, she noticed a smudged white business card taped to the chassis of the machine. It read: Lung Fat Trading Company. There was a highlighted phone number and address down in Wilmington, Southern California. Jenny cut it loose and slipped it into her pocket. She hurried over to the thug's car, cut the valve stems off of all the tires with the knife and, as she ran back past Billy, barked, "This way!"

And then they were tearing through the bowels of silence. She guided him up on crates and out of a transom. They flew toward Billy's truck, which she had concealed. Billy felt Jenny disappear from his side. He turned. She had stopped at a crate and peeled at a label free.

"Jenny, come on," he hissed.

The pickup sat in the front of the building, outside the ten-foot chain-link fence, which sported razor wire on the top. It was stashed behind another stack of wooden crates. He noticed a loose label on one, peeled it free and slipped it into his pocket.

"How the hell did you get in there so fast?" he asked.

"Shhh," she said.

Jenny peered through a gap between the stack of crates. Billy turned to watch. The yellow glow of the street and warehouse lights cast a somber light as it snaked through the fog, which had thinned some. A Chrysler slid up to the gate. A man got out and opened it, and the automobile eased into the warehouse.

Immediately, Neeley stuck his head out and scanned the yard. Heiny and the crew walked past him quickly and fanned out. Leonard limped with a rag tied around his thigh to stop the bleeding. They exchanged animated words. Neeley's fury was palpable; it surmounted everything. The driver, Neeley, and Heiny got into a black Chrysler 300C. Leonard hobbled over and crawled in, too. The rest of them wobbled back into the old brick structure. One of the men pulled a cellphone from his pocket and began to dial.

Jenny jumped behind the wheel of the car, urging Billy to follow. She pulled out fast and they were on the streets again. Billy flicked his tongue over the gouges in his mouth as they slid through the sleepy China Basin area and sped around the Embarcadero again, right behind Neeley's car.

TWELVE

Nuke learned to play opossum as a young boy. It was another survival tool for growing up in a rough neighborhood, and a skill he put to use as Brothers Noah and Ezekiel Army heaved him below deck and tied him up.

The pair were anxious to motor *dead latitudes* away from the crime scene before choppers buzzed overhead. They were also deeply troubled with Brother Maxwell's sloppy attitude about getting the Humvees off the Tiburon Peninsula before cops swarmed the neighborhood. His behavior was moving toward madness, they feared. But mostly, they were anxious to save Ezekiel's ear. They moved fast and sloppily. They didn't even frisk Nuke because his mass made moving him so hard.

Nuke knew the sweet, sickly smell of chloroform, but the little dude was so shook up about his teeth that he didn't really give Nuke a hard dose, so he played opossum and worried about how hard the creep had dosed Sam.

They used flex-cuffs around his wrists and ankles and nylon ropes from the lockers in the fo'c'sle to wrap his body in a slapdash cocoon. They whipped the plastic bands around him, but before they could tighten down, Nuke wedged his forearms out from the butt of his palms and the ankles apart by spreading his thighs with enormous strength. He tightened his colossal musculature while they bound him.

When they bolted back up topside with the first aid kit, Nuke relaxed. The ropes slid off easily. Still wearing the flex-cuffs, he snaked up into the fo'c'sle for some protection, fished the Benchmade Resistor, an automatic combat knife, out of his pocket, nipped the slack plastic off and barely eased the hatch cover up to listen for his tormentors.

They appeared to be back near the stern, by the wheel, working on the ear. Nuke was still shaken up about Sam, but he couldn't let himself be. He eased up through the hatch onto the teak deck, bolted to the rail, and slipped over into the frigid water. Once in the water, he started moving around the hull of the big sailboat. He had been sapped hard. The muscles were knotted in the back of his neck, and the base of his skull throbbed furiously. The icy seawater eased the pain and brought him completely back to life.

He was amazed how his street smarts, his basic intuition of what a tight situation required, were still so strong. Automatically, he understood the need to relax and let ghetto savvy take over. He knew that if he didn't let thinking get in the way, he would instinctively see exactly what to do.

Slipping around the hull from the bow, he could make out murmurs from the men working on Ezekiel's ear. The weather had calmed, but the diesel still thumped gently, and the rails were so high that even if he strained, he couldn't make out what they were saying.

He eased through the achingly cold water toward the rear of the ship, but the sounds were still mushy. Finally, busy footsteps became audible and as he eased along, back nearer to the stern, the cockpit served as a broadcast chamber and the voices grew clear.

"Jesus, where is he?"

Intuiting they would peer over to look for him, he dove down into the water and swam toward the stern. He eased his head up when he got to the center of the transom.

"Relax, Noah. There is only one place he could be. We don't have to worry," said Brother Maxwell.

"If that guy's overboard, we can abandon this boat now because he will report us just like the pickup guy turned the ANVIL Special Ops over to the cops in Sausalito."

"No, Noah. Slow down."

Nuke tried to sort out the two voices. The higher pitch sounded like the little man who was a total lookalike for the one whose ear he had sawed off. They had to be

154

twins. The resemblance had caused him to freeze for a beat before Maxwell sapped him: a rare event for Nuke. The nuclear reaction in him hadn't had time to detonate.

"Relax? Can't you come up with something new, Lucien? What are you going to do, sit down and smoke another cigarette? With him gone, we're screwed. We can go save the Humvees," said one of the smaller voices.

"Zeke, Zeke, Zeke. Slow down, son. Relish your life. Go to the head and look at your fabulous ear. What do you think, Noah?" said the deeper voice.

"Looks pretty darn good. Will it stay on?"

"Just calm down."

"Stop telling me to calm down, Lucien! We've got to call Brother Slade."

"We'll call Brother Slade, but first we have to get away from here. The cops will find the Humvees in the parking lot and start sniffing out the whole yacht club. We've already got the engines running," said the deep voice.

Nuke could understand them clearly, but his teeth had started to chatter furiously. He winced at the thought of them hearing him and knew that there was nothing he could do. Hypothermia would soon be knocking at his door in spite of his body mass.

"Come on. You wanted me to pump the big guy, to off him, and now he's gone," said Ezekiel. "Why am I messing with this big old tub? I'm gonna be all alone and I don't understand a thing about nautical stuff."

So they were leaving the ear guy on the boat, thought Nuke.

"For crying out loud Ezekiel, all you have to do is steer the thing under the bridge. You don't have to sail it to Hawaii. The reason you have to *mess* with this *tub* is to search for tips about the intruders at the tree hugger's house. My guts tell me your findings will lead us to them," barked the deeper voice. "If you get into trouble, I will save your sorry ass."

155

"Don't we have to pull up the anchor or untie or something?"

"Come on, Noah. Don't be stupid. How can Ezekiel go anywhere if some big old anchor is dug into the barnacles or clams or Captain Jack Sparrow's casket?" They all laughed.

"We'll help you way anchor real fast, and then we're all outta here. Come on. Let's get it," said Noah.

Nuke could feel his temperature dropping by the moment. He was way too cold; he had to get out of the icy bay. His mind flashed to the moving blankets he had stashed under the dinghy's nylon tarp in case digital equipment needed to be hauled out from Jess' house for their trip to Russia. The little boat hung off the stern above him.

"So where did he go?" asked Noah Army.

The voice was close. *They must be looking over the rail,* thought Nuke. He forced himself to submerge, dove and swam to the other side of the dinghy. He had never learned how to swim as a boy, but his fearlessness made the motions come automatically.

He grabbed the little boat's rail, pulled himself up, and peeked under the tarp. The men were not to be seen at the rails or in the cockpit. They must have moved forward to figure out how to raise the anchor, and it was already chopper time.

Nuke inched himself under the dinghy's tarp, slid out of his soggy clothes and wrapped himself in the blankets. He sat on the floor between the seats and leaned his body back as far as possible, but his head bulged up under the dinghy's cover. He knew that he had a brief window of opportunity. It was urgent because his body temperature had dipped down into the danger zone. They would have to struggle, and the distraction would provide a bit of time for him to generate body heat.

But what if they couldn't free the anchor? What if they abandoned dead latitudes? What if they spotted the bulge of his head under the cover or the lose corner? What if they simply shot holes in the dinghy to make it useless? Nuke knew all about the what-if game. It would make him baulk like he had when he saw the second little weasel. He had to forget the what-ifs and whip things as they came up.

When Nuke sailed up to the prestigious club earlier that evening, he dropped anchor and tightened the slack on the chain to test its fastness for mooring. The winch had ground hard, rather than just digging into the bottom. There was no question; the anchor was jammed tight in something on the floor of the bay. But he had wanted to see Jess, so he had decided not to try to free the mooring. Now he was grateful, because the men were struggling to free the anchor, giving him the opportunity he needed.

Taking a chance, he pushed the tarp up. The men were still at the front and the wind had calmed, so he could hear them.

"Okay, Zeke, come on. This is easy. We'll pull and let it settle, then pull again. Hell, we'll use the boat motor to tug on it, too. We can cut the damn thing or something. You'll go for a little cruise along the beautiful coast of California," said Maxwell.

Nuke arched his neck listening to their voices.

"Okay, it's down, so now we tug again," said the bigger voice.

Nuke had to use their conversation as a guide for his actions. He paused and listened for them to come back toward him. But they didn't.

He had already quit shivering like crazy and was doing the deep breathing that Billy had taught him. He knew that his body had verged on hypothermia, but being wrapped up in all the blankets with his clothes off had given him back the edge. He was already warming little by little.

Nuke breathed deeply and tried to empty his brain of thoughts. Just listen and get warm. The one thought that kept bugging him was Sam; chloroform could kill, and these weird dickheads had chipped gears. They studied evil, and that meant that they were apt to do anything on a whim. He held his breath and listened.

"This damn thing is not moving!" one man shouted.

The Shaolin breathing warmed Billy more and more as he started to retain body heat. He wanted Sam safe. He wanted to put on some dry clothes. He wanted to be aboard that beautiful sailing vessel moving out onto the ocean with his friends. He wanted his new life back.

These dimwitted crackers had simply marched in from nowhere and interrupted all the good things that his existence had become. And them, or some of their Aryan asshole brethren, had murdered Jess right there in his own living room.

As the anchor bucked again, Maxwell said, "He's in one of the boats or he's dead from hypothermia."

"That's right. We'd better check the dinghy."

The more Nuke's mind wandered over the facts, the less just lying still with dry clothes down in the cabin made sense to him. He raised the tarp and peered out over the gunnel of the little boat. Nothing stirred on the stern of *dead latitudes*. He could just see one of the little men leaning over the rail up at the bow. The others must have been fiddling the chain and the wench.

Nuke raised himself pushing the tarp up fast. He reached over and used *dead latitudes'* rail to pull over onto the deck. He propelled himself down into the galley fast. Sam had started to move but was still bound. Nuke cut everything loose with his knife and the dog went crazy squirming around Nuke.

"Easy. Shhh, Sam," Nuke whispered and knelt to put his arms around the dog.

Sam heard noise topside and a deep rumble broke loose from his chest.

Nuke hugged him close. "Easy, Sam, easy. Keep it quiet." He pushed his rump to the floor and the big dog sat still.

Nuke raided the pirate prevention arsenal in the fo'c'sle. He grabbed a Desert Eagle just like Billy's, a handful of clips, some jeans, a sweatshirt and a flak jacket. Billy, always a man to plan things carefully, was concerned about pirates in the Northwest Pacific. He and Nuke had stocked the old sailing vessel with supplies for all types of emergency situations.

Noah and his pal had originally approached *dead latitudes* with the silence of rodents. Nuke knew that he must be cautious with these freaks of nature. He also knew that on the streets, he had taught himself to move like one of the great cats. He eased back through the ship and topside. He quieted Sam. He went to his knees and stole along the teak planking, up toward the foredeck where the men struggled. Sam inched along behind.

Maxwell stood with his cohorts, steadying himself against the main rail for a mighty heave. The anchor budged slightly. Maxwell straightened and took a deep breath. Then, just as he leaned forward to heave at the anchor cable again, Nuke spoke.

"Don't move."

His voice boomed out deep and resonant. It sounded out like a bullhorn over the rhythm of the marine engine. Maxwell straightened up. Off center from wrestling with the chain and from exhaustion, he stalled.

Noah still carried the Marinecote shotgun he had taken off Nuke, but as his face froze in terror, he sat it right down on the deck. Ezekiel felt his ear gingerly.

Though a big man, Brother Maxwell presented zero challenge for Nuke. Brother Maxwell knew this and looked around stealthily for some way to overwhelm him other than physical strength. Noah sensed his ally searching for a gambit and spoke right up, trying to distract Nuke.

"Who are you? What do you want with us?"

Covering Noah Army with the pistol, Nuke stepped over and grabbed Maxwell by the trachea.

"You are going to stay here. My dog is black like me. He don't like Klan boys, so if you wake up don't move 'cause he'll pull your balls right off at the stem."

159

The pack of varmints had tapped the detonator again and the thermonuclear reaction arose without any control. Nuke never slowed his momentum. He used Brother Maxwell's neck for a handle and popped his head on the mahogany railing. With a thick dull sound, Maxwell moaned and passed out.

With the .50 caliber magnum pointed at Noah Army's third eye, Nuke stepped over and grabbed the wiry man's belt buckle with his right hand. He stuffed the pistol down Noah's pants and dropped the grip on his belt.

"You are going to walk around the cabin with me. You are going to walk backward and if you even cross your eyes, I'm gonna shoot your cock off, boy." He gestured toward Brother Ezekiel with his forehead. "Ear, you are going to walk backward, too, just behind this other little freak show. If you so much as wiggle, I am going to open your third eye. You'll get real spiritual then. You so much as hiccup and I will rip that damn ear right back off. Then I'll bite the other one off and troll for sharks."

Nuke scanned them with menace. "I'm going to be a little off balance with my hand down your boy's pants, and that will make me jumpy, which is all the more reason for you to be good little boys," he said.

He walked Noah and Ezekiel around the deck, through the bridge and down below, and then up forward into the forecastle.

"Don't come up through that hatch or I'll kill you. I'll be right up there with the tall one." He looked toward the galley and shouted, "Sam!"

The dog sized things up in an instant, seeing that Nuke needed to make sure the prisoners stayed put but had things to do, he walked over and sat down, growling at the men. Nuke rubbed the big dog's head and laughed.

"Man, there's not five percent of the human race that's as hot as you are, Sam."

The dog thudded his hefty tail on the flooring.

Nuke dug into supply boxes at the workbench and pulled out some flex cables that he used to bundle electric cables and extra rigging lines. He turned back toward the men and they recoiled stiffly. Suddenly, a horrible stench filled the room.

"Oh, Jesus. Come on," said Nuke. "Oh, man. That's really gross. The ear already shit his pants once. Damn."

He wrapped a long plastic strap around Noah's neck and threaded it through the upper cross bracing on the workbench. He did the same thing to Ezekiel and went topside to look for Maxwell. Both men had to stand on their tiptoes to keep from choking. He bound their hands behind them and then their feet. Sam's chest rumbled in a low growl as he sat watching the Army brothers.

Back on the deck, Nuke stuffed the pistol in his waist, picked up the shotgun, grabbed Maxwell—who was still passed out—by the belt and dragged him back toward the others. Noah and Ezekiel stood motionless with Sam still on guard. Maxwell remained unconscious and Nuke, feeling pressured to get onto the open ocean, just tied off the man's wrists behind his back with a flex band.

"Good boy, Sam. Bite their nasty little balls right off." Nuke leveled the Marinecote at Maxwell and shouted, "I'm going to kneecap all of you if you pull any more shit on me."

He checked the engine, then let it continue to idle while he hefted the anchor right up with his own strength. Steadily, the vessel headed out of Raccoon Straight, away from the yacht club toward the Golden Gate. Nuke stayed topside for isolation. He wanted to throw them all overboard and just sit on the bow with Sam and feel the breeze on his face.

He couldn't hear a thing below, but he knew that they would already be searching for an escape. As *dead latitudes* passed through the Golden Gate, adjacent to Kirby Cove, Nuke surveyed his ship, making everything was ready for going out to sea.

He had vowed to quit killing people. He had given his word to his grandmother, which to Nuke was a sacred

161

act. Holding to the covenant when he was forced to deal with pure scum like this group, became very difficult. He didn't want all these nasty devils with him. He could feel that they were already up to more of their scamming.

He took the shotgun and walked back down, pleased that he had decided exactly what to do. Nuke's grandmother sent him to Austin to learn sitting-practice meditation with the Tibetans. They had instructed him, "First thought, right thought."

Maxwell had come to and used his teeth to dig through the supplies for a weapon. Sam lay unconscious on the floor, and Nuke went straight to him.

"You better hope this puppy is still alive. If not, I'm going to troll for sharks with all three of you."

"He's okay, I just head bumped him," said Maxwell.

Nuke leaned over Sam, took him in his arms and shook him lightly. "Sam. Sam. Wake up, son."

The three men signaled one another with their eyes and lunged to attack him as a team.

"Okay. That's it. You can thank my grandmother that I'm not gonna troll with you right now. I'm gonna give you a chance. Ear, you and the big boy are going home." He cut Maxwell and Ezekiel lose, picked them up by the back of the neck, half marched and half dragged them up to the bow, then cut their bindings.

"If you are worth a damn, you can swim over to Kirby Cove." He tossed them both over the rail into the icy mouth of the Golden Gate, giving them the chance for survival that they would have never given Nuke. Then went down and re-bound Noah very tightly, his neck right up against a metal workbench leg.

"I'm sick and tired of all of you Klan boys. I shouldn't even give you a chance, but I'm going to get some answers out of you after I tend to my ship."

With Maxwell's destruction of the electronics, Nuke had to use the compass and the coastline to navigate. He headed off on a southerly course, not sure whether to head on to Los Angeles or what. Then he got his clothes out of the dinghy, took a hot shower and threw his wet clothes with the brass shotgun shell in the pocket into the hamper.

THIRTEEN

Clarence Henshaw and Desi Sandoval crawled out of the chaparral when the caravan of Hummers eased back out to the highway. They walked around the clearing, rubbing their arms and stretching to warm up. Both Clarence and Des felt as if they had fallen into a dream state. Each had seen a lot of gruesome things during their careers but this was way different.

Plenty of horrible incidents took place on a daily basis: baby animals dead in shipping containers, skins of protected species, organs, paws, teeth, and all kinds of parts dug out of wild creatures all over the world. Deep inside they intuited that they had witnessed terra incognita, a new land of soullessness kindred to corporate greed on steroids: a dark foreboding power into which all humanness had vaporized.

The group with the Humvees walked like businessmen. They did not slouch. They did not swagger or stop for a cigarette. They didn't roll up to the bear parting and tailgate off a beat-to-hell pickup. They moved like a detachment of corporate droids. They didn't act like a group of starving locals trying to pick up some spare change to feed their families.

Neither Clarence nor Des had ever seen anything so creepy. The entire group—except for the men in overcoats—performed in the precision format, the highly organized manner used by militaries with a lot of funding. The entire crew understood exactly what the project entailed. The weird shotgun had penetrated plate steel as thick as armor. The blunt force of the gun could make foot soldiers a threat to armored vehicles. The loads and maybe even the shotguns must have cost an unbelievable amount of money. The group had turned parts dealing into an industry like one of the big packinghouse meat corporations.

The fog had lifted a bit more. Veins of the wispy gray mist still swept in, but the full moon beamed through, lighting up the rugged environment. The wind eased up and a breeze floated in off the Pacific, clearing the slow-moving eddies, leaving more open spaces in the fog. The scene of the men in the clearing left a macabre presence on everything.

"What the hell?" asked Des as they worked their way back toward the truck.

"Dunno. Never saw anything even close. It's like the mob merged with Smokey manufacturing. Humvees and armor-piercing shotguns?"

"And those guys in the Chryslers," said Des.

"Yeah. Like Darth Vader's new car."

Des' and Clarence's nerves were raw. The image of the tight formation of smoke-windowed vehicles pouring into the clearing hung in their minds, ominous as a mushroom cloud lingering lazily on the event horizon.

An image of the group in plaid moving so systematically, as if they worked in a factory, lingered in both their minds. To Clarence, the conversations—now on tape for review—carried threatening overtones. Were all of the wild animals in the United States—on the whole planet—now becoming part of some corporation's expansion plan? A firm with a special ops force? Were the politicians meeting with them to figure out how lawyers could make poaching legit?

On his salary, Des would never have the beautiful overcoats, the sleek cars, the vast amounts of cash available like he believed these men had. He had built some assets but nothing grand. The thugs didn't have petty officials over them, no idiots to arrest and watch waltz away from some pathetic power-starved judge. They took in scads of money and answered to no one.

"What did the tall one in the SWAT gear say?" asked Des as they walked around the field.

"Him and the short one moved quick, like ferrets."

"What did he say about inventory?"

"'Alright, gentlemen, we will now move out in pursuit of three items to secure as inventory.'" said Clarence.

165

"No, Clarence. The tall SWAT-type walked into the lights and said the head plaid dude would lead."

"Yeah, right. He said that the technical command leader, Brother Sinclair, was going to demonstrate how it's done," said Clarence.

"So Brother Sinclair, the plaid guy with the beard, moved them out. He's like some sort of field lieutenant or something," said Des.

"And the two in black are generals?"

"Okay, but why the frickin' *Godfather* scene? Why bother to train the thugs?"

"Right. No comprendo," said Clarence.

"They couldn't move in the woods worth a damn," said Des.

"I almost barfed when the cubs went up to their mom."

"Shit, Clarence. They chased 'em up out of the woods to add thrills when fuckhead shot her."

"No, I think they were trying to train the goodfellas—teach 'em about the cubs being saleable."

"We'll put out some feelers and hone in on them. They've got to be going back over to the city or down to LaLa Land," said Des.

They split up and walked around the scene with their eyes glued to the ground, using their flashlights to guide them. Des ran through it all. The truth would unfold during the meeting. Des needed cash to buy property, and he would find out where all the parts money came from when they sold their product and where the funds actually went after the transactions.

"Those two little pups as new inventory items. Man, what a ton of sick shit. It was like he was taking trainees in for some warehouse job," said Clarence.

"Right, that's right. Creepiest thing I ever heard. Makes bears into some slaughterhouse critter, like cattle. All the wild becomes global inventory units."

166

"The overcoats laughed too much; all they did was bullshit. They seemed awful nervous."

"Let me ask you a question," said Des.

"What?"

He gazed up at the moon, at the wisps of fog, at the California live oaks. He took a deep breath of the rich fresh air off the Pacific. "Am I just getting old, Clarence?"

"You *are* fucking old. You've been doing this for twenty years. You were a boy, and now you're a fossil. You'll be a full-fledged dinosaur in a couple years. This is no job for a pretty boy like you," said Clarence.

Des turned his head slightly and Clarence grinned in the pale light.

"Nah. What I mean is, am I old-timey or something? Weren't people nicer when we were boys? A kid rode a bike anywhere, never any shit like this. Poachers, sure. But they wanted to feed their families. Now, some good citizen with an NRA bumper sticker might shoot your ass for a parking space," said Des.

"No question," said Clarence.

"Well, what's coming next? I mean, if these sick fucks are a sign of where we are going, I'm not sure this stuff is worth our time. Crooks, politicians and corporations all owned by the principle shareholders—it's all the same shit. Maybe I *will* start a little Cubano band. I'll marry me a redhead like my namesake, Desi Arnaz."

"Maybe I'll play double bass," said Clarence.

They both laughed and walked along in silence, nearing the truck.

"How's your real estate empire going?"

"The money's happening a little bit, but everything's kinda creepy. I go to those seminars and watch the videos, and whenever I can get away from you, I go out with real estate agents who belong to the network. I slipped in on three rent properties with all my savings and had to borrow against my retirement. Since the recession started, I've got a four million dollars in equity, Clarence."

"Damn, you are a millionaire and you didn't even bring me along for—"

"I tried to get you to come to the investors club, and all you wanted to do was go to poker with your pals."

Clarence whistled real loud. "Dog gone, a *million* bucks! Hard to believe. What are you doin' this for, partner?"

"Not a clue, Clarence. I don't catch on any more. Maybe we *should* start a band."

"Jeez, you've got the money now."

"Oh, I forgot to tell you. Since were going to be down in the Southland tomorrow, I'm going over to Long Beach on Thursday to talk with some guys about a property. I'll be gone for lunch—about ten 'til two," said Des.

"If we're going south, we gotta scram. We'll take the Richmond Bridge, beat the Bay Area traffic," said Clarence.

"We'll get the CHP, Sheriffs, SFPD and everybody else to locate and watch these guys. And we'll have our lab boys sweep the place. They can run registration and find their headquarters. We'll put tails on them. Heck, we've even got the funds," said Des.

They cut through the scrub growth and neared the pickup.

"There are too many humans," said Des. "Einstein said, 'The only mistake God made was the Human Being.' Something like that. Einstein or somebody."

"Man, what's gonna happen? The woods are gonna be paved over. All those bootlickers in Congress are lobbyist slaves. They'll pave over Alaska because there's too much mud.

"They've slashed and burned all the tax payers' cash. The Interior is not gonna get a damn thing. We just got this big budget 'cause Hicks' panties are in a bunch. Oh my god, black bears sold for parts. All the grizzlies, the other critters, who cares? But hey, can't let Smokey get hurt. Always the votes. Old

168

Hicks can just hear his fellah Amurkans when they read about all the black bears getting poached," said Clarence.

"I try to shut my head down so I don't think that stuff, but I can't ever turn it all off."

They gazed out at the rugged location: the windswept coastal hills of Marin County, the full moon, the wisps of fog. Tomales Bay rested nearby. They were close to San Francisco. The area felt like the country, but would any true wilderness be left by the middle of the new millennium?

They were both sick at heart from seeing such surreal devastation first hand. Clarence resolved to re-double his efforts. Des fully understood the facts. Rich human beings just wanted more stuff. Their greed made them stupid and robbed them of any foresight.

But the Mother Earth would only take so much shit, and then all the Homo sapiens would be wiped out like the dinosaurs. Des knew that no matter how much he believed in his straight-runnin' dumb-ass of a partner, Clarence would not be able to change greed heads like the uber rich, the one percent that owned the United States. Like it or not, there was no hope.

Neither one was able to speak. Clarence started the truck and pulled out of the thicket. He drove back toward the clearing. The memory of the Humvees circling its perimeter, driving right next to the live oaks, came back. The group had mobilized for their operation like building contractors, like film makers, oil drillers, like any production professionals working in the field. They rigged out a processing plant on site. Only the product had not been oil or minerals. The men in plaid and the weird dudes in the topcoats were just like some mafia movie shot in a picture-postcard setting.

Clarence stopped the truck in the clearing and they both got out with their flashlights.

"Let's scan for whatever they dropped. Do you think we can get a forensics team in here tomorrow?"

169

"Hey, we've actually got some funds. We'll put all this together," said Des.

"Right. Old Hicks'll die from tertiary syphilis and they'll melt Interior into Homeland Security and bust you and me as terrorists. Then the judge will slap these guys on their butts and send them home," said Clarence as they fanned out.

"Clarence, you've been schlepping around out here too long. You gotta get out."

The big man scoured the area in front of the pickup with the beam of a large Maglite. He walked slowly, sweeping the beam back and forth across his path. He saw the black shape on the ground before getting up close with the light. He stooped and picked up a small, vinyl wallet used for business cards. Careful to handle only the edges, he slipped it in his pocket and walked back over to the truck.

Clarence opened the door and reached under the seat. He pulled out a box of surgical gloves and slipped a pair over his large hands with some difficulty. Then he pulled the little wallet back out of his pocket and opened it up.

He slid another box from under the seat, pulled out a baggie and went to the hood of the truck. He spread the baggie out, slid the white business cards in it and then laid the vinyl case on the baggie. He began to examine the cards in the beam of his Maglite. On top a plain cheap bulk card that could be printed at any mailbox store in any shopping center, anywhere in the country, faced him.

LUNG FAT TRADING COMPANY
THE MYSTERY OF THE ORIENT AT YOUR COMMAND
4357 Sanford Street, Wilmington, CA 97342
Telephone 310-453-5347
Email – lungfat@lungfat.com

"Hey Des, check this." Clarence fished a little spiral pad out of his shirt pocket and jotted down the address and the phone number. Des came walking up as Clarence examined a second card.

"What'cha got?" asked Des as he peered over at the card. "Well, I'll be damned. Bingo. Bingo. Bingo. We got a Lung Fat in Wilmington and one from what's gotta be the main group. Two addresses. Look at this one."

Des displayed another card for Clarence to read.

ANVIL - THE AMERICAN NATIONAL VIGILANCE AND INTELLIGENCE LEAGUE SPECIAL FORCES - BROTHER NOAH ARMY - PO Box 14251, TEMECULA
5220 Seventh Street, Costa Mesa, CA 92130
Telephone 714-621-2631
Email – vigilance@anvil.com

"This card makes it look like they might have sent some worthwhile info down from the Hill for a change. Man, that is smooth. Lung is right there in San Pedro. Looks like we're headed south for sure," said Clarence.

"Man, this group fucked up big time. I wonder how the packinghouse stuff in the file fits in."

"I don't understand that, but this is one bunch that has screwed the pooch," said Clarence.

"ANVIL. Those are our boys. Way to go, partner," said Des. He grabbed the card. "ANVIL. Man, what a name. Sounds like some vigilante blacksmith pounding on everybody's shit."

"Yep, this is pure evil. American National Vigilance League, are you kidding me?" said Clarence.

"Let me see the other one," said Des.

Clarence aimed the flashlight. Des bent over and squinted.

"Lung Fat. Gotta be a tie to Seoul or Hong Kong. Asian supply and distribution. ANVIL is the hyena pack and they are going global for sure," said Des.

"We're gonna find out. We'll stop and see our boys at LAX. Turn 'em onto all this stuff," said Clarence.

"I'm tired as hell," said Des.

"Yeah, me too, but we gotta beat traffic. I couldn't sit on the freeway at five miles an hour right now. Let's roll on through Bay Area traffic right now. Neither one of us can drive, we'll get one of those motels down on the I-5," said Clarence.

"American National Vigilance . . . This thing gives me the willies. They're some kind of religious freaks," said Des.

"Yep. True believers. Kill you faster than any gangbanger," said Des.

"Yeah. And they've got a lot of money. Look at this card man—five color printing. Touch the paper. We'll get the lab to find out where they're printed. Probably Shanghai or wherever they'll sell the gall bladder out of that bear. What did you find?" Clarence asked.

Des' hand hung down at his side. Thinking about ANVIL, he had forgotten all about the brass shell casings. He had wrapped them with a leaf to avoid touching them and done the same with one strange little loaded shell. Clarence took them from Des using the rubber gloves.

"I thought those overcoats would start a war after the sniper shot the branch," said Des.

"No lie," said Clarence.

Clarence plopped another baggie on the truck. "I think these guys goofed real bad. Look at this thing. This is motive. They're not just into animals."

"Damn," said Des, picking it up. "This is some powerful stuff for a shotgun. Look at the props on this little missile."

"Blew the hole in the steel plate."

"These are the shells that dropped when he blew out the fast spray from the shotgun." Clarence turned one of the plastic casings up on end to study the brass butt.

"Korean. This writing is Korean," he concluded.

"Same here, on the side of this projectile thing," said Des. "What is this stuff?"

"Some brand new weapon. These guys must be as rich as God. Probably sell them to everybody: China, DOD, North Korea, Israel, and al-Qaeda."

"We've gotta go to this Lung Fat thing. The place is in the report, too. Says it's a packinghouse. What the hell is old Lung trading? He's over in Wilmington. Right there at the Port of Los Angeles. Very convenient. We'll get a room down in San Pedro," Des suggested.

After sweeping the area, they scoured closely for traces of the strange meeting.

"Let's get all the casings and shells."

"So we might end up with some stuff for the lawyers. We'll get forensics to run all that stuff down."

Both men walked around and crawled into the truck. They had come back some, but still, an awful lot spun around in their heads. This type of poaching changed Fish and Wildlife forever whether people on the Hill understood or not. A common band of poachers, a gang of cammy-types from the boondocks, the "usual suspects" showed up regularly. But true, highly trained professionals?

As they drove around the clearing for a final look, they saw that both of their careers as agents for the Department of Interior, as men who had worked hard for the preservation of one of the world's most precious natural resources, had changed radically.

Even though they were bone tired, they had to move fast. They had to get on down to the Los Angeles Basin before traffic built up. They wanted to know what this vast change meant, and being tired to the bone was nothing new to either of them

They eased out onto the blacktop county highway. They took Nicasio Road, then headed East on Lucas Valley, out toward Highway 101. Then they drove south toward San Francisco.

They both liked driving all the way to LA on Highway 1, down through Big Sur, so they stayed in the countryside for most of the ride. Clarence detested cities and Des liked to spend most of his time in the country, but loved to go to town and party. Even if the drive took longer, they stayed out in the country whenever possible. But as they neared San Rafael and the exchange to Highway 580 they decided to head south on Interstate 5 because they would be on this fresh trail faster.

"That reciprocal saw worked too damn good," said Des.

"Makes me sick."

"Everything is going to shit, Clarence. I'm going to end up as cynical as you are. I'll drive for a while. Then you can for a bit. When you're whipped, we can get a motel."

"Yeah, we'll stop somewhere way down on 5. Take off at three thirty or four tomorrow. Gotta beat the traffic so we can get on into LAX," said Clarence.

"Okay, but I'm gonna push you out on the porch if you start snoring like a bulldozer," said Des. The big man chuckled. Then he put his head against the door, closed his eyes and was full-out snoring in three minutes.

As Des drove, heading out toward central California and the long boring stretch of I-5, he listened to Clarence snore but he did not feel sleepy. His mind raced at top speed. The Butchers File: now the strange name made absolute sense.

He boiled inside. Over and over again he tried to quiet his thoughts but his mind would not stay calm. His thoughts wandered off and then his brain got stuck in the angry thoughts. Each of his five years with Fish and Wildlife he had spent with Des. He glanced at his partner.

Clarence had never done anything else with his life. Des understood that he would be in the same boat real soon, and he no longer was convinced that he wanted to end up like his partner.

Clarence lost a wife and two long-time girlfriends because he couldn't get past being an absentee sweetheart. Des lost his first wife. The women all loved Des and Clarence deeply, but in the end they couldn't take their men being gone so much and the endless danger. Des' first wife, Marge, said in her parting note, "No way I can get you to quit playing cowboy. I finally catch on that it will never happen. And there's no way that I am going to tell you to choose because I would lose for sure. You might even drop Fish and Wildlife, but you would be a broken spirit and I cannot have that on my conscience. So I am leaving. Please do not try to find me. I will always love you."

Des had been up at Brooks Range with Clarence. The dickheads up at the Range were businessmen. They shot grizzlies out of choppers with assault rifles. He caught a young congressman with a bad holier-than-thou complex. A born-again Christian. A clean bust. Secret Service went straight to Interior and the guy waltzed away like he was at his high school prom. Clarence went to trial with the rest of them.

Things burned hot and nasty in the civil action courts, and the mouthpieces bartered. Charges were filed against Des when he almost beat one of the CEOs to death with the hardwood butt-stock of the prick's own AK47— slugs from which Clarence knew forensics would find in the grizzly carcasses. The rich man hired three full-bore trial lawyers. They went after Fish and Wildlife for 50 million dollars. The Silicon Valley billionaire thought that he had an air-tight case. The big pile of cash would be slam-dunk. For him it was just another business deal: invest in the lawyers then collect from Uncle Sam.

Des wanted to get a band of merry men together and become Robin Hood. He liked Jess Hayes' Free Range. They'd pay better than the Interior. He wanted to go out and kick real butt. Try these fuckers out in the woods with some real men—not all these pussies in suits. Men with dirt under their fingernails. No corporate double-speak types. Men only. They could grab these pathetic characters, put a chain around their necks and pay homeless dudes to guard them while they cleaned up all the trash in a thousand-acre patch of a national forest.

Jess Hayes' new organization, Free Range, was for real men who wanted to take real action. The Interior would call them terrorists and call in Homeland Security. They'd be on everybody's tree hugger shit list.

Fortunately, up at Brooks, there hadn't been any witnesses except the chopper pilot, and Clarence had locked the prick up in the trunk of his Caddy. Des lied point-blank to the jury—he even passed a lie detector test—and Clarence got off without a blemish. It was the only time Des had lied in court but he didn't care. He had finally given up on bullshitting himself. Justice is just a seven-letter word. He had seen the law twisted so many times by then.

But the worst of all possible things seeped into Des' mind as he drove south. The worst question of all: *what for?* The thought kept blinking through his head like a neon sign. *What for? What for? What for?*

This was the only job Des knew until his real estate could generate cash. What else could he do? If he had some real cash flow he could buy apartment buildings fast. He could open a little bar by the beach and listen to retired duffers watch television and talk about the old days. The thought made Clarence sick. He couldn't stand a bunch of armchair heroes. He couldn't stand televisions. He didn't have a choice. He belonged here.

The so-called "ordinary citizens" sat in their chairs every day, hiding, scared shitless, asleep, and dying in front of a whispering television. They believed all the pathetic crap the politicians told them. And if a few tortoises, a few rhinos or some tigers died, fuck it. John Q. Public no longer had a clue how to leave his TV long enough to do anything about it.

176

How many old Ford pickups had Des driven? How many times had he had to buy tires or a car battery out of pocket because they were over budget? But this night changed the playing field. First the little file was couriered down from the Hill, and now the tip about this thing in Marin.

And on top of the business-like parting of a black bear and the inventorying of her cubs, there were these guys in the Chryslers. They seemed right out of the movies or something. And the cedar choppers with the plaid coats. And big funds for the op. And those shotgun rounds like a CIA operation. Des' head was spinning.

Operation Butchers Data. Now he knew why the name had sounded weird. But nothing in the title was weird at all. He could see those men in the clearing as if he were still there. His mind slipped back to when they had arrived and to all the stuff he had seen through the years: whorehouses with bear bladders in the fridge, cases full of monkey paws in software packing, tiger penises stashed in candles. Desi wanted to scream, to burn a lot of rounds out of his weapons, but most of all he wanted to cry and didn't have a clue how to go about letting the tears out.

FOURTEEN

Adrenalin burned right through Billy and Jenny's lack of sleep and the rum they had taken hits of earlier. The pair bolted through San Francisco again. A thousand questions churned fast in their minds so quickly that it seemed impossible to thread them together. Neeley's 300C flew down Brannan, then all the way around the Embarcadero. They were going 50 miles an hour until they swung onto Bay. There, the blacktop slid down toward the marinas again. The car was going so fast it leaned almost up on two tires as they tore into the entry drive of the Empire Yacht Club.

Jenny eased the truck into a service alley, which ran parallel to the main drive. A twelve-foot row of bushes lined the club's chain-link fence, so they lost sight of the Chrysler. She stopped the truck. Billy jumped and she followed him. They pushed the bushes apart so they could see into the grounds. Neeley's car sat still at a gangplank that rose up to a vintage 50-foot Chris-Craft powerboat,

Neeley and Heiny paced while the driver carried big, heavy, burlap bags up off the Chrissy and dropped them into the trunk of the car.

Leonardo rose from the back seat with a bandage around his head. He shouted, and then after a few minutes, they all crawled back into the car.

Billy and Jenny jumped back in the truck, anticipating another chase. Just having one lane in the service alley, she wheeled right up onto the lawn to turn around. She eased forward, and the Chrysler shot back out the gate and flew up to Marina Green. The vehicle repeated its earlier route, past Fisherman's Wharf, and then ripped back around the Embarcadero at 60 miles per hour.

They both expected the car to roll all the way around the waterfront, back to China Basin. But this time it whipped onto Harrison and headed uptown. Billy and Jenny thought they might be taking a strange route back to Union Square, to the Saint Francis, but instead the car continued up on the Bay Bridge.

"How did you get to the truck and follow them to the warehouse?" asked Billy.

"Sleight of hand." She looked around at him with a churlish grin but it faded quickly. "Billy, your mouth is bleeding. Do you need sutures?"

"It's already slowed."

"You sure?"

"We can't lose them."

She pulled some tissues out of her pocket. "Clean it up. We're glowing cop bait already."

"How did you get in the warehouse?"

"Quickly," she said.

They laughed. Jenny held the truck a few lengths back from the smoked windows of the car in front of them, and they both watched the view of San Francisco Bay as they slid over the bridge.

"Where did you first meet Jess?" asked Billy.

She turned to look at Billy for a moment and a couple of tears came to her eyes immediately.

"I first met Jess in martial arts classes," she said after she had wiped the tears away with the back of her hand. "We both practiced continually over a period of ten years. We worked with some amazing old masters from several forms: Shaolin, Tai Chi, the Ninja arts. We both studied Aikido as the base form of our work in the arts. That's how we got to talking."

Billy looked at her. She watched the road with her head slightly cocked.

"There was a man who affected us both very deeply: Dutch Chan. He was kind of a legend like Bruce Lee. He was known all around the Pacific Rim. We had both studied with Dutch. He was a world-renowned Aikido Master.

179

Master Chan was rumored to have been many things: a global Robin Hood type who stepped in for the poor and persuaded the rich to help them, Chairman Mao's bodyguard—the teacher of Bruce Lee's teachers.

"Like that Kung Fu guy my dad liked on TV, Master Chan carried the tiger and dragon scars inside his wrists. Supposedly, he became a branded Shaolin priest in China. He gave me mine. I carried the brazier with the tigers embossed on it in iron across his deck up in Pacific Heights."

"Jeez, let me see," said Billy.

She held her right wrist out, but kept her eyes ahead. He slid her jacket sleeve up and, even in the sulphurous light, the image of the tiger stood out, etched in her creamy skin as distinct as a carving in a stone tablet.

"How far did you carry the brazier?"

"I don't know. Maybe 25 yards."

"Damn, you're something else. That's a long haul."

"Dutch has a big deck."

Billy laughed and smiled, looking at her behind the wheel. "You really are too much."

"Both of us were amazed by Dutch's presence: his speed, his robust sense of humor, his grace, and most of all, the notion of non-violence on which he based all of his teaching."

"Non-violence?" said Billy.

"Right. 'There is no battle, only psychosis.' That was one of the first things he told us.

"As we went further into Dutch's work, the other martial arts began to seem like foolish cartoon antics. What Dutch showed us was the power of non-violence. He always kept a picture of Gandhi up on the wall."

Jenny glanced at Billy, then back at the car in front of them.

"'Greatest warrior that ever lived,' Dutch would say. 'Stopped the entire British Army without using weapons. That's one badass dude.'"

"Of course we lapped up the romance of it all: the venerable old master, his accent, his superb sense of humor, and of course, his badass fighting. But what he taught us was how wonderful it is to be alive, how we don't have to be all uptight, walking around proving ourselves. He taught us that in real life, if not trapped, people actually just step back from the unkindness of others 99.9 percent of the time. The trick is to disappear, then you're never around disgusting people and you don't waste your own time."

They moved along with the flow of traffic. The Chrysler paced itself exactly with the motion of the other drivers.

Billy had been through a lot of barroom and sandlot brawling, Golden Gloves boxing, and Marine Recon training, but he didn't really know how Jenny did what she did in that warehouse. Her ability to *do* amounted to an extraordinary foundation of intense training. He still looked at her as she watched the freeway. She kept pace with the 300C as it blew through Oakland, then farther away from the ocean toward the boring-sounding places like Pleasanton and Livermore.

"I sure hope Nuke got out of there," she said.

"My intuition says he did."

They rolled on, stuck on the thought of Nuke.

Finally, Jenny said, "Does it also say we're doing the right thing following these wannabe godfathers?" She looked at him and smiled slightly. "That was one of Jess' few rules—always trust your intuition."

"Yeah, I know. Luther Four Fingers taught Jess that," said Billy

"Luther? The same Luther Jess carried on about?" Jenny asked.

181

"Right, he's not only the best quarter horse trainer in the world, he's one of the most important spiritual teachers alive."

"Isn't he a full-blooded Comanche?"

"He is," said Billy.

"I thought they were grotesquely violent."

"They were. What seems grotesque to us was a part of life with many indigenous peoples; I mean like headhunters and cannibals. So called 'civilized' people just gloss it over with rhetoric," said Billy.

"Pretty wise stuff for a rich white boy," said Jenny.

"Hey, don't forget, not only am I a filthy rich white boy; I'm a jarhead to boot."

"Well, yes sir!" said Jenny, laughing.

"What I mean is, the white man came in and exterminated the Indians like cockroaches, and the Comanche were the greatest warriors since Genghis Khan, so the fought hard to keep their land as it was," said Billy

"Yeah, right the Yankees were as disgusting as the indigenous people," said Jenny.

"Jeez, it's disgusting; we sent small pox into Indian villages in blankets to kill the women, the babies and the warriors. And we still do that stuff in the Middle East; I was over there and a lot of sick shit takes place."

"I know, Billy, I know. The human story is so twisted," said Jenny.

"I was trained to kill by the US Government, really trained well, and I can tell you for sure that if you look at the totality of the destruction we cause, we are still as grotesque as the Comanche were," said Billy.

"So Luther is a spiritual teacher?" asked Jenny

"Right, passed down from the Indians as they were ripped away from their land and stuffed in the reservations. They were already very spiritual people, but the Earth was their life. The reservations were prison camps for them. They had to pull inward and do spiritual exercises to stay alive," said Billy

"I didn't know that the Comanche were spiritual teachers."

"I know, nobody does, except Johnny Depp. They just made him a member of the tribe for that great Tonto part," said Billy.

"He's so good. Nobody gets that kooky part of human beings like he does," said Jenny

"I know. Right. Luther laughs his ass off at that wacky Indian in the movie. He's watched *The Lone Ranger* a hundred times and still goes nuts."

"So Luther started you on the spiritual path?" said Jenny.

"Right, Luther and my mom. Luther is deeply involved in the Sundance, which saved the Indians after they hit the reservations," said Billy.

"Peyote. Like the Toltecs, right?" asked Jenny.

"Yup. Everything's about living impeccably, getting off it with the self-pity crap that humans always bog themselves down in."

"I want to meet, Luther," Jenny said

"I know. You're going to," said Billy, "We're going on to Texas after we meet with Harlan, so we've got to think through everything to meet with him."

"Texas? Why in the world would we go to Texas?" asked Jenny.

"I don't know yet, but my intuition is telling me it's what will happen," he said, slipping on latex gloves, then reaching behind the seat. He pulled out the clues he had stashed at the Saint Francis and dumped everything in the lap of his poodah pants.

"We've got to think through all this to keep our memories fresh. We don't have any other leads. There's nothing at the Saint Francis. We can't go to Jess' house. We can't go back to the scene of the Humvee shootout. We lost those bull-necks. It's not time to go on that boat of Neeley's—"

"Yeah," said Jenny, "you're right. Thomas Edison said 'you've got eleven minutes to write it down.'"

"He got that right," said Billy. "We've got plenty to keep us busy. All the stuff we've seen go down is getting more foggy by the minute."

He started sorting as he rattled clues off. "The crime scene investigation: Heavy hitters because they are using a Frag-12 with two different loads on Jess and the walls like they are government ops. Hand severed and reciprocating saw left at scene . . . ."

"That's because Nuke walked in on the perp; that's why he ran," Jenny added.

"We don't know that it was a he," said Billy.

"Right, that's right. Good point. My statement was simple sexism, which throws everybody off. It may be a woman. Could your Texas pal, Harlan, handle that?"

"He's a dinosaur, sexist pig. He might not take the case. He just likes to fight. He doesn't care about anything else."

"Jess' house was awful clean," said Jenny.

"There wasn't any dust under the couch when Sam found the datebook."

"Yeah. And his desk, the shelves, and the equipment were all tidy."

"He had some funny tics. He once told me that whenever we were going somewhere for a hairy bungee jump, or to take boards to some hellacious surf out in the open ocean, or ride Buzkashi with the Kazakhs—"

"Some what?" Jenny interrupted.

"You know. That Mongolian Polo that lasts for a few days and everybody beats the hell—"

"You two went and did that?"

"Many times," Billy said

184

"So anyway, when we went where we might not make it back, he kept his house spotless."

"Maybe he thought something was going down in Washington, so . . . ." Jenny began, but she get choked up at the thought.

Billy reached over and took her shoulder. "It's really fucked, but we've gotta keep rolling."

"I know," she said, taking her eyes off the road for a moment to look at him.

"Maybe he expected he'd get hit because he was pushing so hard with Free Range."

"Why would Jess put note in the printer?"

"Had to be hiding it because he knew they were coming, but why the animal parts?" wondered Billy.

"Boy, that's a good one. It's got to be Free Range, right?"

"Gotta be."

"I never had time to really talk with him about Free Range because the report was so important, so the only thing I know is that Jess wanted to grow Free Range. As a part of the growth plan, he wanted to drag more poachers, especially the big guys that pay off the cammy guys that go out in the woods, into litigation and press Senator Hicks to set up a gang on the Hill to come down on the judges for stiffer penalties."

"That's why the report, right? He scared Hicks about the *Washington Post* and the *Times* picking up on the end of Smokey in the wild story," said Billy.

"You got it."

"So he was back there on the Hill, and part of his trade-off with Hicks had to be a witch hunt on judges."

"Bingo," said Jenny.

"Where does Free Range fit in?"

"I heard him talking with the guys at the Wildlife forensics labs who really liked him a lot. He dumped a huge amount of funding into their work."

"The federal Fish and Wildlife?"

"Both Cali and federal. Jess always raved about those people," said Jenny.

"So Hicks' payoff was beating the reporters to the punch on the devastating end-of-Smokey headlines. Jess got judges cornered. And the Wildlife guys got money. And Jess got. . . ." Jenny started crying again.

"God, Jenny. I'm so sorry. I—"

"It's okay, Billy. Jess hated poachers more than words could ever say, especially the big guys that make the real money. Not so much those dudes you were watching at the office."

"He already had a guy from Fish and Wildlife talking with him. Some guy named Des."

"So what's Des' payoff?"

"Funding for deep cover, field sleuthing and research via Free Range. Jess was after the big fish; he planned to drag them back into court *ad nauseum*."

"Wow, Jess was an amazing dude. What a guy, making the frickin' government earn the tax payers' dollars."

Jenny broke down and stared at the road like a zombie as she cried. Billy undid his seatbelt and moved over to put his arm around her. He sat next to her in silence until she finished crying and looked up at him.

"Thanks, Mr. Clayton. Maybe you're not such a bad guy after all."

Billy chuckled and they both sat still until Jenny said, "Free Range won't quit, but funds may get rough."

"No," said Billy, moving back into his seat and buckling his seatbelt. "The funds will grow to five times what they are now. You and I are opening the Jess Hayes

186

Wildlife Fund. I'll get Harlan on it immediately and they will attach the cash to it and open the fund to Free Range."

Jenny looked over at him and raised an eyebrow. "You're a real man-of-his-word type guy. The world needs a lot more real men. It's all run by pouty little pussies."

"Are you going male chauvinist on us, Ms. Warren?"

She reached over and slugged him hard. "You know, I've got a nice-sized trust that a great aunt just left for me. My favorite aunt: Aunt Sophie. She lived over in Martha's Vineyard and thought it marvelous that I am considered a black sheep in my family. She thought it added color to the Warren clan just like in the 19th century when there were still some real American individualists around.

"She would demand that I put her funds into the Jess Hayes Foundation. And that we help Free Range find these poachers, and these disgusting judges and politicians that help them get off with a pat on the butt."

Billy laughed as Jenny continued. "I can hear her. She would say, 'It's about time we got some real Americans back. All we've got are these scum-sucking spies: the CIA and the NSA and the FBI and all the turds in the punchbowl. But these boys . . .'"

Billy was cracking up as she tied up her narrative.

"'. . . they sound like the Green Mountain Boys who fought Indian style and won the American Revolution.'"

"We've got a lot in common, Jenny. Aunt Sophie sounds like my mom."

"That's what the rattlesnake is, isn't it, Billy? It's not a diamond back; it's a timber rattler like the Gadsden Flag, *Don't Tread on Me.* Luther's making the timber rattler into the Free Range brand."

"Haven't talked to him, but it's gotta be. The heaviest thing so far is the Frag-12 loads. Whoever shot Jess was involved in something much bigger than animal parts. I tested those loads and they definitely turn a foot soldier into a very hefty opponent without any air power or artillery. Everything is designed to besmirch Jess' name."

Billy skimmed through Jess' notebook and then went through everything they had.

"We've got a lot of stuff here. I'll just take some notes, but when we get holed up, we'll write everything down so we don't start to forget and so we're ready for Harlan," said Billy.

"All we know now is that they couldn't touch Jess because he didn't give a shit about reputations, and his money is deep and tied up in trusts. A lot of heavy people really hated him, and now they've paved a story for the media that he was funding violent eco-revolutionaries. The lobbyists have tried to hire the president to brand the greens as terrorists, though that may not work with him, even if it does with Congress. The NSA sent in a hit crew and bam," she said, shaking her head.

"Pretty damn good, Ms. Warren. The bull-necks were watching, setting everything up for the shooter, and we are a breach in security. We can identify them in a lineup, and we can validate one another's story. We have their plates, though they've got to be bogus."

"Right," she said. "Both vehicles have to be rentals or stolen or something."

"Do you watch a lot of movies?" he asked, raising an eyebrow.

"Hey, listen here, Colombo. Thank your lucky stars that I'm good."

"Colombo? Jeez, you're showing your age," he said.

"Watch it, my mother and I were Colombo enthusiasts."

"Okay, so we could go back to Animalfund and see if the bull-necks are—"

"Oh, come on. That is too lame," she said.

"No, I am going to cover every base and contingency. That's what separates the wannabe sleuths from the pros."

"Fine, whatever."

"And I'll call Harlan and his office can run the plates. He can bring the senator and Claire Hicks out with him." He continued to write as he spoke.

"Why Hicks? Do we want anyone watching us?"

"My mother has worked on funds for animals and children for years. Senator Hicks is an old-line conservative, not one of these neocon, type-A freak shows. One thing that a true conservative has is honor. Abraham Lincoln was a Republican. Teddy Roosevelt was a Republican and he started the national parks. We can trust Hicks."

"Wouldn't he hate Free Range?"

"Not if they are legal and not performing outright violent acts. He might even like them being a pain in the ass for the presidency. He's a fiery old boy. But no matter what else, saving nature is very important to him," said Billy.

"So it's obvious they're still watching Free Range, not Animalfund, but it looks like several things are taking place," said Jenny.

"Something bigger?"

"There's got to be," said Jenny, looking around at him. "But I can't sort out yet what's bigger than what. Neocons aren't going to risk being tagged as the guys who heartlessly let Smokey the Bear get offed, so if they got pegged with Jess' death it could slaughter them for the 2016 election. Voters already see them as greed head idiots. But how are they going to stand up against corporate shareholders wanting to fight off environmental snafus, which Free Range is pushing with no sign of retreat."

"Jeez, you pegged that. The demise of Smokey and Jess being offed to stop Free Range with the Butchers File report on the Hill could be a nightmare for the whole Republican Party. "

"Right," said Jenny. "Those guys following me, these thugs we're following, there's got to be some focalized, determined power who will gain from all of it."

"Jesus, Jenny. That's it! Some power shaker is playing everyone. What are those bags Neeley got from the boats?" asked Billy.

"I don't know, but we keep following and we'll figure it out," said Jenny. "What's with the card?"

"It's the same address as the label on the crates. A business called Lung Fat Trading Company. The card says, 'The Mystery of the Orient at Your Command,'" said Billy.

Jenny laughed aloud. "Where is it?"

"Wilmington," said Billy.

"The Port of Los Angeles," said Jenny

He read the label twice, then stared out the window. "Harlan will run all of this stuff down fast. He'll put hackers and gumshoes on it all. He's got snoops from all the spook shops: FBI, CIA, NSA, all of them. Has them on the dole, they don't make much money."

"When do I meet this Harlan person?"

"Just as quick as we hit ground for a couple days."

"We just follow the trail around Jess," said Jenny.

"Yeah, Harlan and my friend, Angel, can get it all fast."

"Somebody goes into one of the wealthiest communities in the world and drops a citizen right there in his living room and leaves military vehicles out on the street. Who has that kind of cheek?" she asked.

"You're right, they've got cast-iron huevos, and that means huge cash in the background." They watched the big car snake through traffic at 90 miles an hour.

"Neeley has a Brit accent."

"The movies make Brits look really vicious."

"Think it's true?"

"Guess we'll find out. I'll try Nuke," he said.

"You really are a boy scout. I can't believe you've got those safe phones and all this gear."

190

"Hey, I'm still going sailing just as quickly as we put a wrap on this, and you gotta watch for pirates."

"What's the story with all the credit cards? I am beginning to think you that you really are some spy type. Did you steal those cards?"

"Like I said, you've got to have them to do business in the Far East."

"Plastic leaves a dangerous trail," she said. "Remember that John Grisham thing where they blew up the car and Julia Roberts takes off? They kept tracing the card."

"That's why you have tons. You just keep changing and the trail goes goofy for the trackers. I remember that movie; it was *The Pelican Brief*. Good story. She busted some creeps that were ruining the Louisiana coast," he said.

"You wouldn't believe how many enviro-rapers there are, and it will blow you away that they do not give a damn at all about our lives here. It's like shitting under the carpet in your front room and playing like the turds aren't there," said Jenny.

"Wow, you *are* a total tree hugger."

"So what is a non-tree hugger? A tree hater? Where do we get oxygen without trees?"

"Whoa, Jenny. Wait a minute. I'm only kidding. I think we're both on the same page, but I'm the new guy on the block. I was a real cut-throat, tax-dodging, off-shore business man—the guy everybody's supposed to love and respect no matter what. I made Gordon Gekko look like Minnie Mouse. He just jacked around with markets; I bought and sold the whole shootin' match. I generated his markets."

"What's your point?" she questioned.

"I was Marine Recon for a while and caught on to the fact that all soldiers, no matter what side they are on, are just dupes for rich men. I watched the VA dump on my amigos, tell them to take a hike when they had radiation poisoning. I witnessed officers being destroyed because they were Muslim. Outside of being a red-hot businessman and part of the Marines, the rest of my life has been with my horses.

191

"Outside of my family, quarter horses were the only things I ever really loved. Luther turned me around, taught me that I was wasting all these precious years fucking around and fattening up secure bank accounts. I'm new to this tree hugger stuff."

"Don't call it that."

"Well, excuse me, what should I call it?"

"Living from Enlightened Mind, rather than from jerk-off mind will be just fine, Mr. Clayton."

Billy grinned. "I like that. I've always liked the look of the Beatles sitting around with those gurus: George playing the sitar. Looked like a hell of a lot more fun than a bunch of deranged gimps in business suits with lying eyes, crooked grins and nothing at all to talk about."

Jenny looked back at him and her eyes held his. "You are stepping onto the Path, the Way. You are a good man and it's high time you felt real delight with life instead of wandering around as a sleepwalker. But the Way is very difficult; it pounds your ego thin as jeweler's gold, which is a very painful process and may take a long time."

"That's exactly what my mom said."

"I am looking forward to meeting her."

"Whoever was in that Humvee probably got the plates when the truck was in Jess' driveway," he said.

"Subject too heavy? Gotta change it?" asked Jenny.

"It's registered offshore," Billy continued. "If they have somebody with the highway patrol or the cops, they could hunt us down on the street, but the paper is a dead end. We'll buy something else when we stop. My guess is that sleep is going to become a much-needed commodity."

"Yeah. It looks like we're going to LA for sure," she said.

Neeley and company had melded with the southerly flow through the interchanges toward the long boring stretch of Highway 5. Billy kept thinking about Sam and Nuke, and he grew more tired by the moment. Jenny drove smoothly and she appeared to take control without any effort.

The conversation ebbed. They became monosyllabic, and nothing could be done about that vacant state of things until Neeley's men got to wherever they were going, until rest soothed their minds. Jenny looked at Billy leaned against the door, submerged in sleep. She was pleased. It made her feel good to see him relax.

. . . .

Jenny sat on a jeweled throne. Stunning beyond belief, she wore a white brocade gown with a platinum and diamond tiara lacing through her magnificent hair. A giant pigeon-blood ruby served as the center stone in the headpiece. It looked just like the one in Neeley's ring, only ten times as big. Neeley lurked behind her in his overcoat. He was scoping out how to steal the tiara off her head.

Several court agents—statesmen of some kind—came in urgently and began to read the long scrolls they carried. Jenny leaned back on her gem-studded throne, trying to pay attention to all the boring crap these guys read from their parchments. Billy caught her eye, and she smiled sweetly. She did not part her lips, just eased the sides of her mouth up a bit and locked her eyes on his.

She pulled herself back together and listened to the men in robes read their blarney. The absurdity of scrolls caused Billy to stare in wonder; they were at least twelve feet long. One man finished and the next one read. Then two more walked up. Jenny started drumming her nails. She tried to sit regally and pay attention, but she fidgeted. She shifted her legs.

Billy took a deep breath and walked right up through the crowd. He started talking some kind of gibberish. He didn't even know what he was saying.

"When in the course of the events of statehood, time draws nigh and the elders look for a course of token to strengthen the powers that prevail and move through the aura of being in half-tones and an indignant pod of rabble

193

lift the clouded plane of smothered conscience...." He sounded like the modern-day politicians on TV.

Billy couldn't even keep up with his own words, but the audience stood hypnotized by this dribble. He reached out for Jenny's hand and his heart jumped right out from his chest under the skin, creating a cartoon-like bulge on the front of his tight shirt.

Jenny took his hand and they walked regally, moving off slowly. But the attendants started to follow them, so they began to move faster. Billy knew that he had come in a black titanium space cruiser, and that if he could find it, they could go.

With her head Jenny signaled to turn left. They ran and ran, down a long granite hall. They came to a dead end and the crowd was gaining fast. Jenny shoved on a bookcase that spun and they moved into another hall. They ran again, and just as Billy saw the gleaming black cruiser, Jess opened the door of their room at the Saint Francis.

Billy sat bolt upright in the bed, wondering where he was. Was he still in the dream? He focused on Jess. The confusion overwhelmed him. He couldn't tell whether he was dreaming or not.

"You were dreaming, sorry," said Jess, who wore some kind of Comanche sorcerer's getup. Around his neck were two shaman pieces: a strand of bear claws and a necklace made from the vertebrae of a diamondback rattlesnake. Billy could tell what the pieces were because they had labels on them like they were from a museum.

Even Jess himself was labeled. The large parchment label hung from a wire through his ear: HOMO SAPIENS SAPIENS, LATE TWENTIETH CENTURY, WHITE ANGLO SAXON SORCERER: SPECIES NOW EXTINCT. The diamond back and the bear totem labels also listed the creatures as extinct.

"You're dreaming, again, Billy. You're beginning to tap your power," said Jess.

194

"Yeah, right. Jesus, I was having a great dream. I had all kinds of power and you were extinct," said Billy.

Jess broke into an amazingly loud laugh and mountains appeared behind him. "Extinct but never gone. Extinction creates the true power. The human will lose the Earth because he is not quite bright enough to learn to quit fouling the nest," he said.

His voice seemed to billow up out of a canyon. A group of men and women in corporate suits came up behind Jess, whispered in his ear while looking at Billy. "We are from the New Church of the Good for Humankind and we have been dispatched to return Mr. Hayes to Whacker Avenue, to our Chicago headquarters, where he will be safe," said a severe brunette in a slick, razor cut pageboy haircut.

Jess looked at all of these characters, sizing them up. "Don't go with them Billy. They're not Christians; they're shape shifters. They're not even diamondbacks."

Suddenly the brunette turned into a coiled timber rattler right at Billy's feet—the rattle going like mad—and Billy started kicking at the damned thing.

. . . .

His whole body was sweated and vibrating, and after what seemed to be a millennium of total darkness with nothing but the rattlesnake, Billy's eyes opened slightly and Jenny had a hand on his shoulder and she was shaking him.

"Billy! Billy! Quit that damn kicking, it gives me the creeps," shouted Jenny.

Gradually Billy realized that she had hold of him, and his eyes opened a bit wider.

"Billy! You're dreaming too loud."

"It's Luther," he said.

"You were kicking the firewall really hard; what does that have to do with Luther?"

"It was a powerful dream, a message from Luther. You and Jess and some weird woman from a corporate church. The woman wore a suit and turned into a rattlesnake and was coiled and rattling right in my face."

"You were making this strange noises and kicking. It was weird. Now I'm tired and irritable," said Jenny.

"Luther has something important to tell us. We have to see him."

"Wait a minute, you're all 'I'm gonna find Jess' killers, and now you're sounding like some New Age screwball from Sedona. You dream about a snake and now you want to go see your horse trainer."

Jenny looked at him closely and smiled. She put her hand on his thigh and squeezed gently.

"Maybe you'd better go back to sleep," she said.

"No, you need to sleep now," he said.

"Looks like they're taking us right into LaLa Land."

Neeley took the 110 toward Angels Gate, the entrance to Los Angeles Harbor. They sped down onto Gaffey Street in San Pedro and rolled fast through amber lights. At 22nd Street the driver slid through the signal in a hard left and gunned it toward the ship channels. Forgetting that the truck looked like it had been through a war zone and was easily spotted, Jenny whipped through the light.

The car slid smoothly past the hundreds of boat slips of Cabrillo Marina and into the cul-de-sac for Whaler's Walk. They drove toward the water and Jenny saw that when the car turned at the end of the lot, Neeley's crew would see them.

She stopped, jammed into reverse and moved back to the parking lot in front of the Angels Gate Yacht Club, a small commercial building that sat adjacent to the Hilton. Billy rolled his window down to get a better feel of the night. Rigging and lines tapped lightly against the boats as they rocked gently in their moorings. The smell of salt pervaded the still morning.

196

Jenny killed the lights and drove by the sulfur glow of the street lamps. She stopped the truck when she saw that they were in a business drive that dead-ended at the paths beside the water.

They eased out of the truck quietly, not even latching the doors. Billy grabbed a Desert Eagle and a flair gun. Jenny baulked for a moment and then snatched a Desert Eagle out of the bag for herself.

They ran toward the docks and hid behind a hedgerow that grew alongside the yacht club building. Billy held a hand out to stop Jenny. He slipped his head around the line of bushes toward where the car had disappeared. The Chrysler's lights flicked off just as Billy peeked down the walk between the club and the boats. In the early morning light he saw that Neeley's men were out of the car with the trunk opened.

Leonardo and Heiny started walking back and forth from the rear of the car to the railing, heaving the bags from San Francisco to two men in a dinghy. It only took a few minutes to empty the car, then Leonardo said, "Yeah, we'll see you tomorrow."

The men from the dinghy didn't say anything, just nodded. They rowed the small skiff out to an elegant old motor yacht. The others piled back into the car.

Billy jerked his head back into the shrubs as the car turned around so the front pointed toward where they hid.

Jenny had backed into a parking space. They sprinted toward the Dodge, but the dark phantom car took off up the driveway. All beat up, Billy's pickup stood out like a road sign. Billy went to his knees and whipped the pistol up in a shooting triangle. He looked over to see if Jenny was safe. As always, she surprised him by being fully ready for action. She had gone to a prone shooter's position with the pistol clutched in her grip.

The car stopped, and two of the men in overcoats got out of the back. Billy knew that these men loved guns, and that their pistols were oiled and could sight in on them easily. He knew that the clips were in excellent shape and that two clips of .50 caliber rounds would destroy the engine block of his truck, as well as a good part of the suspension and interior, and wipe out anyone inside within a few quick moments of action.

For a split second his mind roamed. Billy wondered if Jenny would be all right with such a heavy pistol that had so much recoil. In another instant, he recalled her performance in the warehouse, which would have staggered anybody in Force Recon. He took a deep breath, and the thought passed out of his head. He steadied the Desert Eagle.

Even with the distance and the dim lighting, Heiny stood out like a beacon and Billy could see that Leonardo sported a bandage. The men walked around the car and exchanged heated words. After the exchange rose to shouts and some shoving, they both looked around.

Then Neeley got out. He scrutinized the area. His gazed locked on Billy's truck for a second, and then he barked at his men. His words were not quite audible to Billy and Jenny. Then Neely got back into the car.

Leonardo went to the trunk and pawed at the contents. He slammed the door shut, stood up straight, felt his bandage and looked over at the truck again. He cocked his head, then turned and looked around the lot.

Billy wanted to move his pistol up with both of his steady hands and drop all of them right there. They were responsible for Jess' murder in some way, and the law would never touch them because they were men that could afford expensive lawyers that knew how to tweak the system. But who else had been involved? Had Neeley actually masterminded the events or was there a bigger badder wolf? A Mr. X?

Billy looked at Jenny and concentrated on his breathing, readying for accurate shooting.

Leonardo looked around the lot again. Heiny got back in the car. Neeley barked out his window into the dark night. Leonardo stretched, walked to the door and slid onto the seat. The car eased out toward the street.

The vehicle picked up speed slightly, and Billy and Jenny ran hard. They jumped in the pickup and Billy fired the ignition. He eased out of the parking place, stopped at the sidewalk, looked to make sure they were not being watched, pulled back onto Via Cabrillo Marina and swung right.

They were both concerned that they would lose track of the car after all this work. Billy kept the lights off and followed carefully, but the car simply hung a right into the drive of the Hilton.

FIFTEEN

Billy and Jenny walked around the wall in front of the Hilton just in time to see Neeley's whole crew. Very cramped and totally exhausted, the men lumbered out of the dark Chrysler into the cool salt air and stretched. Then they continued on through the sliding glass doors into the lobby.

Billy and Jenny held back, watching. They stood among a few other people who lingered outside in the loading area. As they edged up toward the entry, two outdoors-type men moved past them. Something about the men grabbed Billy's attention. He sensed that they were some sort of law enforcement, and saw that they observed Neeley's group, too.

One, massive with a weather-beaten face, wearing a long brown denim jacket, appeared to be generous of spirit. The other, wearing a tight jean jacket was young and handsome. He had big brown bedroom eyes and thick black wavy hair, and he sported an attitude of arrogance. In need of a laundry, a shave, a shower and some rest, the men seemed oblivious to their surroundings. Their unkempt look, so much like Jenny's and his own, held Billy's eye.

Through the glass, they could see Leonardo dispatch a bellhop to the car as the desk finished their check in. The bellhop walked right out to the stand, got a ticket and stepped over to the Chrysler 300. The scruffy pair hung back and watched as Neeley's men headed toward the elevators. After the doors slid shut on Heiny and the crew, the two men moved up to the registration counter.

Billy and Jenny looked at one another in the light from the valet station. Billy's lemon-yellow slacks had collected several large grease smudges from brushing against machinery while he was trapped in the warehouse. Jenny sported her sky blue jacket with the puce plaid trousers. Both were scruffy from combat. They started laughing aloud.

"Hey, come on. We're golfers. The poodah pants gang. A little rumpled but that's no reason why a couple of party-animal, PGA types can't have a room," said Jenny.

"Let's wait and make sure they don't just turn around and leave. If they're not back down in a few minutes, they'll call room service. They're guts are too big to wait long for food."

"No, I'm tired. You can come back if you want. They won't leave until tomorrow. Like you say, they want massive doses of grease, carbs and booze to wash it all down."

"You reckon?" asked Billy.

"You can hang around down here with the front page up to your face, but I'm ordering a bottle of champagne, a big breakfast, and then passing out just like them. Sleep will change everything."

Ten 100-dollar bills folded neatly behind a Charles Yeager credit card as a tip quickly persuaded the young woman at the desk to abandon the company's privacy policies. Immediately, she put them into a bank of five suites adjacent to, and on either side of, Neeley's party. Billy asked that they ring both his and Jenny's rooms whenever the Neeley party called for their car.

An additional five crisp hundreds tucked into his Charles Yeager passport from Great Britain and the clerk assured Billy that the front desk personnel on all shifts would contact his room whenever the party required their car. He explained that they were scouting with Neeley's party, finding shooting locations for a James Bond-like film about the CIA, and naturally, everything had to remain discreet. To foil paparazzi, communications must remain solely between the clerk and Billy.

The intrigue and the absurd gratuity inspired the young woman to lean over the desk and, in a hushed tone, tell Billy that the Neeley party planned to eat breakfast, then be in their rooms throughout the entire day. She bent closer and added that they requested to be awakened at four in the afternoon for appetizers, which included all the choices on the menu, with emphasis on the deep-fried items. The cocktails would also be delivered at four. Then, dinner would be served in the room at five-thirty with champagne, followed by coffee, brandy and a sampler of all desserts at six-thirty.

As Billy turned from the young woman, two valets came through with burlap bags on a cart. They were the very same type of sacks that Billy and Jenny had watched the men exchange on the boat for those they picked up in San Francisco. The bellhop proceeded to the elevators with the load.

With some apprehension, they followed the cart down the hallway toward their rooms. They each took the other's spare keycard, and went separately to their rooms, located on either side of the two suites the gang moved into. Jenny wanted to shower. Billy retrieved the duffel, their clothes and the phones. He paid the parking attendant to get rid of the truck. In his room, he spread all the evidence they had collected in the Saint Francis laundry bag onto his bed and phoned Nuke and Harlan.

Calling Nuke produced nothing; there was no connection at all. Billy thought that whoever had lurked outside Jess' in the Humvee represented something big: some group to which the bull-necks and the attackers in Sausalito belonged. Did they know about *dead latitudes?* Had they privateered the old vessel with Nuke aboard? They could have destroyed all communications equipment and switched to their own gear. An image of Sam floated up before his mind's eye, and he wanted to put his arms around his dog so badly that his knees felt weak. Nausea struck as he hung up.

He punched in Harlan's personal line and the tough old lawyer's rich and gravelly Texas voice filled up the earpiece.

"Dammit, Billy Clayton, you better not be in trouble again. With your daddy dead, I'm stuck. Now I'm the one's gotta whip your young ass into shape. You were enough damn trouble with all those inscrutable offshore businesses. I think you're turning oriental, Chinese or something. Your mother with all that damn Sun Tzu and Lao Tzu, all that religious crap, Jesus as a Tibetan mystic, Mexican sorcerers, Gandhi, Sufis, Danillo Dolci, the Friends Service Committee, Saint Francis. Good lord. How can such an intelligent, class-act woman have so many kinky ideas? A drop-dead gorgeous gal to boot. With your daddy gone and you as headstrong as you are, I'm afraid you could go off the deep end, son."

Billy pictured Harlan as he spoke: six-foot-four, he wore the short hair of an Air Force major. After four decades of pounding the bar, he remained one of the five toughest defense lawyers in the world. As counsel, he had been a member of the family all those years, and one of Billy's father's few close, forever friends.

"Thanks, Harlan. Please try to remember that sharing is caring."

"Just cut the crap with your cute digressions."

"I've got crappy news for you. I'm probably wanted for assault, as a batterer, a murder-one suspect, a terrorist and who knows what all."

"You didn't listen to a damn thing did—"

"Look Harlan, I didn't choose this, I assure you. Some people who—"

"Oh for god's sake, Billy Clayton! I just now, finally, after a year or more, got your mother calmed down. She persevered in staying pissed with me for letting you get into that thing in Malibu last year, and now I'm going to have to go through it all over again."

"Harlan, *get a grip*! I need you here as fast as you can pile into your jet. One of my best friends was murdered: shot dead with a high tech .12 gauge. Slaughtered and mutilated on his own living room floor. You need to grab the reins on the judge, the DA, the cops, and on all discoveries."

"Where the hell are you?"

"The Hilton at the Port of Los Angeles. It's a comfortable little hotel by the Cabrillo Marina Yacht Basin."

"For god's sake, Billy. That's as bad as Malibu. How do you expect me to sleep in a rotten bed that doesn't even have cotton sheets? Los Angeles Harbor has always been a cesspool. The money boys will want the politicians and the DA to inject poison in you immediately."

"No, it happened up in Marin. In Tiburon."

"That is a million times worse! At least they are just plain old crooks down in LaLa Land. But everybody in fucking Marin County and San Francisco thinks that their pooh-pooh smells like rose water. They won't care who, any old hapless perp will do, but it'll have to be ASAP. They'll want homicide to put a wrap on it in 48 hours. Are you in jail?"

"No, I'm not going to jail, Harlan. The law would be a complete waste of my time. I'm going to figure out what really happened and you are going to take care of the bureaucrats. I'm down in San Pedro and I'm going to bag this perp. Maybe right here."

"Did you run?"

"I left. I picked up some clues and a hot lead. I'm in pursuit before the trail goes cold."

"Dammit, Billy Clayton. Only a lawyer, a judge or a politician can take the law into their own hands."

"You forgot the rich. I'm the richest man in the world."

"Listen to me, William Clayton the Third: do not get smart with me. I changed your fucking diapers. Do you remember when I took your pants down and whooped your scraggly little ass with a willow switch? Remember? You left my million-dollar Lipizzaner stallion sweated, and it gave old Major pneumonia."

"You better think twice. Remember Mama? She said she'd cut your pecker off with her daddy's meat cleaver if you ever laid hands on me again. They'll call you Harlan Bobbitt, abbreviated counsel," Billy retorted.

Harlan broke into a belly laugh that Billy was sure even Jenny could hear in her room. "The problem with your mother is that she reads books. You're only supposed to do that in college, then you're required to forget all the drivel and dumb down like everybody else, or NSA will put you in a database. She reads books and she loved that goddamned

Dr. Spock. 'Spare the rod and save the child.' You're both a couple of kooks."

"Harlan, it's extreme. It appears that some fed spooks like NSA are in on it, too."

"Aw shit, Billy. Don't run some conspiracy theory on me. Ok, find an airport where I can land the Lear and call me back."

"Long Beach. You won't have to wade through LAX."

"I'll be there in a few hours and get a limo."

"Thanks, Harlan. You're a prince."

"We'll see. The DA in Marin may be a real baby boomer: a boomeritis asshole. Maybe I'll put your mother on retainer to torment his sorry butt."

Billy knew that Harlan would force the prosecutors, the defense and the judges to take a long, slow tour through judicial hell and drag the perp with them: a ride drawn out forever, and packed with the kind of clout that only knowledge, endless cash and heavy political connections can produce. At first, the prosecution would be scared shitless by Harlan. Then they would regroup, sit back and grin at him. Then they would get pouty and act out, but they wouldn't win. They'd see him pouring millions into a team for discovery and a media blitzkrieg. Later, they would buckle because so much information would become public. No prosecutor alive could match Harlan for pure down-to-the-bone brilliance, doggedness, media massaging, downright showmanship and being ornery just for the hell of it.

He didn't even wait for Billy to say goodbye. He just slammed the phone down. Without pausing, Billy punched in Luther Four Fingers' cell number.

"Shoot," Luther answered.

"Hey Luther, I've been dreaming about you and a big rattlesnake."

"I know. It's about that revivalist pimp with all the TV shows: Jet Slade. Like Jess said in that note—he's the one who carries on about God's plan. He's all into Revelations and all that sick-ass fear stuff. One of those car-sales, shuck-and-jive artists who's forgotten all love—the only thing Jesus cared about. I'm telling you, it's scary. Thank god there are still the Quakers, and all those other Christians who actually practice kindness."

"You already know?"

"This guy is a criminal, milking the congregation for their hard-earned, middle-class dollars. He's up to some kind of real bad shit, besides his Klan-like itch to lynch Indians and Afro-Americans, probably Latinos too, he's doing something to animals."

"You're dreaming this now?"

"Yeah. I've been doing a six-month purging exercise, so my system is very clean and so now all of these visions keep popping up. The important mental imagery, like Jess, is fine. But you start getting all these little piss-ant insights about where your horse just crapped. After you settle into the enlightened mind, the clean out is worth it. You don't latch on to thoughts at all, so things get real clear and peaceful. But the human mind is like a psychic vacuum cleaner on methamphetamine; it picks up any damn particle of information that blows in the window, so you've gotta pump the psyche's bilge water out once in a while.

"This Slade is the bad guy for sure. He's a real creeper. First off, he is cursed with being a white guy and he's got a real pale face to boot; his skin is the color of a maggot. He does have black eyes like my own, and he is lucky enough to have straight raven-black hair, so he's got a few of my good traits. But the hair is limp, not thick and wonderful like my own. The more blanco men are, the more vulgar they look."

"Jesus, Luther. How can a fully-enlightened sorcerer be such a disgusting judgmental retard and racist?"

"Hey, Billy, I didn't mean to hurt your feelings. You're family. I'm just sayin'. Hell, it's not my fault that your people are so damn ugly. But don't go gettin' all pouty like a white man on me."

"What are we going to do?"

"There's this guy is up in the hill country at a ranch somewhere. He brings in honchos for those canned hunts. At the same time, he's having critters out in the wild slaughtered by the thousand. Not to eat or stay warm, not with respect for Mother Nature. He's just ripping her off for the cash flow. He's also doing some kind of a kinky, Christian retribution rite with rattlers—all that blood and yuck shit that pseudo-Christians like—but I don't think he's a cannibal. Anyway, I turned his sordid rattlesnake vision back on him, so I'm sure he's sweating his ass off.

"Right there in Texas? So close to the ranch?"

"Yeah. Real close. I'm pouring my dreams into his daydreams and night dreams, so the fucker feels like he's totally cracking up. I haven't figured out what his whole scam is yet, but it's real nasty. He's not just a poacher. Not a two-bit cracker, tailgating bear bladders. He's taking animals all over the globe. Wants to corner the market. And he's branching out, re-investing his cash, starting to deal big-selling weapons like rocket launchers."

"So this is some Christian cult or something?"

"His whole congregation is innocent. Clueless. They just want to learn the real love that Jesus taught, not the twisted crap from this sick dude."

"They shot Jess in the chest with a .12 gauge. Used a FRAG-12 armor-piercing load on Jess and ripped his house apart with a fragmenting load."

"Damn. What is this sick dick white boy doing with FRAG-12s?"

"Right. That's the first thing I thought, Luther. They cut off one of his hands with a big reciprocating saw. Looked like they started to vivisect, just like they were parting an animal as a warning to this new Free Range group Jess started. He was trying to scare them out of business."

"Damn. Maybe Slade *is* a cannibal. I wouldn't put anything past a white boy, especially a preacher." The line went quiet for a moment as Luther digested the information.

"So what do you really know about it?" he finally asked.

Billy plucked the sheet from Jess's printer out of the pile on his bed. "Not much. I found this note right out of the buffer on his laser printer: 'Slade is poking around, doing something weird—something big is going down. He is not a happy boy. Why is he mixing with Neeley? Why is Neeley pissed? If I can't make it, Billy and Nuke could . . . too much dangerous shit. I have to do it. He will be at a table in the back of Tosca at midnight. We have to stop them.'"

"So you met this Neeley."

"Yeah, he's some kind of a Brit mobster."

"Must be Slade's business partner. Maybe he's a preacher too."

"I don't think so. Don't think he would even bother with religion."

"Slade's the real bad guy. The big cheese. I want you to come out here within the week, Billy. Whatever has happened to you, we will open it up when you're with me. We have to go to the hill country and stop this bastard immediately."

"It'll be a few days, but I'll fly right out."

"Make it snappy," said Luther.

Just as soon as Luther set the line free, Billy called the Los Angeles Sheriff's Department and they switched him straight through to Angel Orozco. Angel had pulled Billy through the year before when a murder had launched him out of making money and into solving his first crime.

"Billy. *Amigo, mio.* Damn, it's good to hear your voice."

"Same here, Angel. I wish there were another six billion around like you."

"Billy. Billy Clayton. Where are you? I got your message. It's time we get together for dinner and some calvados. We'll tell Toltec stories, I've been down in Don Juan country studying with a Naugual. Just stopping over in the City of Angels before going back up to the frigid Bay Area."

"Let's do it. I'm here in SoCal. We'll do it immediately. I need your help. Give me your home email and I'll send what we know. We're having a meeting with Harlan, if you can come."

"I'll be there for sure. Bad trouble?"

"A murder up in Tiburon."

"Damn, Billy. Tiburon's full of *ricos*. They'll crawl right out of the woodwork, moving fast like *cucarachas* in one of these coffee houses."

"Cockroaches high on coffee. That's good, Angel. Best description of the rich I've ever heard. You're a born writer, not a flatfoot."

"I do have a bit of the poet. It's because of my Latino heart and in my *alma grande*, Billy: my big soul."

"I know that poet, Angel. You need to share it with the world."

"Ah man, you're talking like a damn yuppie. I'm too lazy for all that typing. It's all I can do to get my reports out. It's torture. Anyway, I hate computers."

In her room Jenny ordered a bottle of Moet White Star with three-dozen iced prawns immediately. She also requested three New York steak dinners, two for herself and one for Billy, to be served ASAP with another White Star. When she heard the cart in the hall, she strolled over and knocked on Billy's door. She ducked inside just as eight dining carts rolled up to Neeley's doors.

"Hey, neighbor. Come on over. I have your dinner on its way."

"Good move," he stood there in his towel. "I'll slip into my poodah pants and we'll have a hell of a time. We'll go over to the *Queen Mary* and do some ballroom dancing."

The champagne and prawns arrived and Jenny dove in with gusto. Billy took a couple prawns and downed a flute of the cool wine.

"I called Nuke and there's no answer on his cell or the on-board phone," Billy stated.

"We've got to find him. But we can't lose these guys. We'll have to rent a helicopter and scour the coast to find *dead latitudes*," Jenny said in between bites.

"Harlan will be out this afternoon."

"So I get to meet the most terrifying trial lawyer in the world?"

Billy grinned. "You do. And you have to go to Moon Willow in the next few days. Luther has something very germane to this case that we have to attend to," he said.

"Luther Four Fingers? We can't go out there. We have to find Nuke and Sam. We have to follow these guys and—"

"It'll all work out."

"I don't know. It seems. . . ."

"I do. I know it will work out," Billy emphasized.

"What does Four Fingers mean?"

"When he was a boy, back in the early part of the twentieth century, he took off with a string of stallions. His father, Brown Bear Growling, was a very serious guy. He was ranch manager for my grandfather and bred some of the first quarter horses. Old Brown Bear took off on the trail of his son. Luther had gone down south to the gulf on an unordained vision quest. He saw the great water in a dream and knew that it represented his own noble visionary powers. He had to see it personally in order to launch his ability to see at great distances."

"Is Luther actually a seer?"

"He is; you'll be amazed. Anyway, the teen took off and a band of Karankawa found him."

"Karankawa?"

"Mortal enemies of the Comanche. They were cannibals, so the Comanche always murdered them on site. But there were too many, and they dragged the boy by his little fingers, pulled them right off. Luther bled the wounds, cauterized them, and hid in a swamp bottom, under the scum, breathing through a reed.

"Brown Bear Growling read trail like we read a search engine. He cut the hands off all the Karankawas. The hatred between the two nations was very, very deep. He tied the rest of their bodies to trees for the alligators."

"So, how does he run a horse ranch? And, you said that he went to college and learned to program in assembly language. How does he use the keyboard?"

"Luther's quite a guy."

"I get to visit the ranch, meet Luther and see some of Texas. I wish I could connect with your mother. Jess said an awful lot of good things about her."

"When she gets back from Italy, we'll spend some time." Billy really liked this woman. He couldn't put a handle on all of it, but one thing stood out for certain: everything about Jenny felt refreshing to him.

The steaks came and she inhaled both of hers quickly. She gobbled the massive baked potatoes with sour cream and chives and butter brimming over the top, and she sopped up all the juices on her plate with dinner rolls. She wolfed both bowls full of salad like a foraging buffalo, then finished off the champagne.

Billy laughed as he cleaned his plate after his one steak. "Damn, girl. You sure can eat."

"Well, Mr. Clayton, I've gotta say: you know how to show a girl a really weird night on the town. Gives her an appetite. I'm going to bed."

"They've seen me. Think they'd recognize you?" asked Billy.

"Possibly the one with the bandage on his thigh. But it was too dark in the warehouse for the others. I, ah . . . I surprised them," she said, lifting an eyebrow with a roguish grin.

"That you did. Must be where you got that appetite," he said, grinning. "Do you think they saw us when you stopped for gas?"

"I don't think so. I was clear across that big station, but I did get out to pump. You were slumped over. They would have come after us if they'd seen you. I watched them closely," she said.

"We have their suites surrounded. The woman at the desk said they want a wake up and have dinner and coffee at five. So you're right. We should sleep."

"I'm ready. That food did me in."

"I called Angel too. He's on his way, and he already texted that he talked to a buddy up in Marin."

"Do we follow them if they go back up north?"

"I want to board that boat. It's *The American Eagle*."

"How do you know?" asked Jenny.

"I saw it on the stern."

"Mr. Clayton, I swear, you have that anal-retentive stuff written in your gene code." She yawned and smiled at him.

. . . .

When Billy awoke, he felt very clear and well rested from the brief sleep. He stood right up and did deep breathing exercises. He worked into a sweat with a few rounds of calisthenics. He gripped molding at the top of the bathroom door with his fingertips and pulled his body all the way up in five slow groups of six. Then he stretched out thoroughly with Tibetan yoga and took a cold shower.

At the front desk, he gave the clerk two additional hundred-dollar bills in appreciation to the staff for helping to keep the men in the adjacent rooms on schedule. The young woman informed Billy that the wake-up plan remained the same, and that the best place to buy a computer would be up at Target on Gaffey.

"That's the closest," she said, smiling dreamily at Billy.

He eased up to Gaffey and an overwhelming wave of sadness about Melissa swept through him. The incident from the year before, when he learned that Angels Gate was the entry to Los Angeles harbor, had launched him as a sleuth. The name of the lighthouse that marked the entrance to the world-renowned harbor still gave him chills. She had been—before businessmen murdered her in Malibu—the first true love in the life of a 41-year-old, ex-Recon man with nothing but money in his life. How had that angel who had been dropped down to him been forced through the gate so early?

Billy emptied his mind of thoughts. He corrected his posture and breathed deeply. As the thoughts evaporated, he thought of how to get rid of the truck. He didn't know who, if anyone, wanted to find it. The cops? Angel would fill Billy in about what the law was doing in Marin when they got together. But the others? Neeley, the watchdogs from out in front of the Animalfund building, the SWAT-like characters on Bridgeway, and whomever else conspired in Jess' murder: were they looking for Billy and Jenny?

After another cold shower, he hooked up the computers and spread all the clues out on his bed including the shotgun shell, the flashlight from the Humvee and the CDs. Then he went to Jenny's room.

She crawled out of a deep sleep and grabbed the menu. She ordered three more New York Steak dinners, but Billy broke in and changed his to grilled salmon.

"Damn, Miss Marple. I confess, I chased those two bull-necks impulsively. I didn't discuss it with you, and I brought a lot of hostility into your life. But, are you so pissed that you're trying to kill me with cholesterol?"

"That is an excellent idea, thank you."

"A pleasure to be of service. Come look at this. All the information so far is here on the bed, and the new

213

laptops are over there, ready for us to charge. Harlan and Angel will be here any minute."

"A quick shower and I'll be over. I need clothes, and shampoo and soap. Let's send our street clothes out for laundering."

"We need to change hotels. It's too chancy, having this pack of bozos right here. If they see us, they'll go on the offense, or the defense, or run and hide. Whatever. They don't appear to see that we're trailing them yet, and it's important that we keep it that way."

Billy looked at Jenny with a calm smile.

"Right. We should change hotels. This is too risky even with the front desk thing. They'll be eating soon, so we've got to see if they decide to leave," said Jenny.

As Billy inhaled a couple bites of salmon, a solid knock shook the door in its jamb. It was Harlan. Billy hugged the man and didn't have to invite him into the room.

Harlan's voice filled the every crevice. It was deep, sonorous and intimidating. Since his youth, Billy had always felt thankful that this unflappable man stood by his side, always ready to go into combat with the legal system for his family.

Harlan's build resembled Dirty Harry's, only with a couple extra inches of height and more beef. He pulled the listener in with his eyes as he talked. Imminent peril oozed from the lean man's pores.

Long before peeled heads were *en vogue,* Harlan wore the coiffure of a drill sergeant. Like Billy, he sported a ghastly scar. Billy's started at the center of his hairline and dropped down across his nose to his cheek. But Harlan's started at the left side of the hairline and snaked down across his cheek, clear to his chin. A nasty, jagged, vertical gash from the champagne bottle of an irate oil baroness.

His roman nose emphasized the fleshy wound. He had a great mouth full of huge, sparkling, square teeth. Jenny stared at him and Billy couldn't help but laugh; he had known the man for so many years that the rough exterior didn't project anything but warmth to him.

214

"Harlan Jenks, this is Jenny Warren."

"Good lord, Billy. You didn't tell me that she's drop-dead gorgeous, just that she worked for Jess and she's good people. You tryin' to keep her all to yourself?" Harlan broke into a robust hoarse laugh and hugged Jenny. He stepped back with his hand on her shoulders. "Where did you ever get those eyes?"

"From my mom and dad," Jenny responded, matter-of-factly.

"Damn, she's not just a knock out. She's brilliant too."

They all laughed. Billy grinned, and Jenny looked around at him and blushed.

"So the venue's Tiburon? I can't believe that anyone would harm someone like Jess Hayes. I knew his grandmother. What a doll. A fabulous family. Not your ordinary rich stooges. They were real, dignified, old-line San Franciscans. Came around the horn. Lived through the quake. They moved into the Saint Francis after the shaker, right in with Caruso and all the rich refugees. But the family did so much for so many people. What a good boy."

Harlan walked around, looking around the room as he talked. "God, I can still get amazed at how disgusting human beings are."

"Harlan, are you okay?" asked Billy.

"I didn't get enough sleep, thanks to you, young man. It makes me cranky. I am an old fart and we need beauty rest. At my age you know what actually feels good and what is just the usual BS. So, are you're going to play detective on this one too?"

"I'm going into the salvage business with Nuke."

"Salvage?"

"Yeah, like Travis McGee."

"Dammit, Billy. You are a businessman, not Phillip Marlowe. Playing LA noir is just slumming. A rich boy acting out Mr. Marlowe. You don't really know what sorry

215

shits humans are. You've been listening to your mother with all that loving-kindness crap. That woman can abandon her senses at the drop of a sunbonnet. All that goddamn forgiveness, turn-the-other cheek, Christian mumbo-jumbo, kindness practice from the Buddhists, and that poetic goodwill from the Muslims. Good lord! And the Marine Corps is play-acting; they are not in the day-by-day mess of real life. Stick to money, Billy."

"Harlan, I heard this last year. I'm going into salvage with Nuke. I'm mooring *dead latitudes* in Marina del Rey and moving onboard. The treasure we intend to salvage will be the units of Homo sapiens that have unwittingly been sucked into the folds of the jurisprudence system and similar vipers."

"Alright, alright. Let's just get on with this. I need some facts." He looked at Jenny, and laughed. "This is the most hard-headed boy in the world, even more so than his father. It's why they're so damned rich." He winked at Jenny. "Okay, we need to know what the cops have done."

"Angel Orozco is coming down, should be here any—"

The door vibrated against the jamb with a powerful thump. When Billy opened the door, Sergeant Angel Orozco stood tall and thick in the chest. His upper body muscles looked as if they would burst him lose from his corduroy jacket at any moment. He was like a real-world Incredible Hulk.

The year before Billy asked him why his arms and chest were so big. "I have a huge garden, just like my father," he had responded.

"A huge garden?"

"Yes, Billy. It saves my life."

"Saves your life?"

"My father boxed as a boy, then he taught boxing at a gym in east LA. He raised me up together with some farmworkers when my mom died. He took them into the house for the Cesar Chavez movement. Dad and all of them slipped up from Mexico, but Dad didn't like to work the fields. He loved to fight. Fighting another man was heaven

216

for him. The way he kept powerful muscle was by working his garden."

Angel bulged out of the same corduroy jacket he'd had on the first night Billy met him. The night they met, Billy had just dialed 911 and the LA sheriffs drove out to Malibu to check the scene of Melissa's murder. While the other cops spun around like a pack of clowns out of the circus, Sergeant Orozco saw things exactly as they were.

"Billy, it is so good to see you again. Always a man of great *alma*, great soul, as we say in Spanish."

"Jesus, Angel. You saved my ass. You always knew, didn't you?"

"Billy, you read like an open book. It could get you hurt, *amigo*."

Harlan grabbed Angel's hand and hugged him. "Damn, what an honor. One of three decent cops in the US right here, honoring us with your presence," Harlan said.

"Angel, this is Jenny. Jenny Warren."

Angel took her hand with both of his. "It is a pleasure to meet you, Jenny."

"I've only heard good things about you, Angel."

"How generous. With Harlan here, you know that we have won this case already."

"Angel. Damn. You're the only decent cop I ever met. I'm surprised they haven't fired your ass."

"Too much paperwork, Harlan. That's all homicide is. I'm good at it so I'll never lose my job, but it is very painful for me to pay attention to it."

"That's it, Angel. Not only are you a decent cop, you're smart. You actually see what's going on. I forgot about that because it's so unusual."

"You offer me too much praise, counselor. Here are all the printouts from Marin County, all that has come down the pike."

217

Harlan thumbed through the file quickly. "Okay, this is just what they saw at the scene. Not a whole hell of a lot. But no problem. Let me have your card, Angel. You can shoot info out to me as it comes up. Here's a card with my FedEx number on it."

The door shook with another knock. Billy opened it and in came the food. "Here are your steaks and iced teas," said Jenny to Harlan and Angel.

"Boy, you found a keeper, Billy. When's the wedding?"

"You've got to have fuel," said Jenny, ignoring his question. "We intend to work you plenty hard. Will you please bring us up three pots of coffee too?" Jenny asked the room service man.

"Billy and I are going to have to leave."

"What?" asked Harlan.

"The goons we followed down from the city are in the two suites next door, to the left as you step out in the hall. My room's just past them. Your rooms are the two immediately to the right of this one. And our office is to the right of your suites."

He handed out magnetic key cards. All of them got one for the office.

"Keep these rooms for now. But you need to move all of us out of here, up town in San Pedro, over to the Crowne Plaza at the Harbor immediately. We can't have them get suspicious about us. Get suites on the eighth floor in the corner that overlooks the ship channel."

"What the hell are you doing, Billy?"

"You've got to trust us right now, Harlan. You have to move us while these guys are out. They can't see any of us, especially Billy, or they won't act natural anymore. We're following them and it's important, and we will tell you all about it when we get back," said Jenny.

"So you're just waltzing out the door?"

"Yes, and you are going to go through everything on that bed and the stuff Angel brought and do some in-depth discovery together. Dig out everything that every bureaucrat, cop, spook, government agent and anyone else knows about the guys we chased from Animalfund and the spooks that jumped us on Bridgeway in Sausalito. Sift out everything that happened at Jess' and figure out where the fuck my sailboat, my dog and Nuke are."

Billy handed Harlan a credit card. "Keep the rooms so we can come back and watch the thugs, but get an extra limo and make sure you get everything out of here while they're gone."

"What do we do with these steaks?"

"Take them or order more over at the other hotel on this card. Get five suites."

Neeley and his group stood outside the entry doors lollygagging while the valet brought the car up. Billy bought a newspaper for cover. He walked over to the desk, shielding his face. He had ten more hundred-dollar bills folded in his palm and handed them to the clerk.

"Part of our party will be checking out now. It appears that we have more people coming in for some unexpected script changes and shooting so we will keep all our rooms."

"What's the name going to be?"

"Angels Gate."

"Wow, that's so cool. Of course you already know that this is Angels Gate and that it's the only green lighthouse on the West Coast. Seamen from all over the world know where Los Angeles is because of the beam."

"We did know," said Billy looking at her nametag. "You obviously have a real feel for the movies."

She looked down at the slippery new hundreds.

"I want you to have the ten yourself. These five," he said handing her more bills, "are for the rest of the front desk staff, if I am not being overly presuming to ask you to hand them out."

"Oh no, don't be silly. You are not being presumptuous in any way."

"Here's my cell number. Please call it whenever they come or go."

"Consider it done."

Billy looked around. Neeley's Chrysler had just started to ease out the driveway. He walked through the doors fast and headed for the fencing behind which Jenny sat in the truck. The gang's car moved back out onto Villa Cabrillo, picking up a little speed. At 22nd Street, they rolled past Gaffey, which would have delivered them back to the Los Angeles freeway system.

They turned right and dropped down toward the ship channels. Reaching Harbor Boulevard, the main thoroughfare in lower San Pedro just above the busy port of Los Angeles, they swung left toward town. They glided along the boulevard, past the mountains of shipping containers and the hammerhead cranes that lifted the steel boxes off the gigantic ships.

Billy and Jenny glanced out over the main channel and the ports of call tourist area as they tailed the car at a safe distance. Neeley cruised on, past the LA Maritime Museum and the Crowne Plaza Hotel that sat mid-town just up the hill from the vast maritime complex.

A still cruise ship took on passengers readying for a voyage to the warm waters of Baja, California and Mexico. They traveled on past it quickly. Billy and Jenny breathed a sigh of relief as their quarry slid right past both of the on-ramps onto the freeway system. They had been on their feet for a long time, the brief sleep helped but nothing could take the place of a long, deep rest, no matter how butch they had learned to behave.

But the black beast sailed under the Vincent Thomas Bridge and on around Front Street to John Gibson Boulevard. They glided past the police station and continued along the Turning Basin for large sea craft until John Gibson swept right onto Harry Bridges Boulevard. Abruptly, the dark car turned a sharp left onto Wilmington Boulevard, then right onto Anaheim.

The automobile never slowed, it moved steadily and swept along through the old warehouse area of Wilmington. The remnants of port expansion caused South Wilmington to look like a war zone. There was a combination of slumlord deterioration: ripped down buildings replaced by razor wire, chain-link fenced lots, a sparse population of warehouses that withstood the developers' hammers; longshoremen caught in the middle; gang bangers listening to powerful bass speakers; never ending sixteen-wheel trucks; the onward press of the shipping industry for one of the busiest ports in the world. All of this left the whole area looking like a marginalized city in a war-torn country. An overwhelming sense of danger prevailed.

Neeley's car cruised along Anaheim Street, gliding through several stoplights in the darkness and swung an easy right onto a side street. Billy drove on past the intersection because an abrupt turn would draw attention.

As they eased by, Billy and Jenny saw that the car stopped about halfway down the block in front of a small warehouse. It felt like artillery fire would break out any moment. Billy drove on to the next street, turned left and swung around the block, crossing over Anaheim again. He stopped so they faced the rear end of Neeley's vehicle.

"Back there at the freeway, I thought they were going to jump on and head north again," said Jenny

"Me too. Wonder what they're doing."

"I don't know, but I could inhale a couple orders of eggs benedict or a trio of big juicy cheeseburgers smothered with grilled onions, drink a couple bloody marys and fall out for sixteen hours without batting an eye," she said.

"A trio? How the hell could you eat again? Three cheeseburgers?"

"Hey, I starved for hours. I'm a tall, healthy woman. *And*, I'm PMSing."

"Oh, well *excuse* me. A woman's plumbing system is well beyond my comprehension."

"You'd better be careful; I'm not always in the best of moods when my plumbing is behaving devilishly. My plumbing...you really have a way with words, Mr. Clayton."

"Can we talk about something else?" asked Billy.

Jenny laughed aloud. "How are we going to stay awake? I'm not in the greatest of shape and I can't see you doing a third run up the state if they don't go back to the hotel."

"No choice, we have to follow," said Billy.

With the truck's headlights off, he eased over onto the shoulder. They could see the Chrysler in front of an old brick building. The building was smaller, but otherwise it was just like Neeley's warehouse up north in China Basin. It sat behind an eight-foot chain-link fence topped with barbed wire. A marked difference stood out at this location; the angled brackets above this fence also supported multiple spirals of razor wire.

They watched while Leonardo got out and unlocked the gate in the fence. The car pulled on through into the yard. The men unloaded the bags they had taken from the boat over by the Hilton, and then went into the warehouse.

Out of the dark, a low-slung beefy old Chevy with four men approached in the opposite lane on Sanford. As they drew nearer, they heard the rumble of rap music; the baseline throbbed so loud that they could feel it on their skin. The vehicle slowed, the dark windows lowered, and the men peered straight out at Billy and Jenny. The car stopped. The speakers pounded.

Yanking into reverse, Billy hit the gas hard. He screeched around the corner onto Anaheim and shot forward. The dark car followed, burning through the turn. Gunfire spat toward the pickup. Billy screamed into a left turn onto a side street, scorching past a cop car. The gunfire from the Chevy blasted right through the black and white car.

The cop pounded the brakes and seared into a U-turn, whipping on his lights and siren. The Chevy shot through and swung left on Alameda Street and the siren cannonballed right behind them, the cop returned gunfire.

Still without lights, Billy hauled into reverse. Wheeling into the skid, he turned the truck clear around and fishtailed as he regained control. An oncoming big rig missed them by inches, and Billy slid around the corner at Sanford.

He eased back up to where they had parked before the low-slung Chevrolet had driven up. As he stopped, Neeley's phantom of a car backed out through the gate. They cruised down to the intersection. At the corner, they turned right and headed back toward the hotel. He let them clear the corner and eased down toward the warehouse slowly.

"Billy, what are you doing? We've got to get out of here."

"There's no way. Nobody else can do this. Look at the sign."

Jenny looked up at it.

LUNG FAT TRADING COMPANY
THE MYSTERY OF THE ORIENT AT YOUR COMMAND

"Mystery of the orient?" Jenny asked. "What's that? What does the inventory look like?"

"Probably a shipload of giant water rats from Indonesia," he said, looking around at her as she cringed. "Fresh to you grocer and shelved weekly." He sniggered.

They caught up with Neeley's car and followed it back to the hotel. The men emerged from the truck and handed the keys to the valet. Billy sat and watched the front as Jenny eased out of the truck and ran around to the outdoor dining patio behind the restaurant. All four men bellied up to a table.

SIXTEEN

As the pilot prepped the Gulfstream for the flight to the coast, the driver picked Jet Slade up at the lodge. Slade asked him to make a quick detour on the way to the plane. Rather than drive straight across Paradise Ranch to the runway, they doglegged out toward a 25-foot high structure well hidden from the ranch's central lodge.

Soon the fence drew near. Strange, high tech and threatening, it swelled up to giant proportions in his mind's eye, filling Slade's entire event horizon. He was triumphant and appalled in the same moment. The stainless steel enclosure looked like a prop for a scene in *Star Wars*. Punched evenly over its entire surface with half-inch diamond-shaped holes, it had the look of a very unusual palisade designed for battle. Slade began to sweat.

The driver pushed hard right up to the gate and jammed the breaks. He hopped out, opened the locks and stood at attention as his boss walked through. Slade craved to turn around without looking the fool, but he made himself pick up each foot and step forward. He seemed to traverse a hundred miles.

Once inside enclosure, the most curious aspect of the space was the pit. The 100 by 40-foot excavation in the earth appeared to be an illusion, a performance artist's attempt to help people think outside the box. Nothing seemed real. Slade's knees shook. His muscles twitched all over his body and he ground his molars. Knowing there was no turning back, he wanted to crawl to the edge of the pit. Walking upright terrified him with a horrid notion he would soon lose control and fall right over the rim. The sweat of his brow formed rivulets down into his eyes, and he had not yet even peered over the edge.

The rattlesnakes had been imported from many areas in the United States in an attempt to find out if sidewinders and timber rattlers could exist with the diamondbacks native to Texas. If they could coexist, other vipers would be introduced from more exotic continents.

During construction, the excavators dug down 25 feet into the earth. Next they dropped a small grading tractor and a horizontal drill rig to the floor of the hole. Earth-moving men etched out caves all the way around the base. Concrete men bored into the sides for tiebacks, laced the 30-foot bolts with engineered rebar and sprayed the sides with concrete to avoid cave-ins. Gardeners planted thick chaparral around the rim of the enclosure, providing shelter and an abundance of fodder for rodents. Sales of the reptiles would always be brisk. Snake freaks everywhere would order tons of product.

Jet got to the precipice and struggled for breath. His heart beat like crazy; he couldn't even begin to stay with the thought of his blood pressure. He rubbed the perspiration from his eyes and forced them to peer downward straight to the bottom. Everywhere, every square inch was covered with rattlers that swarmed more thickly than Slade imagined in his wildest fantasies. They coiled and slithered around each other.

Slade's throat caught, his brow dripped, his eyes bulged and he forced himself to breathe. His legs grew weak. Vertigo took over and he swayed on his feet.

Slade jerked his head up to check out the fine concrete block building on the other side of the pit. He thought of how hard he had worked with the architects. He had been through every phase of design and development, and made the building as friendly for the environment of his beautiful ranch as possible. "Sustainable architecture," that's what the design team called green building practices. Every structure on Paradise Ranch was environmentally friendly.

"Sustainable architecture," he said it aloud as he admired the fine-looking lodging. He smiled to himself, musing that the earth-friendly dwelling would be perfect for disposing of Mattie and Lucinda and converting his new woman, whenever he happened to find her, to the ANVIL lifestyle. He didn't know where this new woman hid from him, but already sensed her and knew that only a matter of a

225

very short time stood between them until she belonged to him alone. When he thought about her, everything stood still.

"You alright, Mr. Slade?" asked the driver.

"Ah. . . ." Slade cleared his throat. "Ah, yes. Yes, I am wonderful. Thank you," he said to assure the man. He grabbed the moment to turn and scoot away from the hole. He trooped straight out to the Humvee. The driver let him in, secured the gate and roared off toward the runway. Slade never looked back, he simply crawled on the airplane and they lifted and flew toward California.

He knew how problem solving would keep his mind move away from his glimpse over the edge. He thought about the mess in San Francisco and Marin County. Never had ANVIL faced glitches like these. Sure, all businesses weave in and out of a myriad of problems continually; to think that they would not amounted to folly. Challenges, the continual arising of challenges, kept business invigorating. Without them, the monotony of the day-to-day would become dreadfully boring in a very short time. Slade forced his mind to zero in on what needed to be done.

This series of events held potential for serious damage to all of his most consuming ambitions and the devastation come down quickly. What problems did ANVIL face? What triggered them? And what caused new headaches to continue to be unleashed? Was a relationship with the government a huge error? No, they were as crooked as anyone on the earth, so they had millions of Achilles' heels. How could he put an end to the mess quickly, quietly and terminally?

Slade loved lists and prided himself in his agility and competence in whipping them out. He composed them all the time, but he had no need to write them down. His brilliance amazed him. He allowed his mind to drift and roam through every threat, and sort out what needed to happen in order to bring the threats to an end immediately. He grabbed a cellphone.

"Yeah. Right. Buy another surveillance team for ANVIL's special ops group. Use them to watch those NSA freaks. Steal the new hires away from China, Israel, anywhere. Offer salaries ten times what they would get from working for their government." They would terminate both the ANVIL and the government's surveillance and special ops elimination teams that had failed him.

Yes, he could solve his problems, no sweat. He would use Eastern Europeans who were completely without mercy. If they proved themselves, he would send them to Temecula for full ANVIL boot camp. Otherwise, he would give them a million dollar down payment on a faux mission in Hong Kong, use a Cambodian crew to dispose of them and be sure to get his cash back. He would find the best teams available on the planet.

Slade exhaled, leaned back in his seat and gazed out the window.

"Tell Maxwell to get four choppers, scour the coast from the Golden Gate to LA," he said into the phone. "Yeah, Noah said the name is *dead latitudes*. When he finds the thing, he must send in the whirlies and inflatables and capture everything with an overwhelming force. No errors will be tolerated. No excuses. Then they must tow it with a powerboat and get it hidden in Wilmington. Tear it apart for clues to the whereabouts of the guy in the truck."

Slade started smiling as he beheld the lovely blue skies and sensed his closeness to his maker.

"Yeah, after the new teams terminate our current squads, they are to destroy the Animalfund building, Hayes' house, and all evidence the bureaucrats have."

The sky, the earth, his wonderful jet airplane—his *jet* airplane—he observed it all as he scrunched down in the luxurious chair and knew that everything was alright.

"And Buster, I want you to hand select a crew from our boys down in Temecula. They are to go to Sausalito, on Bridgeway, and scour the entire area for evidence the cops missed. Yeah, disguise them as surveyors. No, I can't talk now. Okay. Later."

Slade hung up. His rest had been tenuous ever since they had started after the tree huggers. Since the situation in Marin arose, he had not really rested at all. But launching this new approach made him relax. Dozing off on the Gulfstream, his slumber was jittery, putting him on edge rather than enfolding him into calm. As sleep finally took over, his breath leveled out and his body sunk further into the plush seat. But as he fully relinquished to the great calm, he began to sweat again.

The vision appeared as a huge timber rattler, darker than the diamondbacks, that crawled across the bottom of his reptile breeding pit. He sensed he laid spread out flat on his back. He couldn't tell for sure, and worse, he had no idea of his actual location. Suspicion that he rested prone in the middle of the pit made Slade very tense, even in the middle of what should have been a soothing slumber.

Coiling before his eyes was the great reptile. He couldn't tell where the snake had perched itself. It appeared to be suspended in the air directly in front of his vision, crawling in place. Then it stopped, looked straight at him and coiled very quickly. Behind it, the weather-beaten face of a man appeared. He had long, coal-black hair with a big smile and a diagonally chipped front tooth. He stood next to the snake and looked straight into Slade's eyes. The rattle started growing in size and volume until it was as big as a pineapple. The noise deafened him.

Slade awoke and jumped right out of the seat, rushing toward the toilets. He stopped at the door and rested his head against it. He walked back to his seat and a sense of falling grabbed him. He steadied himself for a few moments, and then lashed out at the leather armrest with his foot, in frustration. He staggered around the room striking anything near him, ripping pillows open and kicking furniture.

The pilot announced that they would be landing in Long Beach in about fifteen minutes. With a tremendous effort, Slade managed to rein in his fear and anger. A plain rental car awaited him on the tarmac. He drove around to public parking and walked through the art deco airport.

He had talked with Desi Sandoval three times. A good deal of risk would rear up if he needed to dispose of yet another government employee, but Slade now saw that taking ANVIL to its full potential and following the Lord's commandments completely, would require shifting to a new paradigm. Complete diligence was required of him. If Sandoval screwed up, he would be terminated, but things looked promising. The information from inside would be priceless.

Slade sensed great promise for the meeting. He intuited that Des Sandoval had fallen from the pathetic stance of the optimist and seen how useless governments are. Des now understood God only put other creatures here for service to mankind. Slade knew that Des would serve ANVIL well because of the extra twenty thousand dollars he received each month on top of his Department of the Interior salary and benefits. The money would make him a loyal servant for several years. Then Mr. Sandoval could experience an unfortunate mishap in the viper pit. Oops.

Slade walked into the restaurant and recognized his man right off the bat. Des spotted him too. They shook hands and sat right down, looking around for observers before they plowed into business after a very brief introduction.

"Well, for sure, Mr. Sandoval, a person only has one life, and we must take care of ourselves. How can we do good for others if we ourselves are not strong? We will only sink the boat if we can't row our own."

"Yes. Well put, Mr. Slade."

"May I call you Des?"

"Sure, what should I call you?"

"Brother Slade will be fine. I suggest we get right down to business. Wild animals are no different than cattle or hogs; the Good Lord put them here for the use of his chosen children."

"Right, Brother Slade. A hog is an animal too."

"Precisely. And, as you must well know, a robust global economy is to be gleaned from the creatures in the forests. The bleeding hearts do not understand reality. They go down to the market and buy a steak and don't ever complain about the deaths of steers. Liberals don't make sense. ANVIL uses the forests to raise wild animals as livestock. Livestock is livestock is livestock. We raise free-range critters, tend to the inventory and harvest with care, just like an organic farmer with free-range chickens. We are developing large ranches where we raise the animals as stock for outdoorsmen to hunt and feel like real men."

"Right, Brother Slade. The do-gooders need to get a toehold on reality."

"Exactly. We don't want to hurt anyone either; we are very careful with animal husbandry, but God has commanded that planet Earth is for the humans. We are merely shepherds."

"So how can I be of use to you, Brother Slade?"

"You can join us in service. I am prepared to give you specific directions for shifting an account in Grand Cayman over to your own name. It now has twenty thousand dollars in it and will receive that amount each month for the next five years, at which time we can renew, and raise your salary."

Des Sandoval had to strain to keep his composure when he heard this fabulous information.

"In exchange, you will begin to make a list of how you can supply us with inventory from your department's stings and special ops. You will also supply us with pertinent information that you are aware of and make your list. Then, we will pursue your leads. You will receive a ten percent finder's fee for these deals. You will also inform us of any

230

sting and other special ops that could affect ANVIL. It's that simple."

They closed with a handshake and Des felt a tinge of sickness raise its head through the amazing thought that he now had a staggering cash flow. He had a number in Los Angeles that he would call from a safe cell that Slade gave him, along with the instructions to tweak his new account in the Caymans. He had his own offshore account. He couldn't believe it.

Slade drove the nondescript car around the block on Broadway in Long Beach, giving Des plenty of time to take off. He went back in the restaurant and there was Neeley, who had assured Slade that he couldn't miss him.

The man was right; Slade's intuition guided him straight to Neeley though he had never seen him before. All of Southern California felt like summer in the middle of winter. Slade prayed that global warming would not hurt ANVIL's wildlife cash flow. He didn't see how it could harm arms dealing. Wouldn't people begin to fight even more?

The restaurant was open to the wonderful sea breezes and Neeley already had a table. He was immaculately dressed and people turned their heads for second glances at this debonair gentleman. His lightweight, teal, wool suit fit to perfection and his lavender, baby-soft silk, Fabergé tie stood out handsomely without being gaudy. His onyx eyes looked straight into Slade's, calmly. A waiter appeared smoothly and both men ordered Manhattans.

"This is indeed an honor, Mr. Slade."

"Yes, absolutely, Mr. Neeley. The Lord works in wondrous ways."

"So true, Mr. Slade, so true. May I call you Jet?"

"Please do."

"Call me Paul."

"Ah, a powerful name. Straight from scripture."

"Well, power comes from follow-through, but the name is straight from the good book thanks to my dear departed mother."

The waiter came right back with the drinks.

"Follow-through. I see that you are also a man of knowledge," said Slade, smiling.

"Hey, Jet, let's not get carried away. I'm just an ordinary guy trying to make a couple bucks."

"Ah, and a sense of humility-based humor. Man's two finest attributes, humor and wisdom, in that order."

"You appear to be a philosopher as well as a man of the cloth and a business man."

"Why, what a generous thing to say, Paul."

Neeley lifted his glass. "To long-term business relationships between men of like minds."

"Why yes. Yes, indeed. To like minds."

They toasted.

"So how are we with the general business plan?"

"Things couldn't be better. We are now finished with this Free Range group of Mr. Hayes', and your men have now had their first inventory training."

"My boys were carping about being out in the woods, but they'll be okay. I met with Hayes, but he's just a pissy asshole. I took him into custody, but some girl broke in and freed him from one of my warehouses in China Basin," said Neeley.

"What are you talking about? When did you meet with him?"

"I met with him over at Tosca in North Beach on Sunday night."

"At what time was this meeting?"

"At midnight. I planned to make him a deal so he would join us. Having a super-rich enviro-nik on our team would offer us a great many opportunities. The snafu was that the guy is an asshole. I planned to hold him until you and I discussed the situation, but the girl broke him loose."

Slade's face turned red with rage. He choked up in a fit of coughing, then tried to clear his throat with his drink. He snapped his fingers for the waiter who was only a table away. "Yes, bring me another cocktail and make it snappy," he demanded.

"What's wrong Jet?"

Slade grabbed his water.

"We terminated Jess Hayes at approximately seven-thirty on Sunday evening."

SEVENTEEN

"They're dining luxuriously beside the sea," said Jenny as she got in the truck.

Billy took off through the parking lot and back along the route Neeley had followed to the warehouse. He moved through downtown San Pedro fast.

"Out on the patio by the boats?"

"Roger that."

"Were you military?"

"No," said Jenny. "Where are you going?"

"Back to the warehouse."

"Billy, the whole place will be swarming with cops. Look over there," she said, pointing to the horizon as they swept around the harbor. "Those choppers are after the guys that shot at us. They shot at a black and white too."

"I'll drop you with Harlan, but I have to know what's in there."

Jenny said nothing. She watched the helicopters and the searchlights as Bill flew north. He slipped back along the route Neeley took when they returned to the hotel.

A couple of forlorn mercury vapor lamps mounted on the sides of the building flooded parts of the yard with yellowish light, but the majority of the parking lot rested in threatening shadow. Cop cars sped through the neighborhood. Billy pulled the truck through the lot and around behind the warehouse, away from the street. He eased right up to the fence.

He took the flashlight from the glove box and fished out some surgical gloves. He stuck the pistol in the back of his waistband and Jenny followed suit. They slid out of the truck and Billy pulled the back of the seat forward to grab a quilted mover's blanket. They jumped into the bed of the pickup and Billy flung the blanket over the razor wire. Stepping up onto the roof of the cab, they used the moving pad for a footing and launched over onto a stack of big shipping crates. Jumping to the ground, they dog-trotted for the cover of dark, near the rear of the building. Old crates stood in stacks all around the property like at the yard up in San Francisco. They shot right in behind a pile standing next to the wall.

The sound of the choppers and screeching cop cars flooded the whole neighborhood. Jenny peeled some packing labels off the crates fast, and they shot straight over to a dark area, moving in the shadow of the building.

The thick electric mast that dropped from the weather head for electric power started a few feet above the roof and snaked down the wall to the breaker box. Metal brackets resting on wooden blocks secured the pipe to the concrete block building. The space created by the boards left enough room for them to get their hands around the cool steel and shimmy up to a narrow ledge.

Jenny crawled right up the pipe behind Billy and paused. He moved along the ledge, trying to open the transom windows. None of them budged. He handed her the flashlight, slipped the pistol out of his waistband and knocked a hole in the glass above the lock, expecting an alarm to wail.

They had not seen any tape for warning systems on the windows or any kind of box, nor a bell or transformer anywhere on the exterior. But that didn't mean the inside of the warehouse was clean from other devices that could detect them.

After dropping to the concrete floor, they crept through the building fast. They expected a motion sensor to cut loose at any moment. But all remained still. A bit of light came through the windows, otherwise the building remained dark. Their hearts pumped hard. Were a couple of Neeley's men stationed in corners of the building?

Shipping cartons in neat stacks filled the floor. A light fork truck rested silently in an open area near the doors to the rest of the warehouse. They moved silently even though it began to appear no one else lurked in the building. Billy turned the light on and off several times for a few short-lived beams. It appeared that the room served as a receiving station for unloading all the crates they had seen in the yard at both facilities. Across from them, a pair of double wooden doors provided an opening into the larger area of the structure.

Billy stepped out from a pile of crates with the pistol and the flashlight in front of him, and a solid thud on a crate resounded in the dark. He pivoted, drawing aim at the sound with his pistol, and froze. Jenny stood by his side.

They scanned the room for something correspondent with the sound. After an extended silence, Jenny elbowed him lightly and strained to squeeze back laughter. She pointed up at the transoms. The silhouette of a gargantuan wharf rat scurried across the ledge a few feet below where the noise had sounded.

They opened the doors and, not ten feet into the main room, an aluminum-faced door with a commercial refrigerator handle on it spanned an entire wall. Billy tugged it open and flipped on a light switch.

The scene caught them off guard. They both groaned. The whole ceiling was hung with beef carcasses. The dull odor of bled-beef suspended everything in their minds. They paused for a moment to get their bearings, and then pushed through the endless slabs of rib and flesh.

"Jesus, I haven't been in a packing house for a long time—my uncle, Red Clayton, used to wire them. He took me into some when I was a boy and I understood why my grandmother was a vegetarian."

"Yeah. I'm going to a Chinese joint for tofu," said Jenny.

236

"What business are these guys in, anyway? Are these beef sides or some exotic antelope they brought over in a container?"

Jenny checked him out and broke into one of those deep laughs. "Will you please help me understand why it says 'Lung Fat Trading Company—The Mystery of the Orient at Your Command' out there?"

"Maybe the carcasses are some rare Asian buffalo, an herbivore in complete control of its chi, with some kind of animal realm enlightenment. And the buffalo pass the chi on to the creatures feeding on them. You know, big cat chi and all."

She laughed again and elbowed him. "Don't be a jerk. Neeley must be in the meat business; it's a perfect fit for some creep selling bear parts."

"Disgusting," he said.

"Wonder how many more veggie-types there would be if we had to butcher in the backyard instead of buying cello-packs?"

"Watching some guy pop the cow on the head with a sledge hammer would create a lot of vegetarians."

"Oh come on, Billy. That's grotesque."

"What isn't?"

As they pushed on, working through the solid hunks of bone and muscle. They found another door on the back wall. Billy pushed the flat door handle with his palm and they walked into the next room.

Neither of them could have begun to expect the hideous scene that unfolded as they passed into the other side of the meat locker and through the door. It felt like some macabre waltz they were performing with all the butchered bodies hanging from sharp meat hooks. It was as if the scene had been set up purposely as a preface for the grotesque canvas about to spread out before them.

Billy and Jenny's bodies moved in perfect harmony and the noises coming from them filled the room. First they gasped in unison and their exhales turned into a pair of soft moans.

The sounds intoned that deep, ancient disillusionment that overwhelms someone when they discover how disgusting the human race really can be.

They both thought of Neeley's burlap bags. Until now, they hadn't given the contents of the bags much thought. What had lodged in their minds amounted to a cartoon image from a bang-bang shoot-shoot movie. Neeley, Leonardo and the other men looked like plain old sleazebags. Until that moment, Billy and Jenny had no idea what depth their potential for evil amounted to.

They had expected that in the burlap bags they would find some animal parts along with cocaine, heroin, and maybe money. Simple things. The bags were large enough to contain a good-sized stash of cocaine or heroin, or maybe methamphetamine. They had no preparation for the true perversion.

They both stood there numb. The sodium-vapor lamps outside the building cast a sickly yellow glow through the windows. They could hear their breaths moving deeply—in and out, in and out.

"Oh my god," said Jenny, taking Billy's arm.

Everywhere the eye fell there was a heart-rendering trail of murder. On one lone oak school desk sat what appeared to be the bags Neeley's boys unloaded the night before. All over the rest of the room were the remains of beasts and fowl: ghostly stuffed herons, great horned owls, three or four types of eagles including the national bird of the United States. There were piles of animal skins with the heads in place: tigers, leopards, raccoons, otters.

Tables made of smoked, three-quarter-inch plate glass with the massive round feet of pachyderms for bases were stacked on one another and interspersed throughout the ghastly collection. The pelts of Siberian and Bengal tigers, heaps of black bear and grizzly feet, hides of Tibetan antelope were placed in random piles atop the crates. And skulls of all sizes—some appeared to be human—sat here and there atop the collection. There were several bags and boxes that must have held bladders and tiger penises.

The mounted heads of endangered beasts hung from the walls. Their empty eyes all seemed to rivet on Billy and Jenny. Billy swept the room with the flashlight, his heart beating like crazy. Fifteen cages hung from hooks in the ceiling. Billy lifted the cover of one and a magnificent scarlet macaw gazed at him lazily, as if it had been sedated. He dropped the cover in an emotion-crazed attempt to keep the exhausted creature from viewing the carnage around it.

Zombie-like, Jenny stared at the piles of pelts and the hides of reptiles and mammals. Billy had to sit down at the chair behind the desk and let the pistol flop down onto the wooden top. As Jenny took hold of the edge of the desktop, her stomach started heaving. She retched everything out of her body and then began to cry.

A powerful urge to take the parrots to their hotel room, and then buy ten gallons of gas to raze the warehouse and at least give the dead creatures, and those that were only present as severed parts of their bodies, the dignity of cremation roared over Billy. He took some paper towels off a pile on the desk, got up and led Jenny toward a door in the rear corner of the building. The sink still worked in the old bathroom and he put an arm around her as he helped her clean up. She melted against him.

"We've got to get a grip," he said.

"What we've got to get a grip on are these live birds."

With his arm around her, Billy guided her over to the chair. She began to shake with rage. He massaged her shoulders deeply at the pressure points until she quit shaking. Then he began to examine the bags and cartons. Still and blank, Jenny watched as he opened a few with his pocketknife. Inside rested more neatly packed piles of those same dried sack-looking bladders they found in the basement at Jess' house, as well as other organs and other animal parts he didn't recognize.

"What is this stuff?" asked Billy, pointing.

"Organs—bladders, hearts, kidneys, anything they can make a buck from," said Jenny in a terse voice as she rose to her feet. Her tears had dried and now she sounded menacing.

239

But she sat back down in the chair because her knees felt weak. She straightened her spine, sitting up with her hands out on the old desktop. She did ten rapid tiger breaths.

"We have to leave," said Billy.

As Jenny stood, her hands brushed a business card tucked neatly in the corner of the desktop blotter. "We ought to dig into those file boxes and in the desk," she said, slipping the card into her pocket.

Some of the large cages with the tropical birds and draped with mover's blankets, sat on the file cabinets. Billy couldn't bear lifting the covers to look at whatever rested inside. He could imagine their penetrating eyes haunting him forever. He went through the file cabinets while Jenny dug into the desk.

"Nothing here except this card," she said, putting the paper in her pocket.

"Yeah the cabinets are all empty too."

"Let's get away from here," she said. "We've got details to straighten out with Harlan. We have to get to the bottom of this pronto. We'll break through the front and load the cages."

"We can't tip them off."

"What?"

"We can't break anything or take the birds."

"Whoa. Wait a minute. How can you see these creatures in this situation and even think such a fucked up thing? Of course we have to take the birds."

"Jenny, I want to take them too, but this is much bigger than our emotions. The lives of so many creatures are at stake. We have to cut the loses for them all."

"I can't believe you're saying this, Billy."

"Jenny! Trust me. We have already discovered a mountain of information. And we've done more than the cops would do in a year. We can't stop now. We are talking about Jess' murderers and, obviously, they are harvesting thousands of wild animals every day. The macaws will make it but these bears and tigers and lions—these freaks are going to exterminate them all."

"No, Billy. Don't patronize me. I'm sick of standing by. Don't stand around like a replaceable, grid-head male. Get with the program." She didn't even look back, just fled with two of the cages.

She ran through the putrid bulwark of beef, and outside to the fence. She had to stretch up and across the blanket to set the cages onto the roof of the truck. Then she pulled herself over the padded razor wire and onto the cab of the truck. She didn't take time to retrieve the blanket. She jumped to the ground with a cage in each hand. She placed the cages on the dirt over to the side of the gate and out of the way. Then, before the car door slammed, she humped the truck into motion.

Billy stood there locked in a hypnotic gaze, watching Jenny run away from him. Even though he knew it was a mistake, he grabbed four of the huge cages. Hugging two under his arms and carrying the others with his hands, he tanked through the sides of beef like the Incredible Hulk.

The truck seemed to roll of its own volition. Big parts of Jenny seemed missing. She understood that humans were the most horrid creatures on earth; they were so adroit, so cunning, and so clever with their opposable thumbs, but so maladroit at practicing what they preach. She knew that Homo sapiens came with an organic computer that burned at fantastic clock speeds when sorting data. And, she saw, from the burst of a major epiphany, that the species Homo sapiens drifted haplessly through existence, thoroughly bereft of mental acuity and of decency. The human species sat perilously close to destroying itself.

She ripped the truck out into the street, wheeled around, and fishtailed as she jammed the gas to the firewall. She never let up as she plowed through the gates and crashed through the front doors.

Billy put his cages in the bed, scooped up the two she'd left near the gate and dug behind the seat for bungee cords. They inspected the great, beautifully plumed macaws: red fronts, blue and gold feathers. The birds were snugged in their steel cages against the rails of the truck bed.

Jenny quickly climbed into the passenger seat. Billy turned the truck around, and then eased back out to the street.

EIGHTEEN

So muddled with emotions they couldn't talk, Billy and Jenny stared at the road.

Numbly, Jenny took out the business card she found on the blotter. Looking down at the words she mumbled, "We've got to touch base with Harlan and go check out this ANVIL place in Anaheim."

"What do you think they do?"

"The American National Vigilance and Intelligence League. They seem like Nazis or Communist block parties. They probably started in the south and still lynch African Americans. Got to be a big boss somewhere but it's not Neeley," said Jenny.

"Right, they're too much like Larry, Curly and Moe to be the grand dragon or the commander in chief or *führer* or whatever."

Jenny managed tepid laughter. "An astute observation, Holmes. As always."

"Why, thank you, Miss Marple. I had no idea you were one to lavish others with compliments."

"You ain't seen nothin' yet, big guy. Have you checked out this truck lately?"

"Yeah and we're planning to drive behind the Orange Curtain among Orange County cops." They both laughed.

Their voices began to draw them back into reality. They forgot about the dangers in the neighborhood: Neeley, smoked glass cars, choppers, cops. They returned from the immediate revulsion of the warehouse but still sat locked in hypnotic gazes.

The pickup seemed to drive itself. It seemed to Jenny and Billy as if it was floating. Billy recognized how parts of his and Jenny's humanity had been stolen in that building. He felt the same void resultant of seeing with absolute clarity, the harsh understanding wise men surely experience every day. He'd encountered this revelation twice before— once when surveying the burning oil wells during the Gulf War, and then when he saw that all he had left after breaking the trillion dollar barrier was more of the same empty pursuits of business deals.

They hurried away from Lung Fat Trading Company and turned onto another street. As he rounded the corner, Billy spotted an old pickup following them with the lights off. In the glaze from the street lamp, he distinguished two burly men sitting in the cab. They didn't appear to be city slickers, like Neeley's men. Billy hoped they were simply a couple of yahoos out prowling around the local honky-tonks, too well lit by longneck beers to remember to turn on their headlights.

Billy's hopes were not well founded. They did finally turn the headlamps on, but the truck still tailed them. Billy drove slowly, and the driver kept back at some distance. From the dull aura of the streetlights he could make out their brimmed caps, the baseball style displaying logos for earth-moving equipment, tractor-trailer manufacturers or guns on the brow. He couldn't tell which. They wore old wool jackets, a costume Billy couldn't imagine on Neeley's men. Maybe they worked here as warehousemen and were standing members of the Longshoreman's Union.

But they were definitely following the truck. Billy's gut told him that he and Jenny had been seen prowling in the building. He couldn't believe Neeley would want random locals to know about the inventory. Few normal human beings would find forgiveness for such a gristly mess. They had not seen any workers in action at Lung Fat even when he

243

and Jenny followed Neeley's Chrysler. There had been no butchers, truckers, loading crew, guards, no one. Who rode behind them?

Billy watched the mirror. He followed the dingy, sulfurous streets; the Nazi-like fences enclosed entire city blocks, winding around buildings. There was a creepy emptiness. Turning right, then taking the next left and sliding back out onto the busy streets and off onto slower dark avenues, Billy gave the men every opportunity to turn in the opposite direction. But the truck remained steady, always tailing at a slow, even keel.

"What the hell are you doing?" Jenny asked. "We need to go find Harlan and tell him about that horror show."

"Sneak a look in your mirror. Two cracker-looking guys are tailing us."

Billy kept weaving. He glided casually through several neighborhoods, ducked along alleys, and every time he got near the end of a stretch of roadway, the vehicle in his rearview mirror came around the corner at the same studied pace.

They rode along in silence all the way across town, and the vehicle still followed. Finally, as Jenny leaned back and rubbed her eyes, Billy snapped. He hit the gas and spun onto Avalon Boulevard. The choppers still wove through the neighborhood south of them, and sirens wailed in spurts, then died off. Billy flew south heedless of the cops' search for the low-slung car and the occupants who shot at them. He had come to what his mother referred to as the William-Boils-Over Event, which the family had experienced throughout his life. Nothing stopped him when he got this worked up and the needle swept off the gauge.

He sensed the foul current of power; someone more supercharged than Neeley propelled the carnage. Like an iceberg, Neeley only represented a minuscule portion of the massive organization. What kind of sordid group ran the American National Vigilance and Intelligence League? A multi-national corporation? Jess' body cut up on his living room floor resulted from the part of the iceberg lurking below the waterline; the ballast was enough to sink the Titanic.

The same foul people had stripped away all human decency and made those animal remains in the warehouse into cold, calculated product. How many warehouses in how many ports hid the lopped off parts of wild creatures?

Fins, hoofs and paws: sanctified elements that had once amounted to a real, gorgeous, living creature. Now the components equated nothing more than vapid numbers on a spreadsheet, a meaningless inventory. Nothing but a mountain of cash, stirring up the same macabre chill he had every time he rode a chopper over the oil wells Saddam had lit on fire during Desert Storm.

Sides were not the issue—the US or Saddam—all governments revolved around maintaining the cash flow of the super wealthy. Politicians, cops, preachers, military, corporate honchos: the working stiffs always lay under the jackboots of these cash mongers. And no one cared if all the mammals disappeared from the wild. The riddance would simply open up more natural resources for harvesting.

At the end of Avalon, Billy whipped a left through the stop sign back onto Harry Bridges. He hit 50 miles-per-hour and lurched right through a six-foot-deep drainage ditch. He whirled sideways and ripped the truck up the other bank. He cut the wheel again and they cruised parallel to the track on the railhead easement. They drove along the gravel without lights.

Billy turned between two concrete loading platforms, crossed the track and pulled in behind a block wall. They jumped out, grabbed their pistols, ran hard, hit the earth up against a hillock and slid into the cover of another platform. They checked their pistols and they waited. Everything seemed distant and surreal.

The followers were nowhere to be seen. All of the streets appeared empty. Billy raised himself and surveyed the surroundings. Nothing stirred. He grabbed Jenny's arm, hopped up on the concrete loading platform and moved to an area where all nearby automobiles could be observed. The two men appeared behind them as if they had melted right out of the night.

"Drop your weapons."

The muzzle in Billy's ribs wasn't from a rifle; the bore was much too big. He knew .12 gauge shotguns covered them both. Jenny looked at Billy and followed suit as he threw his Desert Eagle to the dust.

"Ok, straighten up and come with us."

Billy and Jenny did as the men commanded, but as they walked toward Billy's truck, Jenny threw a turning back kick. The smaller man grunted with pain, still holding his .12 gauge. Billy elbowed the barrel out of his ribs and tried to take the big man. It was no use whatsoever; the man stood steady and unmoving like concrete. He brought the butt of the riot gun down on Billy's bad lip and the wound spurted. He clobbered Billy again on the head fast and pushed him down with the shotgun.

With his one free hand, the other man grabbed Jenny's leg when she tried a front kick. He decked her like he was punching a side of beef. *Definitely not city slickers*, thought Billy. They held their ground like they were tree stumps. They must have been men who lived outdoors among the elements and who dealt with things much more taxing than a martial arts expert.

The big man dropped his shotgun, grabbed a piece of rawhide out of a pocket and wrapped their necks together, as if he was bulldogging a steer. He pulled the strip so tight that Billy and Jenny were gagging and losing their breath. Then the man shoved them down onto the ground. The smaller man stood over them with his riot gun. The big one picked his weapon up and slid the action real quick, chambering a shell.

A strong wave of déjà vu swept over Billy. It all clicked into place in his mind; these two had also been watching Neeley's bunch at the entry to the Harbor Hilton. They had shaved and cleaned up, but they still wore the same jackets and gave off the law enforcement vibe. The big man still appeared to be generous of spirit, and the young, flashy one still looked arrogant.

"You two had better relax or somebody's gonna get hurt."

"What kind of trailer trash are you? If rape's your game, let's get going," Jenny hissed, seething. She didn't care about the rawhide around her neck, or about being tied head-to-head with Billy. Like Billy, she had slipped over the edge. Too many adversarial events cause some people to give up and slither into shadows of their former selves. Others become cemented in place and forget their intent. But Billy and Jenny clicked into their lock-and-load mindsets.

"Lady, get a muffler on it. Nobody's gonna do anything to hurt you."

The leather cut into Billy's neck. He had to hold himself back from jumping for the Eagle and dragging Jenny with him. It was a powerful handgun, but there was no way could a pistol match two .12 gauge shotguns.

"'Get a muffler on it.' Cute. That is really cute. You are a walking cliché, *and* you are obviously terrified by a woman who can kick your butt and stare you right in the eye."

Jenny sat up straight with so much force that she pulled Billy upright. Writhing with anger, she fumed at the two male lumps in front of her. Clarence and Des stared at her with their mouths hanging open.

"Maybe you can muster up the balls to tell me exactly what in the hell you want. Are you able to articulate anything?"

"We want to know what you were doing in the Lung Fat warehouse, ma'am. Do you work for Neeley?" asked Clarence.

"Neeley? Who are you? What do you know about Neeley?"

"We're law enforcement, ma'am."

"Well if you are such forthright, upstanding citizens, why didn't you approach us in a business-like manner, present your calling cards, and allow us to decide whether we wish to speak with you or bring in counsel?" Jenny barked. "The last I heard, they call this place a free country."

"Jeez, ma'am. For crying out loud, we didn't mean to scare you. Look it, I'm Clarence Henshaw and this is Desi Sandoval."

"Well big freakin' deal! Clarence and Desi, the rapists."

"Aw, come on, don't say the R-word. Just simmer down. You don't seem like a criminal to me. We're Special Projects Officers for the United States Fish and Wildlife Service."

Clarence pulled the leather case that held his badge out of his shirt pocket, flipped it open and handed it to Jenny.

"How am I supposed to know that this is real? Any old, fat, hamburger-head like you could have this made downtown in LA in two hours."

"Here's mine," said Des, pulling his shield out.

"Ok, so why do you have us out here trapped in a rail yard, ready to molest me and shoot my friend? Why aren't we in some boring, little, antiseptic, federal office, being offered some bland, bureaucratic coffee in Styrofoam cups?"

"Well, to tell you the truth, ma'am, Fish and Wildlife doesn't have much money for offices and coffee and luxuries— that type of thing," said Clarence. "Des and I had to buy our last set of tires out of our own pockets. Got 'em at Sears."

Billy sensed Jenny starting to cool down. It was as if their words were a breeze blowing in off the ocean.

"Okay, Mr. Henshaw. I'm getting the idea that I'm not going to be sexually assaulted right here, but you're still coming down our throats with two weapons identical to the one that just murdered our very close friend."

"Murdered your close friend?" Clarence questioned.

"It's a long story."

Clarence was transfixed by Jenny's extraordinary eyes riveted on his own. Their .12 gauges were still pointed at her and Billy. Clarence moved his weapon from high ready to the cradle-carry position, and elbowed Des, who followed suit.

"We've had a tail on bear poachers up in Washington state who are connected to that warehouse, ma'am. Never fired our weapons. We did stop in Marin County, but the only murder we got near was that of a mother bear. We were out in the boonies—out by Nicasio on a stakeout."

Both Billy and Jenny perceived that these two men were exactly what they claimed. The smaller one, Desi Sandoval, appeared to be a bit shifty, but Jenny warmed toward the big guy. He probably had a wife and two towhead kids at home. He wound his way along, trying to live a decent family life, in spite of all the gruesome stuff he must have seen all the time. His voice shot up an octave every time Jenny spewed out anything related to rape.

"Ok, so maybe you're not gonna turn us into cadavers on a deserted railroad spur, but what do you want?" asked Jenny, still in no mood to back down.

"We just want to get some ID and find out what you were doing in the warehouse, and what you are doing with these endangered species, and why your vehicle is full of bullet holes, ma'am," said Clarence.

"The macaws are on their way to our lawyer. We broke into the warehouse because some gnarly animal parts dealers kidnapped my partner and we think a group called the American National Vigilance and Intelligence League shot up Billy's truck," she told them.

"What type vehicle were they in, ma'am?" asked Clarence.

"Those new Chryslers. The Darth Vader cars, and some were in Humvees," said Billy.

"Chrysler 300s, and Hummers or Humvees?" asked Des.

"Humvees," said Billy.

"What do these guys look like?" asked Des.

"The Chrysler gang are right out of *The Godfather*, and the Humvee pair wore SWAT gear."

Des looked at Clarence. "Maybe the same bunch we had staked?" Looking back to Billy, Des asked, "Did you get close to them?"

Billy pouted his lip so the men could see his wound. "They opened it up, and like a good little federal employee, you did it again," he said, spitting blood.

"Good lord. You need to get some stitches," said Clarence.

"No time. They leave a pretty wide trail, but things could dry up any minute. You must know all about moving fast on a fresh trail."

"Of course we do. No time to stop."

"Where did you hear about ANVIL?" asked Des.

"I found a business card in the warehouse," said Jenny.

"We're gonna have to tape you and get a full statement."

"Fine," said Jenny. "But the first thing anybody's going to do is take care of these parrots. You just come along like good little fed-heads and you will be allowed to grill us in front of counsel."

NINETEEN

In front of the Harbor Crowne Plaza Hotel near Los Angeles Harbor's ship channel in San Pedro, Clarence and Des lifted the birdcages out of the bed of Billy's Dodge. Jenny gave several of the valets crisp hundred-dollar bills. They grabbed birds and the parking attendants took the trucks. The drivers who walked over to Billy's pickup ran their fingers over the bullet holes furtively then looked up at Billy and Jenny in awe.

Heading across the lobby for the elevators, Des and Clarence fell back to talk.

Billy turned to at Jenny and grinned. "You must be hungry?"

"God! Don't get too close. I might start gnawing on your arm. You want another steak?"

"I thought the warehouse threw you for a loop and turned you veggie."

"Salmon?"

"They are truly majestic when they jump up the rocks."

"Billy." She slugged him. "What do vegetarians eat? This place isn't Chinese; I doubt the chef has any tofu in the kitchen."

"My guess is that veggies eat veggies."

"Thank you, Mr. Clayton. I'll order for both of us from my room. We should be served by the time we step out of the shower."

Still carrying the big cages, they all went straight to the suite Harlan had taken as an office for the duration of the operation.

When they entered, Angel helped them find a place to put the birds. Harlan's IT staff had decked the headquarters out as a war room: monitors, snoop devices, video

251

production set up, cameras, tape recorders, banks of CPUs, a big cardboard box full of cell phones, white boards, big writing pads on easels, cases of Starbucks espressos and bottles of water in a cooler chest, a case of Wild Turkey. The electronics clicked, beeped and flickered.

Harlan stood at a monitor. "Nasty," he said. "Don't have any feeling for the bears at all; this is perfect jury material. The men just hack off the animal's paws with a chainsaw and cut out the bladder. Don't even check to see if the bear is still alive."

"You don't even have a clue, Harlan," said Jenny.

"Well, I've never been much of a yogurt head, but Billy's mom is really into this stuff. She's been talking about ecology since Rachel Carson wrote book about the virgins and the spring water."

Jenny laughed then said, "*Silent Spring.*"

"Right, there you go," he said.

"Right. So who are these gentlemen?" asked Harlan, helping situate the cages before sizing up Clarence and Des. Jenny made introductions all around. Harlan beamed, pleased to have members of the Department of the Interior on board with their mission.

"What's all this stuff?" he asked as everyone sat their cages down. Jenny pulled the cover up on a majestic Hyacinth Macaw.

"WHERE THE FUCK'S MY LAWYER? I REQUEST COUNSEL IMMEDIATELY!" squawked the giant bird in an unbelievably loud, hoarse voice. One of its big eyes fixed on them.

"Damn! I like this guy already," said Harlan. "Had to have belonged to Bill Gates."

Everyone in the room broke into deep laughter.

Billy called the desk and checked Clarence and Des into their rooms. Jenny ordered food and the four retired to their

252

suites for a shower. Within the hour, they all rendezvoused in the office room. Clarence and Des came in with their hair slicked back. In their new quarters, they had taken damp towels to their clothes, wiping some of the dust off as they stared out over the immense view of Los Angeles Harbor. While everyone chatted about the case, the food arrived along with six pots of coffee.

"Funny. Jenny's buying us a steak," said Clarence. "This case is well funded. Came down as a special op, straight from Senator Hicks' bear committee. They may actually be supplying us with enough cash to get things done."

"I spearheaded the report from Animalfund," said Jenny.

"You?" questioned Des.

"But we thought it was Jess Hayes," said Clarence.

"I worked on—" Jenny broke into tears.

Harlan put an arm around her. "I am so sorry, Jenny."

Everyone stared at the big, gruff man, amazed at his compassion and gracious demeanor.

"Well now we're all working on this together. A team like this will speed things up a lot. Interior's even given us a good budget for this one," said Clarence.

"You bet. And I'll make them cough up plenty more cash. Hicks is up to his ass in the glue factory; the end of Smokey is here. I can see the headlines in *The New York Times*. A bunch of ass-kissin' little toads up on the Hill are going to become tree huggers all of a sudden," said Harlan.

"Well, in that case, I'm not picking up the tab," said Billy to Clarence. "You can bill the president, that guy's one hell of a tree hugger." They all laughed and he continued, "But I don't catch on. If Washington already has enough information to start an op, why did Hicks order Jenny's report? Wasn't it a little late for Animalfund to do massive, in-depth research?"

"No," said Clarence, "Hicks moved ahead because the end of Smokey is political death and big fat reports must be in place for politicians to look solid."

"Right, Animalfund's info will work out fine. His staff will dig through Jenny's work. Then they'll bring in the senator. And any prosecution teams will find juicy tidbits for building their case. They'll leak some scandalous facts. They'll use Jenny's info to dig deep. Every little bit of information the senatorial team and the paralegals can find will help hang the people they go after," said Harlan.

"Then they'll spill each of their fabulous efforts to save nature for the Amurkan people to the *Post* and the *Times*," said Billy.

"Perhaps you are not as asinine as I think you are, William Clayton," said Harlan.

They sat around the conference table finishing off their food and drinking coffee. Jenny was already on her second omelet.

"It looks like Hicks' snoops have found some perps. We've had these guys we staked out. They're part of this American National Vigilance and Intelligence League. The ANVIL thing Jenny found the business card for. The senator pushed through the Interior and got the file right down to us. That's why we were up there in Marin County. We have some leads like the warehouse location. Anything we pile up now is possible evidence and may lead to stuff the lawyers can use to hammer."

"Let me tell you, boys, Billy retained me for a shameful amount. He's got more money than you ever thought of having in a lifetime. I'm gonna build one hell of a case for your team. We'll kick some butt," said Harlan, and they all cracked up again.

"What happened up in Marin?" asked Angel.

"The weirdest thing we've ever seen. We're out there in the freezing coastal fog. I don't know if you've spent time in Marin County, but it's pretty rugged. This squad of

Humvees rolled in off the blacktop and shot into the woods onto a dirt road," said Des.

"You mean Hummers," said Harlan.

"No. The real thing. Humvees."

"A Humvee attacked us on Bridgeway in Sausalito and another one sat across from Jess' house. Black with plain commercial plates."

"I need those numbers, Billy. But let him finish," said Harlan.

"Right. I got a flashlight out of the Humvee too. There may be prints."

"So we got out, skedaddled down into the trees and set up some primitive sound and video. The men in plaid is what we called them. The guys in the Humvees, they're runnin' around, getting stuff out. They all wore those plaid lumber jackets. Every one of them wore those jackets, like some little pod of robots or something. The only difference was the two that seemed to be in charge wore SWAT gear and walked around with their cellphones up to their ears," said Des.

"Is your vid privileged or can I take a look?"

"They're privileged, but you seem like a tough old bird, and you're—"

"TOUGH OLD BIRD. TOUGH OLD BIRD. I DON'T WANT THE FUCKING CEO. I SEEK COUNSEL IMMEDIATELY," barked the macaw. They all broke into laughter again.

Harlan cocked his head, his eyes brightened and a warm smile broke on his face as he scrutinized the cobalt bird.

Des could barely talk. "Hey, we'll copy the whole shootin' match for you, Harlan."

"HARLAN! HARLAAAAAAAN! GET YOUR BUTT IN HERE BOY."

Clarence had to pucker up his lips to get a handle on his laughter. Once he calmed down, he continued his story.

"So the Humvee group set up a professional parting factory in the field. They're in Marin among some of the richest people in the world. Right there. A few miles from George Lucas' films. They had those big industrial floods and a carpenter's reciprocating saw with a long, fine toothed, metal cutting blade. No chain saws. These guys were real sophisticated. An operatory on wheels. Used one of those .50 caliber sniper rifles."

"Heavy equipment. Good for a thousand yards," said Angel.

"They dropped the bear with it. A sow with two cubs," said Clarence.

"Oh no," said Jenny. "They cut the cubs up?"

"No, they shot them with a tranq and caged them. But listen, they had to have come in before they flushed the sow up out of the bottoms—they had to have planted her before the event. Anyway, it was real weird. A new Chrysler, those Darth Vader-looking—"

"A Chrysler 300," interrupted Des.

"Right. Well, two of them pulled into the circle the Humvees had already made. Eight guys piled out of the Vader wagons," continued Clarence. "Four of them had riot guns. These punks were wearing two-thousand-dollar cashmere overcoats. They followed the woodchuck types down into the bottoms and flushed out the momma bear. Some sleazebag dropped her with the sniper's rifle. They took her gall bladder and paws, and then a fight broke out between the men in plaid and the overcoats. I think we can hear it on the audio file, but we had to head on down here to keep the trail hot."

"You've come to the right place, boys. *Mi casa, tu casa*," said Harlan. "If you need some electronics, we'll go online and get them here overnight."

"The overcoats are Neeley's men. He sounds like he's from the West End. Leonardo's got a Brooklyn accent, and Heiny—did you see a big, ugly blonde?" asked Billy.

256

"Yeah. Nasty."

"So what do you guys make of all this?" asked Harlan.

The room went quiet.

"The big boss was the guy setting up the bear parting. The men in plaid were his manufacturing company. His boys were training the overcoats who are going to take care of distribution," said Des.

"What's the name of the op?" asked Harlan.

"The Butcher's File."

"Jesus," said the big, horse-toothed man. "Must be some deep shit. They usually gloss over the heavy stuff. Does it have an apostrophe?"

"We call it the Butcher's File for short, but Operation Butchers Data is the real title," said Clarence.

"Right, that's the name of the senatorial report that Animalfund was commissioned to put together; the one that I have worked on for months," said Jenny.

"Like I was askin' Des up there in Marin: does that mean there's a guy named the Butcher and this stuff's about him, or that it's data they grabbed from the Butcher, or that it's data about all of the butchers?" wondered Clarence.

"Does Butchers have an apostrophe?" asked Harlan.

"That's just what I asked Des. Not on the folder, but the way we use it, it does. The Butcher's File."

"Interior must mean all the butchers," said Harlan.

"Maybe it's a freakin' type-o. The Butchers cut 'em up. Who cares about the apostrophe?" asked Des.

Everyone stopped to think.

"This file is more on the ball than most. They say the animal parts trade is global, and the US is the biggest participant," continued Des.

"It also says we are heading up the whole op."

"So more of the parts trade is covered than black bears?" asked Harlan.

"They talk about the global trade. But they want us to stick with Smokey."

"Is this ANVIL bunch global?"

"Yeah, but the politicians care about votes, not animals."

"I thought we had a lot of black bears," said Harlan. "Aren't they sort of like raccoons?"

"Too big. We brought the population back up, but those ANVIL guys in plaid can pay Bible Belt clodhoppers to go out and harvest."

"They can wipe out any population fast?" asked Harlan.

"You got that right. Business as usual."

"You start with these guys on the stakeout, build a case with a tiny budget you perceive as big funding, use some tired, low-salaried prosecutor and these ANVIL people contribute big time to everything that every judge likes. So you bust traffickers, the judges kiss their asses in typical good-old-boy crap, and the perps walk."

When Harlan got off his rant, Des laughed loud and hard along with Angel.

Clarence sniggered. "Boy you got that right. You must be a damned good lawyer."

"I REQUIRE A DAMNED GOOD LAWYER IMMEDIATELY," the extraordinarily beautiful macaw exclaimed threateningly.

"That-a-boy. You tell 'em," said Harlan, and everyone roared again.

"I'm scary. Real fuckin' scary. I like pro bono best, but I always get some rich greed-head like Billy to fork up a mountain of cash," said Harlan. "Shame the rich and rip the balls off sleazy judges. But of course, if they've got big *cahones*, they do the right thing."

"RIP THE JUDGE'S BALLS OFF."

"That's it, Blue. I use my teeth, then grill 'em. Just like Rocky Mountain oysters. Do 'em with a few tequila shooters. Me and my buddies."

"There's more to it than just animal parts," said Clarence. "Take a look at this." He threw the baggie with the strange projectile from the hunt onto the table.

"Looks like a mini drone—some kind of nano missile. Something spooks use," said Angel, looking at it closely.

"Probably that too. But this one's a shotgun shell," said Des.

"A what?" asked Harlan, and Angel handed it to him.

"We've never seen anything like it," said Clarence. "It blows a hole in half-inch plate steel."

"Who the hell are they?" asked Harlan. "Spooks? Grunts? Weapons shills? Animal part traffickers?"

"Parts and weapons," said Des. "Too much presence to be spooks. Too many. They'd be seen for sure. Gotta have something legit covering all that activity. It would be easy enough with cash from the parts trade."

"It looks like big, wild animals are outta here. Next it's humans: breakbone fever, plague, flu strains, malaria, a few earthquakes and storms," said Harlan.

"That's about right," said Des.

"You guys are correct, it should be the Butcher's File; Operation Butchers Data is a mistake," said Harlan.

"Hey, are you accusing the United States Department of the Interior of making a mistake?" questioned Des with a smirk.

"It should have an apostrophe. I can feel it all over and my hunches are always right," continued Harlan. "It's not a bunch of butchers. There's one boss over all of these guys. He's some kind of a CEO. He's not a politician, and politicians are the only other people that are psychotic with self-importance to this degree. He's got cash flow and he's also head of this ANVIL.

259

He's got to be one of those freaky patriot Bible thumpers out of a Coen brothers movie. Which means that he is totally hysterical like a Klan leader. He's got a business plan. He's a business man through and through: assembling a harvesting infrastructure, training his staff, working on distribution."

"He's the perp. Look what he's done to Jess, Nuke, Sam, the bears, *dead lats*. I'm going to help him get in touch with his conscience like Dr. Phil would," said Billy, jumping up.

"Billy Clayton, I don't want to hear any of this *Bourne Identity* crap. You have to stay here until I've got you clear with the law," said Harlan.

"Hey, we'll come with you," said Des.

"No, I'm going to move too fast."

"Billy, you've got to—"

"No. I'm the richest man in the world, and I don't even care about money. I don't have to do anything. I've got a dynamite lawyer and, funny thing, I only want to do good things. So I am free. Stone free."

"Look, I'm comin' with you, Billy," said Des.

"I don't want company, Des. No badges. Go through all this stuff. Help Harlan and Blue." Billy pointed at the big parrot, and they all broke into histrionics again.

"WHERE'S THAT DAMN LAWYER?" said Blue, scanning them with threatening eyes.

Billy strained to quit laughing and speak. "Help set up a case. I want all of these turds that killed Jess. I want their nuts in a vice forever. Then I want them to row a little boat down their own version of the river Styx while the vices squeeze. The only nuts they have left is their money, so we're going to tighten up all nice and legal, grab them where they really hate it, right through the courts.

"I want all of the snoops that Jess had dispatched working with an above-board nonprofit that files endless actions, over and over and over. And I want all of you to read this."

260

Billy gave everyone a flash drive and tacked a file up on the wall.

THE FOSSIL FUEL JOYRIDE - PART III - NOTES FROM HELL:

The fog rolled in thick like a tissue. Like a big sheath of cells forming a membrane in which I could finally lose myself from thinking. It was as if, at last, I'd found a choice where there had been none before. I could make a difference, as the boomers like to parrot. Could finally change something.

I inhaled nine, neat Wild Turkeys and walked out of North Beach through the fog. The bourbon invaded as if it came from the fires of some ring of Dante's hell, which I was preparing to face. For quite some time, I'd thought that I had dropped all fear. The martial arts can be very confusing because most of us are completely screwed up from our parents and society by the time we stumble across a real teacher.

There are so many layers of fear. Losing fright in combat is simple: you just ride the anxiety rushes. All real fighters know this. They are fully aware that they are adrenalin junkies. Only the wussy-boy politicians—the puppets that use warriors for the cash flow addiction of the wealthy—throw out the term "brave." The old-line, wealth freaks use it to hypnotize the masses into thinking that warfare is good rather than psychotic. But dropping fear during the mundane activities of the day-to-day—the time when we are truly collared by our egos—can only be done by people like the Dali Lama who practice kindness continually.

I'd been blessed with opportunities, and dropped sheath after sheath of fear fast, like the impact dispersion of the fuzzy ball of gasses and particulates launched by a vanishing asteroid. But I still had so much to learn.

The first major epiphany took place during the fourth year of black belt work with Sun Chu, my Aikido mentor. As he'd instructed me many times, I simply turned my hand over and let the scary voices slide from my palm like beach sand. I emptied the vessel and rode the fear like a long board off the

261

North Shore. I told Jet Slade this when he first came in with NSA to kill me. He liked the idea that he could jump on fear and big boards so much that he made T-shirts for his congregation. Naturally, he changed the imagery to the terror of going to Hell.

As I walked fast along Columbus, then out toward Fort Mason, I felt the apprehension coil up in me like a rattlesnake. I hadn't eaten in several days and the whiskey had detonated into hellfire and brimstone inside of me. Every neuron in my brain fired pure and clean from the fasting. The whiskey emulsified the spacey-ness and brought my feet completely to the ground—feet on terra firma.

One of the fears that could still jelly my grit swept in like napalm, clinging to and burning my psyche. The Earth is lost already. We are clever creatures—we keep our opposable thumbs very busy, but Homo sapiens are not as intelligent as a dog. We don't even have the sense to move out of the heat into the shade, or the basic wisdom of how luscious a midday nap is and how lusciousness is actually the only important thing in a life. That thought is terrifying to the lost, vacant creatures that control the power on the planet.

Again, I experienced the most fearsome revelation that I had ever known—Homo sapiens do not have the data-sorting skill to know, and to remember, what a life here on the blue planet means to the creature that it is. A great message like forgiveness can come from a wise person, but human beings are simply too dumbed-down with fear and confusion to recognize abundance and to implement the message further than lip service.

After Jenny Warren's research began to clearly illustrate that Homo sapiens will no longer exist after 2075, the decision to push Free Range to the limit fell into place instantly. What's the point in fooling one's self. The greed-heads are right. They won. Not because they have anything on the ball, just because they are blind hogs. They never cared about doing the right thing—they intuited that we would never make it.

Though certain people have offered us guidelines for a good life here, humans simply do not have the software in place in their minds for living correctly, and the earth is not going to sustain us long enough to see if it will develop. I saw clearly that we enjoyed 9,000 years after the cultivation of grain in the Fertile Crescent and did nothing—now Bush is shitting on Iraq, the place we all came from. It's too late.

Images of The Divine Comedy blew up in my mind as twisted and surreal as Fellini doing Peter Breughel. I walked swiftly toward the merge of my being with my death. Neeley, ANVIL, and now NSA. The Neander-cons—Billy's epithet for neo-cons as lame, completely self-absorbed, curmudgeons. They were hot on my trail. Trying to take me out. It was okay because I now knew that humanity would be extinct before the 22nd century.

But I would fuck with them all the way. Free Range really pissed them off and since it was all in vain, I would have some fun anyway. One of the NSA's economic take-over, financial hit groups—The Hoyt Financial Group—wanted to buy Animalfund. Only a pack of government, suck-egg dogs would perform the dirty takeover of a non-profit.

NSA's financial consultants had given up on their quasi-legal buy-out techniques. We buried them in publicity and lawyers. Terminators from the whole bunch of US government suck-eggs would close in at any moment. The consultants had issued their ultimatums. The FBI had picked me up. I was dead meat. Maybe they would take my gall bladder and cut off my paws like a black bear. If I published the disks, there would be no way I would survive. They wanted to crush Free Range. Our ninja-style financials scared them shitless. With Billy Clayton as the first trillionaire and building wealth horizontally, using all the old eco-warriors—the so-called terrorists—making billions of dollars, and using the internet for jumping funds around, I was in deep doo-doo.

But none of it made a whit of difference. We are a string of frames in a film that we call life. No more, no less. One experience after another. They unfold relentlessly and because of the fear of not being able to maintain that continuum, we start grasping, holding on for dear life. But what is the point if Homo sapiens are not programed well enough to make things work on the blue planet, and why waste a bunch of energy when you already know that the outcome is nugatory?

I could see the beautiful bridge as I strode past Fort Mason. I could see that massive web of steel looming. As I extended my stride past the yacht basin, I could see the structure as if I were inside a mental video. The vicious streams of automobiles blurred together. I could only make out the hordes of people wandering amongst one another on the walks. They looked like a 21st century version of a painting by Breughel the Elder.

The dreams I'd been having kept coming back. I was being hunted like one of the grizzlies. Scads of different characters appeared in them: my father fought with my mother; my sister Elizabeth, perched on a rosewood stool, an ancient cello between her legs, played the Sixth Bach Cello Suite; Gurdjieff and Rudolph Steiner tried to take a group of car salesmen through a eurythmic game that looked like croquet; George Bush sat on a stool lecturing Ronald Reagan about b-westerns; Reagan got up and announced that it was not a fossil fuel joyride that his generation had been on—they implemented progress—the planet was not in trouble; Fellini walked up to the pair and adjusted them, tightening the skin on their necks and elbows as if they were some type of Gumby-droids; emaciated, Reagan appeared to be nearing death; squads of cops roamed through the crowd in Third Reich uniforms; Howlin' Wolf, big and dangerous, stood on a small stage playing a national guitar, singing "Maggie's Farm"; across from them, Martin Luther King and Mohandas Gandhi talked with Tony Blair, seriously; Fidel Castro and Rush Limbaugh had been cornered in a whorehouse by Hillary Clinton. Chaos reined, and not a soul appeared to be bothered at all.

I picked up my pace and moved onto the walkways across the Golden Gate. In great pulsing curtains, the living fog breathed past the thick cables of the bridge. I approached on the west side moving with care so that no one would stop or restrain me. I knew they were back there in several cars. I made myself very obvious in North Beach to get them away from the staff. They were all too slow and stupid for me—bureaucrats always think dull and slowly. I was the ideal weight and in perfect physical condition. I was the sword of Manjushri. No one could touch my physical being. I was the tiger's eye. Even the mad fire of the whiskey could never touch my time.

Nono of them would ever cause a change, but I could torment them like a big cat enjoying the hunt. They were all after me just like they were after all citizens concerned with sustainability. Neeley or one of NSA's own hit men would move in soon enough. Serious assassins always slip through the darkness. But I could have fun and stall them. Jenny, Hicks and Billy would find ANVIL out. Billy was very dangerous. He could close a net and take them down with their own devices. But no matter what, Free Range was launched without central management just like the Green Mountain Boys—the real founders of the USA. The irrevocable trusts were so tight and powerful that it would run as a perpetual, financial engine. We would drag the swine into a vice-grip of litigation for so long that the corporations would never enjoy freedom in the wilderness.

I stopped and looked over, off the bridge, at the cold water. I could jump—could leave the rail in control. A perfect triple gainer turn as I dove into the water like a flying swan. I would pass the Gates of Bardo and face every demon of the ego as simply as Gautama. But I finally had a very urgent mission. I was ready, and I walked in a quick war stride. More quickly. A Cape buffalo battle gait. I was out pacing fear, ready to meet those demons head on. The great mask of terror could never overtake me now that I'd been set free. There was nothing left. Clearly, none of the bonds of ego are real. They are all chimeras and had at last allowed the being to shine as the tiger's eye. Burning bright.

At one of the towers, I took a look over my shoulder. There were a lot of them, maybe eight different cars with two in each. The bridge pulsed with a surge of kinetic energy. They wouldn't do it where San Francisco cops would move in on an immense pile up and expose them.

I stepped up the pace thinking of what it was like for those who'd made the dive: ready to make a change, a conscious choice to jump rather than stumble along with this wishful-thinking crap until Homo sapiens extinguished themselves. Continuing to kick the asses of the NSA and the power freaks that owned it, doing it legally, using the courts just like they do, and using all this money to buy back the media.

And that, after all the bullshit, is what it is all about. Enjoying the short time we have here in this amazing environment. I hadn't spent enough time having fun. I was too fucking serious. I needed to drop that self-centered earnestness, just like people who are trying to drop the fear of death. I would walk them down under the bridge and have some fun. Kick some bureaucratic, greed-head butt.

TWENTY

Jenny carried the baggie with the business card in her hand as they headed out of San Pedro, over the bridge through Long Beach and on toward the 405 South. She sat leaning against the door of the truck, quiet and pensive. Billy knew something inside her had changed. He too had felt the shift into sickness the more they uncovered about the antics of these disgusting people. The determination to end this thing and wrap the honcho up fast in his own web was getting stronger.

Finally, Jenny rolled up her sleeves and pulled the card out, holding opposite edges between her thumb and index finger. He sensed this shift in her mood had to do with the tiger and the dragon burned into her forearms, with tapping the immense heart strength—the profound centeredness required for carrying the searing iron basin of coals.

Anyone who trained away the constraints of ego as thoroughly as she had when she seared those scars on her flesh, didn't have a prove-it trip left. They didn't need to play the pathetic little mind games ordinary humans who depend on leaders, nationalism, the kudos of friends, commanders, bosses, and other so-called superiors to maintain existence. The interior integrity required to boost the presence of awareness while gripping the searing load, had opened Jenny's being so thoroughly she would enjoy crystal clear understanding for the rest of her life. She would forever remain present to the moment, her life the main event, each instant an enlightenment.

She replaced the card. She held the bag out toward the windshield and looked at the card. Her eyes fixed on the text and narrowed.

ANVIL, thought Billy. The acronym sounded like Darth Vader's cousin. Anvil Vader. Everything stank of evil.

267

"Jet Slade," she said.

"Can't be a real name. It's got to be some kind of a stage thing—a preacher's handle. It's the name of a bad guy straight out of the comics. The kind of character you see in Batman or something."

Jenny laughed. "Sounds like a motorcycle manufacturer from Orange County."

"Aw, lord, I hope not. It's too corny, even for Orange County," said Billy.

"Did you ever see *Giant*?"

"James Dean, right?" he asked.

"Right. One character's name is Jet Rink and he strikes oil. Texans are weird."

"Hey, come on. How many Texans do you know?"

"How many does a person need to know?" she asked.

They branched off the 405 South and took the 22, the Garden Grove Freeway, over toward Anaheim.

"That's the Crystal Cathedral," she said.

"Right. I've come across some articles. Pretty wild Christmas show," said Billy

"I know, I'd like to see it," she said.

"Right, sounds like quite show. What do you make of the two bull-necks?"

"They're some kind of spooks—maybe NSA. Big Brother is all over them. They, or a fellow op, may have been Jess' perp so we'll never get retribution, which doesn't really bother me. Like Jess, I find this entire, never-ending, eye-for-an-eye addiction a pathetic waste of a Homo sapiens' energy—deeply twisted shit that we are too stupefied with fear to drop."

"So, Mr. Slade randomly uses the federal government to fix things?" asked Jenny.

"Sounds like."

"So he thumps the Bible well enough to tap on the action buttons in the Capitol."

"I'll bet he thumps plenty of things besides the Good Book."

"That too," he said. They both laughed.

"I reckon," she said.

"What's with this reckon, partner?"

"You said we are going to Austin to meet Luther."

"You practicing?"

"Maybe I'm getting some Texas on me, getting Texicated. It's a scary thought."

Billy glanced over as Jenny studied the ANVIL card again, trying to imagine what the place would be like, envisioning those men looking up across Grant Avenue at her with their dead eyes.

The building sat near the grounds of the Crystal Cathedral. Gaudy, like the Cathedral, ANVIL's building bore no relationship to the surrounding structures. The structure stood out from the Orange County sprawl as if from another planet. The built environment in the OC stood tasteless and dreadful, just some more of the meaningless expanse of the great Southern California maze. One boring building after another, dotted here and there with a touch of lonely-looking green. This is all was surrounded by endless mile after mile of concrete that eventually merged into on-ramps, and then drifted onto the sad and exhausted freeway system.

The area sat lifeless—no humans, just cars. And Slade's building sprang forth from the dreary scene, unexpectedly imposing—similar to the way Las Vegas springs forth from the vast calm of the desert as a human-less heap of building materials.

The American National Vigilance and Intelligence League said the sign out front. Eight stories in height, the building appeared dead except for the retail space on the street level.

They parked around the corner, on the block behind the League's building.

"Why is it so blah around here?" Jenny asked.

"My mother refuses to visit the Los Angeles Basin. She says the void you are experiencing results from Vegas and LA being built for auto sales instead of for human beings. She claims the curse of the automobile causes separation, isolation and the sense of nothingness in all the suburbs, all these places all over the world are the same," he said, as they walked along.

"This mother of yours sounds more and more interesting. A woman who is not afraid of being judged? Who actually thinks in depth?"

Billy laughed, thinking about how abrasive some people found his mother. "She is what is often referred to as a high-toned Texas woman."

"I want to meet her," said Jenny.

"It's gonna happen real soon. She was crazy about Jess, and I can't put off telling her about the murder for long," he responded.

"Some of these things she says have a elegant ring of truth to them. The only other person I've heard talk about the built environment and how structures affect our psyches like that is Mike Davis. Did you read his first book, *City of Quartz?*"

"Yes, I did. My mother demanded it. "

"So she stays out of LA and all nouveau sprawls?"

"Religiously."

"The sprawl makes us dull too; it's one big anesthesia table."

Yeah, right. That's good. Reminds me of another of her favorites, Henry Miller's *The Air-Conditioned Nightmare.*"

"Mr. Miller is a bit artsy-fartsy, but the book, even though it's sixty years old, really hits home," said Jenny.

An obelisk of reflective walls, the building stood out from the other buildings on the block. It's plain aluminum storefront composed the street area of the ground floor. In the lobby near the elevator, an older man sat in a pea-soup green reception booth.

The badge proclaimed him as Harold Beal. His eyes pierced them, mean and empty. His mouth rested in a great flap of flesh draping from the downturned corners of his lips. Somehow, he managed to push the skin upward in a ghoulish imitation of a smile. The smile was betrayed by the coldness of his eyes.

"And how may I help you folks?" At his waist, he wore a Colt King Cobra in a western holster. He kept the odd rig strapped to his thigh with a piece of rawhide.

At the hotel, Billy had sorted through his sheaths of false credentials. An old friend, Emanuel Paz, in Ciudad Juarez created mountains of identities for him through the years. Manny networked with Mexican artisans: engravers, printers, digital wizards. He worked for spooks from every place on the planet. Manny claimed the folks from Spookland didn't care about what side they were on; they simply enjoyed the snoop games. He worked for every government: for twisted individuals from Lahore, Rio, Petersburg, Shanghai, Sydney, Pyongyang, Tehran, Langley, Kuala Lampur, Tel-Aviv, Berlin, Antwerp, you name it. He produced any kind of document including government IDs, license plates, and passports for any place on Earth. With a wave of Manny's magic lantern, a known client—he only worked with corporations and entrepreneurs who had been carefully screened—received any order within 72 hours. Manny had opened many doors for Billy. He helped him move in fast on many a takeover. Helped make him invisible. Helped make him wealthy.

Thinking through his and Jenny's approach, he had agreed with Harlan—journalist would be the ideal cover, the most malleable disguise they could choose. Billy knew from experience that the ego is the most powerful, most quick and most certain inroad into the real life of almost any warped individual. And love, in its universal sense, is the quickest path into the knowledge of healthy human beings. The more the individual fancies their own self-importance, the more damaged their psyches are and the more personal the information they will readily reveal by opening the ego spigot. And the nastier they are, the more self-worth they have invested in ego.

Billy pulled his old Leica camera out of the duffel as he left his room. He would pose as Jenny's photographer. She was doing a scoop for *Texas Trailways*—"The American Dream is Alive and Well in Southern California."

"Yes, Mr. Beal. We have a meeting with Mr. Slade." A natural actor, Jenny looked a tad rustic in her old Leddy's and down vest but Mr. Beal couldn't get past her eyes. As Billy listened, he found himself believing her entire story without a bit of trouble. Mr. Beal hefted the tired corners of his mouth up into a full smile and pointed to the elevators.

They shot upward quickly with an elevator moderne interpretation of a Brandenburg concerto dribbling from the speakers. The doors opened directly into the ANVIL suite, to another reception desk, without any passage through hallways.

The entire entry buffeted the senses with fruity pastels. The lime green, close wale corduroy couches and armchairs sat between light peach, ceramic planters overflowing with chalky pink, silk geraniums. The nauseating elevator music swarmed softly with a wretchedly slow version of "Spring" from Vivaldi's *Four Seasons*.

A buxom, young blonde sporting white-rimmed, rhinestone, cat eyeglasses and a pink, button-up, cashmere sweater smiled bigger than the Cheshire Cat.

"Hello, how are you? I'm Miss Marple, Mavis Marple, and how may I be of service to you?"

Sticking out her hand, Jenny smiled wider than Miss Marple.

"Good morning, Miss Marple. I'm Jane Rodgers from *Texas Trailways* magazine and this is my photographer, Mr. Duncan Autry. We're here for the interview with Mr. Slade at ten o'clock sharp."

Miss Maples looked down at her calendar immediately and grew flustered. She punched her phone, panted a few words softly, and another girl in a cashmere sweater appeared. The ANVIL offices swarmed with a breast-o-rama of rarefied, wooly girls. Young women scurried about to the copy room, the kitchen, the toilets and their desks. Heaven only knows where they all disappeared to, but Hugh Hefner would have been salivating, roughing out a friendly takeover. A Miss Parsons slid in from an inner office with her bosom and her hand extended. Her color was pastel, powder lemon and she had a big smile.

"My, my, my," she said, with a deep, buttery drawl. "I just don't know whatever happened that we didn't have notation of your engagement with Mr. Slade. But being the gracious man he is, he doesn't think it would be fittin' to turn y'all away."

Miss Parsons minced off in her three-inch, sulfurous heels, signaling Billy and Jenny to follow. She opened a solid maple door, which displayed an engraved, brass plaque—Jet Slade, General Director.

"Good morning," said the director, extending a warm, milky hand. "I sure hope we haven't put you out." He stood extremely commanding with his onyx eyes. A frightening intensity in them screamed past his calm exterior. Miss Parsons hurried out for Billy's and Jenny's coffees, and tea for the director.

Paneled in bird's-eye maple, with an old-line, honey colored, wax finish, the huge office had an air of grave importance. There was nothing high tech. The space looked as if it belonged to an oil executive from the early 20th century. The wall behind the desk was covered in maple bookshelves, except for a bank of locked, lateral file cabinets right behind his leather executive chair. Every inch of one wall bore hunting trophies—the heads of domestic species including a magnificent grizzly. The site made Billy and Jenny sick to their stomachs but they carried on with their charade, not missing a beat. Beneath the heads, a leather couch big enough to serve as a bed rested with a striped Hudson's Bay blanket draped over one arm.

Another wall of glass presented a sweeping view of the Crystal Cathedral. The fourth wall bore a massive gun cabinet with beveled glass doors covering the front. Billy quickly calculated that there were well over 200,000 dollars' worth of weapons behind the stately doors; there were several magnums including Weatherbys, Steyr Mannlichers, Heyms, and match rifles including a big McMillan M87—a repeater just like the one Billy owned.

Though hunting was a common rite for boys growing up in Texas, Billy had quit many years before. His father had never taken trophies, only enough game to eat fresh or smoke for the winter season. And later, Billy found the random slaughter any of the few wild creatures remaining disgusting when so much slaughter took place at the packinghouses on a daily basis.

Billy did love to shoot and continued to collect guns with his father right up to his death. They went out to the range and spent time doing what his mother called male mental groping. She never referred to their outings as male bonding—she loathed baby boomer expressions.

Director Slade's collection took up the entire wall. Not only high-powered rifles, but many thousands of dollars' worth of shotguns and, to one side, an arsenal of automatic weapons—HKs, Sigs, Colts, Berettas, a Calico and sundry units from around the world. Billy knew they were illegal, but he didn't say a thing—after all, they graced the world headquarters of an upstanding Amurkan.

Slade seated them in a pair of leather, wingback chairs facing a grand, black, walnut desk and handed them each an embossed business card.

"So y'all are with *Texas Trailways?* I must say I haven't had the good fortune to see your periodical."

"Doggone," drawled Jenny. "I walked right out and forgot to bring you a copy. But we'll send you a pile of 'em when your interview comes out." She fished the small digital recorder out of Billy's old attaché case, which she'd brought along as a part of her costume.

"You don't mind if I flip this little guy on, do you Mr. Slade?"

"Why, of course not, darlin', tools of the trade, that type of thing," he said, adjusting the lapels on his gray wool suit. He had a maroon tie and a matching, engraved, silk hanky in his breast pocket.

"So, tell us Mr. Slade, what are the goals of ANVIL in this chaotic world we now live in?" she asked.

"Well, Miss Rodgers," he said, looking down at the cards. "You are a Texan, aren't you?"

"Sure am. Both of us are."

"Well, it sounds like your names take you back quite a ways as Americans."

"Yep, we go way back there in the Lone Star State, even before it was named so."

"Well, let me be candid with you; our beautiful country is in a lot of trouble and it runs very deep. How can I say this? Terrorists are insignificant, practically of no importance. Our real malignancy is right here at home." Slade made certain he talked toward the tape recorder.

"There is a beautiful document written a few centuries back. I'm sure you know what that manuscript was and that the purpose of this document was freedom. A lot of you-know-what has flowed under the bridge since our forefathers signed the paper, and its purpose is being gravely threatened as we move fully into this new millennium. The people of the United States had suffered a lot of tyranny before the Constitution was written, and our grandfathers and all of their forefathers before them, worked real hard to make the concept of freedom a reality."

Jenny and Billy adjusted themselves in their chairs in order to stay with the harangue.

"Today, a family isn't even free to let their babies walk to school, Mr. Clayton," he continued, staring into Billy's eyes. "If a man needs to protect his family—his babies on their way to the schoolhouse—he isn't even allowed to bear arms for their safety. What do we have?"

Slade cleared his throat, adding significance to his statement. "Fascism is what we have."

He nodded his head slowly, then it bobbed up and down in a signal of confirmation.

"We are not allowed the freedom of choice when it comes to taxation. We have more government than ever with new agencies popping up like maggots and the old ones spying on us without any reason whatsoever. Our forefathers signed the Constitution and later, the document proclaiming our inalienable rights, opposing a sad, demented monarchy. And now we are facing a peril more insidious than a monarchy—an oligarchy."

Slade paused with perfect aplomb, letting his pronouncement settle in with his audience.

"Everyone has heard of ANVIL now; we've been around for 35 years, working to keep our country whole, facing communists, protestors, hippies, liberals, many groups which are in opposition to this great nation. But now, within the last couple decades, the darker forces of amassed corporate greed and avarice have taken hold. The common man is no longer in control.

"For this reason, we have beefed up the American National Vigilant Investigation League. ANVIL was designed as an organization for real Americans, and now we have empowered the investigative arm with deep training. This is an organization for citizens—a platform. Many wish to contribute more than financial donations: citizens who truly wish to make a difference in the noble U-S-of-A. We will pound the information from our investigations into sabers of truth."

Billy and Jenny let him talk until the machine beeped indicating that the memory was full. He was a man with a mission, and judging by the appearance of ANVIL's staff, he had a following that listened closely and found tremendous consensus with the pronouncements and goals of their director. They all appeared to be mesmerized by Slade. Out of the clear blue, he boasted that their nonprofit revenues, thundering in as small contributions, subscriptions, and information sales that already exceeded 67.5 million dollars per month and was growing steadily.

The general director loved to listen to the acronym resonate from his breast. "ANVIL," he said in a thick baritone, as if the truth were being forged on the spot. He got up, took hold of his lapels and beamed with pride as he paced around the room.

"As the name suggests, we are involved in forging the vigilant pursuit of clear information in order to make our training programs imminently successful. We have developed unsurpassed graphic global modeling software entwined with an interactive, mixed-media database. We are modeling Christianity, Muslims, terrorism, the Big Brother syndrome, the weather, natural resources, population, disease, and the global financial spectrum in order to truly understand the forces undermining the very fabric of our society."

Slade looked at Jenny, and then at Billy, sizing them up from head to toe.

"Terrorists don't cause many casualties, and the dead and maimed are your moneyed types. Forces lurk behind all things. Human notions harm freedom and Christianity much more than terrorism. Legal drugs from the corporations, for instance. Why, cigarettes kill 50,000 working people a month and stick the ordinary citizen with a huge healthcare burden the tobacco companies do not pay for at all. Usurious lenders keep our people enslaved with debt."

The director walked back to his desk and picked up a couple of brochures, which he handed to Jenny.

"But we are watching. We are much more vigilant than a bunch of gimpy bureaucrats. Politicians are obsolete. Now is the time for Americans to replace them with computers.

They are worthless liars owned by the super-rich. We are at the forefront. We put our funds to work carefully, why we owned a couple of these beauties for years. Recycled Cray C94s. Super computers, in case you are not familiar." He handed them a brochure.

Billy and Jenny looked at the huge black computers as Slade continued. The hardware looked like it was straight out of Darth Vader's IT department.

"This is the age of information, and we are now completely online. We are a part of the super highway—the infobahn—and the first goal is to insure freedom. I want y'all to come to White Dove Retreat and visit. Your stay will be on me. We'd love to have you. The visit will make your *Texas Trailways* article a rich reading experience."

"Where are you going?" asked Billy.

"Down to San Anton; don't you just love the River Walk?"

"Well now, that's a yes for sure, Mr. Slade."

Slade puffed up with pride.

"We are preparing for all events coming with this new millennium. Corporate greed and crime is our primary target. Without an end to the corporate tax evasion and crime plaguing our ordinary citizens, there will be an end to the middle class, and therefore an end to freedom before the turn of the decade. The major shareholders own the politicians: Presidents Obama, Bush and Clinton, Boehner, the Tea Party, Democrats, the Right Wing, it doesn't matter. They are all stooges for the lobbyists.

"The country, the counties, the cities are all bankrupt. They can't even afford a database, and they bungle them when they do spend our tax dollars on them. They can't develop policing bodies. Homeland Security is just another boondoggle of bureaucrats: a cash drain. Soon there will be nothing but the major shareholders and the enslaved. It's just like when King George taxed our forefathers to death.

"The US still has some potential, but time is of essence in getting the voters to the polls, to get off our oil-junky syndrome, to break the citizen from being stoned on television and the internet, and to run the major stockholders' bureaucrats—the puppets of the oligarchy—out of office. Today is the day to seize the moment as our founding fathers did." His face lit up with a distant, knowing smile.

"When the powers in office can't provide services for the ordinary public—heck, just a good subway, trolley and train system would get us off the oil fix—it's time for the citizenry to take care of itself, and the Good Lord put ANVIL here for that purpose. The only thing the United States has ever had to set us apart was a middle class seeing hope. Now the working people are nothing more than droids, subjects of television." Slade cocked his head and looked off into his own world.

"Towergate was simply a front. The NSA and their buddies in the company trained those Arabs to aim those aircrafts at their targets. The super-rich lost their fear symbol when the Commies fell. The towers gave them a new fear mechanism: terror so they could put in Homeland Security to keep the middle class from protesting." He continued with his deep-voiced oratory. His final invective came out cavernous and sonorous. "America must be returned to the ordinary person. Without a democratic middle class to control the greed of the wealthy, healthy capitalism cannot work."

He stood abruptly, his oratory at an end. They packed the recorder, and Slade took them on a tour of the building. In the vaulted cellars, after passing through a series of bank vault doors, a big, dark Cray sat like a purring animal from somewhere in Darth Vader's galaxy, its fine-tuned brain humming with information.

Slade dismissed them with a syrupy goodbye. As they walked through the upper lobby, Jenny took brochures from a lemon-yellow rack on the wall and Miss Marple escorted them into the elevator.

TWENTY-ONE

A dead-still fog arose from the Pacific Ocean and a chill began to surround trees and stumps, barbed wire and fence posts, grasses and the earth, the shore line, the ocean and vessels out at sea. With the doldrums on the water, an eerie quiet spread out over everything.

Though Nuke decided to wait before he inched through Angels Gate and docked in Los Angeles Harbor where he'd grab a rental car and pick up parts for repairing any serious damage on *dead latitudes*, he would not allow himself to sit still out on a dull, cold day and lock into wondering if Jenny and Billy survived their trip.

He had to get his mind off their safety until something real could be done. Worrying would not help them. He directed his mind toward the practical. With Sam at his side, he swept through a cursory survey of the damages to his ship. He began to work his way around for a closer assessment and stopped to zero-in on the electronics.

He examined the equipment and focused in on three goals, allowing them to completely flood his mind and drive him forward. He had to get Sam and *dead latitudes* far enough away from the cops in Tiburon to keep them safe. After *dead latitudes* sat secure and moored in Wilmington, he had to find Jenny and Billy. Next, working with Harlan to mop up anyone or anything that threatened him or any of them would become the number one priority.

After Jenny, Billy, Sam and the ship rested out of harm's way, he would take care of extermination. The perp and everyone related, all those involved in any capacity with murdering Jess, required decommissioning, whether in the court system, in jail or whatever.

Intuition told Nuke all of the characters related to Jess' death, their whole organization, had to be eighty-sixed. He predicted a boss lurked somewhere, probably the guy on the phone, that controlled a large cash flow, and with so much of that, nasty, white-bigot, good-ol'-boy following he'd be tweaking the good fella types, the Aryan trailer trash, all the power freaks in Washington, every level of judge and, of course, any bunch of cops.

The pest control operation would present exacting challenges, but Nuke loved riding the edge. He would continue following his grandma's instructions for a healthy day-to-day life, but events that did not fall into the day-by-day arena required special attention. The average white man moved through life as a lost, grabby, pathetic creature. Mentally stable white people sat way up on the endangered species list. The death of a truly decent white man was something God would notice. All four of the horsemen would be descending from the heavens, coming down for the swine who'd caused Jess' death.

Nuke realized the little freak whose ear he'd sawed off would always remember him—always walk around looking over his shoulder—and he would doubtless put out an order for Nuke's head.

Nuke planned to rent a big SUV so he appeared to be moneyed but ordinary. He would take four Desert Eagles and a hand grip full of clips and .50 caliber ammo, and hunt every one of them down. The plan emerged instantly, and he fine-tuned each detail as they headed south.

Being zenned-out since birth, Nuke had the ability to zero-in on events without effort. Two things mattered at this stage in his strategy. First, pumping saw-ear's brother so hard he started pouring out information about where to find Billy and Jenny, and then getting *dead latitudes* docked and secured.

The fog bank had spread over them as if it was some vast animal coming in off the Pacific. It created the shroud of chill air, which was invigorating to Nuke. The cool air gave him a lot of energy. With the noise all stilled, his senses rose to a high frequency. He surveyed the storage and felt the clear need to protect Sam and *dead latitudes* from the onslaught of blood-drunk pervs that had clouded his memory.

281

Billy prepared all things in life as if he dealt with his last stand. He didn't just live by some fatuous book about the Tao of business, the Tao of management, the Tao of this, that and the other: he breathed the Tao. He lived the Tao. He never stopped. Nuke realized that Billy had grown so rich because of this clarity. Most business types, and not just white people, but all races, were greed-heads, always grasping for more cash. This caused them to live in fear of losing all the crap they grabbed, so they ended up being ruthless, self-centered wusses. They were rudderless. They play-acted as if they were able to direct their energy and be business-like, but they lost barrels of power in pathetic ego trips. A real man like Billy jumped in and kicked those pitiful types' asses without even breaking a sweat. The zenned-out quality raked in a trillion dollars. The rest of the wealthy didn't have a tenth of his power. They existed for the chimera of ego.

As Nuke steadied his mind, he slowed down and inventoried the supplies. Next he began the repair of the radar and his thinking fell right into place, settling down to normal. The fog bank proved penetrable. The radar steered them onto a course toward Angels Gate, toward the Port of Los Angeles.

When Nuke saw he needn't wait until the fog lifted to continue south now that the radar was working, he cut Brother Noah Army lose. The guy didn't know what to do with the freedom. He couldn't look straight in Nuke's eyes. He rubbed all the parts of his body, the parts that hurt from being bound.

"I want to know where the computers are and where your boss is. Tell me now and I'll do better by you than you would by me: I'll drop you off on land next time we get near it."

"Don't act like a dumb nigger."

"Man, I just don't get it. What makes all you Klan-geeks so dumb?"

Nuke stood still, looking at the man. His reaction was slow. People never understood this part—the time he took assessing a situation. This brief period always proceeded the next phase. He came to a decision. He dug into a sail locker and pulled out a long nylon line. He picked the man up with one hand, broke his nose with a left hook and wove a basket around his torso.

"What the fuck are you doing? I'm tied up enough."

"I broke your nose so you'd remember that you can't call me a nigger, and so it would bleed a lot to help guide the sharks in for your ugly little maggot ass."

Nuke wrapped him through the crotch, around the shoulders, under the arms, and applied numerous loops around the abdomen and chest like a spider securing prey to its web. He picked the man up by the line and walked straight to the stern.

"Hey you stupid fuck, what you think—"

The voice disappeared as Nuke hurled the man over the transom. The heavy fog had thinned through the morning and would soon be gone. *Not good*, he thought, as Brother Noah Army's wail of terror melted and Nuke went back to work on the radar.

He took a minute to look at the communications equipment. He investigated the supply lockers more closely and decided he might be able to repair everything. Getting to Angels Gate was pretty simple. The fog would burn off and he knew the shoreline like he had known the hood as a boy.

He loved California in the same way he loved his grandmother and with the same passion. He loved it with all his heart and soul. He never loved the hood, but he fell in love with the ocean the minute he laid eyes on it.

After pulling out his supplies, he moved them topside and then returned to the stern.

Hand over hand, he heaved the line—a task few men would be able to perform. One meter at a time, he retrieved the body from the ocean and then stopped to leave the man dangling over the back rail. Brother Noah Army had clinched his fists so hard his nails had cut his palms and his face declared a state of mindless panic.

Nuke stood and stared at him. The man's legs were dangling as shark bait. The situation lasted so long the little man started screaming. Finally, Nuke reached over for solid purchase on the line and hefted the man onto the deck. Brother Noah Army flopped and floundered on the teak like some bizarre creature straight out of a dark place deep in a furrow.

"You will pay for this, you dumb nigger-assed freak show."

Nuke threw him over the stern again and the man let out a wretched chortle of terror. Then, Nuke went below and sat to work on the communications equipment. When he had examined what required work and sorted through the supplies, he went back topside again. He heaved the little man up and over the stern. The man no longer flopped or floundered, instead he choked and blubbered up water.

"When you get tired of me trolling you, you can give me what I need. I had hoped to catch me a big old shark for lunch, but you must have really stinky, bad vibes."

"Jet Slade's the big boss. We have two compu—"

As Brother Noah Army tried to save himself, a helicopter swooped in over the bow, passing so close Nuke thought the pilot would break one of *dead latitudes'* long, thick masts.

Just as the chopper lifted and headed away from the sailboat, six rubber assault boats rushed in across the water toward *dead latitudes*. The street fighter in Nuke understood what came his way automatically. He ran below, grabbed pistols, shotguns, and assault rifles and threw them up on deck. The boats were loaded with men in black SWAT uniforms, just like the Army Brothers'.

They rushed straight in on all sides, looking as if they would ram the boat. At the last moment they put a back thrust on the inflatable attack boats, tossed grappling hooks and pulled in to swarm the deck. As they began their assault, the chopper roared back over, flooding everything with a windstorm.

Nuke dropped all the men in the inflatables who had bounced the stern and piled over the mahogany transom. As they rolled into the water, the inflatables worked loose from *dead latitudes* and without passengers, flew off across the ocean. He turned the Desert Eagle on one of the rubber boats hanging off the starboard side. Again, he blew the men right off the rounded sides of the craft. They rolled neatly into the water and Nuke noticed two great white shark fins moving in toward the ship, slowly.

He grabbed two more pistols with the safeties already off and shells chambered. Firing with both hands, he dumped more men into the ocean. He worked smoothly and simply, as if he stood at the rail of a shooting gallery at the Los Angeles County Fair. It was like tipping over steel ducks to win a kewpie doll for his girl. But as fast and precisely as Nuke handled himself, his effort was hurriedly overshadowed. The invaders hurled massive force at him.

This time the chopper hovered and six men repelled onto the deck. Brother Lucien Maxwell carried an ultra-modern shotgun and wore a couple belts full of shells. He eased the trigger, and the weapon hardly recoiled while battering the ancient teak and mahogany topside of *dead latitudes*. Nuke thought the gun was the most dangerous weapon he had ever seen, it had to be what killed Jess and messed up his house. It had to be the weapon Billy was talking about.

He emptied the huge .50 caliber slugs into the heads of several trespassers, and then he felt two deep stinging probes in his neck. And then, what he recognized to be a powerful downer like Thorazine—maybe a horse tranquilizer—invaded his body as a regiment of the Khan's armies might have overwhelmed the hapless cities through which they swept as they rode out of China. He watched the fins roiling with ripped-loose flesh in the bloody water as he slumped over onto his right side.

Brother Lucien Maxwell walked over to Nuke as Ezekiel Army slid down from the chopper.

"Take him below and bind him thoroughly with steel handcuffs on all his limbs. Put a half dozen flex cuffs

285

around his neck and bind the flexies to a cabinet frame. Bust a hole in the cabinet door and use steel cuffs from the frames to the nylon."

Six of the men, including Brother Ezekiel Army, started to move below.

"Be sure to take good care of the dog. Keep him in the head. Don't let him get hurt. Keep him watered and fed. He's bait for this yahoo who owns the boat," said Maxwell. "Then, sink the empty inflatables and let the sharks get rid of the floaters, shoot them in the head to chum for sharks with the blood. Make sure they are all being eaten so the Coast Guard doesn't get cute and dig evidence out of their stomachs."

The SWAT-types obeyed quickly in complete silence.

The chopper took off as Maxwell said, "I'll take the wheel Zeke. You take care of your brother. If the big guy starts to move, give him another dose. I want to get this damn boat into Wilmington and search it. We'll start filling our rap star with truth serum."

Brother Ezekiel looked at Maxwell and wrinkled his cheek with contempt. His ear made him look grotesque like he was a character in a cheap horror film. "You know sodium pentothal doesn't do anything, Brother Maxwell."

"But Zeke, this is sodium amytal—the real thing."

"They are all the same, Brother Maxell: pentothal, amytal, scopolamine. They don't do anything but make a terrorist like this man more loose of tongue and less inhibited. Forty-ounce bottles of King Cobra malt liquor would work just as well. But this character is already uninhibited." Brother Ezekiel Army put his hand to his ear as he continued. "He will just loosen up more but nothing will force him to tell the truth."

"So where did you dig up this information, Zeke?"

"It's common knowledge, Brother Maxwell. State courts find evidence from confessions unreliable and dismiss it."

"Well, whatever you say, Zeke. When we get him tied down good, then we'll switch the rhino tranqs to Valium. We'll keep him so stoned he can't do anything."

When the ship finally sailed through Angels Gate, they fired up her steady four-banger, diesel engine again. Nuke lay dormant under a canvas and Brother Ezekiel continued to check him out every half hour. He did not want Nuke conscious again until he rested securely in a straitjacket for deep interrogation.

Brother Lucien Maxwell did not want anything to blow the situation for them. He had to keep Jet Slade hypnotized in order to keep his position for just a while longer. Typically, mesmerizing him would not be overly difficult because of Slade's enormous ego, but the series of snafus had made his attention to security a lot more arduous.

However, tracking financial data, as Brother Lucien Maxwell had for so many years, had always kept Slade chained to his insights. His undergrad degree from Wharton and his PhD from the London School of Economics, coupled with his vast knowledge of constitutional law, had offered him profound power in any organizational situation.

And now, with the trillionaire, his years of in-depth studies of the wealthy on Earth also gave him an edge few humans enjoyed. He smiled as he thought of how he stood alone as one of the few people on Earth who fathomed the life of William Clayton III in great detail. Journalists, hackers and sleuths on all seven continents had attempted to pry into information about the man's life and various holdings in Liberia, China, all down through Oceania and the nerve center in Dubai, with little success.

But Maxwell had broken through enough secrecy to see what things appeared to be true. Clayton had probably, in fact, broken the unheard of barrier of netting one trillion dollars. A total outsider. Never available to the pop money, Forbes magazine types. Clayton stuck to making money, not blowing off his mouth. He was not interested in nationalism, community, clubs, or memberships. The guy was a loner. He had only a few friends: some old Comanche horse trainer on

287

his father's ranch in Texas, his deceased oilman father, his mother, some woman who'd passed on a year or so ago in Santa Monica, and a handful of tree huggers.

Brother Maxell assumed Clayton perceived he had become involved with serious forces when he saw Hayes' body. He strode in with the girl from Animalfund, and the gangbanger was already there. He entered just after the shooter left, right after the op had removed Hayes' hand with a carpenter's saw. The thought gave him great pleasure. The perp wore a hazmat suit and heavy gloves. With the intrusion, he simply ran out the bottom of the house and disappeared.

Slade hated to be thwarted. People who had lousy parenting remained insecure all their lives. Jet Slade's anger toward Billy Clayton served every one of Brother Lucien Maxwell's personal ambitions. Even if all of his plans failed—if Clayton didn't help him at all—he would go to Dubai himself, buy an Irish or an Eastern European hacker and set himself up with cash downloaded from Animalfund.

But that was silly. One thousand billion dollars easily netted Mr. Clayton fifty billion in tax-free income a year. The man never had to pay a bit of attention to his funds again. Twenty-five billion dollars for the lives of his dog, one of his closest friends and what appeared to be his new sweetheart, would be nothing to him, but everything to Brother Maxwell. The rich man would be able to dump money into one of Brother Maxwell's accounts within moments with nothing more complex than a cell connection.

Brother Maxwell ached to get the boat tied off and start questioning the Afro. He would use the Army Brothers. They would do the hammering and he would protect the gangbanger as he interrogated. It would be a game of good cop, bad cop. He would dig out more information to use when he spoke with the rich man in private. He would be accepted by the trillionaire.

The old sailing vessel chugged gracefully up to the dock, cutting the still water with her sleek bow. Below, Nuke's face glistened with sweat. Even with his massive body drugged so heavily, he twisted in anger. He'd bunched his brow up so tight the worry wrinkles above his nose plowed a half-inch furrow in his forehead. It looked as if the embittered thoughts inside him were hard-wired past the effects any substance would have on his mind. Every time a voice spoke, Nuke's facial muscles went through contortions, making the deep, gristly scars on his face stand out.

TWENTY-TWO

"We are headed for Temecula," Jenny said, reading the brochure Slade gave them for White Dove Retreat.

"I'll be on the freeway in a minute."

"God, I feel worse than I did after the warehouse," said Jenny, looking down at the brochures again.

"I know he's the one," said Billy as they burnt toward the 415 South. "I wanted to take him down right there. All the training in the Corps really took hold of me, allowed me to suck it in and not attack."

"Me too. Funny how, in the end, the idea behind most violence, especially authentic martial arts is to get to non-violence."

"I know. And humans are too slow-witted to get there en masse. It's like Jess said on his CD; there's always some excuse to start wars and kill each other."

"Yeah, I could have dropped him right there and had a million excuses," said Jenny. "My mom and dad went to Joan Baez's, she's an old folk singer—"

"Right, my mom listened to her records. Loved that she had the school for nonviolence in Carmel Valley and pissed off all the neighboring fascists," said Billy.

"Yeah, my mom and dad went there. It's why I went into Shaolin. Teenage angst and rebellion. They chose being peaceniks; I chose fighting."

He smiled at her and she looked in his eyes for a long beat.

"Anyway, a real gentleman, Ira Sandperl, taught the classes. Mom has always thought Ira was one of the few important people in the 20th century, right there with Dr. King and Gandhi. One of her favorite aphorisms from Mr. Sandperl sums up how this whole ANVIL thing feels: 'The world is a play written by Kafka and acted out by the Marx Brothers.'"

"Right. That's Slade 1,000 percent. What do you make of all his conspiracy theories?"

"A lot of it's true. I'm from the Connecticut super-rich and you're the same, only from Texas."

"We're oil barons like the Bush family," Billy agreed.

"So Slade has some real truth mixed in with his spiel. There is no way to have a democracy and capitalism without a healthy, thriving middle class; it's what's made America work since the Second World War."

Billy laughed. "Right. Only throw some sadistic Larry, Curly and Moe with some San Fernando Valley porn in the ANVIL sauce."

Jenny laughed aloud. "Well, I must say, that is a spot-on analysis. He's hysterical and sounds a great deal like Herr Hitler did."

"Correct. Absolutely. No question about it. These places of his are so weird. And his credo: wow! What do you call him? A neo-repub-demo-nazi-freedom-fighter?"

They howled with laughter.

"Man, you got it. He's our boy," said Billy.

"Our perp?"

"He's the big bad wolf."

"You don't have any—"

"Trust me, Jenny. I don't need proof, Harlan will find that. It's visceral. I smell it. The big boss is a perv, maybe a child molester. All evil. I wanted to take hold of his neck."

She looked around at him closely. He felt the gaze, turned his head and smiled. Neither said a word.

They rolled onto Highway 15 and headed down the state toward Temecula. Billy punched in the number for *dead latitudes*, but when there was no answer, he tossed the phone back onto the dash.

"Nuke?" asked Jenny.

"Nothing."

"Maybe Clarence's Coast Guard guy will find them."

"Damn. Where is he? Where's my dog?"

He dialed Harlan. "This Jet Slade at the American National Vigilance and Intelligence League is the bad guy. He may not be the shooter, but he caused Jess' death, and he's up to some really lousy stuff. You can bet he's in cahoots with some big cheeses on the Hill; they're afraid of him because he's a Bible thumper. I'm sure he's in with the NSA. They probably provided the trigger man. They have been following Jenny and Jess and the Animalfund staff. Gotta be because of Free Range. One of their *Bourne Identity* types offed Jess."

"Yeah, we met him face to face. Just got out of the place in Anaheim. No, I won't kill him. I want to, but I won't. I have to go to Austin. Luther has something on Slade, too. Don't talk like a politician's wife. Luther's not stoned, he practices the sacraments of the Native American Church. Trust me, he's got more on the ball than all you fucked up old white men will ever know."

Billy could barely finish the conversation through his laughter. "Hey, don't threaten me, counselor. For your own welfare, you must remember, I am stuck with being a white guy, too."

Using the map on the brochure, Jenny guided Billy to the ramp. They pulled off the freeway, drove through Temecula and onward. They sailed past the Pechanga Indian Reservation and the big casino.

They wove down through the hills and, pulling into the ANVIL grounds, they slid down the switchback to the valley floor. Both stared in amazement at the size and gravity of the camp. Where were the real headquarters for the American National Vigilance and Investigation League? This looked like the place.

The camp sat in silence. It was easy to imagine times when the small, white, saltbox cottages swarmed with believers. Covered with thick white paint, all of the buildings on the grounds showed signs of diligent maintenance. Just outside the gate, Billy pulled out pistols. They stuffed them in the backs of their waistbands.

The main house rested stately beneath its blue asphalt shingles. Billy and Jenny walked up the steps then across the vast porch that ran the length of the mansion. Wearing a thin, white cotton, dress, the very pale, blank-eyed, dark-haired Mattie Slade sat in one of the swings. She pushed off the gray floorboards with a bare foot and glided the swing gently.

Billy and Jenny walked straight up to the nine-foot front doors. There was no doorbell, only a big brass knocker shaped like and anvil. Billy banged, and the sound reverberated all over the acreage. He looked around quickly, half expecting Neeley to drive up in a cold-looking car.

Lucinda, pale as a morning star in the heavens, in another white, cotton, summer dress, opened the big door. Barefoot and voluptuous, she spoke with a deep southern accent.

"Ah, travelers descending at our doorstep. How fortunate we are. I am Lucinda Osmond and I am here for your calling."

"Good morning, Ms. Osmond, I am Duncan Autry from *Texas Trailways Magazine*. This is my lovely partner, Jane Rodgers. She's the brains." Lucinda laughed and offered a limp white hand, palm down.

"My pleasure, ma'am," said Billy before kissing it. Jenny strained to keep the disgust on her face low keyed.

Lucinda made no attempt to hide her sensuality. Her cheeks flushed as she sized Billy's big, lank, raw-boned frame up and down with a quick, genteel reconnaissance.

"Mr. Autry, I assure you, the pleasure is all mine."

"We're here on a little research project, all the way out from Austin, Texas."

"Ah, the great state of Texas. I have so many friends down there, even a few, scattered relatives who moved over from the Carolinas after the Comanche wars. A horrible time for all, dealing with savages and the likes."

"Well heck, ma'am. My folks walked over to Texas from Kentucky. There were many restless spirits who had to move on, like so many Americans did in those days."

Lucinda whisked them in the door. In spite of the frail beauty she presented with her wispy garments—the bone-white complexion and the warm-butter tonality of her voice—Billy could see she controlled everything in her environment.

"My, this is an honor. The journalist's profession is hard row to hoe as my daddy, Colonel Malcom, would have said. Y'all are just always on the go, travelin' to all those lonely, plastic hotel rooms," she put a hand to her cheek in a swoon. "Why I just can't even think of all the travail you must encounter."

She stood very still after the hand left her cheek and looked at both of them with care.

"Well, ma'am, it can be a bit of a workout at times."

"A modest gentleman, just like the Colonel."

"Obviously, this is not one of those excruciating encounters." Billy winked at Lucinda and she blushed. Jenny choked back a nauseous look that strained to spread over her face.

"We are visiting everywhere, just like Huell Howser did, doing a—"

"Oh my god. I just adored that man. He is such a big ol' gentleman."

"Right. You're right. Our story is a lot of fun, just like Huell's episodes. We think the American Dream is alive and well here in Southern California. It's some encouragement for all of our many readers."

"Well, I suppose it is just fine here. Everything does seem to be alright."

Lucinda closed the massive portal and swept them into the formal parlor, furnished primly in the French provincial style. Billy and Jenny perched on an extremely uncomfortable, straight-backed settle, and Lucinda sat on an equally stiff armchair.

294

"Oh, Raymond," she said, in a firm, commanding voice.

She looked them over assiduously and said, "We will have tea."

Raymond came into the room in creased black trousers, a white shirt, a black bowtie and a spotless, full-length, white, cotton apron. A small, slim man, Raymond looked as if he calculated every movement in his life to achieve maximum results.

"Raymond, our honored guests are journalists. Will you please prepare tea?"

"Yes, of course, madam."

"And, Raymond, I think a fine old bottle of Armagnac from the cellar would be most appropriate. Thank you."

"Yes, of course, madam," he repeated.

Raymond served a magnificent tea on silver: thick scones laced with tiny currents and dripping butter; Irish breakfast tea, hand nurtured all the way through the process from wherever it came in India; bone white China straight from the potteries in England; fine Dutch linen.

"I am not familiar with your periodical," said Lucinda.

"*Texas Trailways* covers a great many topics. Right now we are doing a series on—" Billy didn't have time to finish the sentence.

Two of the most cold, blue-eyed, blond WASPs Billy and Jenny had ever seen walked into the parlor. These Anglo-Saxon Protestants dressed in black tactical uniforms like the men who had attacked them in Sausalito. They carried brand new HK416, special ops assault rifles.

Both of the men stood trim and appeared to be in excellent physical condition. They wore their hair sheared-off and, like Brother Maxwell, they had no wrinkles on their faces, though they each looked to be about 45.

They patted Billy and Jenny down, took the Desert Eagles, cinched their wrists behind their backs with nylon cuffs and led them out. Billy's and Jenny's minds went rabid with questions. Had someone followed them from Slade's? From the Harbor? Were Harlan and the other guys safe? Were they in a Quentin Tarantino movie? Was this a new version of the Klan with encampments all over the US? How many were there? They both breathed very deeply to quiet their minds.

"Let's go over to our data center and make you comfortable," said the apparent leader.

They were forced through the kitchen and out the back door. The SWAT-types jammed their gun barrels into Billy's and Jenny's backs and prodded them out across the grounds.

They marched through a door into one end of a long building and down a staircase into a cold, high ceilinged, underground area of cavernous proportions. Concrete block walls surrounded a number of fabric-covered office cubicles arranged in various configurations. In one corner, through windowed partition walls, a Cray sat black and looming. There were two dated, but very powerful, super computers. Billy wondered what the two Crays did, especially the more vulnerable CPU sitting underground in the building full of pastel ladies next to Crystal Cathedral. Had they stumbled into a Stepford-Wife-Tim-McVeigh-Reverend-Jones-CIA-NSA madhouse?

Their minds worked very fast, and they each thought the same things. Why would people simply worried about the state of the nation need so much data clout? More than distribution of Christian newsletters took place here. ANVIL enjoyed more cyber power than many small nations.

"Sit down," said one of the men in a flat voice, pointing at the floor.

He nudged them to the concrete with his gun barrel while the other one covered them. He strapped their ankles so tight with plastic cuffs that Billy was concerned about the nylon band stopping the circulation in Jenny's wrists and feet.

"Let's warehouse our guests' ordinance," said the leader. He looked at Billy and smiled. "Hand cannons. Vintage Desert Eagles, so well known for excellence. We thank you for this fine contribution to our arsenal."

As if programmed in Stepford, the pair walked over to a massive steel door in the wall. One put his eyes in a goggle-like devise to have his retinas scanned. His voice commanded, "Open, please," and hydraulic arms slid the door open, slowly. Inside the connecting room, racks brimmed with assault weapons, rocket launchers, pistols, grenades, and explosives. A huge supply of ammunition rested in crates on the floor.

As Billy studied the arsenal, he noticed the potent array of Class III weapons: machine guns with boxes of belt-fed ammunition, launchers, and a rack of round-magazined, auto-loading shotguns. Tucked in with the shotguns sat shelves of small, rocket-like projectiles that looked like miniature rockets. They had to be the new ANVIL weapon Clarence mentioned. Cases for both with oriental lettering sat in the background, piled to the ceiling.

While the man with the pistols placed the Eagles on a shelf, the other covered them with the assault rifle. He placed his brow against the eye-scanner again and said, "Close, please." The doors swooshed shut and the locking mechanism crunched with steely precision.

"Now, gentlemen, we need to expedite taking care of this nice, surprise visit, and after, we will head on back to the *Queen Mary* to help with the preparation for our event," said the leader.

The second man nodded and took off obediently. The leader rolled over to a secretarial chair that looked as if it came right out of Slade's reception area in Anaheim. The seat and backrest stood out from the stainless steel and concrete of the cellar. It was covered with a synthetic, pastel lavender fabric matching the cubicles in this overwhelming computer cavern.

Both Jenny and Billy wondered how huge this operation might be. Did facilities like this sit hidden all over the United States? All over the globe? Were autocrat spawned, Stepford-like creatures being trained to destroy the basic fabric of freedom all over the world?

297

The man sat erectly, the padded rest centered in his straight back, and smiled. "Brother Slade informed us that you just visited ANVIL's corporate headquarters. We are very much interested in your journalistic practices."

He leaned back on the chair, a complacent grin on his face, then raised his arms and clasped his hands behind his head. The big black computer moaned through the walls of the air-conditioned room as it sorted through reams of data.

Billy wondered what kind of information, and about whom, whirred through its registers—who would be labeled a terrorist? What data raced through the chips? Was it information about animal parts, unions, school teachers, humanitarians, wild creatures, peaceniks, born-agains, believers in the apocalypse, tree huggers, animal lovers, white supremacy types, enviro activists, Free Range?

"So, Mr. William Clayton the third and Ms. Jennifer Sales Warren: two citizens from families of great influence for many generations. Things are not looking up right now, are they? But, never fear, you appear to be an inspired man. And you, Ms. Warren—why would a beautiful young woman of such wealth be tromping around in the Fairie City, wasting such a promising life? You would both be excellent members of ANVIL. You could be reborn in your country's only religion. Regain you faith, become brothers and sisters in the good fight. Avoid the charge of the four horsemen, which is now upon us. You are obviously looking for a calling in life; what better than to promote constitutional freedom and peace on earth, good will toward man? Think of it. You can support the president, homeland security and put an end to all this silly, tree-hugger terrorism. Spend your time securing the endowments of your forefathers."

"Jeez, dude, we're so darn busy with our journalistic pursuits we don't have time for clubs, but it is swell of you to ask. Right, Jenny?" said Billy.

"Oh heavens, yes. Praise the Lord and pass the napalm. It's all very pastel of you. Will I get a pointy bra and a cashmere sweater?"

"Now, now, now. Let's hold our tongue like a good girl, Ms. Jenny. And Mr. Clayton, you threw us a bit of a curveball up north, battling our men as you did and interrupting our mission. But you need to realize we are not talking about a little gathering of slobs slurping up beer and cholesterol while watching crummy television. Wasting away on drunken football escapism. No, this is not some white trash undertaking as you so smugly think; our organization is very high caliber— the upper strata of businessmen from all around the world."

"Does that include women?"

A petulant demeanor spread over the man's face. He looked at Jenny for a long beat with a dismissive sneer. "You will find out soon enough. We are delivering you back to Mr. Clayton's home state. You will enjoy the luxury and thrill of one of our many hunting facilities so you can meet the real shakers and movers."

The man stood, always covering them with the automatic weapon. "This is not anything like sitting around with a group of GOBs—good old boys—promoting one's dinky little business. That is not what ANIVIL is about. It appears you are worth a good deal of money from your takeover work, but what you obviously need is inspiration."

"Wow. You're offering me a job, aren't you? What a guy. But darn, I'm just a good old boy, like you say. A GOB. Just a plain old guy. Nothing in your league. Of course, we are talking about a subject a photojournalist can get his or her teeth into. Maybe I could hire you. I actually have enough money to cover your salary, but I don't think you could cover mine."

"Anyway, you don't enlist a person who's looking down the barrel of an assault rifle," said Jenny.

"There, there, there, Ms. Warren. You are a journalist and moved by great stories. We are talking about major concepts here. What is the film industry cliché? Ah, yes: 'high concept.' ANVIL is high concept to the max."

"Like blowing holes in the sternum of truly good citizens and sawing their hands off?" Jenny spat.

"My heavens. Do you always like such spirited fillies, Mr. Clayton?"

"I know from your background check, Ms. Warren, that with your doctorate in computer science, you are fully aware that our little computer in that room is a Cray X1E, and that we have more than one. You understand it's a bit dated, but our X1Es can push over eight thousand processors and pack a punch of almost 150 teraflops—a trillion bytes of data—a second, all in one magnificent black and maroon box. It does not appear that your gentleman friend is aware that we can throttle so many processors and have them sing together in our choir. It's plenty of firepower for business operations."

"So you've got a big hunk of iron that set your slavish followers back *muy mucho* bucks. But none of it means a damn thing without human smarts. Who's your code jockey? Only a limited group of people around the globe can put the pedal to the metal on a machine like this."

"Buster Bush is our driver—the best in the world."

"Oh, for crying out loud! Buster Bush was in my classes when I was getting my bachelor's. He's a jerk off. Thinks he's sharper than Seymour Cray. He does have good processors in his head. His brain has fast retrieval speed, but all he knows is how to load data and shove it around, not to mastermind anything. It's a wonder that knee jerk can get his shoes on."

"Thank you, Ms. Warren. We are very much aware of your computer skills and we have plenty of consultants at this time."

"You put those two creeps out in the car watching me at Animalfund."

"Let's get back to the subject at hand. The high concept. Freedom, freedom, freedom. Don't you see? We are dealing with the same major issues of 1776 even now. This is the United States of America: the land of the free and the home of the brave, and we must keep it that way."

The man's phone rang. He spun away and talked with a muffled voice. He clicked the phone off and turned back to them.

"Alright. Let's not wear things out. Much to do in preparation for our event on the *Queen Mary*. Our honored guests will begin to arrive soon."

He walked over to Billy.

"First, there are a couple of things I need to know. Your cooperation will make this simpler for us all."

Billy lay on his back and the man kicked him in the kidney area, hard and quick. Billy controlled a gasp, making it barely audible.

"Lord, what a man," he said and kicked Billy in the jaw.

Billy closed his eyes and opened them again quickly, controlling a deep moan. Blood started to ooze out of his mouth as the cuts from Neeley's men reopened.

"I really like a good strong man. We don't have many in this age of wimps." He kicked Billy's head again, higher up, at the ear and Billy groaned aloud.

Jenny pushed off the block wall with her feet and turned the energy into a lunge with her whole body. As she neared the man, she managed to whip her neck and hit his knee so hard with her head that he crumpled on the floor. She pushed again off the floor with her feet and hit him in the nose with the top of her head. He grunted and fell back. She grabbed his neck with her teeth, looking as if she might bite right through his carotid artery.

Billy rolled over. He attempted to spread his knees and grab the man's head between his legs, but the man elbowed them out of the way, scrambled away, got to his feet and grabbed Jenny by the hair. He clobbered her in the mouth. He kept hold of her hair and pounded her face with his fist.

Billy lunged across the floor, but to no avail. The nylon kept him from using all his strength. The man sprang to his feet and kicked him away. Jenny lay still on the floor with a bloody face.

"You have missed an excellent opportunity, so now we must get to business. Answer the questions and you are free. Even though the plates for your pickup are from offshore, we are finding more about you every moment. We believe you were the people at the shootout with our men in North Beach—in Sausalito—and that you went to Tosca, posturing as Mr. Hayes," he said with contempt.

He kicked Billy again.

"Do you want to explain these things for us? Life will be much simpler. We know it was you, so why not clean the slate."

"You don't know or you wouldn't ask," said Jenny. "And you better not act so smug because, as a matter of fact, numerous parties are after you, like the authorities in Marin County. We heard about you through the grapevine. You're more well known than Starbucks."

The man stared at her for a long beat, then Jenny said, "Oh, and I forgot to mention that Harlan is after your sorry ass."

Billy and Jenny laughed.

The guard pulled out a black special ops knife, swishing the nasty serrated blade out of the scabbard, and grabbed her hair again as the second man returned.

"I am going to cut your feet loose, Ms. Warren. We are taking you out for a special interrogation with Mr. Slade. We will let Mr. Clayton spend some time meditating, getting his mind collected. If you try anything foolish, your boyfriend will suffer beyond your imagination."

Jenny stood reluctantly. The guards followed her out and Billy heard the big bolts slide into the steel doorframe over the leader's voice. "Get somebody in here to watch him."

Billy slumped back, laid still and listened. At first, he heard the humming of the big black computer and nothing else. But as he relaxed, sounds began to invade the event horizon over the throbbing machines. He could tell that the front door at the entrance to the building had been left open. The guard posted for him apparently stood just inside it. Billy heard the man's feet shuffle. A lovely clean breeze flowed in off the Temecula Valley floor. A cricket whispered its vespers, automobile doors slammed shut and the sound of heavy tires, like those of a Humvee, scrunched in gravel.

As the tires crunched into motion, a horrible feeling seized Billy all over. From deep within, his emotions grabbed him in the middle of the stomach, as powerful as the jaws on the clamshell bucket of an earth-moving crane. Tightening like a great steel fist, his most profound, primitive understanding of the condition of being in the moment seized him. The part of him that was designed to keep him alive in times when he had been kicked over, the part that knew much more than the thinking parts of the brain ever knew, began to work. Up from nowhere, from the ancient cradle of understanding, Billy knew that Jenny—like Nuke and his wonderful dog—would be completely removed from him. And then he heard them, somewhere out in the expanse of night; the jet engines screamed down the runway.

TWENTY-THREE

Billy worked his hands down behind himself and pulled his feet through, between his arms. The constraint of the flex cuffs still hampered every movement, but his hands, now in front of him, and his eyes could work together.

He crawled to the open door of the bathroom. The toilet stood next to the same wall as the lavatory sink, about three feet from the end of the room. The basin sat perpendicular to the plumbing wall, so Billy pulled his knees up to himself with his back against the bowl. He put his feet on the sheetrock and lunged with his legs. He repeated the motion several times until the base of the commode snapped.

The force fractured the porcelain lip at the bottom of the toilet. The bolts holding the bowl to the floor cracked the porcelain at their holes. Though the toilet didn't tumble over, the rear basin sloshed water against the wall, soaking his jeans.

The fractured base of the commode produced a six-inch porcelain spear. Billy pulled a huge wad of toilet paper off the roller and wrapped the spear. With the tip of the makeshift dagger pointed toward himself, he held the wad of tissue with his bound hands. Using a constrained sawing motion, he cut through the nylon around his legs and lay back and ground through the binding on his wrists with short, powerful strokes.

Back in the main room, he lifted a roll of duct tape off a shelf, grabbed a handful of paper towels, wrapped them around the tissue, made a firm handle for the knife and slipped the weapon into his waistband. He grabbed a five-legged swivel chair and took the man guarding the door to the floor with it.

He went back to the computers and clicked on the screen. Someone had been working on it recently, because he could get right in and browse directories. He turned and

304

shuffled through papers at the Cray's workstations. In a tray he found a bound-in-house ANVIL directory. Inside he discovered a list of websites and phone numbers: ANVIL Corporate Aircraft 1, 2 and 3, the Slade Residence, the Red Line. He folded the document and wedged the information into the rear of his waistband. Back at the Cray, he sent Luther a note to hack the site.

The entire room whirred with the intense concentration of the computer, but over the purr, he heard the sounds of men as they found their downed peer. Billy went straight for a large air duct in the ceiling. He grabbed two edges, harnessing his weight and anger, and ripped the sheet metal screws loose from the steel flange beneath.

He inched along the three-foot shaft toward light for what seemed like a lifetime. The sounds of big fans whirling hard reverberated through the ducting. Billy had no idea how many of the ANVIL mercenaries remained on the grounds. He kept expecting the SWAT men to scoot through the cover he'd pulled lose. He wondered if he would even be able to hear them if they pursued. No sound rose above the wind blowing through the shaft. There was only the sounds of the air whistling against the metal edges and the bearings for the fans and motors, and him scuffling along the passage, which sounded like a buffalo stampede.

At the first turn in the sheet metal tunnel, he pushed up on his forearms. Ahead, a big fan blocked his way. The air blasted a cold draft, but was clean and fresh and the chill helped him avoid focusing on claustrophobia.

He crawled on, and before he had to tackle getting past the fan, a shaft appeared above him with light coming through it. Billy stood up in the airway, bent at the knees as well as he could, and sprung upward, hard. He had to hit the grate above him with his head because his hands were forced to remain down at his sides.

He banged over and over again. Finally, he stooped, worked his arms up above his head and hefted the metal over the edge. Pulling up and jumping, he lifted his body out. He emerged outside near the garage. The steel grate lay on the ground. He touched his head and didn't find any blood. He shot along behind the garage, stopped and peered around the corner.

Billy flew to the back of the nearest building. He peeked in a window. Everything was dark. Another building. Nothing. He ran hard and fast. As he was skirting the pool, his left foot hit something small and round. His foot went out from under him. In the grass sat another of the singular shotgun shells, identical to the one they found at Jess'. It was the same shell Clarence had seen in action up in Marin County.

He pushed his weight off the concrete deck fast and pumped toward a concentration of light glowing above the camp. Before he got to the main lights, he spotted a glow from an airline hanger. He hunkered up against the metal and caught his wind. Voices arose from inside.

"Aw, come on, forget it. I don't want to go outside. Just play! You're afraid I've got a fistful of aces. The noise came from one of those old Toms in the dumpster. Some little pussy's in heat. Let's play cards. Quit worrying."

Billy backed away to look through the window. Inside, four gruff, sunbaked men drank straight from a bottle of cheap bourbon, smoked thick cigars and played cards. They wore casual clothing. Billy guessed they were another group of the SWAT-types lounging through a slow shift. If so, guards probably stood watch in other areas. He slid into the shadows and moved around the structure quickly.

The big lights came from an expensive landing facility. A Gulfstream sat on the runway. Billy didn't look for guards. He ran hard, straight up the stairs and into the cockpit. After firing up the aircraft, he ripped along the runway, lifted over the subdivisions, casinos and vineyards of the Temecula countryside and roared toward Texas. The serene hills of San Diego's eastern county melted beneath the wings.

He hadn't heard the details from Luther yet, but everything inside him understood the old warrior would guide him, and together, they would find Jenny. He grabbed the phone from his pocket and called Harlan on his scrambled line.

"You what?" Harlan asked in disbelief.

Billy could visualize Harlan's face, could hear him wading through the authorities, the power-freaks, and all the other dreary, self-righteous types with whom he'd dealt for so long. As always, he was thankful Harlan was the family's lawyer.

"Yeah Harlan, I'm on a Gulfstream flying to Morning Star."

"Did you buy one?"

"No. I borrowed it."

"You stole an airplane? Damnit, Billy, get out to the ranch and ride horses with Luther Four Fingers until I get a wrap on this thing. He keeps calling here and pushing me around like I'm his hired white boy. I want you to get the old fool off my back."

"I'm on my way. Luther's got something. What's with Nuke?" asked Billy.

"The Coast Guard didn't find *dead latitudes*. There's been a lot of fog, but your boat may be lost. Tell me where you've been and why you stole the—"

"Listen," Billy interrupted. "I just crawled out of an underground bunker of ANVIL's. They store Class III ordinance in a vault and a couple of old Cray super computers. The new shotgun and the armor-piercing rounds are available in mass. They are probably supplying Iranian soldiers, US Special Ops, and you name it. US Military has a vendor in England. The Iraqis and Afghans are buying them from Slade's people in Pakistan and they're all shooting at each other while Slade laughs all the way to the bank. You'll get him for sure; I just slipped over one of those shells while running on the sidewalk."

"I am reviewing judges and prosecutors. This guy has enough funds; he may own them, so you may need to cough up some huge cash. I want to video these places, too. The ATF and fibbies might be in his pocket. He might work for the CIA and NSA and be commissioned to bring another huge load of total chaos in on the Middle East so the corporate boys can finally grab Iraq's oil and all its minerals. Nobody can figure out who's doing who. Hell, this guy might be the one who hired the dudes who blew the World Trade Center for the CIA, for all we know."

"Got to pay attention to this bird right now, Harlan, but my intuition tells me I won't be out at Luther's long. I found the ANVIL directory and the list appears to be an amazing cluster of information about the whole organization. I'll be sending everything to you with the information about the locations as soon as Luther scans the material into his hardware."

Billy's father's ranch, Morning Star, had been handed down through the generations by his forefathers. But when his dad's will passed the property on, Billy thought the land really belonged to Luther Four Fingers. Luther had lived on the ranch all through the years with Billy's mother and had taken care of everything. So Billy deeded the buildings and acreage to him. But the old Comanche warrior didn't give a damn about paper, about who owned what; he simply wanted to raise breathtaking quarter horses.

Luther also served as the spirit master for Morning Star. He refused to live in the big house and Billy's father had paid contractors to build him a concrete block home on the high ground, above the lake and the lowlands where the creeks converged. He spent the winters in the small house, with the old Kalvuki stove Billy's father brought over after one the family trips to Scandinavia. In the summer he would hitch his tipis to a stallion, travois style, and move them regularly to avoid the modern human's stuck syndrome.

As the slick corporate airplane roared east, Billy could picture Luther's hands. The brilliant horseman lavished untold hours of equestrian training on him as a boy. With those rugged hands, steady as granite, navigating every situation with royal dignity, he guided Billy. He taught the impatient young man to place a hackamore over a skittish yearling with aplomb, rub a two-year-old animal down with

308

sage to calm it, place a loose line around his mount's neck and disappear over the side during a full-hand gallop.

Billy ached to be near Luther's glow of sanity. Everything corporate—bloated egos, pitiful lying, pathetic infighting and tedious money grubbing—made Billy sick. Luther's deep-rooted knowledge made him the steadiest human being Billy had ever met.

He sat the plane down on the Morning Star airstrip. Lined with tall elms, the walk up the drive caused him to begin to relax. His mother's ancient, International Harvester Travelall, a huge station wagon predecessor to the yuppies' SUVs, sat on the gravel. Billy could hear her voice: "I was just practical. I bought my old International for practical purposes, a down-to-earth piece of machinery just like anything else off the farm. Thrifty and solid. My generation is pathetic. Only a boomer could turn a silly artifact like an automobile into a prestige object. A ridiculous erotic fetish. It's one thing to be praised for how high your stallion struts, but SUVs? Please! They are actually SRVs—self-realization vehicles. They are just icons for the spiritually famished."

Billy laughed. Her voice was so clear in his head. He wished she had returned from Rapallo or that he could hop in a jet with Jenny for a jump over to Italy. The ranch brought so many of his deepest values to the foreground. In spite of the grinding events at hand, he stood strong and grounded as he walked up to the front door.

He thought of all the amazing teachings his mother bestowed on him as a young man. Wisdom he let slip past like water rolling off the body after showering. Unconsciously, he had imitated his father and allowed money to become his entire existence. The Marine Corps changed everything quickly. On a ridiculously low cash flow, he began to appreciate how important truth and wisdom actually stood out as parts of one's life. After the active time in the Corps, Billy remained changed forever.

He walked down out of the big house, past the giant, red barn and the stables toward open pasture. He poked around and came upon Luther with a gorgeous, quarter horse filly. A grulla. He had a rubber snaffle in her mouth and crinkled a big bundle of thick, brown wrapping paper all over her back, teaching her to be steady.

Billy walked quietly as Luther's father, Brown Bear Growling, taught his son and as Luther schooled Billy. He muffled all sounds, but Luther didn't even need look around to know that Billy was there.

"These bastards didn't have the smarts to leave your new woman alone. She's the best thing ever happened to you. We've got to go get her fast. I talked with the peyote buttons, while doing the half-moon ceremony. I can grab hold of her spirit through brother peyote already; she is a very powerful tantrika. She is my sister. They want to throw her in with rattlers. These are those really evil white men. Let's go on a raiding party."

Billy felt as if he stood there as a twelve-year-old boy again. As always, Luther knew exactly what had taken place. He put his arm up under the mare's neck, patted her, slipped off the tack and slapped her on the rump. She pushed off her stocky hindquarters, blew a rush of wind through flared nostrils and bolted off toward a thicket of oaks.

Luther walked toward his concrete block home, and Billy followed him inside. He sat cross-legged and pulled out a small bottle of cheap bourbon.

"Alright, drink some white man poison. Old white eyes' Supreme Court doesn't like us working with big daddy peyote. They like booze. This evil shit makes you a nasty, fork-tongued killer like those old honkey lawyers."

He took a draw off the bottle, handed the bourbon to Billy and grinned wide with his broken front tooth making him look like some kind of a pirate—one of Captain Jack Sparrow's brothers. Billy followed suit. He had listened closely to Luther since he was a little boy. He might have dismissed the old man as a nutcase, but they rarely sat around for teachings. They roamed the backcountry. They whispered to horses, broke colts and took care of lame animals.

Luther never acted phony, tried to chip away at Billy's being, or spoke falsely: none of the habitual behavior that inspires children to close down their listening when they are around so-called adults. Plugging his ears to the old horseman's great knowledge would have been like shutting off the choir of the birds singing in the morning.

He contemplated Luther's weathered face.

Luther rarely talked about his personal story; no one was privy to his age for sure, though he must have been at least eighty. But anyone could perceive how alive he remained in old age, how vital and engaged he was with every part of life.

"So, my boy is back to me without his blood father. My own blood, my great-grandsons are off at the big-time, white man colleges. They only come to me when they have problems, just like you. It's good for boys to work with a trusted elder. The practice of having staunch old farts like me indoctrinate young men is about gone, and it's got us in some sad shit."

Luther smiled at Billy. "Let's get your stuff out so we can take off."

Billy gazed at him and shook his head. The old man's ability to read his mind like a sign on a restroom door still blew him away. He had completely forgotten he had the ANVIL directory stuffed in his waistband. He handed the list to Luther who roamed about, getting the thing digitized. A massive tunneling into ANVIL iron started with Luther's hacker buddies; it would be a transfer pipe dumping the information to Harlan.

"I encountered father peyote and had a vision. Part of the broadcast is an old, tired insight. Whitey making evil into a business pursuit. What's new? Nothing. It's the same old story that everyone has down. Raping our mother, the Earth, 'til she's about ready to kill all of us, like now."

Luther took another pull off the rot-gut whiskey. He sat the bottle down and gazed at Billy.

"It comes from the sadness. This great country of a hundred thousand rivers is sliced up like a crappy cut meat

311

on a plate—like opossum or muskrat or something—and it may never be well again."

Billy watched Luther straightforwardly, as he had always done. His eyes never dodged in fear.

Luther sat down and Billy joined him. He reached over to a wonderful table of woven willow branches with a hundred-year-old Navajo blanket on top. It held a few of his possessions. He picked up a pack of American Spirit cigarettes. He shook one out for each of them and reached over for a light. He scratched a big old kitchen match on one of his thick thumbnails and lit the cigarettes.

They both sucked deeply on the cigarettes. The draw on the little cylinder made Billy feel dizzy, like he would fall over. Luther gawped at him closely and laughed.

"To help you understand money, the world came down hard on you, Billy. You lost a wife and the beautiful girl last year, and now you've lost your new one. You've lost the gangbanger, Nuke. He is a real man. Most men today are wimps, but he is a man of great courage. He is powerful enough to actually practice wisdom. He engages even though he never got out of the city except over by Buda, Texas at his Grandma Moss'."

Luther leaned his keyboard against the wall as he continued, and they both pulled on the cigarettes. "You can feel people of African lineage, you know. You start getting soft and genuine around African-blooded people because all religion came from their heartland. Yes, sir. Right after the last ice age, back when old Homo sapiens started traipsing up to the steppes of Central Asia."

Luther took another drag off the cigarette and blew perfect smoke rings. "You see. The smoke says Grandma Moss is damn cute for an old woman. I might even think about going after her. Maybe I'll slow the urge down with these young fillies, the barrel racers and whatnot. They're cute, but they take me away from my own horses. Those Afro girls can really dance. I could get some Al Green CDs and go court her. Damn cute. Fifty-two: the best sex you can get."

Luther's face took on a sly grin and he winked at Billy.

"A 50-year-old girl will knock your socks off night and day. They quit being scared of old age, so they get really fun again and not so grabby anymore. They don't talk every second, night and day, like young ones do. I'd go do something wild with her, but a damn woman wants to take up all your time if you get in thick. Your mature chicks are sex fiends. She'd pull me away from my ponies. No good. Hell, after 60 years, or whatever it's been, I'm startin' to get good with women and horses both."

Billy and Luther howled.

He blew more smoke rings slowly. "Your daddy was more linear as a boy; he always recognized what he wanted. You still aren't tuned into your driving desire. If a man can't instill purpose around himself, the world hammers his life force out and leaves a very weak man. He doesn't catch on to what to do. You're weird. You're strong, but all you've got is a bunch of money and a few scars."

"I'm a private eye now. Nuke and I made a blood vow."

"Well, you're not any good. Where the hell is your dog? Your girlfriend? Your fucking partner can't even find himself, son." Luther laughed so hard Billy had to join him.

"Remember all those Travis McGee books I read when I was about twelve?"

"Hell, yes. I read 'em too, remember?"

"I know. I always liked the way that guy lived. We're going to be in salvage, too, just like Trav."

"Well you better salvage your own damned boat or you guys are gonna be a joke, not PIs. You'll have to buy a houseboat like that Trav had." They laughed again.

"How are the horses?" asked Billy.

"Rivers are rivers. Trees are trees. Horses are horses. Some are mean, some are kind, and some love to learn, same as people," said Luther.

They finished up each of their cigarettes. Billy was wobbly—high as a kite from the smoke and whiskey. Luther flipped his cigarette butt into the fire pit in the center of his home and stood up. Billy did the same, following him outside.

"Let's get down to business," said Luther. "Father peyote has been rustling like silk sheets. He told me you were coming. He told me the rattlesnake is ready for war, and I need to protect you. We've got a lot of dumb white boys foolin' with things they should leave alone. White boys never were too smart."

Billy cracked up and reached over, grabbing Luther in a bear hug.

"Clever, sneaky and mean, but not smart. The feds in on this—looks like they killed Jess. So they're all bound to be real stiff and lame. It's easy to kick the butts of stiff people," said Luther, laughing too. He stepped back, smiling. "Damn, you are lookin' good, son, even if you *are* lame. This new woman must be hot."

Luther opened his right hand, slapped his breast and brought his flattened hand, palm down, out from his heart while looking straight in Billy's eyes. "I hear the truth. I speak from the heart," Luther said. Billy made the same, solid gesture in return.

Luther continued to stare into Billy's eyes. "Remember that, Billy? I taught you when you were ten and you still went off and did the money crap." Luther pushed Billy's chest with his hand.

"I remember the sign every day of my life, Luther."

"But you didn't live true." He put an arm around Billy. The old, crag-faced man swept his hand out at the slope, down toward the lake and the great stand of white oak and sycamore trees.

Tears came to Billy's eyes.

"You earned a trillion bucks, but what can you do with all that crap? The white man jacks off his time. He plays with his own dick because he's starved for power and

314

has never really had any good lovin', only a little tiny squirt when he gets 'em off. Why do you think those white girls think us Indians are so sexy? You can't eat money, or dive into some juicy love medicine with the stuff. All you get from the white man's temple is paranoia. Now all those bytes of data are streaming through your hands representing your big wad of money, and you have to watch out for every little government bureaucrat and two-bit thug who is too dumb to make money. If being lame at grabbing cash is someone's problem, then they are real fucking dumb. The cheeky ones get more vicious by the minute."

He turned his hand over and gestured toward the expanse of voluptuous landscape as if he was reaching to hold it. "There's your wealth, son. Nothing can match those oaks. The Marines was okay. You learned how to take care of yourself and didn't waste a lot of time with those dumb military politics. But this money-grubber stuff. White men are just plain old dumb, aren't they? White boys being so dumb blows us Indians away. We don't get it. You let 30 years of your life slip by, and you can't kiss money or ride on it. It's nothing but some numbers on chips."

"Things are different now, Luther. The unheard of string of numbers, my trillion dollars, those twelve zeroes, finally piled up in the global financial crunch. I saw that I was like the zombies in a casino, like a TV junkie: too stoned on bullshit to look around at how beautiful everything was around me."

"Are you spending time on your big sailboat?"

"Yeah. As soon as I get this mess tidied up, I'm going over to Russia to look at the tigers."

"Damn, you *are* coming back to your senses, son. This planet is spacious. She is beautiful. She is a smooth lover and as wily as any woman. You need to mix with her. Father Death sits on your left shoulder like those old Toltec Naguals say. Those guys are crazier than the Tibetans, but they're real smart. Your grim reaper is right there ready to take you at any time. You never have a clue when. You better enjoy this beautiful little planet. She's all heart and soul, and the white man's temple, the land of the dead numbers, means nothing, same as the white man stealing too much from the earth means nothing. Plenty of Indians like the Karankawas and the Aztecs were as disgusting as old white eyes and look where mean shit got them. The Earth will spit old whitey off, exactly like she did to all those other people, if he doesn't catch on to what an honor it is to live here."

"Yeah, Luther. You're spot on. I probed the number with the dollar sign and all the zeroes and one little period. One trillion dollars. I finally caught on to what you had been trying to tell me all along about what my life would come to. I would have no woman, no friends, no kids: nothing but a string of numbers. If I hadn't hid out, all the money boys would have known I broke the magic number; my name would have been plastered all over the *Wall Street Journal*, which would really suck."

Luther pulled him back inside the house. "I introduced you to your Protector when you were ten. Rattler is the guardian at the gate of knowledge. No one can touch rattlesnake power. You got captured by the white eyes' weakness. Got drunk on money like any junkie. But your daddy is gone now, and he asked me to make you my boy while he lay dying. He said he finally understood how he messed up, how he screwed up wasting so much time hanging around with the oil sheiks in Dallas and Houston. He understood how few moments a person has on Earth; he finally saw clearly as he finished his life. He saw he should have stayed out here raising horses."

Luther stepped over to a stunning table made from a three-inch-thick maple burl with a honey-looking beeswax finish. The table rested under one of the huge windows set in the cinder block. He scooped up a bundle of sage.

They walked out and down to Luther's tipi. Inside the flap, Luther sat on a fabulous, Tibetan carpet with snow leopards on it. The carpet was believed to have belonged to Chuang Tzu, the great Chinese philosopher. With his forehead, Luther signaled Billy to follow as he fanned up the embers from the fire pit. He placed the sage on the glowing coals, sat down cross-legged on another Tibetan rug—one with icons of the monsters ego can produce. Such frightening figures were woven into a carpet that Billy's mind stood still as he looked at it. Luther swept his hand in a "be seated" motion. Billy sat on another rug.

"Those are snow lions. My buddy, Chogyam Trungpa, gave me the weaving. He was some kind of a wild Tibetan monk. I guess he was a Buddhist, but then he got enlightened and stopped clinging to his thoughts. He helped people in dharma jams, like you're gonna help end this salvage business because it resonates with your principle predilection: kindness. You're getting your madcap sense of humor back. You really were funny when you were a boy. Sit down and lean into the vibes of this durn rug. It's yak wool. Trungpa was one wild-ass son-of-a-bitch; you'll feel him all over the place. We laughed our asses off all the time. He rode a horse like it was a goddamn yak."

Billy understood that Luther and his buddies all rode on a great cloud of energy from the highest spiritual centers on Earth.

"You always did take to mescalito, I put some in the smoke. You're also getting a contact high off me. It's your best vision portal. Damn, I can feel you opening right up. You've never been this clear in your whole life—not since you were five. I like it. Back to a pure mind like the little kids."

"This is a hell of a rug, Luther."

The old man cracked up. "Acerbic wit and the beauty of understatement: you and your daddy both lived it like my old Tibetan buddies. Bring humor to the top, Billy. After the Hikuri kicks in good and strong, we're gonna get in the plane you stole and let doctor peyote guide us to the beautiful, Texas Hill Country. I can visualize your girlfriend, and the bad guys have her up there. I also know this jet you stole has sat down on a runway on Slade's ranch before. I also sense the main bad guy, this Jet Slade character, is a pasty little white boy who declares he's a Christian. But he ain't. I'm close to some true Christians. Real Christians don't plant fear

317

in people's hearts and they do some really good stuff that you can see. It's called bearing witness; they don't bullshit about how good they are. Hell, there were Quakers who sailed medical supplies right into Vietnam when the fat-cat, white boys were agent oranging everybody."

The aroma of sage pervaded the entire space. Billy inhaled deeply and as the spirit took hold; the power made him completely aware of everything. He mingled with the vastly spacious contentment arising from not thinking, not dwelling on any thinking. The thoughts arose but they never overwhelmed him. His intuition told him exactly how to find Jenny, Nuke and Sam. He relaxed to wait for the plan to arise. Luther handed him a gourd. Billy turned back the acrid peyote tea without flinching.

"Okay, you've stopped time. You finally worked through the typical white-boy, business-freak, fear-of-not-being-enough thing: the rushing through to grasp onto some more greenbacks and gizmos. You're back to your real self. As soon as you're getting enough nookie from this beautiful girl, she'll cool your jets so you can sit still. Then you're coming back here and I'll introduce you to Choogy."

"I thought that guy was dead?"

"Well, let's say everything is dead," he grinned, "*and* everything is alive; it's the divine paradox."

"Luther, you are too damned mystical. How the hell is anybody supposed to know what you're talking about?"

"You got me," said Luther and they both laughed so hard they rolled over on the rugs.

"These Tibetans are some cosmic cowboys. They can ride the rangiest stallions around and don't even need a rope. Just walk up, put their hand on the horse's snout, take the mane and hop on. Like my people, they don't need a bit, a bridle, a hackamore, nothing."

Luther handed the whiskey to Billy.

"This will give you a grounded edge with these nasty swine. We're going to take off now and you need to get the damn airplane up and not let brother peyote fly to the frickin' South Pole. We'll finish the little drink, and then we'll be able to find Slade and Jenny right away."

"Well hell, Luther, I'll tell the air control boys I'm stoned out of my ass on peyote, I stole a corporate jet from a dude named Jet, and I'm flying up to the Hill Country of Texas."

They both laughed like wild animals. Luther looked like a hyena to Billy.

"Damn, you are comin' back to life, Billy."

Luther handed the gourd to Billy again and he drank the horribly bitter tea without any complaint. The pungent alkaline fortified the long march into Billy's subconscious. Now, he had no choices to make, so he was completely liberated.

"I think this stuff is legal if you're an Indian, but I don't know. You white boys may become felons for entering peyote's temple, even if you become a member of the Native American Church." Luther howled with laughter so infectious Billy had to follow suit.

"If you get stoned for religion it's okay, but what the hell is religion? If you did some father peyote to get thick with a young horse, they'd say you were a sicko and a drug friend. No way you were engaging in a religious activity. If you did anything just for some good old fun, our most deeply religious act, they would croak. Most white men never had any fun their whole lives. It's why they walk like there's a cucumber up their ass. They're too damn stiff."

"Luther, in case you hadn't noticed, I'm a white guy."

"Nah, you don't care about race; you're not scared. You're not stuck on anything. Racists are afraid they're not good enough, so they put others down. The insufficient-funds syndrome happens to every brand of human. People play 'prove it' all the time. You've seen the games. You're people, too, Billy. But you're brain's not stuck. You can *see*."

Father peyote swelled up over everything. Time and other fetters began to take a back seat, a position out where Stephen Hawkins roamed, past the constraints of a frightened ego. Billy's thinking took a straight leap through the prison of society's mental shackles and lapsed into pure understanding: into the place where he actually knew about being alive, knew his life first hand and knew how short it was.

TWENTY-FOUR

As quickly as the as the pilot eased the corporate jet to a stop on the runway at Paradise Ranch, the driver packed Jenny into a Humvee. Cuffed at her wrists and ankles, she was placed next to Jet Slade. They drove fast, straight across the expansive facility. The giant fence stood out as they sped toward it. The construct loomed massively, threatening everything around, as if it controlled the entire environment, demanding and ominous; nothing took place without express permission because Slade and his edifice reigned supreme.

As they moved in closer, Slade tried to focus on the diamond-shaped holes in the stainless steel. The heat of fear rose in his stomach, and to calm himself he glanced around at Jenny. This woman's beauty overwhelmed him. He wanted to reach out and caress her face, to fondle her breasts. He needed to be close to Lucinda soon. He hoped she had already been flown out from the Temecula facility, from his beloved White Dove Ranch.

The driver slid up to the gate, stepped right out of the Humvee and worked the keypad for the lock quickly. Once inside, he stood waiting for Jenny and Slade to pass. Slade's throat caught with fear, but he simply turned and looked at Jenny's body. His whole body grew light, formless. He was high, stoned out of his mind on things to look forward to. He would put the fear of God into this woman. He would bury her stupid friend buried right here on the White Dove property. Without his sick input, she would come around.

Slade had turned many a person around—congregation upon congregation. The most twisted sinners like Lucien Maxwell had accepted Christ completely. They had fallen on their knees in honor of the Lord. Look at Lucien now. He made mistakes, true, but study the results of his human sculpting. Jet Slade definitely has the "right stuff," he thought. He was a ridiculous, high-classed pimp, supplying the oil barons of Dallas and Houston with extremely expensive broads flown right in from Paris, from London, from Milan. *Actually quite a clever cash flow,* thought Slade. But Slade had reinvented Lucien absolutely. Now that Lucien was a servant of the Lord, Slade knew for certain that this new man would wade through ANVIL's challenges and tidy up the mess in California.

Yes. With this Clayton character recycled, shredded and applied as fertilizer for the tomatoes, this gorgeous girl would be at his beck and call.

Past the fence, the huge excavation seemed to rise up from within—to expand from its own void and to take over everything. Beads of sweat erupted on Slade's brow. Spasms of fear shot through the muscles all over his body. All he had to do was avoid looking down, to turn away and focus on the new building. His building. And imagine his new woman as a guest. So much love, sweat and so many tears he put into the design of this domicile for his new ladies. There he would live with them: training them, caring for them, disposing of them appropriately. He thought about the endless passion and beamed at the berm and the sod roof. Slade reveled again at his own genius—recycling the earth from the excavation into the structure. Brilliant. God, he loved his own brilliance, and he would become a green himself, join the tree huggers, and turn environmental friendly. Even that dumb shit, Al Gore, was an enviro-weenie.

As he and the driver walked toward the building, around the great pit, Slade couldn't help but squint over the steep drop. The serpents seethed with boiling motion: hissing, rattling, striking, crawling over and under one another like a roiling cauldron of wanton flesh.

Slade forced himself not to lose it. He punched in the code on the front door and walked right into the building through the coded lock on the thick, steel front door. Inside, the driver followed him and he punched through another device on yet another steel door. Inside the containment room, Jenny sat drugged out on animal tranquilizers. She balanced on the edge of a prison-like cot with fine, floral cotton bedding. She sat atop the big, fluffy comforter and stared vacantly at the wall in front of her. Her arms were manacled behind her back.

"Ah, my dear. You have awakened from your little nap. Come with me. You need to stretch out a bit."

He took her by the arm, eased her up and they walked out the front door, past the viper farm. Slade forced himself to keep himself together in spite of the snakes and tried to lead her out into the yard beside the building.

"What in the name of god is this?" asked Jenny, when she zeroed in on the bottom of the hole. "What are you doing?"

"You needn't worry, little lady," said Slade. "We are rattlesnake farmers. The flesh tastes a lot like chicken."

"Good Lord. You are one weird creep."

Slade clamped down on her arm without looking into the abyss. He urged her toward the grass. "Don't worry, my dear. You will grow to love my lifestyle."

Jenny jerked away, jumped around him and tried to push him into the pit with her shoulder. The big driver moved in fast and took hold of them both, pulling them away from the precipice.

The man overwhelmed Jenny with size and strength because he surprised her by moving in so fast and taking hold of her. Slade nodded toward the door of his seraglio, his den for taking care of his esteemed guests. As they moved back into his den, he noticed Mattie. Pallid and waif-like, she stood on the second floor landing, rag in hand, dusting the upstairs railing. The slight woman held her ever-present bottle of lemon oil. Seeing her, Slade was trapped, never a moment's peace, a little space to be himself.

Here he stood, having found a dream woman and . . . and Mattie's accident would soon come to pass. Such a tragedy; he had sacrificed so many years taking care of the poor thing. Slade could envision the entire scenario. Announcements in church and to any media people that stumbled across the story. A viper pit made for fantastic headlines, for living clichés, for collateral damage from gossip. Even though the ranch sat hidden in a very remote location, tucked away in Central Texas, an awful lot of people roamed in and out all the time.

"Put her away. Lock everything down. Go in the basement and check the alarms and the electric circuits. Make sure the locks all click into place. I'll wait in the Humvee."

The driver checked over his shoulder, around the grounds and scrutinized the facility as he locked the gate. He popped into the Humvee and spun round in a big circle toward headquarters. Slade locked in on more excitement than he had imagined in his wildest thoughts ten years earlier, when he still writhed with the pain of his youth. Now he would end up living like Hugh Hefner: hot and cold running women on tap. Though frightening, the viper pit added to his intoxication: coiled, slithering fast, striking, every action imaginable took place right in front of his perspiring eye lids. The adrenalin rushes kept him living on the edge.

Deep inside, Slade loved quandary. Every snafu hurled his way, screaming to be taken care of, brought him to life, shielded him from the boredom of the day to day. Peaceful people seemed like freaks of nature to him—like the living dead. Working on difficult situations always kept his mind away from the true horror of human beings. He thought about the plan, about his reaction; he heard his own sonorous voice expounding to his flock, to the media: "Oh Lord, please have mercy. I never thought to put a fence inside the big one, a barrier right around the excavation itself. Our serpent farm is a pure and simple service for the human race. Humankind is in big need of inexpensive protein. And snake lovers, there *are* so many of them now. The project stands strong as a copasetic profit center on ANVIL's animal sanctuary. I mean, after all, they *are* snakes—cold-blooded reptiles. But some things always break my heart, my wonderful Mattie, all our years together. We didn't think to fence the breeding ground."

He felt how wonderful and sonorous his voice would grow in timbre, modulating an edge of sadness, and he would pull on down to the true basso profundo range as he spoke over Mattie's grave. Deep, secure, powerful. *God this is a wonderful life*, he thought as they drew closer to the front porch of the grand, Victorian headquarters building with its immaculate white paint.

The international businessmen—the arms dealers and their friends who manufactured ordinance, the brilliant capitalists who provided weapons ready for international distribution—stood on the porch, on his fabulous ranch, holding cocktails and hobnobbing. They already treated him as a star. This new work equated the true Jet Slade, elicited pride and satisfaction, more so than preaching or ANVIL. Though he would never tell a soul, using animals for human purpose made him the liberator of himself and Mattie when they were little captives. But he wouldn't dive in now; cash flow is the American way. The bleeding-heart liberal had already done enough damage.

A smile spread all over his face as they moved in closer. Everyone was dressed to the nines. They would soon go and change into very expensive khakis from the finest men's clothiers. They would go out and get their blood thundering through their bodies with the hunt. The jet full of women would be landing soon, flown in from the west side of Los Angeles. The women would be in place and very ready for cocktails by the time the hunt wound down. They would be showered and enjoying drinks as the powerful men returned from the hunt.

Slade spread his warm, gracious smile, raised his brow to emit power and lowered his voice to that deep timbre that commanded the audience. He moved from group to group and on inside—into the great room and the massive parlor. He worked the crowd like a presidential candidate.

He slid from handshake to handshake quickly, taking hold of an occasional shoulder as a part of a show of genuine camaraderie and he patted a back from time to time. But right in the midst of the advent, Jenny came to mind. He wanted her so badly that the CEOs started to seem like a bunch of big, fat, florid-faced, fatuous swine. He wanted to be with her, not them. Or, he wanted to be alone with his vision of her. The thoughts, and the swarm of emotions attached to them, overwhelmed him. He moved up the stairs to his office and bolted the door. He perched at his computer and brought the 20-inch monitor to life. He called Buster Bush.

"Hey boss, you soupin' those sleepy ole pussies up with speed. Damn, they're lucky. Be sure and save me some."

"You know, Buster, you are not as funny as you think you are."

"Hey, don't go all weepy on me 'cause you used to be the meth preacher. I never was strung out on the stuff. I was studyin' assembly language at Cal Tech while you were stoned on speed, dippin' born agains. Keep the facts in mind, boss."

"Cut the crap, get all the links fixed for the demo of our databases on the *Queen Mary*, and get that goddamn snake off my screen, Buster."

As he spoke, he wanted Buster and everyone else to disappear. To leave him alone. To let him sleep. Maybe he would dream about the two startling, different-colored eyes. Sleep had been a horrible quandary for some time. Had someone had pulled off an arcane curse on him? Santeria, hoodoo, Christian apocalypse hocus-pocus, whatever. Slade didn't believe in any of that hooey, but it did seem odd that sleep had been his one true ally all his life. He often sat down in a party to sleep for 20 minutes and wake fully rested. When he put his head on the pillow at the end of the day, Jet had always known the Lord fully in his heart and he fell asleep as soon as his eyelids clicked shut.

But since this disgusting, tree-hugging geek in Tiburon had started his Free Range group and that fucking idiot, Hicks, had gone nuts to protect Smokey, to hold onto his precious little seat in the Senate, sleep had become terrifying. Legal terrorists, that's what has was going to create. Only entitled people were allowed to do such a thing.

But Hayes. They had so much goddamned money and now all they spent it on was lawyers, terrorizing businessmen with the stupid court system. The judges should be terminated. The horror manifested every night. Stretching out in bed, preparing for slumber no longer brought joy and peace of mind. No, bed delivered the most disgusting part of the day. He crawled into the clean white sheets, lay still, and his mind latched onto the thought of how long he would take to fall asleep. Some nights churned with the thought until the morning light slipped through the shades.

He gazed out a window as his mind raged with the thoughts, but finally he brought himself present and a looked at the screen. His breath leveled out and his body sank further into the plush leather executive seat, but as he faced the screen, he broke into an intense sweat, barely gasping down a scream.

The timber rattler sat coiled, ready to strike. It was darker, more thick and threatening than the lighter, less formidable diamond back. Slade's skin always crawled when he watched them slither among the other vipers. Their coil, their preparation for the strike, caused more bone-chilling fear than any terrorist ever churned up in a person. The snake's eyes bore straight through him and then a weather-beaten man appeared. The man had thick and black hair, plaited down the back of his neck, and a chipped tooth. He was the very same character for certain. Just as before, he stood beside the thick rattler, piercing Slade's eyes with his own, and as before, the rattle grew to the size of a pineapple and the sound it made sought to shear Slade's mind into a pile of sizzling fragments.

Slade tried to dial Buster back but the keyboard sat frozen. Slade stood and slammed the big, flat screen on its face. He picked up a straight-backed chair that sat to the right of his desk, raised it over his head and came down hard. He threw the chair on the floor and skulked right out onto his deck.

The fresh air invigorated him, brought his thoughts back around to power. He leaned over the railing, inspecting his guests as they milled about out on the grounds anticipating a fabulous day. Some of the executives had already shed their business suits and changed into their field attire for the hunt.

Slade stood up straight and shook himself. He inhaled, raised his brow, pushed his shoulders back, and stretched his neck in an effort to get his composure back.

Below, Lucien Maxwell stepped out of the house and into the crowd, and immediately Slade knew that Brother Maxwell had changed.

The moment Brother Maxwell disappeared into the lodge with a coterie of Europeans, Lucinda stepped out on the porch with a cocktail. She slipped up behind him and put her free hand over his eyes.

"Boo."

"Oh my golly, is this the big bad wolf?"

"Yes, and I've come to eat you," she said, laughing luridly.

"You naughty girl."

"Oh lord, you don't know how naughty I am."

She was more voluptuous than ever. He pulled her into his arms and grabbed her with his lips. They kissed deeply, and he reached the top of the light summer frock she wore. He groped her bosom and Lucinda pulled back.

"Guess what this is?" she asked, holding the cocktail out to him.

He glanced at the cocktail. "Damn, you are the best woman a guy could dream up. It's a gin rickey isn't it?"

"Your favorite," she said.

"Darlin', you are too much." He took the drink and chugged it straight back and then pulled her up over his shoulder, walked through the door into his bedroom and threw her across the bed. They sunk into one another and smooched until everything faded away. He lost himself until a shout came from outside, down below the deck.

"Jet, it's time for the hunt." Lucien Maxwell's voice rang out distinctly from everything below. He didn't even bother calling him Brother Slade.

Maxwell had turned completely and Jet Slade knew it. The voice alone told all. He knew that things would never and be the same. He had saved the man, dragged him out of perdition, cleansed him in the water with his own hands, protected him and the man had now turned back. Maybe only launching him into the beginnings of judgment, into a form of purgatory with the snakes would help cleanse his spirit on into eternity.

Slade got right up and left Lucinda spread out on the bed. "Hey, Mr. Jetson, you aren't gonna run right out and fight off the big bad wolf, are you?"

"Darlin', I gotta go hunt tigers. When I get back, I'm gonna give you a real ride. That was a little quickie to hold you over."

Brother Maxwell's voice rang out from below the deck. "Hey, boss, are you comin'? We are ready to get the big bad tigers."

Slade grabbed a freshly-pressed, heavily-starched khaki shirt and trousers out of his closet, hobbled into the pants, slipped on the shirt and ran to the rail.

"Get us a car, Brother Maxwell. We need to go into the outback and make sure that things are okay."

"That's a ten-four, nutty buddy."

Every inch of Slade was grated by Maxwell's new, horrid attitude. No organization hung together in such disarray. He would have to recycle Maxwell. The snakes would make excellent fertilizer of him and the tomato field would serve as a burial ground.

As the Humvee flew out toward the animal shelters, Slade kept all complaints to himself. Nothing to discuss, he had decided what to do with Brother Maxwell. The man had slipped off the deep end again and part of the load of being in command required very difficult decisions.

"It won't take long," said Brother Maxwell.

"Nah, we're good. We can move fast. Heck, we've rehearsed enough."

"Yeah, the methamphetamine kicks them out of the torpor from the tranqs. I've never seen anything like it. Big cats and their amphetamines—who'd a thunk?" Maxwell turned to Slade and grinned evilly.

As the Humvee slowed, the driver hit a remote, and the gate in a 20-foot concrete wall opened and the vehicle flew through. The cages sat in various groupings, in rows of five, spaced all around the installation. Men shuffled around in the area, tending the cages, which were all full of large cats. Some of the animals were crippled, some were injured, others were very old and tired. All rejects from zoos, some lame and too old, some as parts of litters that the zoo did not need.

The driver pushed the handheld's buttons and the doors on the central building slid into the walls quickly and closed behind the Humvee. Slade and Maxwell hopped out and grabbed the sedative rifle box and the rest of the equipment. Maxwell broke the breech, loaded the first, long sedative dart with its colorful nylon feathers and slammed the gun shut.

The dose of methamphetamine would have killed a man as big as a basketball player. It was huge enough to high wire a rhinoceros. The thought that the tigers might die and ruin the hunt did trouble Slade a bit. They would compost the bodies, after all they were old, tired zoo animals. But if this weighty group of capitalists listened to him flounder through excuses about a canceled hunt, the stealer and the buster might suffer a slower market entry. Slade might even lose his engineers, all leftovers from the Supreme Soviet days.

As they ran out the back door, Slade loaded another rifle with one of the massive doses, enough to make a percheron horse bounce off the walls. At the cages, the old, ex-zoo critters watched with little enthusiasm. Slade and Brother Maxwell delivered the injections and reloaded. They fired five into each critter. Soon, all of the tigers were rangy, pacing, and ill tempered like any common speed freak.

They stopped again before returning to headquarters. An enormous firing range sat in the shade of three-story mounds of earth scraped into place as a shield for absorbing fired projectiles. The three CAT D11 bulldozers that had built the hills sat idle. In front of the great piles of earth, a collection of old, wrecked earth-moving equipment, hummers, armored limos and sheets of steel had been gathered.

Several hundred yards away from the manmade mountains, a 300-foot wooden structure with a tin roof that covered benches and work platforms was designed to offer shooters a bit of protection from the elements and hold their weapons. Most of the shooting gallery sat back from various types of targets: paper, wood, human forms, bull's-eyes. At the end of the structure, in front of the wrecks the benches, was a setup with two-dozen automatic shotguns. With each weapon sat a supply of shotgun shells with small stainless steel projectiles protruding from them.

Slade grabbed a weapon and fired at a Hummer limousine. Though the armor plate would have stopped all other light arms, the projectile launched from the shotgun, flew straight to the handle of the limo and blew out the mechanism.

A smile broke over his face. "That's my baby," Slade said to Maxwell.

"It's a very naughty little baby," he said, laughing.

Back at the main buildings, Jet ran into Desi Sandoval talking with two CEOs. Before the hunt was over, Jet would know this man inside out. Desi looked like any other greedy business dweeb—always grabbing for more, talking out of the side of his mouth, completely void of integrity. It was a lot of risk, stealing a government officer, but the guy spilled over with hunger so much that he would probably drop his Smokey job like a gila monster. By the time they flew back to Long Beach together, Jet would know whether this man wanted to pull off a sting on ANVIL, or just get rich. If Sandoval wanted to play games, he would join the girl in the snake pit.

He shook hands with Desi, watched him disappear into the crowd, and then a heavy hand landed on his shoulder from behind.

"Jet, I'm all dressed and ready to go. When do we take off?"

"We're on our way to the garage. Come along, Mr. Hegel. We have so much to talk about after the hunt, but now let's get out under God's beautiful blue skies and get you your first tiger."

"Yes. Excellent. This is quite the facility. I am very impressed with your thoroughness. Do you have German blood?"

"Nope, just good old Yankee persistence."

"How are your shotgun shells doing?"

"The plant is fully operational. Beta testing with troops in Cambodia is complete. All we need is your distribution genius."

Six inches taller than Slade, Hegel put his arm around his shoulder. As they moved out toward the garages, the driver picked them up.

"Where too, Brother Slade?"

"Let's go up behind the veterinary center."

They flew over the grassy terrain toward a tree line. The shrubs thickened, and at the edge of the forest a yellowish streak bounded straight out of the cover toward them. The driver slammed on his brakes.

Hegel, CEO of several major arms firms in China, wore a ring with a diamond carved into the shape of a bullet in its casing—a load for a .45 caliber pistol. It was mounted on a titanium band. He reached around with his right hand, which sported the ring, and pulled a Krieghoff .470 nitro express rhinoceros rifle out of the back seat.

The blur grew clear. The old, exhausted tiger was snarling and running full blast toward them as if it would attack the Humvee itself.

"Mine Gott," said Hegel. "I didn't expect such fierce beasts, Jet. You have a ferocious attack animal here. These canned hunts are usually stupid. Where did you get it? Animals aren't this wild even in the bush."

With his fleshy hands, he steadied the big game rifle. He wanted to hit low on the breastbone so any damage remained hidden. The rifle was way too big for the job at hand and would cause more damage than Hegel desired, but he paid over six thousand dollars for the remarkable weapon, so he had to use it. He squeezed the trigger calmly and the slug ripped out the nozzle at such a rate of velocity that the impact with the tiger didn't seem possible without the passage of time. The great cat rolled in midair and fell back in a spent heap.

TWENTY-FIVE

Luther carried his saddlebags in off his stout, black quarter horse stallion, Buster, and left the great, sweated animal rolling on its back in the dust. The sacred alkaloid, peyote, had brought Billy to a state of such awareness that Stud, his own black stallion, fused into an extension of his body, like his arms or legs. Luther and Billy checked on the horses' feed and water and Billy swatted Stud on the butt. The horse rose up on his hindquarters, snorted and raced Buster out to pasture.

"I'll go up to the house and get some guns," said Billy as the horses ran out to pasture.

"Don't need 'em."

"There's a lot of these guys and they've got a heavy arsenal."

"They're too ego bound to be good in a fight. Besides, we've got the army up there already; it'll be more fun to steal their guns," said Luther.

As the plane lifted and banked, they watched Buster and Stud roaming. They flew out across the landscape south of Austin and on toward the Texas Hill Country. They used Luther as their compass. At one with his intuition, Luther would set them down in the correct place.

Billy had known Jess Hayes all his life. When the boys first began their rites of passage into manhood, they did Luther's peyote ritual. The old horseman painted cobalt blue swaths on their faces like Braveheart—like many indigenous warriors of the Americas and around the world.

Luther hung the father buttons around the boy's necks, attaching the stiff, brown, dried discs to necklaces made from the rattlesnake spines they both kept. Later, Luther added three large, red jade beads from the Ming period in China—gifts from a Tibetan friend. Tales of certain peoples from the East state that jade brings good luck. The legends express that when a catastrophe strikes a person, the jade cracks, saving the bearer's life.

For the first ritual, they took three, big-hipped stallions Luther planned to lease out for stud work and went on a high-pitched night ride, not coming in until late morning. The ceremony had taken place decades earlier, long before Billy joined the Marines. At the time, as always, Luther reckoned his own age hovered somewhere around a hundred. He glowed with energy and sported a liveliness most men never enjoyed, even in their 30s. His posture on the back of a horse looked as fine as a teenaged child's: erect, supple and in perfect tune with the rangy young stud horse. He could have ridden the animal to California without even trying.

They went down to the river in the afternoon and Luther washed their faces. They hardly spoke at all, but all three appreciated the camaraderie and warmth. They wore the father peyote buttons around their necks and rode out after sundown.

As they walked off through the dark in that lonely hour of the day, Billy and Jess appreciated why Luther loved the quiet and peacefulness so much. On the 5,000-acre ranch, the white man's noisy world grew trivial and distant, and the quiet became more explosive.

Billy and Jess were changed forever after the ritual. Freed, they lost all need for keeping up with the Joneses—from trying to "win" or pursue any other frivolous activity that keeps one stuck in the mind and distant from the magnificent quality of the moment. Though Billy still had years of learning to work through all his kinks, the habitual pursuit of money being the biggest, his freedom from frivolous personality habits gave him the ability to focus his concentration completely.

Jess gained enlightenment that morning. Billy understood the immense quality of the present second one lives in, but it took him many years to understand how his life sat in front of him, wide open: that all he had to do was to decide what needed doing and act. Billy's father taught him that working hard as a businessman and accumulating vast fortune is a man's duty. He pounded the boy's soul from a very early age. Billy, in turn, worked blindly as a takeover, divestiture, reinvestment con man, accumulating billions and billions and billions of dollars, but he never understood hopelessness and freedom and how many people on the planet live in deep suffering—not just the poor but all financial layers of humans.

After the Corps and the massive leak Desert Storm left in his being, he began to see clearly the desolation of the super rich and the how accumulation of wealth actually enslaves them. At that time in his life, at the hour of the wolf, the mental chatter was suspended, knowledge he and Jess had in the morning when Luther came back—knowledge that had always been there with him. The teachings swept over everything in life and felt keener, more invigorating, and even stronger than they had when he was a boy. He sensed it as a total rebirth and began to look for something to do with his time on Earth.

Billy's senses rode all high and rangy as he and Luther floated over Texas in the Gulfstream.

"Billy, you are my son now, one of my boys; you were a good boy and you are a good man. They murdered your spirit brother, and when we get to this ranch of shit your girl will be in big trouble and all the innocent animals will be too. But you have to remember, the rattlesnake travels quietly. Remember not to boast or be noisy like the white man. Travel in silence and strike quickly. Don't even bother to coil, just strike. It's like Bob Dylan said: 'When you've got nothing, you've got nothing to lose. You're invisible now; you've got no secrets to conceal.'"

Billy looked around at Luther. "Invisible, like recon."

"Being with those jarheads was good shit. The training was healthy for you because you had me and your parents teaching you to experience with your heart from the time you were a little bitty man-sprout. It's a shame most of those fine girls and boys are cannon fodder for the majority stockholders: those fat cat, oil baron buddies your daddy hung with. The coat-and-tie thugs that pay their lobbyists to

336

control those boot licker presidents, senators and judges. It's some real sick shit. It's the way of the white man."

The old horseman sat up straight and watched the view of the earth without saying a word; he simply pointed, giving Billy directions. The plane seemed to lift, and then settle in the same beat, without effort. Billy zeroed in on the Paradise Ranch buildings below. With the power of father peyote, he didn't even have to think to fly the big bird; he'd become part of the machine. It seemed as if they were back on the ground within moments.

"This place is some really bad shit," said Luther as they stepped out. Luther stood on the platform without moving. He surveyed the environment.

"The main ranch is right there," he said, pointing toward the big lodge and the outbuildings that served as guest suites. He raised his head and squinted off toward the distance, and an open-topped Humvee rolled right up to taxi them.

They climbed aboard, and the driver hit the gas and let them out at the center of the grounds. As they stepped out, John Long Tool, a powerful Kiowa friend of Luther and of Billy's whole family, rode up on yet another amazing black stallion with a white blaze on his muzzle and four matching stockings.

"Let's go. This place is pure-dee-evil. We've got to get Billy's girl. She's still safe but these are some *muy malo* white boys. Can't trust 'em at all. The stables are over there. See that roof?" asked the old man, gruffly. He loped off in the direction of the gambrel roof on the barn.

Luther and Billy walked fast in his trail. The stalls all held fine horse stock. Luther ran straight to the stallions as if he lived on the spread. He pulled a fine chestnut mount out, just holding it by the jaw and jumped right on its back. As Billy followed Luther's lead, John Long Tool rushed into the barn from the other end, still on his mount.

The old Kiowa, a descendent of Wolf Howling Often, a Kiowa chief who was a close associate of Quanah Parker, broke into a big smile. The descendent of Lone Wolf, and longtime champion of the Half Moon peyote teachings of Quanah Parker, charged the fine stallion right up to them and brought the creature up on its hind quarters. He smiled wide and full. His handsome, weathered face lit up with a wide, deep smile. He wore ankle-height, beautifully-beaded moccasins, a huge, bright lavender, silk bandana at his neck and waved his wide-brimmed, Silverbelly Stetson as if he were performing in a cowboy medicine show.

"Well, dang me. If it isn't Kevin Costner himself," said Luther.

"Bo and I have been riding around this place, hiding out from these weirdoes, doing a shadow dance with the help of father peyote for two days. We've been over to the cages and the breeding place. These are some real bad boys. Disgusting is the word. Bo and I are gonna burn the whole business to the ground."

"How'd you get up here, you old fool?"

"Rode Bo."

"All the way up from home?"

"Yeah, stopped in to get close to a few of my girlfriends. Rested up at their places along the way, hell of a good time. Everybody thought I was a movie star, even some big-gutted, sleazy, cracker cops. People kept wanting to buy me a beer and pet Bo. I'm going to turn all these horses out to pasture."

Bo, quivering with energy, danced in place. "Those rednecks in all those little towns didn't even give me any shit about being an Indian—guess they're all star struck. They kept asking me if Bo is short for Bucephalus."

"Well, isn't it?" said Luther.

"Hell no, Four Fingers. You oughtta know better. He's named after Bo Diddley. I learned all that Greek crap at Cambridge, but the only Greek I like is Zorba."

"You're one wacky old fart, Long Tool. Too many women. All that pooh melted your brain," said Four Fingers.

"Hell, my other stud horse is Wolfie, after Howlin' Wolf. Him and Bo Diddley are the only real rock stars who ever lived."

"You're crazy as a goddamn bedbug, Long Tool."

"I didn't think white boys in Texas could even figure out how to read, let alone them all talkin' about Greek legends and Alexander the Great. Alexander was a gay nut bag. I guess it's what made him smarter than his dad, Philip the Second. Philoneicus brings this unbelievably beautiful, big-assed stud horse up and nobody could ride it. The bad boy would pitch and throw and have a big fit. Even the great Philip couldn't mount up. Alexander was twelve, but he saw that Bo was afraid of his shadow. He takes the big stallion out in the sun where the shadow was in back of him, and the giant stud let the boy ride him."

"Long Tool, what the hell are you talking about?" asked Luther.

"He should have relaxed and enjoyed his rambunctious, erotic exploits and stayed home. Why the hell did he pillage all the way around to India? Who the hell would want to own a squirrel cage like India?"

"You are a real nut bag, Long Tool."

"I'll put all these horses out to pasture while I burn this place down. Then, when we get back from the *Queen Mary*, I'll come take all these horses out of here," said Long Tool.

"How'd you know we're going to the *Queen Mary*?" asked Billy.

"Not everybody's as slow as old white eyes," said Long Tool. "We've gotta smash 'em before they hurt any more animals."

"They're harvesting them all around the world," said Luther.

"I know. I'm not taking any chances. Burn now, then drive the horses back to Austin. Hell, I'll have a whole remuda. It'll be a repeat performance. The rednecks will think I'm an Indian cowboy in a frickin' movie."

339

Bo danced in place, impatient to get going again.

John Long Tool herded the horses out and drove them off into the pasture while Luther and Billy mounted up. As they rode out of the barn, Billy saw Slade ride by in a Humvee with some geeky-looking, business type who appeared to be German. A Bengal tiger lay strapped over the hood, blood oozing from its breastbone area.

Slade saw Billy. He did a double take, but obviously had urgent business with his guest. Billy could feel Slade's anger. He checked his first impulse, chasing the vehicle, pulling Slade out and forcing him to reveal Jenny's whereabouts. He couldn't take a chance before he scouted the situation. What if the sentries were watching Jenny?

He couldn't stand losing her again. He would wait. Slade would lead them to her. Billy would watch, picking up information for Harlan that could be fuel for putting an end to this whole nightmare. They would simply allow Slade to do the work; let him do his own thing rather than taking a chance with him going sneaky on them and moving Jenny to some hard-to-find spot, maybe even whisking her off again. As long as Slade was with his guests, he would not have time to harm Jenny.

Slade's Humvee stopped in front of the main buildings. He entered the front door with a knot of German gun manufacturers surrounding him, pushing him about their turn to go out and take their tigers.

Billy and Luther followed the intuitive power of father peyote and started to go through all of the buildings, to clear each one in a deep search for Jenny. They rode their horses through each bunk house—all over the commissary— through a building decorated with velvet walls, silk cushions and huge, over-stuffed couches, where a porn video was playing, and the rooms were swarmed with scantily-clad women in fishnet stockings, toting whips and handcuffs and other erotic toys.

They pried at bookcases, tapped every wall and shelf, breaking through hollow-sounding areas, searching intensively.

As they pushed through the dining hall, they moved into the kitchen. They popped open the walk-in and searched for spaces which might open into adjacent, hidden rooms, but they found nothing.

As they progressed out of the kitchen toward the adjacent dining rooms, a man with a .40 caliber SIG Sauer stepped in through the back door and held the pistol leveled on them.

"Gentlemen, may I help you in some way? We are always pleased to have guests, but you can't bring horses in the buildings."

"We are looking for the men's room," said Luther.

Billy, at his wit's end from lack of rest and worrying about Jenny, completely lost it. Luther's remark was so simple, so prosaic, so off the wall, and the whole situation with the horses in the building was so dumb, he broke up in laughter. All three of them slid into uproarious hysterics; the trio looked like they might fall from their mounts.

"My friend here got out of the dentist's a little bit ago and they really loaded him with nitrous oxide," said Long Tool. They laughed even harder.

"I assure you, gentlemen. Your levity is lost on me."

"That's because you're too serious. You need to get high on something besides booze, dude; those hangovers will make anybody uptight. You'll end up with duodenal cancer," said Luther, and Long Tool put his head back and howled like a wolf so loud that the man with the SIG backed away.

Luther walked toward the man with his hand extended for shaking. "Look, you hop up on my stallion and we'll run you down to the dentist. He's a charming fellow. He'll get you bombed, too." Luther spoke like he had a mouth full of feathers, imitating a white man's jowly drawl. The trio laughed so hard their jaws ached.

"Okay, chief, that's far enough," said the man with the gun as Brother Lucien Maxwell emerged behind him.

341

"Alright, thanks, Melvin. Go back out and make sure our other guests are behaving. I'll take care of this."

Maxwell walked toward them and put out his hand. Luther spit on it. Maxwell pulled back, wrinkling his brow.

"This guy is a fucking viper, Billy. Don't deal with him. He's the bad guy in all my dreams. Snake man. I used his energy to make the timber rattler pop up on the other creep's computer. They have sister rattler trapped somewhere on this disgusting ranch. They are raising snakes as a kind of livestock and using rattlers as murderers. They will throw Jenny in if she doesn't cooperate."

"Hey, wait a minute. I *was* in with Jet Slade and ANVIL. Yes, I can't deny it, and my activity with them has been reprehensible. But killing the mother bear, just shooting her and taking parts off like she was something in a warehouse . . . well . . . I mean . . . It really got to me. I could feel the gruesome edge all over, feel how far we have slipped away from . . ."

Maxwell stopped in mid-sentence as a corporate jet revved up and took off at the runway. The thrust of the engines and the lift made Billy's solar plexus float. He knew Jet Slade had slipped past him again. He listened to the huge engines put thrust into the great hulk of metal. As they had at the sprawling ranch near Temecula, every fiber in him swarmed with deep, hopeless rage.

He would get his hands on this disgusting little man, and, he would never pause to think about grabbing him again. Not for any reason. He didn't care about the law, the disgusting judges sitting at the bench in all their privilege, with no interest in truth or real justice. Lost in protocol with their fascist phalanxes of cops. The disgusting lawyers in wool, glib and spouting chicken shit.

Billy's eyes followed Long Tool as he slipped out the door. Watching the warrior leave, he knew he would not kill Slade, though he craved the act so badly. Once again, he wanted to grab his neck in his hands and squeeze the life

342

out of him, just the way Angel Orozco, who was now with Harlan, had done to the men who killed his first woman.

But he wouldn't do it. He would break the revenge loop somehow. It was his route to freedom as his mother had explained all his life: "Honey, I can't stop you from being a Marine. You have to learn for yourself. But I can tell you that soldiers are always dupes for rich men like your father. Nationalism is a pathetic—an ongoing curse of the human race. The A-type grabbers' rule. Until human beings can understand that violating other human beings is no longer a workable situation, we will not be able to break the loop; we will remain the same squalid little creatures we have always been."

As the corporate airliner eased out of range, the sound wafted off into nothing. Billy's throat choked up. His solar plexus pulled up into such an intense knot he thought he might barf. He tightened his fists. Jenny sat there, a prisoner, and for the moment he remained completely helpless. He straightened his posture, breathed deeply and pulled his lips up into a slight smile. He saw in a vision clear as a spring morning. He would catch up with Jet Slade real soon, and he wouldn't turn him over to the authorities, and he wouldn't murder him with his hands in mindless revenge, but he would fix things so Jet Slade would never endanger another human being or any other living creature ever again.

"Gentlemen. Let's have peace here. Look, I put the gun away."

"You didn't put anything away, pencil dick, nothing but your spirit," said Long Tool.

"Mr. Clayton, you and I have some things in common. You have changed your ways, no longer tearing families apart with your financial exploits, wanting to be a helper rather than a grabber. I am doing a turn around, too. And, as part of moving away from ANVIL, I am going to return Nuke and *dead latitudes* to you."

"I thought I had put dust all over Billy's cyber-trail on the new laptop, burrowed right into the thing," said Luther.

343

"You are very good Mr. Four Fingers, and so is Ms. Warren, but she left a couple simple little wormholes for us when she put in her fire wall. One thing can be said for ANVIL: Buster Bush is probably the best computer jock in the world."

"Boy, the shit is getting thick now," said Luther.

"I need some air," piped in Long Tool.

"I want Jenny and my dog. And where the hell is Nuke?" asked Billy.

"There is a big meeting on the *Queen Mary*; Slade is pitching ANVIL's environmental program to the Hill: Saving Smokey. The program's for senators and congressmen and their wives. Hicks and all of them will slurp his rot right up like hogs at a trough."

"It's seems like five minutes ago, you were kicking the hell out of me in that computer room. You seem sleazier than Slade, if that's possible."

"Look, I'm as sleazy as I ought to be. Are you perfect? You have all your cash, and we have hungry children right here in the Texas countryside."

"So what happens?" asked Billy.

"I'll take you right to them. He's setting up sales for an automatic shotgun that fires an armor-piercing load."

"Jesus. The Corps will want those," said Billy.

"The Corps is already working on their own. But every army in the world will want them. They make grunt infantry and jarheads lethal against armored vehicles. They don't even have to call in air support."

"They'll sell faster than he can ship them out of China. He'll be richer than I am."

Everyone laughed.

"So that's just one example. I personally am your greatest asset in your war against Jet Slade. I know what pins him to our friend Jess Hayes' murder."

344

"That's a lot of info."

"And there's a hell of a lot more, Billy. May I call you Billy?"

"No. You may call me Mr. Clayton or I may have to salvage you into Luther Four Fingers' guruship."

"Guruship?"

"That's your problem, Mr. Maxwell; you've never had a guru to help you drop some ego. He might make you as decent as you oughtta be. He'll show you why they call him Four Fingers."

Brother Maxwell looked at Luther. His eyes slid down to the long-healed sockets from which the brave man's little fingers had been ripped out by the Karankawas, then he turned back, looking at Billy as if he were stark-raving mad.

"Alright, Mr. Clayton, I can understand you being suspicious of my life turning on a dime. But it does happen you know; people are born again every day."

"Let's get on with finding Jenny."

"Jet will bullshit the Germans who were here today. Tell them to come to the next hunt, which will be out in Virginia. He wants to move fast and get things set before the event at the *Queen*. He will keep her with him; he's madly in love with her."

"Oh for god's sake," said Luther. "This sounds like a Hank Hill script: a wimp in love with Billy's woman."

Maxwell laughed too.

"You're right. It is a bit cartoonish. But it's all so repulsive that I have a hard time staying with any humor," said Billy.

"The best way to find her is to go everywhere Jet is likely to go before the *Queen*."

Luther walked back in. "Where the hell is Long Tool? The old fool must have gotten lost." As Luther spoke, Long

Tool came into the doorway of the barn, pulling a cart full of wine bottles with rags sticking out the neck.

"What the hell?" asked Four Fingers as they all walked over toward the cart.

"I told you I was gonna burn this place down. Poured out a hell of a lot of expensive French wine, never cared for the stuff myself. I like cold Czechoslovakian beer "

Billy watched as John Long Tool grabbed bottles from the cart and ran from building to building. Maxwell joined him, and they threw the incendiaries through every window. Billy wondered about the man's intentions as people ran from the buildings. Completely panicked, the assembly of gruff-looking financiers scrambled out of the buildings and grouped in the yard barking questions about what to do next.

Four Fingers and John Long Tool mounted up and rode from building to building, searching for Jenny, then lighting the structures on fire. Seated on their stud horses like a true Kiowa man of war and a full-out Comanche horseman, they carried armfuls of Molotov cocktails, lit them with Zippos and hurled the bottles through windows.

Men in suits ran fast, leaving the buildings and fleeing wildly out to the fields. Billy pulled Maxwell up behind him, onto his mount, and they took off for the runway in a full hand gallop.

TWENTY-SIX

The old waves of emotion that surround all human beings when their loved ones are in jeopardy overwhelmed Billy as they waited for the rental. Anger and tears were trying to get out at the same time. The fury blew up in waves. He had no thoughts, only the vision of being stuck in place, void of any way to insure Jenny's safety, listening to Slade's jet lift and sweep off with her took purchase of his mind.

When the thought came, the tears pushed at the edges of his eyes, aching to pour out, and right behind them, the urge to hurt the slimy little man. Over and over again, he breathed deeply, calmed himself and knew Jet Slade bore witness in the most horrible of all courts: the 24 hour a day judicature of not being at ease with one's own self. There Slade roamed, trapped endlessly in the only real hell.

Billy accepted complete responsibility. He put this fine young woman in this loathsome situation by charging the bull-necks in their car. Forbearance had never been a strong suit in Billy's deck. Had he endangered Jenny, or had he simply short-circuited the inevitable? Though he felt the tears, the luxury of crying did not tabulate as an option.

Maxwell sized Billy up as they waited for the attendant to bring up the rental car. "I know you don't trust me yet, but you just don't get it. The stories in our minds from our pasts are very, very strong. Jet Slade watched me as I watched him. I stood with our born-again Christian parents.

"Mine owned the Cadillac distributorship and Jet's dad was a booze-hound politician and preacher. Sometimes he had money and sometimes they lived on cornbread and navy beans. But I've talked a lot; you know enough for now, and I am ready to stand with the prosecutor. In the end, it's another dumb story of how disgusting humans can be, and I don't want to wear you out," said Brother Maxwell.

"But you say you're an animal lover, and you stood by and let him butcher everything," said Billy.

"I tried to make myself strong, to become a good businessman. The process was all about learning the American way: do lots of business and fuck the truth or casualties or any of the collateral damage. I never caught on, never enjoyed the turf at all."

"Business. What's this shit with you so-called business people? You think you are above all common decency because you are doing something as lame as turning a dollar? Above thinking through the damages resultant of your actions? Jesus, dude."

"Hey, you're a big business guy," said Maxwell.

"No, I can't stand those arrogant crybabies. I didn't go into business; I jumped in the arena to battle with them, just like a pirate, to beat the hell out of them, to hurt them and take everything away from them like being in the Corps. I kicked the shit out of a lot of them and grabbed a whole lot of cash fast before I jumped off their lame boat."

Billy gazed out at the sprawl of the LA Basin as the Gulfstream eased down at the Long Beach Airport.

"I don't think you have any criterion for comparing our visions. You were raised by good parents who treated you kindly."

"True, but you're using parents as an excuse, like you're on the *Dr. Phil* show or something."

"I know, I'm being practical and taking the high road. It's why I am going to stop Jet, put the brakes on his fortune from this armor-piercing shotgun, and for sure keep him from more butchering. I don't want any excuses. Maybe I can't clean my slate, but I am through. I am good with animals and I am going to go to work with one of the foundations like your buddies, fighting the smugglers. I'll put my whole life into it. I'll never be healed, but I will feel good about my days."

The young driver smiled cheerily about the 20-dollar tip as he delivered the rental car. Billy got in and stared straight ahead, thinking of Jenny again. He couldn't strategize. Couldn't get his thoughts around a plan. His mind went vacant as thoughts of her safety swarmed over everything.

He didn't even remember the telephone in his pocket, that calling Harlan for info on Slade's flight, on his whereabouts was an option. That he could put an army of PIs on Slade. That he could storm all of the places Slade might go. That he—

"So, you are sure about where Jenny is—the same packing house over in Wilmington? The place where Neeley has all those sickening animal parts?"

"Right, he uses the packing house guise to get all the other slaves to the lobbyists on the Hill off his trail; he sends them a freezer full of beef to make them love him, tells them he's in the meat business if he doesn't want them to know anything. The ANVIL preacher bit works on the heavy right-wing dingbats. But he wants to break into the arms business more than anything. He has deals with the Israelis and the Iranians both. Getting the stuff made in Korea."

Billy floored it, straight for the packing plant. The vortex of loss, and of realizing how limited a human being's power really is, kept wiping his mind clean, emptying his thoughts. He swept over the bridge out of Long Beach on Anaheim Boulevard. Big hammerhead cranes laced the full horizon, plucking containers off the ships just powered in off the Pacific. He blew hard down to the flats and onto Harry Bridges.

At the entry to Lung Fat Trading, to his Mystery of the Orient, Maxwell reached into the back of his waistband. He pulled out a pair of Browning automatics and turned one around, offering the grip.

Billy studied him closely. "You could have taken me during the flight."

"Didn't you hear what I told you up there?" asked Maxwell.

"You talk, but you haven't earned my trust. Who killed Jess?"

"An NSA op."

"How did Slade get such hefty clout?"

"Through fear, the rich's hatred of enviro-groups and money; the Hill wants to eradicate all serious environmentalists. All the lobbyists have the squeeze on the Congress and Senate with the crybaby pitch that the greenies cost business people, the job creators, too much capital.

"Free Range had more money than God. They had already filed 50 times as many litigations as the ACLU in their first year. So the corporate whiners were way pissed. Not only did enviro-requirements cost a fortune, but Jess Hayes saw how litigation costs would add salt to the wound.

"That's way too much power for the guys that are the hub for the 'conspiracy theory.' You always hear theories snickered about so a conspiracy of the rich can be dismissed, but it's the truth. I've met with various groups of these cabal fuckers. Slade's a dumb, power-hungry freak like the politicians. Those guys are really evil. They all hated Jess Hayes 'cause he had cast-iron balls. They also knew that Free Range was involved only in completely legal activity, but Mr. Hayes was not opposed to using some really violent greens—decentralized groups that made Green Peace seem like a church choir."

"Who were those two that spied on Animalfund?"

"Part of the NSA op team."

"You'd better take me straight to Jenny. I really have a hard-on for all of you. I want to kill you real bad."

Billy checked the magazine and the action of his Desert Eagle. They pulled right up to the doors Jenny had pulverized. He thought about her as they moved through the door and burst through the sides of beef. He never slowed, just hammered on into the macabre space. He dislodged the office door and toured the room fast. Maxwell shot in behind him and sized up the room.

"Jeez. I can't believe I stayed with ANVIL for five minutes. It's all over now. Jet Slade will never have power over me again," he said, putting his hand on the desk, taking a deep breath. "Swear to God. This is so horrible. I can't believe it, and these people call themselves Christians." Raising his hand without thinking, Maxwell swept up a printout of an email. "I am so glad I told you about this," he said, glancing down at the note.

Billy stopped at the door and looked back. "Let's go to the office over by Crystal Cathedral."

Maxwell glanced at the paper in his hand. Billy stepped over and read the page. It was and email from j_slade@anvil.org to gneeley@pacificpacking.uk. The subject was: *cancelation of subscription.* The message was: *We are all in agreement about the subscription to your nature magazine,* the Maxwell Traveler. *Please cancel our subscription at your earliest convenience. Thank you, The Anvil Group.*

"What is it?" asked Billy.

"My death warrant."

"Jesus. You're right, aren't you? Bring that for Harlan."

Billy walked out to the car and surveyed the area. Smoke poured from the rear of the warehouse and he heard a siren pump up in the distance. He ran back in and Maxwell roamed the room just in front of the leaping flame, pouring gasoline from a five-gallon, metal can all over the product.

"Goddamnit, asshole. That's all evidence and an excellent location for an ongoing stakeout."

"I wish it was Jet Slade."

"Don't worry about Mr. Slade. My intention is to tidy up his life for him. I will give him an opportunity he can't refuse," said Billy, cocking his head to listen. "Let's go. There's already a siren."

Maxwell looked at the door and threw the gas into the flames.

They saw the spire from many blocks away. Billy parked out front in a green zone and they flew up the stairs. The pastel décor of the entire facility blew his mind as before. Plastic lime green couches and arm chairs, planters flowing with pale flowers.

Ms. Marple looked up at them. "Gentlemen, how may I be of service to you?"

"Miss Marple, hello dear. Surely you remember me, your old friend, Duncan Autry. We'll be going on in for Mr. Slade."

Miss Marple stared at him, motionless. She contorted her face. She punched a line and the breast-o-rama girls swarmed toward them. Billy pushed right through all the pastel-armored breasts.

Miss Parsons shot forth from the inner offices with her bosom and her hand extended once again. She wore pale pink cashmere, with her vast smile painted the same hue.

Her syrup drawl stretched her sentences way out. "Mr. Autry . . . ah, Mr. Slade. . . ."

Billy pushed on past and right into Slade's office with Miss Parsons clicking her heels on his trail and Maxwell bringing up the rear. Jet Slade did not appear to be in the facility. The bird's-eye maple gave the whole room a soothing, honey glow, but the composure was thrown out of whack by the animal heads. Billy saw the magnificent grizzly, turned and left the room. He scouted through the rest of the suite, checking every room. Ms. Parsons followed right behind him, her feet clacking against the floor.

In the ladies room, she skidded right into him as he stopped abruptly. "Mr. Autry, I assure you Mr. Slade is not here, and he does not use the ladies' room."

Her breasts pressed against Billy. She was wonderful in her cat eyeglasses. Her breath rolled over him, inviting and warm. He stood up straight, breathed, and stepped back. Then he smelled smoke.

"Oh fuck," said Billy and Ms. Marple jumped back with a loud clickety-clack. Billy put out a stiff arm and shot past her. Back in Slade's office, Maxwell ran past Billy with his a huge-flamed, throw-away lighter up in the air. Right below a wall of heads, Slade's Hudson Bay blanket shot up in flames under the leather pillows for the couch. Maxwell had piled the bedding to use as propellant. Billy scanned the room and saw at least 100,000 dollars worth of Weatherbys, Steyr-Mannlichers, Heyms, and all sorts of match rifles ready to go up in flame. Director Slade's entire collection— HKs, SIGs, Colts, Berettas, a Calico and all the magnificent maple paneling would end up a charred pile.

Maxwell had his pocketknife out in the lobby and, after slitting cushions and the backs of the furniture, he flared them with the big slash of flame.

"Okay, ladies, you all have to leave," said Billy.

The women started screaming and ran for the door. Bill moved fast and toured the whole suite again. Nothing stirred. He ran back to the front and Maxwell held the lighter to the edge of a throw rug in his hands. Billy grabbed it, threw it and took Maxwell by the back of his neck. He marched him out to the rental.

"Goddamnit. What are you, a pyro? You're going to have every cop in Southern California after us," he said flooring it.

Maxwell pulled out a cigarette. He dug in his pocket and pulled his *Manifest Destiny* Zippo out: the lid clicked, the rubies glittered. Maxwell tapped the white cylinder on the death's head ten times, then thumbed the wheel and the big flame licked up to the cigarette.

"Give me one of those," said Billy.

Maxwell turned to him and frowned. "What?"

"Don't act dumb. Why do you thump the cigarette on the lighter so many times? The habit makes me want to beat the hell out of you," said Billy, exhaling.

"You have to pack a smoke for maximum, tight draw and to keep the tobacco particles away from the tongue for full palate."

353

"Makes sense."

"Sure does," said Maxwell.

"I always wondered about that. I thought people who thumped were some kind of power freaks that liked to torture others. I've always wanted to strangle them with my bare hands. I bought five businesses from an old dynasty lord in Shanghai and he always thumped. Wanted to slap the shit out of him every time, but I made many billions of dollars off old Li Po. He sold me one thousand businesses all down through Oceania. Tipped me over the trillion dollar scale."

Maxwell whistled. "That's more money than I can understand."

"One thousand million dollar bills, except they don't print them. It's pretty simple. Mounts up fast if you don't pay tax, which is how the US tax laws work if you have scads of cash. Of course you've gotta be stinking rich before the IRS lets you off the hook, and you keep a lot of funds off shore and busy. A working person is just a slave in the US now."

"It's true, isn't it? Do I get a reward for Slade?"

"How much are you thinking about?"

"Fifty million."

Billy whistled. "We need to stomp Jet Slade out like a forest fire. Let's see if you can earn it. Take me right to him, drown him and every person he's ever known in the jurisprudence system, bury them and their entire families in a hundred year's worth of civil actions. My lawyer could have used all the evidence you burnt."

"You don't know the ANVIL system, the computers, all the twists and turns. You need me so you can tie all this up fast." Brother Maxwell grinned with a leering look in his eyes. "The devastating evidence is on the Crays—the big computers here, and down at White Dove."

"You just burnt this one."

354

"No way, some of the synthetics in the office will burn but you couldn't burn the computer vaults with a hydrogen bomb."

"So, is Slade down there?"

"I'm taking you to these places in order of probability."

"You're not doing very well with your statistics. Why should you get any money?"

"I can help the prosecutors smash him and the entire organization with the real-world facts."

"They'll take you down, too."

"No, I'll bargain."

"So you want off scot-free with a boatload of my money," said Billy.

"Hey, why shouldn't I want to take care of myself? I am busting my employer. You didn't pull your cash together with charitable intent."

"No, I really enjoy fighting, but only with bullies— with big guys that use weak people. So business guys are really fun to kick the shit out of; it's probably some Freudian thing because my dad seemed lame to me when I was a kid."

"All hot kids go through that rebellion stage," said Maxwell.

"Well, I forgave my dad and love and respect his memory, and I really enjoy pulverizing business thugs. You know that the sick A-type grabber attitude has destroyed the United States. We don't stand for any kind of integrity any more, nothin' but greed."

"What do you think, I'm some kind of neocon or something?"

Billy laughed aloud. "Maybe not that bad. I don't like you at all, but you are really quick, you're kinda funny and, like you said, if you rat them out to the feds, you can help me wrap this up, pronto. You're just like the Congress; you never think about anything but you and your buddies'

355

wallets. But I'm going to give you the most amazing deal you ever heard of. If you work with my attorney, take over Animalfund and manage things for the next 25 years, actually achieve results, and Harlan will set up a—"

"Who's Harlan?"

"My attorney. You will meet him real soon. He'll set up a trust that provides a salary of 50 thousand a month. He will dispatch attorneys and PIs every quarter to write up a brief for me about what you are doing with Animalfund. Any failure on your part will cause the trust to evaporate and we will lock you into frivolous litigation for the rest of your life. Harlan will send you the paper to sign, a check for the first year's pay, and he will help you with your plea. Jenny Warren will be your boss. You will go out and stump for funds, at which I am sure you are very powerful. Thirty-seven percent of your funds will go into Animalfund, but you won't have to pay income tax 'cause you'll be one of the rich."

Brother Maxwell had his head cocked to the side and turned toward Billy. He stared with his mouth open.

"Where is Jenny?"

"Slade has to be on your boat in Wilmington. He's got to be hiding over there, near the *Queen Mary*, prepping for the event. "

"Why didn't you take me there first?"

"I am taking you to the most likely places, one location at a time; we are clearing them from the list systematically. Narrowing down so we don't miss him. She may not be on your sailboat, but I think it has the most potential."

Billy's emotions had fused. Within the fusion process, they melted down into one knowledge and came out fully tempered as grit. He couldn't believe how good it felt to rest his eyes on *dead latitudes* still afloat, and Maxwell had to run to catch up with him. He charged past Billy and took the lead.

They flew right up the gangplank onto the big, old, catch-rigged yawl just as Brother Ezekiel Army pushed his head up from below. Immediately, he ducked back into the galley, then sprung through the portal again with one of the Heckler & Koch MP5/10s Billy had stowed for the voyage to the tiger country of Russia. The long magazine swept down out of the stock, giving the automatic weapon a look of evil. The little man wore his black SWAT outfit and glowered at Billy.

"Ah, Brother Ezekiel, I am proud of your preparedness. You are one of the trusted within the ANVIL ranks. Keep this man covered while I go down to speak with Brother Slade."

"Brother Slade is not here. Why would you assume he is here, Lucien? You are second in command. You're supposed to be abreast of everything."

"I just flew in from the tiger hunt and what with everything so hectic, I—"

"Lucien, I am sick of you sneaking around, bad mouthing Brother Slade behind his back and undermining ANVIL. Brother Jet Slade may have kinks like we all do, but he is all we have. He is in charge and you are not. You are either a part of us or you are against us."

The sound of running arose from below deck, and Brother Noah Army came flying through the portal. He carried an HK in a raised position. The muzzle caught on the lintel at the top of the doorway and swept back over his head. As he jerked loose, his finger clinched the trigger and several rounds flew off over the yacht repair yard, out across the water.

Brother Maxwell shoved the barrel of Brother Ezekiel's weapon out of the way and grabbed Noah Army by the arm. "What the hell are you doing, Noah?"

"I am, I ah. . . ."

Brother Maxwell jerked him up close to his own body and took control of the gun. As he turned toward Brother Ezekiel Army, he said, "Give it to me." He reached toward Brother Ezekiel's HK.

"Don't make me do this, Lucien."

"Give it to me, Zeke. Don't be an assho—"

357

Brother Maxwell grabbed the weapon by the barrel so quickly that it appeared not to happen. But as he strained to make the transfer take place, the barrel, now lower, in close to the body and pointed at the little man's heart, jumped slightly to discharge the cartridges and filled the scene with the roar of the explosions, blood and the smell of cordite.

As Brother Ezekiel Army went down, Nuke's head pounded through the door from the cabin. With manacled wrists leading his charge as if he performed a massive prayer, he pounded forward. Two gigantic, tranquilizer darts hung from his neck. A fresh dose of the drug still clung to his mind, and, overwhelmed, he tried to charge these disgusting men.

Sam growled deep and ferocious in the background. Billy stood still, knowing one of the men would make a mistake soon—someone would forget, would drop their guard for an instant. He wanted to get Sam to safety, but his guts knew he would not have to wait long.

His head was cloudy in a strange, drugged dream. Nuke still saw shark fins roiling with flesh in bloody water as he mustered every ounce of strength to use his head on his captors again. Everything looped together as if they were in a slow motion film. Billy strained to hold himself back for that instant. Spread out over the teak decking, Brother Ezekiel Army raised his weapon and dropped Brother Maxwell.

Billy grabbed Brother Noah Army by the neck, threw the HK into the water, and squeezed until the man gasped, pleading for his life. Billy grabbed a line coiled near the stern and lashed loops around the man's neck. He tied him over a yard arm so he had to stand on his tiptoes to keep from being hanged, and jumped over Nuke to find Sam, whom he heard whining somewhere up toward the bow. He took his first stride toward his dog and all went black.

TWENTY-SEVEN

Billy remembered Brother Noah Army. Maxwell going down. He remembered Nuke and Sam but nothing else. Everything appeared fuzzy. He felt very slow, but his heart lifted as he moved his arm and bumped into Sam. He grabbed his dog and the thick Labrador moaned as Billy snugged him against his own body. Finally, Billy looked around and experienced an intense wave of relief. Nuke was there shaking him.

"Billy, Billy, come on. You gotta get up." Nuke hefted him up, threw him over his shoulder and jumped down onto the dock.

"Where's your ride, man?"

"It's the rental right over there."

"Fast, Billy. We gotta move, gotta get to Jenny."

He took the driver's seat and checked the mirror and scanned the back seat, nothing. She remained a prisoner. Billy couldn't fill in the pieces. His mind strained to race off and make her safe, but everything moved slowly as if bogged down in molten asphalt. He looked out, scanned the area. No sign. Nothing. Where had Slade gone? Jenny had to be at the ranch down by Temecula again. Maxwell? Maxwell would be of no help now. Billy's memory slid back together in pieces, but the sedatives maintained a blurry edge.

"You gotta pull it together, Billy."

Striving with last moment hope, he looked into the rearview mirror at the back seat again. His stomach knotted up thinking about Jenny. Then the black Chrysler 300 appeared. He watched Heiny drive into the car hard and push up against their rental, and then he felt their car roll into the putrid water.

He checked the mirror again, and up at the top of the ramp, above Heiny's car, was Neeley. His car sat sideways across the boat ramp and the thug had lowered his creepy, smoked window to see them go down. Watching his bone-cold face, Billy understood the entire situation in an instantaneous flash, a thundering mental image, honed very keen from being with Luther and Long Tool and the brilliant clarity of peyote. Billy's intuited exactly what had come about.

Slade had dispatched his men to the area and an NSA spook went into Jess' home for the fed. They had to exterminate Jess because Free Range presented a set of real problems, in perpetuity. A violent arm of some eco group meant nothing; who cares if a tuna boat goes down or a civilian gets smashed here and there? From experience and close connections, Billy understood that when quick decisions in the face of crisis are required, governments rated certain parts of the population as expendable. But real, everyday threats to authority could not be overlooked.

An endless march of expensive lawyers presented a real-world, nuts-and-bolts, on-going nightmare. So they had put Jess' body on display. The desecration served NSA as a herald of ANVIL's power to greens all over the globe, and they would all know the spook in the shadows. With brilliant marketing savvy, Slade now proclaimed ANVIL's environmental intentions to the Executive, the House, the Senate, to politicians all over the world over. Tree huggers were all terrorists and would be shown no quarter.

And now, with his steady business acumen, Slade had placed barriers between ANVIL and the threat of exposure that came with violence. The NSA did the shooting. They dove into the shadows after an operation. ANVIL provided harvesting and strong-arm work where needed. Neeley would cleanse the urban environment of every hindrance to growth.

An immense, final thought grabbed Billy like a spear of lightening dropping down out of a thunderstorm. In Slade's quarters somewhere, a new, intense love interest radiated from this pallid monster. When she spurned his advances violently, he would obviously want to eliminate her, as he would do with anything interrupting his goals.

Billy understood Neeley's pact with Slade; it was etched in the man's reptilian eyes, which watched Billy and Nuke going down with complete dispassion. Nuke, Sam, Jenny and Billy existed as flesh bags full of parts like any other creature. As far as Neeley was concerned, he had been dispatched to clean up a few snafus as a business task, an improvement in cash flow from an associate. The American National Vigilance and Intelligence League needed to be rid of Free Range and all environmental types thwarting the organization. They had engaged Neeley as a professional to act for them alongside their own ops and government spooks.

Billy looked at Slade's eyes and vowed to remove himself from this immediate situation and then, to engage Harlan with a hundred billion dollar, irrevocable, money-making trust to become a blatant, save-the-planet, eco-babbling enviro-machine. Free Range. A vicious, take-no-prisoners vehicle like the Corps. A brutal apparatus for finally wresting the United States from the bondage of corporate business and handing the wheel to the people as Adams and a few of the Founding Fathers wanted. He could take care of Jet Slade, but only the hassle of the courts, the one power of the American people, could kick butt on the NSA, the politicians, the courts and all the other factotums of the super-rich.

At last, Billy felt completely free in his life. He was happy for the first time since he was with Melissa, the woman he'd lost to thugs the year before. He was as happy as he'd been before they offed her. He knew only ongoing, conscious acts could set him free. And he'd finally found the vehicle. A merciless tool that would wrap every corporation up in furious, never-ending litigation and squash them under legislation from enviro-lobbyists with deeper pockets than Washington DC had ever had. Hopefully, a glimmer of hope would liven the Amurkan people up, get them out from the clutches of television and cellphones and fast food. There would be legislation, pissed-off constituents, nasty judges and very clever lawyers in the trenches against the facelessness of big business for so much as trimming an oak tree on the site of a new building.

Suddenly, the car started shaking. Nuke joggled the entire vehicle as he started moving to the seat beside Sam, straining at his bonds. "What the fuck is going on, Nuke?"

"We're getting ready to take a swim."

Pulling out of the tranq-laced stupor with which the Army Brothers had subdued him, Nuke straightened up. Leonardo was behind them with Heiny. They backed up the ramp and grinned as they watched Billy and Nuke bob out toward the shipping lanes, taking on water.

The looming hulk of a freighter moved menacingly, thundering toward their trajectory on a steady course. Their paths would cross for certain with the rental car and the three of them being keelhauled and swept into the enormous brass propellers. The momentum would position them in the water under the hull, in an absolute death course.

As they gained more and more momentum, Billy noticed that Nuke sat stooped over, fiddling with his mid-section. Billy laughed. Why would he laugh as events plummeted to their most abysmal? He did not know, but it sprang from the same humor always cut loose in hopeless situations. Was Nuke injured? How could humor possibly come to play? It wasn't at all appropriate. But even if it didn't make sense, he did know the strange cackle at the absurdity of heavy situations had cleared his mind many times, allowed him to drop all self-absorption, and saved his life over and over again. He thought of what a shrink might say and laughed louder.

"Damn, I'm glad you're in such a good fucking mood," said Nuke.

"What the hell are you doing? We are easing into a ship channel with a mountain of steel bearing down on us, and you are fiddling with your trousers."

362

"I got a key off the little weasel. Picked his pocket. Now I'm trying to find it if you don't mind. All would be dandy if I could swim with my wrists free."

The car began taking in the cold, oily fluid of LA Harbor while bobbing toward the oncoming ship's prow. Water started to snake into the cab as they began to descend toward the path of the gargantuan propellers. As the inevitable became reality, they both started feeling torpid, dull and sluggish, as if they had passed a threshold, and some great moment in time etched in a logbook with a quill pen, slowly, very slowly, one letter at a time, began to take over.

And then the water. Water, water, water. A nasty brew of chemicals and the ocean everywhere. Crawling over their feet. Up their calves, their thighs, inching upward with grave certainty. As the cab filled, they got a last glimpse of the freighter making steady headway, her vast shadow stealing along the water, casting everything into a tomb of darkness. And there was the water—the patient, pervasive water: cold, smelly and certain. Billy's crotch tightened with the damp. His stomach went cold. The filthy liquid surrounded his chest and elbows. The car gurgled, groaned, and shifted while groping unrelentingly for a place to come to rest.

In the last seconds before their heads were lost in the murky confines, with the freighter slipping upon them, like a vast planetary body gliding through the emptiness of interstellar space, Nuke brought his head up toward the car's roof, emptied his lungs and took a great breath of air. Billy followed suit, preparing for their last act on earth.

And then there was the dark. And wrenching sounds of vast steel rudders, propellers, engines, and hope had come to a final resting place as the vehicle searched for a place to settle its mass on the bottom of the forlorn, back part of Los Angeles Harbor.

Billy could think of a dozen places he'd rather die. To himself, each time the slippery fantasy of death had occurred, he'd always wanted to be out in one of the meadows along the river at Morning Star. The sense of years of family, the closeness to the earth and the trees, Luther and his tales from indigenous

363

peoples, the fish and animals, the easy-going sounds of earth gave the thought of the long descent into whatever happens next a soft, warm edge, coupled with a sense of completion, an understanding that all things remain hitched up together, and death stands strong as a simple strand in the complex weave.

He wasn't afraid, but he was definitely sad. Sad it had to happen in such a rotten, steely, cold environment. None of the softness, the sweet sounds of animals and birds, none of the things we are placed here to live side-by-side with, and to pass on side-by-side with, were present. Nothing but the cold, hard, oily emptiness of human financial exploitation, the same disease that drove Slade. *And*, they hadn't finished their mission. Jenny remained in severe jeopardy. Jet Slade had received collateral damage but not been wrapped up. And he would miss out on honoring Jess with the resurrection of Free Range.

Jet Slade had Jenny. She could handle a lot, but this man had moved on, on over the edge into Joseph Conrad's *Heart of Darkness*. He no longer had any of the real human qualities in place: simple kindness, the ability to care, compassion. Billy couldn't stay with the thought. Too much pain. But the very spark ignited his anger, and he knew again they would get out of this vehicle and check each location off the list of Slade's possible hiding places, and he would continue as he had done with Maxwell.

On the way to the ANVIL retreat, he would eliminate every possibility. Slade wound never be ahead of him again. Next he would go to the *American Eagle*, the boat in the Cabrillo Marina where he and Jenny first saw Neeley's men move contraband as they came south. Working with Nuke would make each element happen fast. If Jenny was not on the boat, they would search the *Queen Mary*. They would go to the airport and take Slade's other Gulfstream apart. Then on to the ranch. Within hours, Jenny would be safe forever.

Then he felt Nuke's hands. Moving fast. Certain. Very strong, and very determined. Billy sensed his friend's drugged state had worn off completely. Barehanded, Nuke ripped loose the thick duct tape binding Billy's wrists to the steering wheel and punched through the windshield using his handcuffs like brass knuckles. Billy slithered out after Nuke with the oomph of the massive freighter's keel moving through the channel, churning up walloping currents. Billy wondered if, in the end, they would all be snared in the immense propellers or snagged in the rudder, or rudders, whatever hung down from the hull. He wondered if all of their efforts had been in vain. He swam deep and hard.

Finally, he shot toward the surface. He pushed away from the tug of the ship's currents, and, after what seemed like a lifetime, broke through the water. The freighter glided without hesitation. Nuke shot up nearby and they ploughed through the murk, escaping the surge. Scanning the surface, Billy grasped how the massive motion of the freighter would attract the attention of Neeley's men.

He scanned the area for Sam as they swam toward the channel walls where they would be less obvious to any of Neeley's crew searching the area with binoculars.

"Where the hell is Sam?" asked Nuke.

Billy's stomach heaved upward as if he would vomit, but he held his emotions at bay. Hypothermia would soon overwhelm them both. Sam could last longer than the two of them. They had to get out of the water. As Billy started to push off the wall to search, Sam's head came bobbing away from the ship's path.

Atop the channel walls, they hobbled toward *dead latitudes*, soaked like swamp rodents. Neeley's men had moved their cars into a formation over at the gangplank leading to *dead latitudes*. They had stationed men on board, and others stood around their vehicles, smoking.

Heiny walked away from the rest and scanned the area where Billy's rental had hit the water. He stared for a minute, then happened to see the three of them. He yelled at the other men and they all stopped to survey the situation. He popped the trunk and came out with a scoped assault rifle. He pulled the piece up, ready to fire.

Nuke elbowed Billy again and pointed at a wannabe cop car sitting about 50 yards from them near a light. The driver appeared to be reading. They moved toward the car low and fast as slugs hit the earth and spewed up dust around them.

Nuke and Billy split up as they came up to the vehicle, starting at the rear and fanning left and right. The wannabe cop sat glued to a girlie mag, sipping coffee and eating a box of donuts. Nuke grabbed a handful of gravel and threw it over the front of the car. The rent-a-cop stepped out quickly and looked around. Nuke heaved a rock over and hit the light post. The man drew his weapon and aimed at the post. Nuke flew from behind and took him to the ground.

Billy moved quickly from the front of the vehicle and grabbed the man's weapon, a .50 caliber Smitty, the kind of hefty iron both Billy and Nuke loved. He stuffed the piece in the back of his waistband. They took the man's cuffs and wrapped his arms behind his back to the telephone pole. Nuke ripped off the guy's shoes, slipped off his long, knee socks, wedged one into his mouth and tied the gag in place with the other one.

As they flew out of the container yard, Billy observed one of Neeley's men piling into a Chrysler and driving off fast. Billy roared around, out from behind the hammerhead cranes, onto the surface streets, pushing the gas pedal as he flew over the bridge through San Pedro toward the Leo Cabrillo Yacht Basin. He called Angel on the cop's cell phone and asked him to bust the guys at *dead latitudes*. They burned past the entrance to the hotel, and around, into the adjoining parking area where they had first seen the hoods unload the bags from San Francisco.

They parked and walked around the building, stepped over the wall, and still soaking wet, eased right back into the water. They swam out to the Chris-Craft, pulled themselves up onto the dock and stepped over the rail onto the boat.

While he spoke softly, Billy chambered a round in the rental cop's pistol. "If Jenny and Slade aren't here, we're headed for the *Queen Mary*. Clarence, Angel and Harlan can dig through any evidence on this tub."

"But we might find papers on this thing," said Nuke.

"I know, Nuke. But now we know for sure that Slade is the bad guy, he's got the NSA working for him, and he has fallen for Jenny head over heels. We can also assume he won't seek Oprah's psychological help when she spurns him."

As they went for the cabin, two ANVIL SWATs pushed through. Billy and Nuke both smelled the heavy stench of their breath; the men were off center from alcohol. They each grabbed the barrels of the men's assault rifles and clobbered the pair with their fists. The SWATs groaned as they melted to the floor.

Billy jumped into the cabin, and the space sat there empty. That same knot the size of a grapefruit tightened in his stomach. He could see Jenny's face. Hear her laughter. Hear her arguing with him. Hear her talking through their leads. See her inhaling massive quantities of food. See her amazing legs as she walked through the room wrapped in a towel. See her smile. Her eyes.

He grabbed a cellphone sitting on a counter in the galley and fished a role of copper wire out of a toolbox. Billy and Nuke wrapped the men's legs over their heads, around their necks, entwined them with their hands, and wired the whole bundle into a ball, their foreheads to their necks. Nuke grabbed a coiled rope off the deck and suspended the two contorted forms off the rail above the cabin, while Billy called Angel to come and get them with Clarence.

They moved fast, tossed the assault rifles in the trunk of the rent-a-cop car and Billy whipped back out of the lot. They screamed off through San Pedro. Nuke called Harlan's cell.

"Where the hell are you?" Harlan barked.

"WHERE THE HELL ARE YOU? I AM FILING AN ACTION." Blue's gravelly voice echoed Harlan in the background.

Billy spoke through his laughter. "We're headed. . . ."

367

"What the hell's wrong with you? What are you laughing for?" barked Harlan.

"WHAT THE HELL ARE YOU LAUGHING FOR? I'M FILING AN ACTION," chortled Blue.

Barely able to keep a governor on the laughter, Billy instructed Harlan to secure both vessels, the *American Eagle* and *dead latitudes,* and that they were to work with Angel and round up Slade on the suspicion of murder on the *Queen Mary* and hold him at the event with any evidence.

"I think you've met your boss, Harlan," said Billy.

"I am your boss now, young Mr. Clayton, and don't you forget it."

"Gotta find Jenny. Bye Harlan."

They screeched back over the asphalt and hung a right into the turn-off lane for the *Queen Mary*. They cruised into the guests' entry. Billy gave the valet a wet hundred to hold the rent-a-cop car for him while they went in to register.

They took the elevator up and went toward the registration desk. Near the counter stood a placard with a list of events at the hotel. The signage indicated that the first international meeting of ANVIL Environmental was underway.

Billy had to control himself consciously to keep from running. He walked out on the deck and moved past tourists who chatted softly, enjoying the wonderful sea breeze. Their words floated through Billy's mind as if they were an infomercial reminding him of something far off. Something he had once known about: soft afternoons with grass and trees and the sound of water dancing along rocks in a streambed.

But there was no way to sign up. Nowhere to put his signature on the dotted line. There was no dotted line. There was no space in the dream for William Clayton III. There was only Jet Slade.

They both walked fast, being careful to hold their pace slow enough to keep from standing out or shoving guests out of their way. They turned into the corridor and headed straight for the woman at the entrance to Slade's event.

"Clayton, Special Ops, Coast Guard."

"Oh, well, is there some way I can be of help?"

"No ma'am. Just a new special op being initiated. Undercover, you know. That's why we are in disguise. Designed to protect citizens. A simple, random walkthrough of all passenger related ships on the coast."

"Well, you know we are not really an ocean-going vessel."

"We are checking them all, trying to observe from the viewpoint of regular folks, nine-eleven stuff, you know," said Billy, moving on toward the room.

The woman stepped back and looked them over. They were two soaking wet, dirty, rangy and exhausted men. "May I see your badges?"

"We don't need no stinking badges for deep cover," barked Billy.

The woman's eyes widened as she followed.

"We can't expose our presence ma'am, so if you will please keep your voice down."

"Excuse me? Please wait a moment while I get my man—"

Billy checked her tag and then looked into her eyes, closely.

"Stacey, I want to assure you that this is on the QT right straight from the Commander in Chief himself. Executive orders for the welfare of your country. Any flourish of management will ruin the entire scenario we are exploring."

Stacey's mouth dropped open as she watched Billy and Nuke walk around the seated assembly, scanning the crowd for Jet Slade. When Billy passed the seating, he walked right up the stairs and onto the stage. Senator Hicks wrapped up his speech and joined his wife. Rather than re-seat themselves, they walked to the wings.

Billy walked in behind the curtains. He moved to another drape, but found nothing. As he stepped around the third wing, he saw that Jenny stood on the other side of the stage. Four men surrounded her. Jet Slade stood with a crowd of participants engaged completely in his never-ending, glad-handing, smiling celebrity demeanor.

Billy blinked in a double take at Des Sandoval doing a soft shoe routine identical to the conman. As the crowd dwindled, Slade reached and took the Fish and Wildlife officer's hand and put an arm around his shoulder. Letting go of the shoulder but still holding his hand, Slade handed him a plain white envelope. Des couldn't quite break into a smile, barely raising his thin upper lip. He slid the packet in his jacket pocket, adjusted his tie and backed up as another group surrounded Slade.

Slade and Billy locked eyes for a moment, and Slade turned to a man behind him. He barked orders, and a group of men surrounded Slade and whisked him away. Des did not appear to them. He didn't even bust through to the other side of the stage in pursuit. He saw that the group played out a well-rehearsed exit. He would have to catch up with them at their destination.

As Slade's entourage disappeared into the other wing, Harlan and Angel came running up the aisle with SWAT-type LA sheriffs. The group, moving fast, didn't appear to phase Blue, the bird, balanced skillfully on Harlan's shoulder.

Billy understood what had happened, knew that the sound of a corporate jet would soon blow out of Long Beach Airport and Jenny would be on it. For the third time he would have to sit by helplessly while the horrid man shot off into the clear blue sky, and, that he would never, ever, let him get away again.

As well as knowing the location of assent, he also knew, very deep inside, from the voice Luther always taught him to listen to, the exact destination of the craft—knew exactly where the descent would take place.

"Billy, snap out of it," said Harlan.

"I WANT MY LAWYER," said Blue.

370

"Did you get the boat?"

"Yeah, a couple of LA sheriff's loving, attentive staff had come down to visit Angel. With Clarence and the Coast Guard they locked down everything."

"Do the same with all the ANVIL types here, and Des as well."

"Des?" asked Harlan.

"He's got a fat envelope on him that has to have Slade's prints all over it."

"Jesus, does Clarence know?"

"I don't have any idea, Harlan. I guess you've got to do the dirty work."

"Payola while on a fed salary puts them both in the slam for a good long breather, but I want to know where this stuff all hitches together."

"It hitches at Slade. Sandoval is just the beginning of the payola. The NSA did Jess."

"Maxwell told me and he's dead. But we'd never be able to do anything with it because it's all buried so deep. Somebody on the Hill dispatched them to get rid of Free Range for the lobbyist cabal. But you are resurrecting Free Range for Jess. After I have Jenny, several banks will deposit 750 billion dollars into an irrevocable trust you can set up with some of your legal beagle buddies in Manhattan."

"Jeez, Billy, that's an unbelievable trough full of cash."

"You'll love it. You are going to enlist a tribe of young, red hot, constitutional geniuses. The ACLU will help you find them. Bring in some from Europe and China. Free Range is going to be the worst so-called terrorist organization ever imagined: nonviolent, completely legal, with a take-no-prisoners outlook and no weapons, but all the jurisprudence systems."

Harlan laughed so loud people turned around.

"TAKE NO PRISONERS," said Blue, and Harlan and Billy laughed hard. Harlan put his arm around Billy.

"Damn, you're coming back to life, son. What have you and that incorrigible old injun been smoking? Your cash with ACLU types will shove a humongous thorn up the real money boys' asses. No revenge like having fun"

"You got it. And the first venue is the Bay Area. Clear Jess' name, any blemishes on Jenny or Nuke, me, then file a thousand actions in Northern California. Is there an honest judge up there?"

"There's a chance, but what are we gonna get Slade for? Bear parting training? I want to give him the full lethal injection just like you do. We don't need environmental toxins like him on the planet. Too damned many humans already," said Harlan.

"Don't worry about Slade."

"Billy, your mother and father opened an enormous fund for me to protect you from yourself; they both knew you are your own worst enemy."

"Jess is dead because he presented an upcoming cash-flow problem for Slade with his new action group and a nightmare for the big money behind NSA, all the gov ops and all the politicians. Obviously, as you should know by now, Harlan, ANVIL is a mega-business. They are developing that new weapon, producing the unit in Korea and selling to all militaries. Businessmen are not on anyone's side. They are only on the side of cash flow. This is an armor-piercing shotgun projectile. A foot solider so capable without air support or burdened by excess ordinance like rockets, changes warfare. Grunts don't need to carry weird weapons that slow them down around in combat. They can run with a shotgun and won't need backup against armored vehicles and other strongholds. They'll be free."

"Goddamn, Billy. Do you know how heavy that is? Every scum-bucket politician, including our own, will want a piece of it. Do you have facts?"

"EVERY SCUM-BUCKET POLITICIAN WILL WANT A PIECE OF IT. I'M FILING A CIVIL ACTION," rasped Blue.

"I'll know today. We'll find out what it means," said Billy, grinning as backstage politicians looked round at the majestic macaw and Claire Hicks, Clarence and Angel came up to join them.

"We've got them all? The prints on the flashlight from the Humvee on Bridgeway are those of two men back at ANVIL," said Angel to Billy.

"Right. Slade is building a global inventory on some old Cray supercomputers, just like you said, Billy."

Billy had trouble looking at Clarence; he was such a true spirit having to digest such grungy news. The inequity made his flesh crawl like nails on a chalkboard. "Yeah. They used super computers, and Jenny says the modeling software for the animal inventory is like the weatherman has."

"Where is she?" asked Clarence.

"As a matter of fact, I have to blow on out of here to meet up with her."

Claire Hicks stepped up to Billy—behind her were the wives of several other senators—and she took the hand he extended in her own. She moved her body in close. "I am so glad you are helping us, Mr. Clayton. They say the trade is six billion now globally, but I think it's more like twenty."

"I need your help, ladies. Right back at home in Washington. The NSA is working with the bad guys. They are killing people who are trying to stop the slaughter."

"My god, that's a very serious allegation," said a small brunette in blue pumps and a matching blue sailor top. "There are so many allegations about the agency now. It's all the rage since that boy ran off to South America or something. They are doing a bit of mole work because of the terrorist threat, but we must control these wildfire conspiracy rants. Do you have facts to back that up?"

Billy smiled, moved in close, put his lips down toward her ear and spoke in a conspiratorial tone. "We are drowning in data. Facts, ma'am. Weapons. Arms dealing."

Billy took her hand and she grinned impishly, thinking he was coming on to her.

"Cutting the dicks off tigers for businessmen and NSA agents that can't get a boner," he continued. The small woman arched her shoulder defensively, stepped back and looked on with alarm as Billy carried on. "Leaving the carcass to rot beside a trail up north of Vladivostok. We have enough facts to make you barf, my dear."

"Oh lord, you are doing such a fine thing, young man," said another—a big, sturdy, Teuton wife with horse teeth like Harlan's. She moved in on the brunette, getting close to Billy's body. "The NSA," she said, "Why I just met that squirrely little prick, Heshaw or Hershey or Hensteeth, or whatever the fuck it was at the Kennedy Center. I'll have my husband over there tomorrow. Then I'll call his sorry little ass up. We'll drag him into the hornets' nest and start some hearings. They're a bunch of meddlesome geeks is all, not a real manly man among the whole building of perverts. They've got more computers than God and the taxpayer plays for them to fondle their own units."

Billy couldn't help but laugh. "Just talk to that big man with the parrot. The bird's name is Blue, and the man's name is Harlan."

"God, I'll help Jan here," said another slinky wife with a black Egyptian pageboy and skin the color of Wite-Out. "I can't stand that stinking bunch of cyber-snots. They think their shit don't stink, just because they got a degree in some stupid geeky crap like assembly language. Think rest of us are twits."

"We'll kick some butt for you, Mr. Clayton," said yet another senatorial spouse. "I can't believe that fucking NSA. Jeez, makes my blood boil. They should be helping you bust poachers. This government is out of control. I read today that a Asian rhino horn sells for a million or so, in the last ten years 70 percent of the African elephants have vanished, 70 thousand a year and 95 percent of the black rhinos have been killed in two decades," said another.

The big one snuggled in close to Billy. "Well Harry's not gonna get laid 'til he gets that little prick to lay off you."

"The carnage makes me cry, a clouded leopard coat sells for, ahem . . . what was that? Ah, yes 750 thousand in Japan, 250 thousand for an American black bear's gall bladder in Seoul, a quarter mil for a corporate executive to drop an old, tired, zoo tiger at a staged 'hunt' on a ranch in Texas, Idaho, Virginia, California, or wherever," said another.

"Where is Jenny Warren?" asked Claire Hicks.

"I'm just going to meet up with her, if you will excuse me, but Nuke, the captain of my ship, will be here to take care of you ladies," said Billy, winking at his friend and smiling to the ladies.

Claire Hicks raised an eyebrow and a slight grin of recognition that something might be going on between Jenny and Billy other than business. Both attracted and ill at ease, the Hill women all moved in to shake hands with Nuke.

"Nuke, why how wonderful. Where did you ever get such a delightful handle, Mr. ah . . . Mr. . . .?"

Billy turned and headed right out of the auditorium. In his interior he could hear the roar of Jet Slade's Gulfstream overwhelming the night again, could feel the bird taking off clear over Long Beach Municipal Airport, could sense the assent in his viscera. He looked down to his side to find that Sam had escaped Nuke and his coterie. He smiled and Sam ran with him as he sprinted hard along the old teak decks. Sam moved right out in front. Billy's spirit ached as if he were in a vice that some force was doggedly tightening slightly every day. He remembered Jet Slade's face in the office in Anaheim. He wanted to be close to the man again. To take hold of him by the windpipe.

TWENTY-EIGHT

Even in a state of unwavering intent, Billy was distracted by the mansion, which reminded him of Southern, antebellum plantations, and of slavery. Grand and elegant, the facade presented the visitor with an imposing and formidable entrance. But there was no room for romantic notions in his mind; Jenny had been at his side the first time he approached, and there was no question, she would be at his side again.

Like before, he walked straight up to the nine-foot front doors of the main building and took hold of the stout, cast-brass anvil hanging from a big brass loop. Billy banged the handmade knocker against the plate behind, and again, the sound reverberated all over the acreage. He turned around quickly, expecting a team of ANVIL SWATs to move up from the shadows and surround him.

Lucinda, the same woman who greeted him when he came with Jenny, opened the door slowly. Her fair skin was exposed by another breezy day dress, this time a lemon pastel, and with her coal black hair and steel grey eyes, she cast the same hypnotic spell as before. The deep Southern accent flowed like a Belgian chocolate sauce spreads over gelato, making every seductive thing about her even more so.

"Ah, a sojourner descending at our doorstep. How fortunate we are. I am Lucinda Osmond and I am here for your calling." It was almost exactly the same thing she said the first time Billy came to the door with Jenny.

"Yes, I am Duncan Autry, and I am as charmed as when we met before. Now I need to find Jet Slade," said Billy to the stoned woman.

"Mr. Slade is not receiving guests at the. . . ."

Billy took her by the arms and moved her out of his way.

"Excuse me, sir, I seem to remember us meeting . . . Oh yes, you are the report—"

"Wrong. A total pack of lies we used to dig into your organization. To you and everyone here, I am Lucifer. I am your worst nightmare. In point of fact, Lucinda, before this evening is over, you will think that next to me, Lucifer is like Bambi. You will wish you had never seen my face."

Lucinda's eyes grew cold as Slade's. The syrupy flow of her voice hardened to tempered steel. "Raymond. Oh Raymond! Raymond! Please come this instant and show this man off the property."

Raymond walked in from the kitchen with a brand new assault rifle. "Sir, I will escort you out to your—"

Billy grabbed the barrel of the weapon and dropped one of his wide fists into the cartilage and tissue just under Raymond's Adam's apple. The man fell over backward, grabbed his neck and coughed violently.

"Mr. Autry, you must leave immediately. These grounds are protected and you enter at your own risk. Sir. . . " said Lucinda.

Billy didn't look back. He ran up the stairs carrying the weapon down at his side. He toured the huge, antebellum house fast. He pushed door after door in with his foot, searching every nook and cranny. Empty. Nothing. No one.

After the last room, he jumped over the rail, down two stories, and landed on his feet right in front of Lucinda. She stood still with a gigantic, double barreled, .10 gauge duck gun.

"Sir, you must leave."

"Lucy, I'm gonna take the pea shooter away from you and throw the thing way down in the pasture. So you better blast away if you are ser—"

The humongous shotgun thundered with astonishing ferocity, and Lucinda fell over backward. The load was bear balls for sure, and the pair of blasts took a good bit of the bannister off the landing. Billy's mind blew up with pain;

377

some other sleazebag with a shotgun had ripped into Jess' sternum, leaving him cold on his living room floor.

Billy took the ancient goose gun, checked the ground floor, and bolted down the stairs into the cellar. When he was certain the house did not contain Jet Slade or Jenny, he bolted back upstairs. As he hit the highest cellar stair, Lucinda dove at him with a seven-inch, fisherman's fillet knife. The long, thin blade barely pierced the skin on Billy's ribs because he grabbed her wrist so quickly. She let out a blood-curdling scream, and the knife slid to the floor as he slammed her forearm against the doorjamb. The bone cracked and the startlingly beautiful woman yelled again, falling to the floor and grabbing her wrist as she gasped in pain.

Billy never glanced back; he flew out the back and went to his hands and knees for cover, crawling as he passed a long garage building. He slipped around past several structures with lights on, trying doors. Nothing budged. He wanted to avoid the noise of break-ins until he understood Jenny's position. With extreme quiet, deeply concerned he might cause Jenny harm, he breathed slow, powerful, silent breaths.

Finally, a door to a building with light in two windows opened. He crept in and eased toward a door across the room. Just as he reached for the knob, more lights flicked on, and two more of ANVIL's cold, steely, joyless Aryans stood in front of him. They carried brand new HK automatics.

Both of the slim men stood around five-foot-ten. They wore their hair sheared off, and like Brother Maxwell, their faces showed no sign of wrinkles, though they each appeared to be about 45 years old. They appeared to be twins just like the Army Brothers. *What's with these people?* thought Billy, *are they into some kind of an inbred, fundamentalist, cloned-sex thing they practice for producing droided-out twins?* The thought caused him to laugh aloud.

"What's so damn funny, bubba?"

"There are an awful lot of twins in ANVIL. Is the organization built around some kind of kinky-assed, white-bread, erotic rites?"

"Your levity is not really necessary, Mr. Clayton."

"Aw, guys, I didn't mean to hurt your feelings. Looks like somebody's spreading my name around, a milestone I have avoided assiduously. Did I make the cover of one of the money comics, the *Wall Street Journal* or *Forbes* or something?"

"Let's go over to our data center and make you comfortable, Mr. Clayton. Brother Slade will give you an audience. Please set the weapon on the table," said the taller man.

Not wanting to hunt for Slade, Billy let them have the draw on him and placed the weapon as instructed. The pair of varmints jammed their gun barrels into his sides and they moved out across the grounds. They escorted Billy back to the long garage building as they did when Jenny walked at his side. They moved through to the cavernous computer area as they had before.

One of the men grabbed a handful of plastic cable connectors and started to tie Billy's hands, the other one stood by with the assault rifle on Billy. The man pulled so tightly Billy thought the makeshift rope would cut the blood off from his hands. He strapped Billy's feet together and pushed him down on the concrete floor. As the man tied off Billy's leg bindings to those on his arms, the other character who stood guard walked across the room and came right back.

"Alright, Mr. Clayton. Richest man on earth. Wow. A trillion dollars. We are so proud to have you with us. We want to take especially good care of such an honored guest while we drain your bank accounts globally. So, now it is time for your medication; we want you to feel at home while we tap your holdings."

The varmint carried glass injection vials. Billy could read the labels: Prozac, Haldol and Halcyon. The guard poked the HK in his ear, while the thin one drew off all the liquid into syringes. Billy bit the weasel's arm so hard a chunk of flesh ripped open. The guard slapped him solidly with the rifle and pushed the weapon into Billy's thigh, to the side of the bone. The stab wound had clotted but still oozed blood, along with the wounds in his mouth. He wondered how much more his body could take without demanding he hole up and sleep.

"Mr. Clayton, let's not be silly, medication is good for all. A flesh wound through the thigh, without a bone fracture, heals, but these things take a while, and are imminently painful." He fired a round through the thigh. Billy's flesh throbbed with the tear, and the searing pain came next along with the pain from Lucinda's gash next to his ribs. He thought about Jenny walking across the Shaolin temple with the dragons invading her flesh and laughed at his own pain.

"See what I mean? It's bleeding a little bit but no big arteries are flowing; we'll just cut your pant leg and tape things up. And what's this?" He pointed at blood snaking out the knife hole in Billy's golf shirt.

"That's a hell of a nice outfit you've got. Kinda rumpled, but you're obviously living to your fullest, the proverbial 'outside the box' thing. What's this little dribble?" he jabbed his finger into the hole, checked his finger, then frowned and licked off the blood.

"Hell, you're bleeding all over. That little doll Lucinda's quite the girl, isn't she? We'll tape that one up too, but I don't know what your body's going to do with this next shot. It's going to take bone, and afterwards the healing process gets a hell of a lot more complex. Mr. Slade wants you calm and reasonable for your consultation with him." The other man tested the needle.

He could fight with the effect drugs have on the psyche, maybe even work on through them. But he could not be certain if, crippled with a bone fracture in the thigh, he could move fast enough to break Jenny out of this poison environment, so he gave in to the injection.

The pair marched over to the door and performed the retina scan, repeating the opening of the armory routine. Everything became very clear to Billy. Slade used the fervor of religious zealots to rake in a TV cash flow. He invested his spoils from fleecing his followers into the massive wild animal trade; it was a remarkable cash flow with no constraints, and unlike drugs, there was only a hand slap for getting caught. But never satisfied, he had invested again in the most certain of all incomes: weapons. All of his cash cows would make businessmen bow at his feet.

The pair rolled two pastel secretarial chairs over near Billy. The droid-types sat erectly, the padded rests centered in their backs, and watched for the drugs to take effect. The whopper of a computer moaned through the walls of the air-conditioned room while ripping through mountains of data. Billy wondered just what kind of information, about what else besides wild things, whirred around on the hard drives: peaceniks, animal lovers, and enviro activists, child sex slaves. Were they tied directly to the National Security Agency as a part of a citizens' vigilante group, in some black op covering the USA? A neighbor-watching network of stooges the news media would never hear about, a matrix from the general population, just like Hitler and the Chinese and the old Soviet Union?

He tuned the pair of puppets out of his frame of reference, took hold of his mind and directed the thoughts gently. *What will move you toward Jenny?* he thought. He began with analysis of the built environment. The buildings enjoyed very simple design: 1940s shiplap siding, white paint, simple, gable roofs. The mind-numbing effects of the pharma-industrial complex began to wrap their horrid, suede glove around his psyche and squeeze the juice out of it.

"Alright, I think Mr. Clayton has arrived. Time to bring Brother Slade over for a meeting of minds." One twin stood as he spoke and walked right out the door. As he left, something in Billy popped.

He couldn't think about what he should do, about how to preserve his presence of mind. He was sick of the whole business. He wanted to be on a big, thick, quarter horse stallion, walking out under the sky on an open expanse of land. All of the pursuits of human beings became totally inconsequential. He wanted to be away from everything: vigilantes, cops, businessmen, judges, courts. *And,* he wanted Jenny to be safe.

He couldn't control himself any longer. Formality, the constraints of the community, the constraints of human beings and all of their total bullshit lost their meaning. He didn't care what the drugs wanted in his mind; they were grotesque and disgusting, trying to take his power, to remodel his head like a limp salamander. He had reached the boil-over point in himself. He knew the state of being very well, and the explosion point felt like a reliable, old friend. All focused on what he wanted and what stood in the way.

The remaining twin still sat in the straight-backed office chair with his back turned to Billy. He wore a nasty combat knife on his web belt. Slouching, he used his feet to push back and forth in a short arc, propelling right with his left foot and back with the right, dealing with his own boredom. The small motion appeared to hypnotize the man. To and fro, left and right, he let his arms swing down behind himself. The tip of his assault weapon dragged on the floor.

Billy got his legs and launched, thrusting forward with his entire body. He grabbed the man's Adam's apple with his teeth and clamped down as he jerked with his head, neck and entire body. The man yowled like some strange, wild beast and caterwauled hoarsely as he fell to the floor.

"Goddamnit!" shouted the man in a horrid rasping voice.

Billy dug his teeth clear through the skin and ripped at his throat. He shook the man's head, digging deeper through to his larynx until the man exhaled and whimpered with resignation, then finally was silent.

Billy let go, and even though his wrists and feet were still bound with the plastic bindings, he lurched and swung his whole body hard, ending up with his hands at the knife scabbard on the man's belt.

Prying the blade open required intense effort because of the bindings on his wrists. Billy strained and struggled as the man started to move. With the blade open, Billy began to cut at the binder straps. He cut through with the razor-sharp, black blade and the plastic started to give. Billy's hands broke free and he grabbed the HK off the floor, flew out the front door and skirted the pool as hard as he could pump his legs.

As he ran, his left foot hit something small and round. The déjà vu slipped over Billy just as his feet started to go out from under him. For a second time, he started to go down, but this time he caught himself. He didn't have time to fall down. And he knew without seeing that he had stepped on another of the shells. Did these guys walk around with them as loads for their .12 gauges? Harlan would have a field day when the dust settled.

Again, the urge to find Jenny came over him ferociously. He drove his thighs like pistons, as hard as they could go, and shot past the edge of the rows of buildings toward the airline hanger. Light came slipping out of the shed-like structure at the hanger.

Billy hunkered up against a wall and listened. As he caught his wind and surveyed the situation, he heard voices inside the building. He couldn't believe his ears; the scene was straight out of a *Twilight Zone* story. The men repeated the same dialogue he'd heard before,

"Aw, fuck it. Forget the damn thing. I don't want to go out there. Just play. You're afraid I've got a fistful of aces. It was just one of those old toms digging in the dumpster. Some little pussy's in heat. Let's play cards. Quit worrying."

Billy edged up to the window. Inside, the same four gruff, sunburned men he'd seen when he first lost Jenny drank from a liter of cheap bourbon, smoked thick cigars, and played poker. A bold, red and white, no smoking sign sat pinned to the wall behind them.

Billy shot to the corner of the building without making any noise. He snaked around the next one and paused beside the small porch. Silent as a phantom, he eased up on the wood decking and blew through the screen door.

The men at the table studied him as if he had just beamed down to earth with the *Star Trek* set. He jammed the assault rifle up under a fat man's chin.

"What the fuck is this? You think you're some kind of transporter or some—"

Billy hit the guy on the bridge of his nose with the barrel of the HK, breaking the skin. Saying nothing, he pushed the HK up under the chin of the smartest looking guy at the table. A thin man with sallow skin, the man shuffled his legs and grabbed his crotch unwittingly, as if his body assumed the act could protect him.

"Get up," Billy growled.

The thin man wore a long-sleeved, khaki shirt and matching trousers with tan, lace-up, sailboat, deck shoes. From his belt a Maglite hung in a round metal loop. As he stood, a fresh stain made a big circle around his crotch and fear etched his forehead. Billy jerked the barrel down and shoved steel into the guy's Adam's apple, and pushed him against the wall behind his chair.

"Let's keep this sweet and simple. One round will take out the vertebrae in your neck, but because I'm nicer than you guys, I'm gonna take a chance that I'm faster than these whiskied up boys, whip this thing sideways, blow out your voice and screw up your breathing and swallowing for the rest of your life."

"Aw fuck, man, get that goddamned thing off him," said the fat guy.

Everyone else at the table sat with their mouths hanging open.

"There is a woman in this compound that none of you horny old fucks could ever miss. She has eyes of different colors, just like an Australian Shepard. Her name, if she gave you the real thing, is Jenny Warren. I want to know where she is," said Billy.

The statement of intentions loosened everyone up. They adjusted their hands and bodies.

384

"You don't know what you're getting into, son," said the fat man.

Billy pushed the assault rifle into the thin man's neck so hard the guy's gag reflex heaved and he sprayed the nearby men.

"Jesus, that's disgusting," said the fat guy.

"Where is Slade?"

The card players all turned to one another. They shuffled and grunted. Billy grabbed the man by the hair, whirled him around and pushed him over to the kitchen sink. Bent backward over the drain board, he strained to turn sideways in terror as Billy turned on the hot water.

"I'll clean him up a bit."

Billy moved the spigot and pushed the man so his head hung backward over the sink. As Billy pulled the spigot, running scalding water over on the man's face. Liquid slid up his nose, and he choked as if he might drown.

"Where is Jenny?" demanded Billy, pulling the water away, then edging the spigot toward him again.

"She's in building one; the first one up by the pump house."

"Good decision. You'll come along and show me."

Billy pushed the spout out of the way, pulled the little man up by his Adam's apple, and readied him for walking backwards.

"Okay, everybody out the door backwards, and real slow. Baby steps. Bring a flashlight."

Billy held the weapon on the rest as they walked. Building one stood totally black inside. Billy let the men go ahead and shoved the one he held through the door.

"Take me to her bunk, fast. Shine the light and let me ID her."

The men led him straight to her. In the beam, Jenny's face was very deeply exhausted as if she had coped with profound stress. Billy took her up in his arms. She acted distant and spaced out. He reasoned she just suffered from the effects of Haldol, of the Prozac and Halcyon. No way could she have handled herself so well in Neeley's warehouse and not be able to free herself now.

Out of nowhere, a cast iron arm clamped Billy's neck and placed a pad that released a sweet, sickly smell over his face. The odor swarmed all over him quickly, causing him to float downward.

When he awoke, he was slightly nauseated and extremely disoriented. He and Jenny lay on the floor next to one another, lashed to the end of the bed. Their feet jutted up in the air above the mattress, bound to the frame with duct tape. Billy smiled at her but the drugs really had a hold of her and she responded with a weak, vague attempt to raise the corners of her lips.

Whipped together in front of him very tightly at the elbows, his arms were bound with pantyhose. Ordinary, black coat hangers secured his bound hands to duct tape bindings at the knees. Billy's arms needed circulation. He looked over at Jenny who appeared to be in a condition similar to his own. Below the bindings, his hands dangled at the wrists, loose but worthless. Getting to the binds would have required a joint in the middle of his forearms.

"I hate pantyhose," he said. "You can't even admire a woman's legs when she's wearing the fucking things."

Jenny managed a soft laugh and they laid their heads back on the floor in unison.

"I feel like barfing. What was that stuff?" Jenny asked.

"Chloroform: the choice of pros," he said. "Don't get the barf on me."

"Oh god, I wouldn't dare presume. I'll projectile hurl right through the window, after I break the glass with my chi. It should be a rather straightforward manoeuver." She looked over at him and smiled deep and warm.

"You're coming back," he said, returning a warm smile.

"Let's not wax too cavalier."

386

Billy's heart felt good. Good and warm and robust and happy, as it had not felt since he heard Slade's plane take her away. They looked at one another, sprawled back on the floor in relief and returned to those weird escape places a human being slinks off to when life is thoroughly hopeless. Those places they had ventured into before are genetically etched into the computer banks of true survivors: the areas in their genomes that keep them from ever getting close to the giving up place. The mildly mad spaces, which clear everything up and, at the same time, keep despair from overwhelming the situation.

"We're a fine fuckin' pair of Vin Diesels," she said.

They broke into hysterical laughter, roared until their jaws hurt. He wondered if they had slipped all the way over the other side of the cuckoo's nest or not.

"So, what's the plan, Stan?" she asked and they howled again.

"Dial 9-1-1 and explain our circumstances to the governing bodies," he said and off they went again, aching from paroxysms of laughter. They relaxed back onto the floor again, and Billy spoke softly.

"When I was a boy, my best friend, Levon Helm and I made these little coat hanger sling shots we could slip into church with and shoot old Rayanne Moore. You know, one of those life-consuming crushes teens have. We would shoot her with dry navy beans and get her laughing. We were both horny as hell."

Jenny turned her face toward him. "Have you chipped a gear?"

They roared until she blurted out.

"Quit making me laugh, my jaw is aching." They broke out again until they couldn't laugh any more. They lay still for a while.

"Come on," he said. "Didn't you ever take clothes hangers out of the closet and start bending them at the corners? You know, at the side part where the shoulders hang on them."

She looked at him raising her brow. "I can't say I have had the pleasure of—"

"Oh come on, you bend 'em back and forth. Back and forth 'til they'd heat up and break," he said.

"Whatever in the world are you talking about, Mr. Clayton?"

"Time to gather up Mr. Slade and get out of here."

Smoothly, he raised himself from the abs and reached for the clothes hangers. He groaned aloud with the pain of the wire digging into his flesh, but he just kept working the metal back and forth. Finally the binding snapped, and with some maneuvering, he got free. But his arms were still gangly like a puppet with cut strings. He began to scrape the panty hose with the sharp ends of the hanger. He worked back and forth, back and forth, again and again.

When the fibers gave, he loosened Jenny up in a hurry. They ran out into the compound and ducked into the shadows. At the corner of the building, two characters from the poker game stood guard.

Jenny grabbed a man by the neck. Billy locked onto the other one by his balls. The man doubled up screaming.

"We've gotta get right down to business here. I can cut these babies off with your knife, or we can go visit Jet Slade."

"Fuck you."

Billy squeezed down hard. The man screamed again, coughed hard and sputtered with his face contorted in pain.

"Slade," said Billy, and the man started walking.

TWENTY-NINE

Billy looked over at Jenny and smiled. She lit up with warmth, then they both looked down at Slade. Billy's gaze locked on him for a moment, before he looked back out at the clear, blue sky. The big-talking businessman looked like another pathetic slob: a great, silk-tongued preacher; a slick, wheeler-dealer entrepreneur; a butcher. Such a terror. So heinous that the Senate opened a file on him, but in the end, the man was so insignificant.

As he watched the immense emptiness of the sky, Billy reflected on what the last few months had dropped on his and Jenny's doorsteps, and gazing across the vast Alaskan wilderness, a major epiphany swept over him. The understanding resonated so obviously his skin crawled, the hair stood on his arms and he shivered. He grasped clearly that next to the broad sweep of mother nature, the majority of the political affairs, of humankind, are vapid, fleeting, unkind and, in the end, empty.

A wave of sadness swept him. Homo sapiens was nothing other than another species, a cluster of breeding machines within the folds of Mother Nature's skirts. She had seen scads of creatures come and go, and she, along with some bodies from interstellar space, had wiped her little blue planet clean of plenty of critters. And there was no real reason for humans to be allowed to enjoy her bounty if they couldn't respect it.

"I can give you anything you ever dreamed of," said Slade from his hog-tied position on the floor.

Jenny sat in the copilot's position as Billy captained the sleek chopper.

"Pahleez, Mr. Slade. You are trying to become a sophisticated fellow with a lot of cash and the political capital huge funds can produce. A robust positioning of yourself, as they say on the Hill. However, one of the first

389

things you must learn as a sophisticate is to avoid clichés like the plague," said Jenny.

"You're not even listening to me, are you?" asked Slade.

"Help me, Mr. Slade: exactly what is there to listen to?"

"I am a minister of the faith."

"What faith?" asked Billy.

"A bearer of the ministry of our Lord, Jesus Christ."

"Jeez," said Billy. "I'm no scholar, but my understanding is that the amazing thing about Jesus' ministry, was how he mandated the actual practice of love, not wholesale slaughter."

"Very simplistic, Mr. Clayton. You tree hugging liberals always avoid the truth with flashy rhetoric."

"You call Jesus' ministry of love 'flashy rhetoric'? And you yourself are supposed to be a man of the cloth? Shame on you, Mr. Slade."

"Another liberal spreading a pack lies behind slick talk. The truth is you are not listening to me, and you people don't listen to the word of the Lord himself."

"Mr. Slade, my attorney assures me you have investigated my estate in great depth, though not as skillfully as he has mined into yours. I am the most cash-laden man in the world. And, thanks to you, I have now stumbled across genuine fortune. I am now one of those people who enjoys true wealth, who can find joy in small things and in turning one's concern away from one's own ego trip. I don't see any way you will be able to help me further with fulfillment, you don't even think love is an important part of Jesus' work. And, as far as personal achievement goes, you obviously can't help me with cash."

Jenny pulled a paper shopping bag up off the floor. She fished around and pulled out a handful of sandwiches. "I don't know about you dudes, but I've worked up a hell of an appetite."

"Is that supposed to be something new?" said Billy.

390

She kicked his leg as she ripped open her meal. "Being copilot, I was going to open one of these lovelies for you, Mr. Clayton, but now I'm not so sure. You are in bad need of an attitude adjustment."

"So, what is the nature of these heavenly delights?"

"Egg salad. I stole them out of the kitchen at Mr. Slade's."

"You naughty girl. Is petty theft a misdemeanor or a felony?"

"Here you go, Mr. Slade, I'll loosen you up. Isn't it ironic, we have a vegetarian meal for the Butcher?"

She reached over and undid his cuffs. "I am doing this on the honor system. Don't be bad boy or you will have to grovel on the floor like a dog."

Slade turned up his nose at the offer and refused to take a sandwich.

Jenny turned back to Billy. "Okay, that makes two for you and two for me," she said as she worked with the wrappers.

"I just want one."

"Good, that's three for me."

He checked her out and laughed.

"I am no longer PMSing."

"Hooray and hallelujah," he said, as a digital squawk broke through all the other sounds.

Jenny jerked around, and Slade had a small cellphone. Bent over away from them, he whispered into the receiver. Jenny flipped her seatbelt, turned and grabbed him. She took the phone.

"I offer you a little kindness and you spit in my face." She jerked his arms and threw him back in the cuffs but with his wrists behind his back.

"This is my jet and you will be in deep shit with the FBI for kidnapping and grand theft aviation."

Billy and Jenny cracked up.

"Grand theft aviation, is it," mocked Jenny. "Great line, sounds like a *Jackass* movie." They roared, and Slade looked more and more churlish.

She threw the egg salad on the floor in front of him, pulled her hand back to her side with her elbow up at her ribs while making a perfect fist. She threw the punch right into his face. The sound of the cartilage cracking rose above all other sounds. Blood flowed down onto his white, stonewashed silk shirt.

"Fuck. You goddamn, stuck-up, self-righteous tree hugging bitch. Let me loose from these constraints and I'll discipline you like your pussy-brained, goody-two-shoes, sorry excuse for a boyfriend hasn't got the balls to do," barked Slade.

Jenny jumped up. "I promised Billy I wouldn't hurt you, so I won't, but I am gonna kick your sorry ass, just for fun. I've been working hundred-hour-plus weeks for months in a row, and your NSA, jack-booted thug buddies have been making me skittish. I'm not quite finished PMSing, and I need to loosen up."

"You won't hurt anything. You're just a dumb intellectual. You'll be begging to suck my dick when I teach you how to be a good girl."

"Wow. How sweet life gets," said Jenny, sliding up the sleeves on her shirt. "I have to show an innocent this dragon and the beautiful tiger I took on as a part of my vows to my teacher. Take a close look. I am a Shaolin priestess and I have been trained as a weapon. I have had teaching in how to steal your life away very quickly. You must rethink going into combat with me."

"Will you quit being a piss-ant, New Ager? Take the cuffs off and you'll be on your knees in seconds, begging to take me up on my offer. You didn't know I'm a black belt in taekwondo, so you're gonna eat your words.

She loosed him, and he jumped right off the floor with extreme gusto. He backed away from Jenny. He bowed and Jenny bowed back. Slade took up a taekwondo stance. Jenny stood frozen, amazed by the weird little man's ornery streak, his obtuse self-absorbedness, his complete misunderstanding of the world around him. She felt open heart from all her years of Shaolin, Taoism, her Christian coworkers, and her Buddhist work. She peered into this man for the spirit of Jesus' teachings, but only felt the cold, dead, vindictive streak in his eyes. She had no plans. She simply felt into Jet Slade with her open-heart wisdom, her amazing, collected, pool of chi, her capital of knowledge.

She saw how deeply the pain on his face had etched into his body, how the torment undoubtedly came from childhood, from so-called adults behaving poorly with an innocent child. Jenny read Jet Slade's being as if she were a machine that ran CAT scans of the psyche. She felt very warm toward the innocence, the basic kindness of that little boy, which the adult world had destroyed so thoroughly. Jenny's deep fount of perception also read that Slade had been injured so badly he would always live in the stuck place—as so many politicians, businessmen, celebrities, those desperate for a sense of power did. He would never enjoy this life of his, not ever. He would always seek more, always. And had no idea how to get clear enough to refrain from harming other people or creatures—not in this lifetime.

"Kai yi," he shouted in a surprisingly deep baritone.

He sprang forward like lightening. Jenny watched without moving. He spun, threw a perfect kick, landing it squarely on her jaw. Her head bounced back and blood trickled down from the corner of her mouth. A pinched, self-satisfied smile twisted Slade's mouth. He stepped back on his retrieved leg, used it for thrust and cast a closed-fist punch straight for her windpipe.

Imperceptibly, Jenny adjusted a leg to steady herself and leaned slightly back from the waist. His fist missed her neck with a whisper. His follow-up punch connected with her stomach, nothing other than a meaty thud transpired. As

Slade's arm retreated, she grabbed the wrist, tweaked slightly and dumped him flat on his back. His head hit a metal brace. He let out a deep groan and passed out.

"Thank god. Maybe we can enjoy a moment's silence," said Billy.

But it didn't pan out as smoothly as Billy hoped. They enjoyed a few moments' peace, but after coming to, Slade proceeded to argue with them, working hard to convince them to release him. When Billy and Jenny turned out to be completely unflappable, Slade buttoned up. Then—much to their relief—he pouted all the way to Anchorage.

They had stopped in Long Beach for fuel and to meet with Nuke at *dead latitudes*, on which the captain had launched repairs. Billy grabbed some supplies and Jenny loaded up a sail bag with food. Billy had a very hard time leaving Sam. They talked with Angel, Clarence and Harlan by phone. Nuke had become Harlan's assistant for this case. According to Nuke, Blue kept Harlan walking the straight and narrow. Harlan didn't even want to hear about what they would be doing in Alaska with Slade. He wanted them to bring the Butcher into Long Beach. They both chuckled at the thought of Slade having to face Harlan and Blue but they didn't want anything to detain their flight north.

Nuke wanted them to stop at the Long Beach airport so he could go to Alaska, but Harlan proclaimed that as Nuke's counsel, he certainly did not want his client exposed to Billy and Jenny's chicanery.

"No, this young man has suffered enough at the mercy of a bunch of adults: racists, LAPD sadists, deadbeat dads, scofflaws, faux-despot honkeys, *les enfants perdues* and other plane old trash. I will not allow a man who is under my wing—"

Blue, who according to Harlan perched with majesty on the counselor's shoulder, broke in on the conversation, "WHERE'S THE G-D LAWYER?"

"Alright, Blue. Thank you for your expertise. As I was saying, I will not allow my client to inherit the brunt of the activity of two bullheaded, spoiled-rotten rich kids. He'll be assisting Clarence and myself—two citizens who are above reproach from the judicial system—rebuilding *dead latitudes*. He will be better off for staying clear of you two."

It took some time for Billy to get a word in edgewise. Finally, he asked Harlan to draw a contract for nature training between ANVIL and the Busted Flush Group which consisted of Billy, Nuke, and now, Jenny's new salvage consultant team—named after Travis McGee's houseboat known to be anchored in slip F-18 at the Bahia Mar marina in Fort Lauderdale.

"I have to sign up your consultancy as a Maryland corporation just the way the IRS is registered. We don't want you to pay any tax. I'll fax the contract so Slade can sign."

Harlan's office wrote out the papers and shot the files straight to the Gulfstream's printer. ANVIL proposed to provide a full wilderness training in bear country for the Busted Flush Group. As far as Billy and Jenny and their counsel were concerned, one of ANVIL's environmental efforts was showing the public how precious the wilderness really is for the welfare of the United States, for all peoples. Slade claimed to be a real bear expert and would provide deep training for Busted Flush. Being nature lovers at heart, the salvage group jumped at the opportunity to spend time in the Alaskan outback with brown bears.

Harlan opined that in front of a jury—where he always reigned supreme—there would be no contest to the obvious, Billy and Jenny stood completely innocent in relationship to anything that happened to Slade, the wilderness trainer. At the bench, ANVIL would look like one more organization—rotten at the top like the Wall Street groups—greased by oily relationships with the Congress, trying to cover its massive clandestine activities like poaching.

But the annihilation of Smokey did not amount to just another group of bush-league poachers. A jury would not let the judge get off with a simple, good-old-boy slap on the behind for Slade. They would be horrified by wild animals being captured and would not let the court off the hook. They would let the magistrate practice cronyism and send Slade to a white, crook's country club like the mortgage banker set.

Harlan could hear the panel of ordinary working-class folks: "A bear ate him? Well, oops, ain't that too bad? Shouldn't have been training naturalists if he didn't understand what he was doing, and he sure shouldn't have been poaching—are you kidding me? How tacky can businessmen get? What would the kiddies do without Smokey? That is not American. These corporations are out of control. And as far as this little mishap goes, any fool recognizes a bear is a very dangerous critter."

Jenny told Slade she would give him a real ass whoopin' if he didn't sign the document immediately and she didn't want him to act like a wuss and whine about any of it. She pulled the sandwiches out of her bag.

"Kicking butt gives me a heck of an appetite," she said. "Do you gentlemen care for a bite? Jeez, Mr. Slade, yours is all over the floor—this one is all fresh and nice."

"Where are the steaks? Did the packing house turn you vegetarian?" asked Billy as they dug into the meal.

"Maybe, but the only thing those crackers at ANVIL eat is fast food—god, is it disgusting."

"They are not crackers. They are highly dedicated professional—"

"Oh, pack it. I have heard enough out of you for one hundred thousand lifetimes. Do you want some egg salad or not?"

"No, I do not want some disgusting veggie food that—"

Jenny rifled through his bag quickly and pulled out a roll of duct tape. She loosened the end off the gray surface, grabbed Slade by the hair and wrapped the tape around his head five times. She tore the roll loose and dug into her sandwich.

"They kept bringing me in bags with logos from corporations selling HAZMAT products free of all nutritional value—no wonder everyone's got high cholesterol and diabetes.

If I see another bag from a burger yuck, I shall disgorge on the spot," said Jenny, raising her upper lip with disgust.

"Is there such a word as disgorge?"

"Of course—I thought you were a Yaley?" said Jenny.

"What are you going to do when we get back, Ms. Warren?" asked Billy.

"I expect you won't be ready to sail to Vladivostok for a while, so I'm flying to Manhattan. I have a suite at the Plaza. I am giving myself a getaway, a culture break—a symphonic, jazz, theater, spa, pedicure getaway, and, as all healthy creatures are want to do, chill out."

Slade grunted and made nasty sounds from his place on the floor, and they flew on in silence for some time.

"How do you know you are the richest man in the world?"

"I don't, actually. Not today. Might change any moment. But the last I heard from a reliable source, nobody else has broken a trillion yet."

"Nobody has a trillion dollars?"

"Well, probably no individuals, but of course other entities hold many assets," said Billy.

"A trillion. One trillion. A trillion dollars—none of us can begin to grasp what the number means. Sounds ridiculous."

"Surreal, like something out of *Star Trek*. Doesn't even sound real."

"No, it doesn't," said Jenny, running the math in her head. "I think the problem is it doesn't sound like an actual number. Most of us mere mortals can't even get a handle on what a billion means. Heck, the word confuses me, and I've spent a lot of time dealing in teraflops."

"Teraflops of data are pretty much the same—just as arcane," he said.

"Yeah. One trillion floating point operations per second. I don't think Homo sapiens can really get their mind around such a huge concept."

"How can the engineers build a super computer if they can't get their mind around it?"

"No, what I mean is, we can work through humongous concepts and build gizmos to work with them one chunk at a time, but we never get them into complete focus."

"Yeah, right. I can't understand a trillion dollars any more clearly than the total concept of a trillion bytes in a hard drive," he said.

"How many bytes does that new laptop hold?"

"I didn't notice."

"God, do I like your thick style. You're a true jarhead: brilliant as hell, all testosterone and completely unconcerned with any yuppie, neocon jargon. You'd rather be on a big old stallion out in the badlands than anything, right?"

Billy blushed, turned his head and looked at her for way too long. He felt drawn to her like crazy.

"Ah, yoo-hoo, Mr. Clayton. You're not flying the airplane."

"Right, I forgot you are a super hacker," he said, turning to peer out at the great blue sky in front of them. "Most of us are carrying around a hundred gigs or so in our laptops and your boxes hold trillions."

"Right. That's it. Sounds airy-fairy, unreal, like your money."

"It does. And there's not really any difference—the money's all digital too."

She turned to see if he still listened. "So what is a trillion dollars, and what do you do with it? No one could ever spend it?" asked Jenny.

"Okay, let's get precise," he said, with a bit of exasperation in his voice. "I'm no hacker like you and Luther, and I don't have a clue about currency beyond a hundred dollar bill, but in the States, one billion dollars equals one thousand, million dollar bills. A thousand times a thousand equals a million. A thousand times a billion equals a trillion."

He grinned and raised an eyebrow.

"To make things easy, let's say a ream of paper is about two and a half inches thick." He held his hand up toward Jenny with his thumb and index finger forming a C shape about as thick as 500 sheets of printer paper. Two reams is a thousand sheets." He grinned and widened the gap between his forefinger and thumb. "So, a billion dollars is a stack of million-dollar bills about five inches thick. Or, could be one million thousand-dollar bills—"

"Whoa. Whoa. Wait a minute. They don't even make million-dollar bills."

"Pretty much a 'duh' type thing," said Billy.

"No, you said to look at this matter precisely, and—"

"Nothing in the book of precision says one cannot use an example."

"That's not an example. That's a magic mystery tour. There are no million-dollar bills."

"Ms. Warren, will you shut up for a minute? Those million-dollar bills would stand five or six inches in height. Or, we can look at it like this: one billion would be a stack of a million thousand-dollar bills."

"Hey, come on. They don't make thousands either," said Jenny, grinning.

"Are you *trying* to be a horse's ass?"

"You said precision."

"Swear to god, I'm going to throw you out of this airplane. A trillion dollars would be a stack of a million thousand-dollar bills. The pile would stand approximately two hundred feet in height—something like a 20-story building."

"A skyscraper of cash."

"Well, not exactly a skyscraper, but a big pile."

"Jeez. You're making me nervous. Let's get to the other part of my question. What does a sailor do with all that stuff?"

"*We* are going into the salvage business like Trav McGee. I may buy an old Rolls-Royce Silver Cloud, take my torches to the rear end and put a pickup bed on it. What did Trav call that vehicle of his?"

"Miss Agnes."

"Damn, you're good. I think I'll be a blatant, Trav copycat."

"And Harlan's setting up a Free Range trust with seven hundred and fifty million of those dollar bills."

"Wow, that's quite a trust fund."

"I thought you didn't catch on to those example stacks?"

"Hey, you never know what we girly-girl types are up to." She winked at him lasciviously.

They flew on and let their minds wander over the past few days. Billy knew most everyone would chastise him for taking the law in his hands and not turning Jet Slade over to Harlan and the powers that be. But he also understood they would praise him behind his back. He also recognized what a well-funded defense team with a slick, play-actor mouthpiece could do.

The time in the Corps had caused him to understand how human affairs actually work. Like the political machine, the jurisprudence system belonged to the A-type grabbers who have gathered up a lot of cash. The ordinary person also belonged to the grabbers, hypnotized with beliefs and indentured to the workaday. In the end, Billy didn't care— Jet Slade had to be confronted, and judges didn't have the balls or the power.

They set down at Ted Stevens Airport in Anchorage and went to the chopper area.

"Jack Henry, how may I serve you?" said the man at the desk inspecting yet another of Billy's fake credit cards.

"We want to rent a Bell Ranger, Irv," said Billy, reading the patch on the guy's shirt and sticking out his hand.

"Not a problem, we have a pilot here now."

"We won't need a pilot."

"Sorry, no can do. We don't let our crafts out to ordinary folk. Insurance stuff. You know."

"Hey, I am ordinary folk but my skills are courtesy of the US Marine Corps."

"Well damn, I imagine you're better than my pilots, but it's the rules."

"Sure are a lot of rules in this day and age."

"Yeah, a hotel chain bought us."

"They're even doing buyouts clear up here."

"Yeah, makes me sick."

"Do you have one here I can buy?"

"Buy?"

"Yes, we'll meet your price, right here, right now."

"Is this legal?"

"Just some tourists on a jaunt, Irv."

"Well, the Bell out there is one I didn't sell the chain when they took over here."

"How much?"

"It's worth about three and a half million. Only got forty hours on her."

"I'll give you four right now."

"Don't you have to go to a bank and get—?"

"No, it's from one of my own banks, and the money will go right into your personal account the minute I make the call. When I return, I'm selling the bird back to you for three million six, so you'll pocket some spare change for a day's work."

"Who the hell are you? You some kind of spook or something? We get 'em in up here a lot."

"No, I'm the salvage guy."

. . . .

Robust and outstanding, she stood ten feet tall. At full alert she would have towered over any Los Angeles Laker—and simply, without straining at all, been fully capable of flattening the entire quivering team, sending them all scrambling for cover. Terror in a pack of humans, wolves, and any other species would only require an easy, slicing swat from one of her immense paws.

Big. She had always been big. The size always allowed her to have her way. Even when breast feeding, she got what she wanted: nourishment and deference from her siblings, from her peers, from males. Creatures all gaged size, weighed fright and flight; the understanding came from somewhere way down in their gene structure where they understand the code of respect. And like any other creature, she knew this.

Males knew this too, and they always gave a giant female berth. They knew that pound-for-pound, she stood ground because she really was an awful lot tougher than any male ever imagined—that in the end, the final determination of a female outweighed the male. No male would ever be able to stop a female this big. She could hang tough through the worst of situations. She would fight viciously, no bravado at all. She knew how to move on through the band standing of the males. And she could do anything with babies clinging to her side.

She weighed eleven hundred pounds. Very rare. She had been birthed in the Chugash Mountains, near Valdez, Alaska, in the shadow of Mount Marcus Baker. And the rich streams, the abundance of fat in her diet had made her grow and grow. All of her neighbors were big.

But the males knew about her. They were careful with her. There was never any threat. Though she had bred rarely, as is the case with brown bears, she had never lost a child. No male ever came close to her children. They might rear up, standing twelve feet tall. Try to put a scare in her. But she knew her own strength, and she would grunt, cuff the little ones and saunter off. Food was more important

402

than the whims of males. She had played in the streams, wrestled with her children, taught them to fish. She was a hell of a mom in every way.

She was fast, handy and long of limb. A couple of times, really big, twelve-foot males had come up on her while she watched her cubs. They wanted to kill her babies so she would get all hot and bothered for sex again. But they would move in towards her kids and all she had to do was push up on her hind, so she was nearly as tall as them, but with very long arms and three inch nails. She would take part of their nose or go for an eye with the first swipe, and the big fools would grasp that this lady was not a bullshit artist. They would grunt and turn, and she would shred an ear and take a big bite out of a flank and the old male would rip off through the birch saplings like a bulldozer.

She loved her life. It was good. The coastal mountains were gentle, the weather more heavily influenced by the Pacific than it was farther inland. More warm weather. More time to make sure everyone took on lots of fat during the feeding frenzy. Her distant relatives were over on Kodiak Island, right across the Chugash Islands and the Barren Islands, across the Kennedy Entrance to the Cook Inlet. She was kin to the giant families on Kodiak Island.

And she was on a full feed with two beautiful new children. She had to put weight on them and she needed lots of fat and berries in order to let them suckle. She was hungry. Very hungry. She was not at all in the mood to deal with a big, stupid male out on some vanity trip. The males didn't have to do a damn thing. They didn't have to take care of anything but their dumb selves.

When he walked around the boulder, she already had the rogue bear's scent. The smell was an obnoxious bother. She wanted to work her favorite fishing hole, and she didn't have time for it.

In order to make the interruption brief, she stepped out a ways in front of the kids and watched as they crawled up in a boulder pocket and watched their mom. The male was around eleven feet tall, skinny and rangy. She simply jumped up on a wide boulder to get some height and leverage and when he came around the big granite bulwark, working hard on their scent with his long, ugly snout, sniffing for her wonderful little ones, she dug at his right eye with a long sweeping left hook. She ripped the flesh near the socket loose and let out a long, shivering snort.

The force of the blow bounced the big guy's head off the boulder and she grabbed an ear with her teeth and ripped it right off his head. She had always been very fast. He shook with rage and fear and loped away from her fury as fast as he could make himself go. She stood to full height, surveyed the area, went back to her children, and sniffed them. They took off, following her toward her fishing hole.

. . . .

The chopper flattened the grasses on the meadow as Billy eased down closer to the sow. She bolted for the wood line, but her cubs moved clumsily as they tried to look up and see what produced the hell-bending noise.

"You're gonna' drop me down with the bear aren't you?" asked Slade. "You neolibs think you're all sweet and good, but you're not. You're stuck up, lazy and thoroughly vituperous. You will rot in hell for this. I can say that for sure, because I am a man of the cloth."

Slade pleaded, cajoled, reasoned, cried his eyes out, and finally screamed like a two year old.

At last, ready for it to be quiet, Jenny opened the door and kicked him out. Billy lifted the helicopter up, away from the glorious meadow, up over Big River, out over Shelikof Straight with Shuyak and Afognak Islands sticking out of the water. Just south of them sat Kodiak Island.

They headed north along the straight and as Billy gazed out over the extraordinary wilderness, he felt a deep sadness. Would this glorious natural environment make it? Would yuppies and all their trashy descendants move north and build big, ugly, cookie-cutter houses like they had in

Southern California? Would global warming make Alaska's weather like the City of Angels?

He turned toward Jenny, who had looked back from watching the islands too. She smiled and reached over and squeezed his hand for a moment. As she lifted hers, she said, "I have decided to join you in the venerable salvage profession. There is, however, one condition."

"What?"

"Our firm will be called Jess' Salvage."

"How about Jess' Busted Flush Salvage?"

"Perfect."

"Next thing we're gonna do is lead a gaggle of senatorial spouses in to find the NSA's hit man. Claire Hicks' girlfriends are going to make sure the boys don't get laid anywhere but out with their concubines until they start fighting the animal slaughter. Harlan thinks we'll have the actual shooter in two weeks and his big *capo di capos* within the month.

"Harlan's gang will lock in Free Range. It's going to be Danish run because they're so levelheaded it's nauseating. All the head lawyers are from the Hague, well versed in international and constitutional law. They will work with the ACLU putting the Americans in place. The hackers are all from Ireland and the sleuths are all ex-Stasi, so the NSA's propaganda and sad stories won't faze them."

"What are we gonna do to the perp and his boss?"

"I think everyone in the NSA sawed Jess' hand off; the whole pack of sneaky dogs is guilty. And I think all of them should be picked up and put to work in hospices all over the world, helping children die for the rest of their lives. Do something real for society, rather than run around playing like they are Hannibal Lecter—completely rangy and above the law."

Jenny zeroed in on his eyes and smiled. "It's not just NSA, dude. It's spooks. They're global. They're nasty, and you can't stop them."

"You reckon?" he said, winking at her.

"Well, you did find out if there was an apostrophe."

"It's definitely The Butcher's File, with an apostrophe," he said.

"Hey, no contest."

They both laughed softly and smiled at one another. He turned his head, looking east, out over the incredible Alaskan woodlands. All the emotions he'd carefully covered as a financial whiz and a highly-decorated Marine came up: the families he'd murdered in the service; those he'd broken as a business type; his own potential family that he'd lost to divorce from workaholism; the time for going out to the ranch with his father that slipped past due to the pursuit of the greenback; the children of his own, the kids he never birthed due to the time gobbled up making a trillion dollars; the animals being parted out as inventory; the fact that Slade's absence would just slow things down for a moment; the certainty that the greed-head, power freaks didn't give a damn about anything but cash—a thing he knew on a personal level; and Jess. Jess. Jess. Jess. He would never see the great man again. Never. Never. Never—not ever.

ANGELS GATE,

THE NEXT BOOK
IN THE **TRILLION DOLLAR MAN** SERIES
CEMENTS BILLY CLAYTON AND JENNY
WARRENAS THE ROBIN HOOD AND MAID
MARION OF THE 21ST CENTURY

THE FIRST TRILLIONAIRE AND HIS BLACK
SHEEP HEIRESS ALLY ARE AT IT AGAIN

WHEN SOME DISGUSTING BUSINESS TYPES
MURDER BILLY'S SWEETHEART
THINGS GET THICK FAST

A SERIES OF DYNAMIC BOOKS
The Trillion Dollar Man books are a series. He is the first trillionaire, Marine Force Recon retired & joins forces with the black sheep heiress of an uber-rich blue blood family. Jenny took off from the constraints of being a rich kid and at 14, after reading *The Catcher in the Rye* took off and studied Shaolin in the mountains of China. She was so brilliant and ferocious and had the feminine single mindedness on her side and became 10th degree black belt with the tiger and dragon branded on the inside of her forearms in just 20 years, a challenge that usually requires 40 years. This supercharged team change things fast. They take down the bad guys who are in charge, not the little guys underneath, and become true 21st Century Heroes.

LOS ANGELES HAS SEEN A LOT OF FINANCIAL TERROR
". . . I used to like this town....Los Angeles was just a big dry sunny place with ugly homes and no style, but good-hearted and peaceful.... Now ... we've got the big money, the sharpshooters, the percentage workers, the fast dollar boys, the riff-raff of a big hardboiled city with no more personality than a paper cup. . . ."

Raymond Chandler

REAL ESTATE FILLED THE BONE DRY LA BASIN AN IT'S STILL A THROBBING MONSTER
- Real estate developers brought easterners to the Los Angeles Basin by the train full turning huge profit for bone dry lardons of raw, dry earth.
- They have been the undercurrent to greed ever since.

THEY CREATE THE FIRE CATASTROPHES AND ARE NEVER CONCERNED WITH ANYTHING OTHER THAN PROFIT
The rotten soil beneath Los Angeles could easily become a gold mine if the developer weren't required to be responsible.

WHAT IF
- You were trained as a special op by Force Recon?
- You retired from the Marine Corps, from Force Recon?
- You re-directed all that can-do from the Corps?
- You put it into the money markets?
- You're the richest man in the world?

DOES BEING THE RICHEST MAN ON EARTH CHANGE THINGS?
- But once a Marine, always a Marine.
- Your sweetheart discovers that the mid-Wilshire developer she works for is poisoning a beach town.
- What if the developers have her murdered?

AFTER *ANGELS GATE*,
THE NEXT BOOK IN THE
TRILLION DOLLAR MAN SERIES
PITS BILLY CLAYTON AND JENNY WARREN
AGAINST THE DEALERS WHO SELL CHILDREN INTO
SEXUAL SLAVERY

ON THE WINGS OF A DOVE
WILL KEEP YOU UP ALL NIGHT

ROBIN HOOD AND MAID MARION
FOR THE 21ST CENTURY

THE FIRST TRILLIONAIRE AND HIS BLACK
SHEEP HEIRESS ALLY ARE AT IT AGAIN
WHEN SOME OF THE MOST DISGUSTING
BUSINESS TYPES YOU HAVE EVER RUN
INTO TAKE THE TRILLION DOLLAR MAN'S
FAMILY INTO SEX SLAVERY

**AND AGAIN, THINGS GET THICK REAL
FAST**